SOUL DANCING

Best Wishes!
Gail Priest

GAIL PRIEST

Soul Dancing
Red Adept Publishing, LLC
104 Bugenfield Court
Garner, NC 27529
https://RedAdeptPublishing.com/

Cover Art by Streetlight Graphics[1]

---

1.   http://StreetlightGraphics.com

In Memory of Charles V. Osborne Jr.

Chapter One

2015, Philadelphia, PA
Shirlene

Next to me, a familiar voice snaps, "She's moaning again. Please do something."

Someone holds my hand against a scratchy face. It must be Stan. Why hasn't he shaved?

"Don't worry, Shirlene," he whispers to me.

The deep burning in my chest intensifies. I groan.

Then he barks, "She's in pain, damn it!" As always, my husband is polite until the pressure builds up, and then he blows his stack.

The panic in Stan's voice forces me to focus. This isn't good for his heart. I want to reassure him, but I can't make my mouth form words. I open my eyes to a blurry environment and glimpse someone fussing with a pole and plastic bag over my left shoulder, but my head refuses to turn fully. I try to sit up.

"Hold on, Shirlene." Stan gently presses me down. "The pain will subside now."

Warmth travels up my left arm. I need to ask Stan if he has taken his blood pressure medicine, but with the warmth comes a shadow, like clouds traveling across the moon. The need to get answers slips away, and my eyelids become heavy.

"She'll be calmer now, Mr. Foster. I'm sorry. That won't happen again," a young woman's voice murmurs.

"See that it doesn't."

"I apologize."

My Stan sighs. "No, I'm sorry I lost my temper. How am I going to live without her?"

"I understand, Mr. Foster."

"I've loved her since World War II. I bet someone as young as you can't imagine that."

"It's romantic you've been together so long. I'll be back to check on her again soon."

After the gentle whoosh of the door opening and closing, the room becomes still.

Stan kisses the back of my right hand. "It's time, Shirlene. I won't be long behind you. It's okay to let go."

Although Stan firmly holds my hand, nothing prevents me from detaching from his grasp and from my entire body. I float up. While hovering near the ceiling, I see myself below, eyes closed and face relaxed. I'm covered with the double-wedding-ring quilt my mother made for us back in 1945. Over the years, the pastel colors of the interlocking rings and corner diamonds have faded. On a table next to the bed is a picture from our sixty-fifth wedding anniversary. I was well back then. We are both dressed up and smiling broadly.

This hospital room is not the same one where my doctor told us there was nothing more he could do. Oh, I remember. He said, "I'm sorry, but it's time for hospice."

My Stan lowers his head of white hair onto his arms on the side of my bed. His shoulders shake. He's crying. I wasn't supposed to go first. Who will take care of him?

I begin to panic when a fierce energy drags me through the ceiling. I don't want to leave him, but the more I resist it, the stronger the pull becomes. I'm swept into a brightly lit tunnel. The light is so intense that I can't open my eyes without shielding them with my hands. I separate my fingers and glimpse the silhouette of a small figure several feet away. Sensing it's the person I most long to see, I keep watching, unable to wait for my vision to adjust. My eyes sting as I blink against the glare. The little boy I know better than anyone exists in the glow. When I attempt to call out to him, a sob escapes my throat. Weeping, I stumble toward him. I would like to kiss his ruddy cheeks, to ruffle his auburn hair.

"Danny."

"Don't cry, Mommy. Everything will be all right now."

"Is it really you?"

"Yes, Mommy. Come with me." He holds out his hand for me to take.

My eyes begin to adapt to the light. He still appears to be four years old, but he speaks as an older child, a wiser spirit. The last time I stroked his soft skin, he lay dead in my arms. And now he stands before me. I ache to bundle him up in my arms, to inhale his little-boy aroma. Behind me, Stan sobs my name. He is leaning over my body at the other end of the tunnel. I want to stay with my boy, but Stan needs me. My heart is being ripped in two.

My voice breaks. "Daddy needs me a while longer."

"But your old body won't work." A pond appears at our feet. "Look at yourself now, Mommy."

I peer at the liquid reflection. My strawberry-blond hair flows around my shoulders. All the wrinkles are gone. I smile at myself with perfect white teeth.

His small hand slips into my palm. For sixty-four years and ten months, I've never stopped yearning for the feel of his hand in mine. My fingers curl over his warm flesh.

I kneel next to him and gaze into his sweet hazel eyes. "I wish I had died instead of you."

"It wasn't your fault." My little boy wipes a tear from my cheek. "It was my time, but now it's yours."

Again, Stan cries, "Shirlene."

I peer through the tunnel and watch him caressing my face. He kisses my lips. He's ninety-three with a failing heart. How will he manage? I'm torn between the two people I love most in the world, but my beautiful son is safe. He's guarded by angels.

"I have to take care of your daddy. We'll both come to you. Soon."

"Your old body is gone, Mommy. You can't go back to it."

"But your father can't cope without me. I don't want to leave you, but I must." I release Danny's hand.

The first time I was separated from my boy, it wasn't my choice. This time, it is, but it's just as agonizing. My chest is splitting apart as the tunnel spirals out of control. I'm still being yanked toward the light.

"No!" I shout. I float up and start swimming urgently away from the light and my son.

"But your body is dead, Mommy!" Danny shouts from a long distance away.

Once I break free of the energy carrying me to the light, a vacuum sucks me through the vortex. The bright light fades. I lose control as I spin like a wash cycle. Blurred images whirl about me, making it impossible to focus on any one thing. I squeeze my eyes closed to avoid vomiting.

The movement abruptly stops. Everything becomes still, and I blink my eyes open. I gasp to find myself hovering above my body and Stan in hospice. A force prevents me from returning to my old body, which is cold and solid. I can't penetrate it.

I cry out, "Stan!"

He glances up, but his confused expression makes it clear that although he may sense me, he doesn't see me.

The energy sucks me through the ceiling again. Determined to stay with Stan, I fight against the bright light. This decision returns me to the swirling vortex. I close my eyes to fight the recurring nausea.

Reverberations pound in my head until an unfamiliar female voice whispers in my ear, "Take care of her."

The sickening whirling stops. Intense pain returns, but it's different.

"We have a heartbeat!" a woman shouts.

"It's crowning," a different lady says. "Come on, Rain. Now that you're back, work with us."

Damn—it feels as if my insides are being squeezed against my pelvis in a nightmarish scenario. I have the urge to push.

"That's it, Rain. Keep pushing," the woman demands. "Can she hear me?"

I feel pure agony. I keep my eyes closed, bear down, and scream.

"She hears me. I have the head."

Panting, I can't inhale enough air into my lungs.

"Try to take deeper breaths, Rain. And push again."

The pain intensifies. I push, grunting.

"Here we go. Shoulders are out. And torso and legs."

A baby cries. Something warm, wet, and squirming is plopped onto my chest.

"Open your eyes and say hello to your lovely daughter." It's a male voice, deep and gentle.

I take in the tiny infant covered with blood and amniotic fluid and wrap my arms around her. I've never seen anything so beautiful. When Danny was born, the nurse immediately whisked him away. I touch the soft, round line of the newborn's cheek. I must be dreaming. A tiny bubble comes out of her kiss-shaped lips. She furrows her brow.

"Do you have gas, sweetheart?" I whisper.

People laugh, which reminds me I'm not alone with this precious creature. There are medical personnel in my dream, women in scrubs and masks, going about their jobs. A small blanket is positioned over the baby. A hat is slipped over the top of her head.

"Rain, give another push. Hopefully, the afterbirth will be easier," the woman standing below my legs says.

Why does the doctor keep calling me this odd name? I'm so preoccupied with the tiny infant that the contraction delivering the placenta feels like nothing more than horrible cramps. The doctor continues taking care of me below the sheet propped up on my knees.

Another person steps into my view. He's young, with black hair and a light-bronze complexion. Perhaps he's Polynesian. He must have been the one who told me to open my eyes. He touches the baby's tiny blanket-covered back and beams. His hand is giant in comparison to the child.

The baby starts rooting around toward one of my nipples, only these firm breasts aren't mine—the nipples are lighter in color. But that's how dreams are.

"She's hungry." I move her to help her latch on.

The man steps back. "You don't plan to nurse, Rain, so don't let her do that now," he says without judgment in his tone.

Who is this guy? I cover myself with the blanket. I wish he'd go away and let me enjoy this dream.

One of the nurses touches my arm. "Some new mothers change their minds about breastfeeding once the baby arrives. It's instinctual for them."

I can't take my eyes off this precious peanut getting her fill, but as I support her head with my hand, I notice my fingers are larger and long. The knuckles are no longer gnarled with arthritis. I shift the baby and brush a strand of long blond hair out of the way. My hair is blond? The doctor lowers the sheet over my legs, which also seem longer, and steps out the door with one of the nurses.

The baby finishes feeding. I gently lift her to my shoulder to burp her. A tiny sound comes out of the infant.

"Is it okay if I wash and wrap her up now?" another nurse asks. "I promise to bring her right back."

I reluctantly let go. Without the newborn to distract me, my heart races. Things are appearing more real.

The young man sits on the edge of the bed. "We thought we were losing you. The doctor said your heart stopped. They had me step away while they worked on you. Then you were suddenly okay."

I am unable to look at his face. I need to hide the panic building in my chest. What has happened to me? Where am I? Who am I? I shiver.

I vaguely hear the man ask, "Are you all right?"

My teeth chatter.

"Nurse?" He rises from the bed.

This isn't my body. Old or young, I'm no longer me. The nurse places a warm blanket over me. The man reaches to adjust the blanket.

"Don't touch me!"

He opens his mouth to speak.

"Please, get out," I say firmly.

Surprise registers in his eyes, followed quickly by disappointment.

The nurse places the baby, now cocooned in a tight wrapper, in my arms. Guilt, horror, and sadness grip my heart. For an instant, I see the reflection of my son in the window.

I hug my tiny girl close to my chest. "Danny," I whisper.

The man hesitates a moment longer before leaving the room.

I read my hospital bracelet. Rain DeLuca. Born twenty years ago on May 1. Not that I expected to find my own identification on my wristband. Still, the truth is difficult to face. I am in someone else's body.

The doctor reappears, and I focus on her for the first time. She's quite young with a smooth olive skin tone and a sparkle in her eyes. It's obvious from her enthusiasm that she loves her work.

She speaks quickly. "They're going to take you to your room, Rain. But we're going to monitor you closely after the heart event you experienced. I've ordered an EKG, which they can do in your room, but that's precautionary." She trots away from me. "I have to go. Another baby on the way. The nurses can answer any of your questions."

"Thank you," I say as she dashes out of the room.

The baby yawns. I think of Danny, and I force a sob back down. Stan comes to my mind. I must find a way to manage a newborn and a new body and locate my elderly husband.

Before I can gather my thoughts, someone arrives to roll my daughter and me out into the hall. I'm relieved to find that the man isn't lurking nearby. In my private room, the nurse, who introduces herself as Sharon D'Alessandro, settles the baby into a bassinet and helps me into bed. Sharon appears to be in her fifties, with short salt-and-pepper hair. I'm hooked up to a monitor and have a pulse thing on my finger.

"Can I take a shower?" I ask, hoping to have a moment alone to try to process what has happened to me.

"Not yet. You had an unusual incident during labor. That's why you have the heart monitor and pulse oximeter."

I remember the EKG the doctor ordered. Rain's heart—now mine—stopped during labor. Why? And why did it start again? What happened to Rain? Did I force her out of her body? Is she dead?

Sharon fills up a plastic cup with water from a pitcher. "It's better to be cautious. Besides, you have to pee first, and we have to make sure the epidural has worn off."

"I had an epidural?"

She laughs. I'm sure she hears that a lot.

"If Mr. Michaels comes back, should I keep him out?" she asks.

Who? Oh, the man. The news that I tossed him out must have traveled from the delivery room. I press the heels of my hands against my forehead. What the hell has happened to me?

Sharon hurries to my side. "Are you okay?"

Although I feel like Edvard Munch's painting *The Scream*, I release my hands into my lap and try to appear calm. "Yes, I'm fine."

"Please tell me if you're experiencing any headaches or pain." She points to the heart monitor. "We need to keep an eye on you. So if having Mr. Michaels in here will stress you, I can tell him to come back tomorrow."

I feel guilty that I told him to leave. If this is his daughter, he has a right to be here. "He can come in."

Besides, where am I going to go with an infant, no money, and a different body with a new identity? It is distressingly obvious I'll have to ride this out for a little while with the young man, Mr. Michaels. But I can't very well call him that. How am I going to find out his first name?

I hope we're not married. Our last names are different, but Rain could have kept her name. Oh. What do I do when we go home and it's time for bed? I'm not sleeping in the same bed with him. Stan would have a fit.

Stan. I could be across the country from him. With the blinds in my room closed, I can't look out the window for anything familiar. If I ask what city I'm in, Sharon will be ordering a psych evaluation. I notice the white board on the wall with the date, my nurse's name, and "Pennsylvania Hospital" on the bottom.

I lost tract of time in hospice, but it must be close to the day I died. At least I'm still in Philadelphia, not far from the Hospice Unit off Rittenhouse Square where I... my God. Stan thinks I'm dead. By now, he and our closest friend, Hattie, have contacted the undertaker. I stare at the hospital phone on the table next to the bed. I need to reach my husband. And say what? A call from me would scare him to death. But if I hear his voice, at least I'll know he's okay.

"You seem anxious. Can I help?" Sharon asks.

I'm as truthful as possible. "My mind keeps racing. I'm disoriented."

"It's weird being in delivery for hours. You can lose touch with what's going on around you."

I've lost touch all right.

Sharon begins opening cabinet doors and drawers. "There are no extra pads in here. You can expect some bleeding. Don't let it alarm you."

I nod.

"I'll go find some, and I'll check on when we can expect the technician to do the electrocardiogram."

"Thank you," I say.

"Push that button if you need me. No getting up without me in the room."

As soon as she disappears, I pick up the phone and dial 1 and our New Jersey number. The phone rings and rings. Why isn't Stan answering? Has anything happened to him? I expect the recording I made to come on, saying, "You've reached Stan and Shirlene Foster. Please leave a message." But the phone keeps ringing. He must have turned off my voice greeting when I was in hospice, and now I'm dead. My hand trembles as I set down the phone.

"I'm not dead," I say, noticing how different my voice is. I watch the sleeping infant in the bassinet next to me. I touch her tiny forehead. "Hello, baby girl. I'm Shirlene. I'm your mommy now." My voice is in a higher register with a slight New York accent.

So, along with my hands, legs, and hair, my voice isn't mine either. I haven't seen my new face. I lift a cellophane cover and snatch up a plastic hand mirror that sits with other hospital supplies and personal items on the bedside table. I slowly scan my neck. Clear, fair skin. No freckles. I used to have so many of them. I raise the mirror to my face. *Tired* is the first word that comes to my mind. Bags under my blue eyes. There are empty pierced holes at my right eyebrow and one in my nose. What the heck? I swivel my head both ways and discover rows of holes in my ears. Yikes. I force a smile at myself. My teeth could use a good cleaning, but my lips are pouty. Not bad. I'd say Rain is quite attractive in a hard sort of way. She—*I* look as if it's been a tough twenty years.

Staring into strange eyes but knowing it's really me inside reignites the anxiety I felt in the delivery room. I nearly drop the mirror before setting it back on the table. Do I push the bell button to summon Sharon back in here? She could bring me a warm blanket.

But I watch the baby breathe instead, inhaling and exhaling with her in an effort to settle myself. She is a precious miracle. Another chance. Unexpectedly, I've been given a second opportunity to be a mother. I have a child, a daughter. But what will Stan think of her?

There's a tap at the door. "Hello?"

I freeze.

Another knock. "Rain, it's me."

The man is back.

"Just a minute."

Who is he? My husband, my boyfriend, the father of my child? Whoever he may be, I can't tell him who I really am. He'll take away the baby and have me committed on the grounds that I'm crazy. Perhaps I am.

"Come in," I say.

The door swings open. He's more handsome than I noticed in the delivery room. He looks Hawaiian. Possibly Samoan. Tall with pale-bronze skin. He has a football player's build. He's older than Rain, in his late twenties. He carries a teddy bear and a bouquet of blue irises, nearly purple, with wide dashes of golden yellow toward the centers. My favorite flower. Stan and I used to have large clusters of them in our backyard until the ivy, which we weren't healthy enough to keep in check, choked them out.

When he hands me the flowers, our fingers brush. A pleasant tingle travels up my arms, and my cheeks flush. His deep-brown eyes register surprise.

I glance away from him and lower the flowers into my lap. "These are lovely. Thank you." He remains silent, so I go on. "I'm sorry I insisted you leave before. It was rude. I apologize."

He stares at me with a confused expression. Finally, he says, "You've never apologized before."

What kind of person is Rain? She never apologizes? This guy is either madly in love or a saint or a fool.

He leans over the bassinet and gazes at the infant. He wipes his eyes. "Hi, sweetie. I brought you a teddy bear."

He's in love all right. With the baby. That's why he puts up with Rain. He's trying to hold his family together.

"So, what's the final decision on her name?"

I can't begin to guess what names he and Rain have discussed. "I don't know."

"You've given up on Storm?"

Storm? How cliché. Rain and Storm. Please. "She's definitely not Storm."

"Good. Did I hear you say Danny before? Should we name her Danielle?"

The urge to cry climbs up my throat. "No, I couldn't."

"Okay."

I take a drink of water before making any suggestion. "How about your mom's name?"

"Absolutely not."

Now what do I say? "Tell me your favorite choice again?"

"Arlene, but you hate it," he says.

"No, I don't. It was my..." I stop. I nearly say it was my father's mother's name. I was named for her and my mother, Shirley. So, Shirlene.

"What?" His eyebrows knit close together as he examines me.

"She looks like an Arlene to me." I hope he releases his interrogating glare. "Unless you think it's too old-fashioned."

His dark eyes shift to the infant. "Perfect. It was my dad's mother's name."

What are the chances this young man and I would both have paternal grandmothers named Arlene? I breathe a sigh of relief. "If you like, we could nickname her Reenie as in *The Dark at the Top of the Stairs*."

Again, his eyes bore into me. "Since when did you ever read a William Inge play?"

I laugh, taking time to come up with a plausible answer. "In high school."

"You finished high school?"

I try to cover my tracks. "During freshman English." I'd better keep my mouth shut until I understand more about Rain. Obviously, she's not a reader, a theatergoer, or even a well-educated person.

"You sound different," he says.

Unconsciously, I must have lowered my tone or opened my vowels. Apparently, it's going to be tough to convince him I'm Rain. In an effort to avoid eye contact, I study the details of the maternity room for the first time. It's homey with two large, framed photographs of mothers and babies on the walls. Things certainly have changed for the better since Danny's birth. Stan agonized out in the waiting room. Our newborn slept in the nursery with nearly twenty infants, and I shared a hospital room with two other new mothers. Across this room, I spy a daybed, presumably for the baby's father. Then it dawns on me that he is staying the night, and I can't have this stranger in my room.

"Were you planning on sleeping in here?" I ask.

"Yes, I'm doing the feedings because you were going right to formula and didn't care to wake up in the middle of the night. Don't you remember?"

"Well, since I'm nursing, you can stay home."

"You suddenly plan to get up at all hours with the baby."

I hesitate. I have no idea how to manage being Rain. "I've changed my mind. That's all."

"Is this some game you're playing, Rain?"

"No. I feel differently after giving birth."

"Differently?" He emphasizes the *ly*.

He isn't buying it, and I have the distinct feeling he's somehow on to me.

Chapter Two

Cameron

After final instructions from the nurses, I maneuver through the Philly traffic with Rain and Arlene in the back seat of my car. My apartment isn't far from Pennsylvania Hospital, but congested streets make it a long trip. I finally reach my block of brick row houses on Spruce Street, but finding a parking spot is ridiculous.

I talk to the rearview mirror. "I'll drop you and Arlene off at the apartment. I may end up blocks away."

Rain seems bewildered.

"What's wrong with you, Rain?"

"Nothing."

I double park, and with my flashers on and blocking the traffic, I hop out to release the infant car seat carrier. Some ass beeps their horn. I lift the carrier out and point to the sleeping infant. The guy shrugs. Rain gets out of the car and tugs at her crop top like she's trying to make it grow into a full-length T-shirt.

"Can you manage the car seat? I'll bring everything else after I find parking."

"I don't have a key." She takes the handle of the carrier.

"Just buzz. Mrs. Haddad will let you in."

"Who?"

I jog around to the driver's-side door. "My landlady. Be nice!"

Rain starts up the adjacent steps to the home next door. Has she lost her mind?

"One over!" I yell and jump back behind the steering wheel.

I pull up to the red light. In my passenger-side mirror, I watch Rain go up the steps and read the bell labels. She knows which one is Mrs. Haddad's. Why is she so baffled? I'm worried that maybe there was some oxygen deprivation when she nearly died during childbirth. The horn blares from the car behind, and I realize the light changed.

"Relax. I'm going." I accelerate.

When I reach home with Rain's overnight bag and various baby paraphernalia balanced in my arms, I find Mrs. Haddad in the first-floor hall, fussing over the baby, and Rain smiling. She rarely smiles, and when she does, it's more of a grimace or sneer. At this moment, her smile is dazzling.

"She's such a gorgeous child," my landlady gushes.

"Thank you," Rain says.

There's that thank-you again. So unlike her. And to Mrs. Haddad no less, a woman she frequently mocks for her hijab.

Rain jumps when sudden hammering starts at the back of the brownstone.

"Sorry." Mrs. Haddad touches Arlene's cheek. "That will stop now we have a baby in the house."

"I hate to see Mr. Haddad delaying his progress on the studio apartment," I say.

"He won't mind." Mrs. Haddad snickers. "He likes any excuse to stop working."

"I wish I could help him." I enjoy doing maintenance and repairs for the Haddads. It keeps the rent down, which is how I can afford my second-floor apartment. But I'm not going to be able to do much with the baby here.

"You do enough, dear boy. Well, I'll let you three get settled, but ask if you need anything at all."

Mrs. Haddad slips into her apartment.

I wait to allow Rain to go up first, but she doesn't move. "Are you ready?" I ask.

"Lead the way."

This is peculiar, but my arms are aching from being overloaded with stuff, so I climb the stairs. Rain follows with the baby. I dig the keys out of my pocket, shove open the door, and dump everything on the sofa. Rain stands still, looking like she's never seen the place.

"I'll put her down." I move to take the baby, but Rain holds on to the carrier. "Would you rather do it?" I ask.

Rain sets the carrier on the coffee table and kneels to kiss the baby's nose. "It's okay. You do it." She takes Arlene out of her car seat and transfers the wrapped little body with surprising gentleness. "Be careful of her head and neck."

"I will." I'm the one who studied up to prepare for this baby, and I have the drill down better than she does. Or at least I did. Now, Rain suddenly seems experienced.

I tiptoe down the hall to the second bedroom, slip Arlene into the crib I bought last week at the used furniture store on Fifth Street, and turn on the moon-and-stars mobile, a gift from the Haddads. She continues to sleep as Brahms's "Lullaby" softly plays. God, she's so small. It's frightening.

Rain comes in with her overnight bag from the hospital and drops it next to the bed.

"What are you doing?" I ask.

She surveys the makeshift nursery—which doubles as a guest room—with the bed shoved against the wall to make room for the crib right next to it. "I thought I'd be sleeping in here with the baby."

"You're not staying in my room?"

The color drains from her face. I wonder why she seems embarrassed about taking my room.

"No."

"You said you didn't want the baby waking you up. That's why I'm staying in here."

"Oh." Her expression relaxes.

"But now that you've decided to breastfeed, do you plan to sleep in here instead?"

"Yes."

I gave Rain my room and closet. She doesn't have much, but what she does have will need to be moved. "I'll take my clothes out of this closet and bring yours in here, then." I step to the door of the nursery.

"Can I help?" she asks.

I'm bewildered by her offer. "It's okay. You relax. Soon, this little munchkin will wake up to eat again. Rest while you can."

"The doctor gave me the okay to shower. Do you mind if I do it now?"

"You're asking my permission?" Rain has never cared how I felt.

She processes my question. "Are you okay with the baby while I take a shower?"

I nearly scoff at her but decide to accept this thoughtfulness. I don't trust it, but I'll take any cooperation I can get. "There are clean towels in the hall closet."

When Rain passes me and opens the door to my bedroom, I assume it's to find clean clothes, but she makes a little surprised sound and tries the other door, which is the linen closet, before going into the bathroom and closing the door. I don't understand her bizarre behavior.

While I'm moving the last of the khakis and Oxford shirts I wear during the school year from one closet to the other, there's a shriek from the bathroom. Miraculously, the drama queen hasn't woken the baby. I bolt down the hall and wrench open the bathroom door, ready to give her a piece of my mind.

Rain stands in front of the partially steamy mirror, staring at a spider tattoo on her right hip. Her long, wet blond hair clings to her exposed breasts. I drag my eyes away. No way am I getting involved with this wackadoo my brother managed to knock up and abandon.

Our eyes meet in the mirror.

"I have a tattoo." She picks up the towel from the floor and wraps it around herself with a modesty I've never seen in Rain before. "Please knock before you come in."

"Of course."

I feel like a jerk. In the months we've cohabited, I've never heard Rain say please. I try to come up with an acceptable excuse for my rudeness. "I thought you'd hurt yourself."

"A tattoo," she mumbles with clear disdain.

"There's another one."

She jolts as if a real spider is crawling on her. "Where?"

"On the back of your left shoulder." I point.

She turns to look at the skull. Her face becomes red. She lowers herself onto the edge of the tub and begins to cry. Another first. Guilt immediately bubbles in my gut. I burst in here to tell her to shut up before she wakes Arlene, but now there are tears.

I hand her a wad of toilet paper. "The doctor warned us about your hormones getting off balance. That's all this is."

I hope this soothes her, but I can't imagine why tattoos she obviously decided to get would suddenly freak her out. I don't dare bring up the one of a snake I noticed on her right butt cheek when she leaned down to grab the towel and cover herself. The skull tattoo on her shoulder has often been revealed with the tank tops she wears, but I never saw the spider and the snake until now.

I fill a bathroom cup with water. "Here. Drink this."

Rain wipes her eyes and nose before taking the cup. "When did I acquire these?"

"What?" Was she so high at the time that she forgot?

"When did I get these tattoos?"

"I have no idea. Maybe Chase can tell you, but they could have been done before you met him."

Her turquoise eyes plead with me. "Could you please leave me alone now?"

The "please" throws me again, causing me to stumble over myself. "Yeah, sure," I mutter as I skulk out the door. I'm left feeling off balance. Something is wrong with Rain, and I need to find out the cause.

Chapter Three

Shirlene

I scurry back to the nursery without running into the man. He seems to be busy in the kitchen. I close the door and tiptoe over to the crib. Watching my sleeping baby calms me after the shock in the bathroom. I have tattoos, and he saw me naked, and I cried. Once I calm down, I realize I'd better get dressed before he charges into the nursery. I can't believe he barged into the bathroom. Fortunately, I'm sleeping in here with the baby. I eye the doorknob. It has a lock.

The only nursery furniture in the room is a white crib and a rocker. The top of a low Ikea-looking dresser is covered with a baby pad to serve as the changing table. The bed is up against the wall, under the room's only window. This nursery isn't much larger than the one Stan and I had for Danny when we were living in a small apartment.

On the adjacent wall is the kind of tiny closet typically found in a traditional Philadelphia rowhome built in the early 1900s. I go through the meager amount of clothes the man moved in here. Most of it resembles what a hooker would wear. All the shoes have impossibly high heels. Even the maternity clothes are skimpy. Rain's belly must have popped out for all the world to gawk at, with the crop tops I find. I tug open the top dresser drawer and find disposable diapers, baby clothes, and the like. In the second drawer, I locate Rain's underwear. After what I found in the closet, I shouldn't be shocked. Most of the underpants have no seat. Just a string. Hattie would roar with laughter over this.

The thought of what my best friend must be going through, believing I'm dead, causes my heart to hurt. I don't want to start crying again, so I hold up one pair of tiny black panties and concentrate on them. Stan might actually find these attractive. I laugh and slip them on. They are tight across the remaining baby bump, and I discover another set of holes in my belly button. How many piercings do I have? I'm curious to see my new firm twenty-year-old butt. I twist in the mirror and barely manage not to scream at the additional tattoo I find back there. The snake's open mouth looks about to take a sadistic bite out of me.

I clearly need to buy some different clothes and shoes but with what? The notion of having to ask this stranger for money makes my stomach flip. I toss on the same clothes I wore home from the hospital, maternity jeans with rips above the knees and a tight midriff T-shirt.

Does Rain have any money? I search through the other drawers and find thirty dollars and half of a photograph in a wallet. It's a picture of Rain standing on a city street. Whoever was in the other half has been torn off. But it's clearly a man, judging by the size of his forearm and large hand angled possessively over her shoulder. The skin tone is similar to the man in the kitchen. Is it the same man, and they had a fight?

I search for jewelry to find out if there's an engagement or wedding ring among Rain's possessions. I discover a plastic sandwich bag. I unzip it and rummage through the pieces of jewelry. There are rings, but not the kind one wears on one's finger. It's a bunch of inexpensive piercing rings and other intimidating studs. She must have taken them all out before going to the hospital.

So, no marriage or engagement ring. The man and Rain are sleeping in separate rooms. Therefore, it could be that once Rain got pregnant, their relationship changed. From the bits and pieces I'm

"Who the hell are you?" His eyes are intense as he runs his hand across his five o'clock shadow.

"That's your name, isn't it? Cameron Michaels." This new body of mine seems to have nervous indigestion at an early age.

He moves toward me. I step back, but he keeps coming. He takes the baby, gently sets her into the crib, and stands between it and me with his feet set apart and his hands on his hips. "Who are you?"

My voice breaks. "Rain DeLuca."

"Whose baby is this?"

"Mine."

He lets out a sigh. "Who is the father?"

I swallow. "You?"

His face contorts. "You don't know, do you? For God's sake, Rain, you lied to me. You said Chase was the father." His eyes become wild. "I willingly took this on because it was Chase's responsibility. He always runs from his own messes."

I can barely keep up with him. Rain slept with Chase, but who is he? Why is Cameron taking care of Chase's girlfriend and baby? Shivering, I rub my arms but remain cold.

Cameron's posture relaxes. He snatches up a baby blanket and wraps it around my shoulders. "I'm sorry."

My teeth chatter. "She's Chase's." It's possibly a lie, but I hope to regain some equilibrium with Cameron.

"I know. Otherwise, why would you have come to me?"

I take several deep breaths.

"Thank you for having the baby," he says. "I realize this is hard for you. I shouldn't have gone off the way I did. It's the stress. But it's going to be all right. We have all summer to get used to this."

I begin to settle down. "What happens at the end of the summer?"

He laughs. "School, goofy. And since when have you called me Cameron or Cam?"

I am back to square one. What do I call him, and how do I find Stan?

Chapter Four

Shirlene

Between the baby's feedings, spending the night in a strange man's apartment, and worrying about Stan, I didn't sleep much. I jump when Cameron's voice comes through the closed nursery door before breakfast.

"I'm going to the Acme. I can't face takeout again. Is there anything you need?"

"No, thank you."

"I won't be long," he says.

"Okay. Thank you."

He waits outside the nursery. I can't stop thanking him, but obviously, Rain never did. I bite my lip. Will he come in here asking who I am again? After a moment, his footsteps go down the hall. The apartment door opens and shuts.

I haven't been able to reach Stan at home. If his heart is giving him trouble, he'll be at Jefferson Hospital. It's where his cardiologist is. I dash to the kitchen. With Stan's history of cardiac disease, I have the Jeff number memorized. After I ask for Stanley Foster's room, I'm told to hold on, which means he is there—not in ICU—and can talk. But I hang up before it rings. I can't take the chance of breaking the news that I'm not dead over the telephone. It could scare him to death. I have to see him in person in order to explain what's happened.

I try on the only pair of Rain's jeans that aren't full of studs or designer rips. They're tight, but I can fasten them. The miracle of a twenty-year-old body. As for the top of me, unless I want to attract business, I need to cover myself up. I dig deeper through the skimpy clothing and find an appropriate maternity blouse with the tags attached. I add a wide belt to cinch it in at the waist and examine myself in the mirror. My appearance is respectable.

After nursing and burping Arlene, I watch her settle back to sleep. This dear, incredible creature gives me such peace, but I must tear myself away today to visit Stan.

When Cameron returns with groceries, I go into the living room.

"Hey, you're wearing the shirt I bought."

I am suddenly self-conscious.

"It doesn't seem like a maternity top with that belt." He sets the grocery bags on the counter that separates the kitchen from the living room. His dark eyes scan my face. "Not putting the nose ring back in?"

"No."

"The new look is nice," he says, but I read uncertainty in his expression.

I open the refrigerator to put away the eggs and butter from one of the Acme bags and finally find words. "Now that I'm a mom, I want to seem more mom-like. So I could use some new clothes." I decide not to bring up nursing bras.

He goes to his desk in the living room and opens a drawer. "Here." He holds out a credit card.

I stay on the kitchen side of the counter. This is unexpected. "I can't charge things on your credit."

"It's yours. I gave it to you to buy things for the baby. Remember?"

"Oh, yes." I don't sound convincing.

He steps toward me. "Honestly, if you're not screwing with me with this forgetfulness and distraction, Rain, then you'd better go to a neurologist."

"I'm not screwing with you. It's the hormones." I take a breath. "Do you mind watching the baby?" I come out of the kitchen and take the card. "She's sleeping. I'll only go to Macy's."

"No problem. Do you have any cash for a taxi?" He slips past me to continue storing the groceries, and his citrus-scent aftershave rattles me.

I remember Rain's wallet. "Yes. I was going to walk, but you're right—the doctor recommends I be careful."

He palms a cantaloupe in each hand, hesitating. "Tell me now, Rain. Are you disappearing with the credit card?"

It takes me a moment to understand the question. Nothing should surprise me, but I'm astonished he suspects Rain is capable of abandoning her child.

"No. I'm just shopping. I promise."

"Okay. I believe you."

But his eyes disagree with his words. I have the distinct feeling he wants to follow me, but there's no one else to watch Arlene. Which is perfect because I can't have him trailing me to my husband's hospital bed.

"I'll be back."

Once outside, I go to the corner to hail a cab. Aside from the normal postpartum abdominal pain and perineum soreness, it's remarkable how quickly I move in Rain's body. There's no knee pain. I'm not short of breath. Although it seems Rain didn't take care of her body, it's a miraculous improvement over my old cancer-ridden one.

Cam nearly passed out when I asked for brown rice and a meatless stir-fry for dinner last night. Apparently, Rain had something against vegetables. Once I put some healthier food in this body, I should be able to do whatever I desire. I'll be able to swim again. Imagine that.

The taxi drops me off at the entrance to Jefferson. I enter and approach the visitors' desk with a knot in my stomach, wondering what kind of shape my husband is in.

"I'm here to visit Stanley Foster."

The woman tells me he's in Room 410, and I go to the elevators. As I ride up, my mind whirls. Now that I'm this close to seeing my dear husband, I'm not sure how I'll convince him it's me in this body. When I tell him I'm Shirlene, he's either going to think I'm a cruel young woman pretending to be his wife or a ghost. Or he might be horrified or repelled by this new body. Either could upset or possibly kill him. He might be asleep. Maybe I'll check on him and not tell him what's happened. I could pretend to be a volunteer. I step out of the elevator and pass the nurses' station.

"The guy in 410 died," a young man says to another nurse behind the counter.

I freeze. I should have come sooner. I allowed myself to be distracted by Arlene and this ridiculous charade of pretending to be Rain.

I force myself down the hall, passing Rooms 404, 406, and 408 on the right. My hands shake as I step into 410. The bed closest to the door is empty. The curtain is closed around the other bed. Stan's body must be behind it. He's gone, and I'm not with Danny to greet him. I should be dead and with Stan and our son.

I have an urge to run away, but I must see my husband's body one more time and say goodbye. I slip through the curtain. He's pale. His mouth is open, and his cheeks are sunken.

"I'm so sorry, Stan!" I cry and take his hand. It's still warm.

A sound comes from his open mouth. I jump. He smacks his lips.

"Oh, my dear. You're not dead!"

He snickers. "Not yet, Shirlene."

I kiss his hand.

"I fell in love with you the first time you did that." His eyes are still closed.

"Wake up, Stan."

"I am awake."

"Open your eyes."

His lids flutter open. First, he regards my hands, no longer gnarled with arthritis. He stares intently at me. "You've changed."

"You're not dreaming."

"I realize that."

I don't understand it, but he knows it's me. Relief floods my body. I kiss his hand again, a hand that has seen years of work, pleasure, and pain.

"I thought it was unusual for a woman to kiss a man's hand. I recognized then how unique you were, and I had to marry you. But I had no idea you were a shape-shifter." He touches a wisp of blond hair at my collarbone. "You look like an angel."

"A fallen angel."

Stan squints. "A little rough around the edges but a sight for sore eyes." He pauses. "I miss your red hair."

"It's been white for years."

"Details." He's tired, but the corners of his eyes wrinkle.

"This must be a shock."

"Sort of, but I didn't really sense you were dead. I told that to Hattie, but she said it would take time to sink in. She's so literal. What happened? Hattie and I had your funeral at Locust Wood Cemetery yesterday."

The thought makes me queasy. "I saw the light and all, but I resisted. It let go of me. I was transported into this body."

He eyes me. "Pretty hot."

"Don't flirt. You'll have a heart attack."

"If I can't flirt with you, there's a cute night nurse."

"But I'm not me." I sigh. "I don't know who I am."

"It's you, Red. These bodies are simply shells."

"Well, I'm very attached to yours, Stan, so don't plan on going anywhere."

"You mean with the night nurse?" He winks. "Why were you crying?"

"I heard the man in here died, and I thought it was you."

"Oh, did Bob pass?"

I nod.

"It must have happened while I was asleep."

"Oh, Stan. I'm so glad you're not dead."

"I'm so glad you're not dead either." He becomes serious. "Well, it's only a matter of time for me, Red. I had another heart attack last evening. The old ticker is finally giving up, and before long, the kidneys are going to quit on me too. The doc told me to figure out a hospice setting. I'll check in where you just left."

"No, absolutely not. I'll bring you home. I'm able to take care of you now." I hug him as best I can while he's in a hospital bed.

"I guess you could." He has a sad expression. "I wanted you at home."

"Stop. It was the best decision."

"I hated leaving you every evening and taking the PATCO train back to Jersey. I needed you in our bed." He swiftly wipes a tear from his cheek. "I slept on the sofa in the den. I couldn't go upstairs without you there."

"We're not going to talk about it anymore, Stan." I kiss his forehead. "It's water over the dam."

"Okay." He glances around the room. "So, tell me—what was it like to die?"

"It's comforting. I felt safe."

"Did you see anyone?"

My stomach tightens. We haven't mentioned Danny in years. It seemed as if Stan pretended we'd never had him. It was the only way he could go on living with me.

When I don't answer, he says, "Some people who have near-death experiences say they see their loved ones again."

I can't tell him Danny was there. Not yet, anyway. I need to tell him about Arlene first, and bringing up Danny could make his reaction worse. "What I saw was a bright light. I wasn't afraid to go, but I couldn't leave you."

He pats my hand. "What was it like coming back?"

"Nauseating, a whirling vortex, and mystifying. But I must tell you something because it will affect things when I bring you home." I can't exactly hide a crying newborn in our home.

"What? You're scaring me."

"Sorry. It's quite wonderful, actually. When I took over this young woman's body, she was giving birth. I have a baby. A little girl."

His expression becomes stony.

"The young mother's name was Rain. I haven't been able to piece much together, but I don't believe she wanted the child."

"And you do?" he says disdainfully.

I refrain from expressing the boundless love I have for my daughter because it could make matters worse with my husband. "Yes, Stan. Definitely."

He turns his head away. I'm disappointed by his behavior, but I realize he is trying to protect himself.

"I have no idea how I ended up in this body with a newborn, but it's meant to be. It's very strange, but Rain died, or her spirit went someplace. I hope I wasn't the cause of her soul leaving, but her body survived for me for some reason."

Stan won't make eye contact. "Who's the father?"

I resent the guilt churning in my stomach. I'm in a different body, but the ingrained reaction is the same.

"There's a father figure, but the connection is a mystery. His name is Cameron Michaels. He thinks I'm Rain."

"Are you sleeping with him?"

I yank Stan's face back to me. "Of course not!"

"I didn't mean you, but are they involved? This guy and Rain." His jaw clenches under my fingers.

"I'm not sure. The man is sleeping in a separate room."

Stan's eyes sharpen. "Just tell him who you are."

I release his face. "He'll assume I'm insane."

"How are you going to take me home? I'm not going to this guy's place."

"Stan, I'm doing the best I can here under extraordinary circumstances."

He softens. "Of course you are. I'm sorry, but I kind of have a full plate too. My wife, whom I love desperately, dies. I have another heart attack, and this time, there's too much damage. I'm going to die, and my wife reappears in a young body with a newborn and likely a new husband."

While it breaks my heart to hear Stan talk this way, the mention of the baby makes my breasts leak. "I've got to go."

"Why?"

"I'll be back tomorrow, and we'll work this all out."

My nipples drip milk as I dash out of Jefferson and along Chestnut Street to Macy's. I buy several maternity bras, go into the restroom, and slip one on. My flow has slowed, and I have enough time to grab and pay for two shirts that don't look too old lady and a pair of jeans with no tears in the legs. I'm running late. Arlene is going to be up and hungry, and Cam will be worried I'm not coming back. As I scurry to catch a cab, the damn thong inches its way up my crack. I forgot to buy real underpants.

Chapter Five

Cameron

I grab my phone because it's a good time of day to text Aimee. I haven't had a second to tell her the baby was born a few days ago. But Rain comes into the living room, wearing a light-blue women's Oxford shirt and skinny jeans. Her hair is braided. I believe it's called a French braid. Her blond hair has various shades of dark and light. I try to convince myself these observations of Rain are about making sure she didn't have brain damage during delivery—or isn't screwing with me—and not the new and disconcerting attraction I'm feeling.

"Are you busy?" she asks.

I can't figure out where this politeness has come from. "Nope. Just about to text Aimee to announce the baby has arrived with ten fingers and ten toes."

Rain knit her eyebrows. "Aimee?"

"Yeah. You remember—my ex-fiancée, Aimee, is on tour this summer, performing in Europe. She's a classical vocalist."

"If she's your ex, why are you texting her?"

"Because we stayed close friends. You know all that."

"Oh. I forgot."

"Like so much else. What's up?" I ask.

"Do you mind if I go shopping again for an hour or so while Arlene is napping?"

Why is she suddenly changing her appearance to be less flashy? "No problem."

"Thanks. I'm recovered enough to walk today."

My churning gut tells me Rain's up to no good. I can't let down my guard and trust how comfortable I'm beginning to feel around her. She's being nice so she can slam me with some demands or disappear.

"You sure you don't mind? I really need more sensible shoes."

"Sensible shoes?" Sounds like what my grandmother would have said. "Get whatever you want."

"Arlene is sound asleep." She goes to the front door.

I follow. "I'll take care of her."

"Thanks." Her smile is different too. Sincere. Cheery. Incredible. What the hell am I thinking?

Just as Rain yanks the door open, Mrs. Haddad appears. It startles them both, and they laugh. When I first suggested Mrs. Haddad might be willing to babysit, Rain's response was ignorant and racist. Now they're laughing together.

"Hello. How are you, Mrs. Haddad?" Rain asks.

"Well, thank you. How are you and your precious child?"

"We're both fine. Thank you for asking."

I can't help but wonder who this courteous person is.

"If you'll excuse me, my time is limited before the baby wakes up." Rain goes down the stairs.

"Motherhood suits her," Mrs. Haddad says as she follows me into the living room.

"I know. It's good but unnerving. I keep waiting for the old Rain to reappear." I wait until my landlady sits before I join her on the sofa. "When she went out yesterday, I thought she might not come back."

"Where is she off to?"

"Shopping again. Out of the blue, she's changing her look."

"Well, that would be an improvement." Mrs. Haddad crosses her arms. "But you don't believe her?"

"No, I don't. I need to follow her if you can stay with Arlene."

"You go."

I stand but hesitate. "I'm not comfortable with this. I don't want to be stalking her."

"You have a child to protect now, Cameron. Go see what our young mother is up to. I think she's telling the truth, but you'll be reassured if you see for yourself."

I place my hand on my stomach, hoping to settle it. "You're right. Thanks for understanding."

"You're not a stalker. You're watching out for Arlene. Go."

I hurry down the stairs and out onto the street. I catch sight of Rain going along Spruce Street. I follow but keep my distance. She turns onto Ninth. She crosses Locust. I expect her to cross Walnut Street to head toward the stores on Chestnut, but she enters Jefferson Hospital instead. This isn't where Arlene was born, so Rain wouldn't have a maternity follow-up here.

Then it hits me. I've heard Jeff has a recovery program for addicted mothers. Maybe she's going to a meeting. She did leave about the same time yesterday. Why wouldn't she simply tell me she's going for some help?

I could go home and never tell Rain I saw where she went. But that feels creepy, like I'm really stalking her. I'm not going to get very far in the hospital without a way to explain my visit to the guard at the desk. So I grab a cold Sprite from a nearby food truck, surf on my phone, and stay. It takes less than forty-five minutes.

When she comes out, her eyes are red. I've seen Rain pissed, stoned, sulky, and moody, but I'd never seen tears until the bathroom fiasco.

"What are you doing here?" She glances up and down the busy sidewalk.

A lump forms in my throat. I wonder how she'll react. Why do I suddenly care how she reacts? "To be honest, I followed you."

"Is Mrs. Haddad with Arlene?"

"Yes."

She seems fine with that. In the past, she would have laid into me for trusting a Muslim. Can motherhood completely change someone's personality?

"Listen, I'm glad you're going to the Jeff rehab program, but why weren't you upfront about it?"

"The what?"

She's fidgeting and begins moving down the street. I follow. She turns onto Walnut.

"I assumed you were going to a recovery meeting. Why else would you be going into Jefferson Hospital?"

"Recovery from what?" She moves around a couple walking hand in hand.

I catch up. "Rain, you know. Alcohol. Drugs."

"That's not why I was there." She picks up her pace.

Before the baby arrived, I would have let her go, but I'm compelled to step in front of her. There is shock in her eyes, and fresh tears well up. I promised myself I would never let Rain get under my skin while I did what had to be done for the baby. She is unreliable, selfish, uncouth, unethical, and an energy vampire. Why am I getting involved now?

"Rain, what the hell is going on?" My voice is angrier than I intended.

She avoids eye contact. "I have something to tell you."

Rain looks both ways before crossing the street and going into Washington Square. I follow her to a quiet spot, wondering what bomb she's about to drop.

Rain settles on a park bench. "Please." She pats the spot next to her.

I sit. She clasps her shaking hands together and settles them in her lap. She crosses her legs at the ankles. For several moments, she doesn't say a word.

"What's going on? Why are you so different? Why were you at Jefferson Hospital? Come on, spill."

"I'm not sure how to tell you this."

"Well, you have to. Just spit it out. What the hell is going on with you?" I ask.

Rain bites her lip.

"All right, let's start with why you were at Jeff. Is there anything wrong? Are you sick?"

"No."

"Did you go there yesterday too?" I ask.

"Yes."

"Okay. Were you visiting someone in the hospital?"

"Yes."

I'm going to lose control if I have to keep prodding her. "Who?"

"My husband."

I leap to my feet. "What?"

A lady walking her French bulldog glances our way.

"Sit down," Rain whispers.

I have no desire to sit, but I do, clenching my jaw.

"It's not what you think." She straightens on the bench.

My head is about to explode. "You're married? Is the baby his?"

"No."

"Is it Chase's?"

"Yes. Well, I guess so."

"You guess so?" My heart is pounding in my chest. I wonder if it's possible for a man to have a stroke before he's thirty.

She blurts out, "I don't know for sure, because I'm not Rain."

"What the hell are you saying?"

She clasps and unclasps her hands. "Rain's gone. She died in the delivery room."

"Have you lost your mind? You're sitting right next to me."

"I'm not Rain," she repeats. "I died too. Well, I left my body, at any rate, and saw the light but fought it because I thought my elderly husband couldn't manage without me. Then somehow..." She takes a deep breath. "I was transported into Rain's body during her final moments of labor. When Rain let go, I took over." She begins to cry again. "And now Stan needs hospice. I want to bring him home to take care of him."

"Stan is your husband?" I can't believe I'm asking this as if the situation is normal or even plausible, but I can't have her crying. I'm overwhelmed with the need to comfort her, but I'm too pissed to think straight.

She nods and runs her wrist under her nose.

"And who the hell are you? Sorry. Who are you?"

"My name is Shirlene Foster."

I instinctively shift away from her on the bench.

"I'm not sure who Arlene's father is. Only Rain could tell you. But nine months ago, I was in my own body, dealing as best as I could with cancer."

I hesitate to ask, but the situation is so absurd that I do. "How old are you?"

"I'm ninety."

I notice I'm tapping my right heel, a nervous habit I stopped back in my teens. I settle my foot on the ground. "This isn't happening."

"Tell me about it. One minute, I'm in excruciating pain. It melts away, and I'm seeing a bright light. After that, I'm in a nauseating vortex. Then I have labor pains in a body with tattoos and enough piercing holes to sink a ship." She finishes her rant, and her voice softens. "But I have a baby." Her turquoise eyes meet mine. "Arlene is amazing."

"Totally."

"Stan sounds like a character I'd get along with. I'm sorry he's so sick."

"It's his heart. I need to move him home before..."

"Where is home?" I ask.

"Just across the bridge in Haddon Heights, New Jersey. They're releasing him soon." She places her palms in a prayer position and folds the fingers over, clasping her hands together. "But you have to understand—I can't possibly leave the baby, so I need her to come with me."

"No way! I'm not giving Arlene to anyone. We're a package deal. I go where Arlene goes."

At first, she seems surprised, but worry creases her brow. "You're staying in my house?"

If I can believe this person is really a ninety-year-old woman who has been nothing but thoughtful and intelligent and who loves Arlene unconditionally and is coping with her dying husband, I won't play hardball.

"You don't know me, but I'm a good guy. Do a background check on me."

"I sense you're a nice person." She blushes.

This completes my heart attack. I'm getting into trouble here, but what other choice do I have? "I have the summer off. It's not a big deal for me and Arlene to stay with you while your husband is in hospice. I'm willing to help you with him. I can take care of chores or shopping. I'm an okay cook. But I won't hand my niece over. I plan to raise her, to be her father."

Her face lights up. "Your niece! Is your brother her father?"

"Yes. Chase. He and Rain were together."

"I'm so relieved to find out who Chase is and that Arlene is your niece." She sighs. "I have so many questions about Rain."

Instinct tells me not to lay too much more on her—not yet. This woman has a lot on her plate with her husband nearing death. "Never mind about the saga of Chase and Rain right now. What are we going to do about your husband?"

"You're right. Stan could be released tomorrow. There's so much to do."

Her devotion to Stan hits me. I am looking at Rain, but clearly, she is someone else. "How can I help?"

"It would be best to have Stan in our bedroom. He'll want to be in his own bed."

"Hold on. The hospital staff certainly doesn't believe you're Stan's wife."

She lets out a tiny giggle. "Stan's only surviving relative is the great-great-granddaughter of one of his sisters, so I told the hospital that's who I am." She grins at her own cleverness.

"What if the real great-great-granddaughter shows up?"

"She won't. We've never met her. She moved from the Pacific Northwest to Australia. We have no contact."

"Who am I going to be?" I ask.

She frowns. "I don't know. Why can't you be yourself?"

"Will the neighbors ask questions?"

Her eyes widen. "My God, this is so complicated. I have to focus."

"Is this great-great-granddaughter married?"

"I don't know. But she could be." She pauses to come up with our story. "And she recently had a baby, which is why she couldn't travel sooner, right?"

"So we're married?" I suggest.

Rain—Shirlene—glances away. "I suppose."

I find her modesty way too appealing. But she's really ninety years old. I must be out of my mind.

Shirlene gasps. "You and Arlene will have to stay in the den off the living room. There's a sleeper sofa in there and a full bath behind the stairs between the living room and kitchen."

"You'll stay upstairs with Stan?"

"Yes. I'll take the baby into the living room for feedings during the night."

"Wouldn't it be easier to set up the nursery upstairs with you?"

"I can't have the baby near Stan." She bites her lower lip. "He needs quiet."

I let it go but sense there's more going on.

"If you can shift some furniture for me, Arlene's crib will fit in the den," she says.

"Sure."

"I can't thank you enough, Cam. Or do you prefer Cameron?"

"Rain called me Mike."

"Mike? Oh, for Michaels."

"Yeah. As a kid, I didn't like Cameron. Chase still uses Mike, and that's how he introduced me to Rain. In college, I went back to Cameron or Cam. But what do I call you?"

"Well, I'm not a weather pattern."

"I can't use Shirlene unless we're alone or with Stan."

"Or with my best friend, Hattie. I'm going to have to tell her who I really am. Hattie was a trial lawyer, and she'll never buy this lie that we're long-lost relatives from Australia."

"When you do tell her, will she believe who you are?" I ask.

"I know things about her no one else does. I can pass any test she gives me. And it will be a relief to be myself with you, Stan, and eventually Hattie."

"I hope your husband and your friend can accept me."

"Hattie will come around. Stan will be another issue."

"Why?" I ask.

"He doesn't approve of strangers in his house."

"If I'm changing my entire life for a time, I want to be helpful, not avoiding Stan."

"You're already being helpful. But it's best if you stay away from Stan."

This seems bizarre, so I plan on meeting Stan eventually one way or another.

Chapter Six

Shirlene

As I step off the hospital elevator, Hattie is coming out of Stan's room. She carries herself with her usual posture perfected from years of ballet training. With her hair in a tight bun, Hattie looks as if she's entering the stage, the prima ballerina, especially when she's gearing up for a challenge. As an African American woman, she's faced plenty of them. There's nowhere for me to escape, so I hurry toward her, hoping she doesn't wait to see if I go into Stan's room. I glance her way and smile. She tips her head quickly the same way I've seen her do a million times since she was a girl. Her eyes are red from crying. It takes all my strength not to bundle her up in my arms and tell her who I am.

She pauses. For a split second, I worry she's reading my mind, which would be no surprise. I purposely go past Stan's room and slip around the corner at the end of the hall. I can't believe I'm hiding from my dearest friend, but the hospital is not the place to tell her I'm alive in a twenty-year-old's body. After waiting several minutes, I step out and march back toward 410. There's no sign of Hattie.

Stan's face is strained. He immediately blurts out, "I'm being released tomorrow."

"We have it all worked out." I pat his arm.

"We?"

"I."

His eyes narrow the way they do whenever he anticipates some harebrained plan of mine.

I go into my lousy imitation of Ricky Ricardo. "You got a lot a 'splaining to do, Lucy."

He smiles. My heart surges with love. I wonder how many days we have left together. If I'd been more patient, I would be with Danny now, waiting.

"What's the plan, Red?"

"I'm taking you home. We have a hospice interview later today. They should be able to set up someone to come and monitor your care and keep you comfortable."

"They'll let you take me home?" he asks.

"Once they want you out, they don't really care about who or how. Remember, I told the social worker I'm your sister's great-great-granddaughter."

"That's what I told Hattie. I'm not sure she bought it." Stan furrows his eyebrows. "You must have just missed her."

"No, I didn't. We passed in the hall. She'll be suspicious, but I'll tell her the truth as soon as I can talk to her alone."

"It can't be too long because I plan to have Hattie draw up a new will leaving everything to you—I mean, Rain DeLuca. She's the only lawyer I trust. That way, you'll be taken care of."

"Let's concentrate on getting you settled first."

Stan grimaces. "The house is a mess."

"I'm going to hire a cleaning service. Cam can be there to let them in and make sure they are legitimate."

Despite my reassurances, I notice his jaw tighten. Stan has never allowed anyone in the house without one of us being there. He could be tense over the cleaning people or Cam or both.

I proceed carefully. "Stan, this baby needs her mother, and for some reason, it's me."

"The baby is staying in our house?"

"Of course she is. Where else could she be?"

"With this guy."

"Cam is staying with us too."

"You must be joking. We'll never be alone together."

"Cam and the baby are staying in the den downstairs. We will have the entire second floor to ourselves."

He crosses his arms. "Why can't he stay at his place?"

I use Cameron's words. "It's a package deal. He goes where the baby goes, and I want Arlene with us. With me."

"You named the baby after your grandmother?" he shouts.

"Sh. Cam named her after *his* paternal grandmother. But what if I did name her after Grandmom? What's wrong with that?"

"Nothing." Stan's face is becoming red with frustration.

I stamp my foot. "No, tell me."

"It indicates you're making her your own." He seems to struggle for the right words. "This isn't temporary."

I long to yell she *is* mine. But I must avoid distressing him any more than he already is.

"So this guy thinks he can move in with us and freeload," he continues.

"Cam wants to help. He's offered to food shop and cook."

"Doesn't he have a job?"

"He's a history teacher. He has the summer off."

"Why is he doing this?"

"I don't know. Maybe he's a nice guy."

"Humph."

"We're both tired," I say. "It's been a lot to digest. I'm going to go down to the lounge and make some calls while we wait for the hospice nurse."

Stan gives in. He's too sick to argue. "You manage everything. You always do." He yawns.

I kiss his forehead. "I love you."

"I love you too."

I slip into the hall. I take out the smartphone Cameron gave me and immediately feel stupid. While we ate lunch, I only learned how to phone him. Otherwise, I'm useless on this thing.

Cam answers quickly and asks how things are going.

I'm surprised to find I'm more grounded when I hear his voice. "I saw Hattie when I got off the elevator."

"And...?"

I take a seat on one of the pale-green upholstered chairs in the empty lounge. "I wanted to tell her I'm alive."

"You'll know when the time is right."

"Sooner rather than later because Stan plans to have her change his will to benefit me, as Rain. Hattie will have to be told it's really me, or she'll fight with Stan about it."

"I thought she was a *retired* trial lawyer."

"Hattie will never retire, but ten years ago, she shifted to part-time estate, family, and civil rights law."

"Doesn't sound like she's slowed down any." Cam chuckles. He has a nice laugh.

A middle-aged woman glances in the lounge but leaves when she notices I'm on the phone.

"Stan's being released tomorrow, but in all these years of hospital stays, they've never cut him loose until the afternoon. He is so miserable waiting."

"I don't blame him. Once they say you can go, you want to move the hell out of there."

It hits me how empathetic Cameron is. If I can assure my husband that Rain and Cam weren't in a relationship, it might help Stan to accept this young man and his intentions. "Do you mind if I ask you a personal question?"

"Go ahead."

"Are you and Rain a couple?"

"No! Oh God, no." His voice bears shock bordering on distaste.

"I didn't mean to upset you."

"You haven't. You just took me by surprise. I figured you knew we weren't involved because we were sleeping in different rooms."

I'm embarrassed to tell him I'm relieved they aren't together.

He continues. "And there's no telling if Rain was going to stay after the baby was born."

"Who would help you? What about Chase? Are your parents nearby?"

He snorts. "My brother wrote off the baby as soon as Rain told him she was pregnant. And my parents are very busy with their real estate business in LA."

"Haven't you told them? I'd certainly need to know."

"They aren't you, believe me. Besides, they don't deserve to know, but I'll tell them eventually, I suppose."

I wonder what they've done to be undeserving of their son's generous empathy and the knowledge of their granddaughter. I remember that when I suggested we name the baby after his mother, he looked at me as if I were crazy. There's a story there, but I don't press. Soon, we will all be cohabitating, and I'll come to understand this young man better.

Chapter Seven

Cameron

I can't fall asleep. Early tomorrow, while Shirlene deals with getting her husband released and transported home, I'll be moving whatever Arlene and I need to Haddon Heights, NJ. The decision to help Shirlene isn't the only thing keeping me awake. I lied to Mrs. Haddad, telling her that grandparents of a close former student have died, and the family doesn't want the New Jersey house left empty while they work out inheritance issues. I said Rain and I decided to take up their offer to stay there so Mr. Haddad can return to rehabbing the downstairs studio apartment. I felt awful deceiving the Haddads, but it was the only plausible excuse I could float for taking Arlene to stay at Shirlene's house.

It's too cold in here, so I go into the living room to adjust the central air-conditioning. On my way back down the hall, I notice the nursery door is open and the light on. I can't help but take a peek.

Shirlene and Arlene are both asleep in the rocker. I gently lift the baby and settle her into her crib. Shirlene stirs but doesn't wake. She has a peaceful expression. Even asleep, this woman is completely different from Rain—not that I've ever seen Rain asleep, but I've seen her passed out.

Back in my room, I check my phone. It's three in the morning, the same hour that Rain showed up here six months ago. I woke up to someone pounding on my apartment door. Worried Mrs. Haddad had a problem, I stumbled out of my bedroom and wrenched open the front door. Rain looked worse than usual, and that was saying something. Matted blond hair framed her dirt-streaked face.

"What did you do—change the lock after we left?" Rain snapped.

"How did you come in downstairs?"

"Nice to see you, too, Mike." She pushed past me and into my living room. She stank.

"Rain. What are you doing here?" I stepped away from the apartment door but left it open until I could get a handle on what was going on.

She held up a set of keys. "I let myself in the front with the key you gave Chase and me, but this key for up here didn't work."

"Where's Chase?"

"Hell if I know. I thought he might be back here." She sat on my sofa, toying with the edge of her tattered jacket.

"Don't you have a coat?"

She shrugged. She must have been freezing out on the street.

I rubbed my eyes. "Why are you here in the middle of the night?"

"I'm looking for your brother."

"I haven't seen him since you both crashed here three months ago."

"I haven't seen him in over two weeks," she said.

"That's surprising. You two seemed pretty tight."

"True love never runs smooth." She was sarcastic as usual but actually seemed coherent.

"Are you clean?" I asked her.

"Yeah."

"Congratulations, but is that why my brother has disappeared—he doesn't like you sober?"

"He doesn't like me pregnant."

I felt my legs weaken, but I managed to land in the recliner.

"I need money," she said.

"Is my brother the father?"

"Of course he is. I'm screwed up, but I'm not a ho."

"Sorry."

"I need money for an abortion. Your brother doesn't want the kid, but he's not around to help me out. He took off."

"How far along are you?" I asked.

"About three months."

I glanced down the hall toward the bedrooms.

"Yep. That would put the conception right down there in your 'guest room.'" She punctuated with air quotes.

Rain and Chase had shown up with about fifteen bucks between the two of them. They'd been on the streets for a while. They needed a fix, some booze, food, and a roof over their heads. Against my better judgment, I'd offered the last two.

"So. Can I have the money?" Rain asked.

I desperately wanted children. I'd hoped it would happen with my ex-fiancée, Aimee, but she called off the wedding. What if this baby of my brother's *is* my only chance? I should take it. Raising a child alone—how hard could it be?

"This is my niece or nephew. I'll take responsibility. If you go through with the pregnancy clean and sober, I'll open a bank account for you with ten thousand dollars in it. After the baby is born, you can be as involved as you like or walk away."

I watched Rain work this over. It was more money than she'd ever had, I'm sure. I knew money would motivate her. Ten grand was a big chunk of change on a teacher's salary, but I worked construction with a buddy during summers, and I'd managed my money—the one good thing I'd learned from my mercenary parents.

"I don't want to be pregnant," Rain said.

"Too late. With the baby due in June, I won't take a summer job. I'll do the middle-of-the-night feedings. By September, we'll have the hang of things."

"What if I leave?"

"The money will be yours one way or the other."

She squinted as a moment of pensiveness crossed her face. "If I can't stay clean after I have this kid, I'll leave. It'll be better off without me."

"Don't say that. You might change."

Rain smirked. "Ever the idealist. Face reality, Mike. I'm not cut out for motherhood. I don't want this baby. I'm only keeping it for the money."

That was so typical of Rain and is completely atypical of Shirlene. As strange as this all is, I finally fall asleep, grateful Shirlene is now the mother of my niece.

Early the next morning, I rush to pack my car before Shirlene leaves the baby with Mrs. Haddad and goes to the hospital. As I drive across the Ben Franklin Bridge, I go over my mental list of things Shirlene asked me to do when I reach her house on the east side of Haddon Heights. Once I drive into her community, all the properties seem well-kept, with manicured lawns, except the one I pull up to, where the grass needs mowing and the shrubs are out of control.

With the strap of one duffle bag over my shoulder, I step onto the portico of the handsome colonial-style house and notice paint flaking off the two columns supporting the roof. It's amazing Stan and Shirlene managed to stay in their home this long. Although Shirlene gave me the key Stan had with him in the hospital, I feel as if I'm trespassing when I twist the knob on the front door, which drags against the pile of mail behind it. I grab the envelopes and advertisements off the floor and set them on the hall table. Standing in the foyer, I face the stairs leading to the second floor. On either side are archways. Through the right arch is the dining room, and the living room is to the left. Since Shirlene said the den—where Arlene and I will be bunking—is off the living room, I head in that direction.

A baby grand piano sits under the back windows. The lid is closed and covered with a fringed shawl underneath several photos in dusty frames. With a beaming grin, Stan stands next to his bride on their wedding day. Shirlene was a petite red-headed beauty. No wonder she is amazed by Rain's lanky five feet, eight inches. I guess Stan to be just under six feet but more than a full head taller than Shirlene. In another frame is a picture of a freckle-faced Shirlene with her arm around an African American girl. The teens are laughing together on the beach with other Black people in the background. Likely, the girls couldn't have gone to a white beach, and Shirlene's presence was tolerated here. The next photo is of two young men in World War II uniforms. I compare the taller one to the groom in the wedding photo. It's Stan. The other guy is fair-haired with freckles. He looks like a relative of Shirlene's. She could have had a brother.

I check my phone. The cleaning service is arriving in an hour. I asked Shirlene why they hadn't used a cleaning service regularly, and she said Stan wasn't comfortable with strangers in his home. I wonder how he'll manage with me living in it.

Two Easter baskets filled with blown, dyed eggs stand on the dusty fireplace mantel. On either side of the fireplace are doors to the den, which, Shirlene mentioned, used to be an enclosed porch. I open the door closest to the piano, and a foul smell hits me. The coffee table is filled with dirty dishes and old take-out containers. I toss down my duffle bag, quickly open the windows, and switch on the ceiling fan. A mountain of papers sits on the desk, which Shirlene said we could use for the changing table. There's a bed pillow and a blanket on the couch. I suspect Stan didn't want to sleep upstairs without Shirlene. But he hadn't bothered to open the sofa bed. Sadness creeps into my chest. Aging is a bitch.

I decide the first thing to do is pitch the empty take-out containers. I'll move the television upstairs so the cable guy, who is due soon, can run a new wire up to Stan and Shirlene's bedroom.

The doorbell rings. I expect to find the cable guy or the cleaning people, but when I open the front door, I see an elderly but spry-looking Black woman. Is this the girl in the beach photo? She scrutinizes me with steely eyes.

"I'm Harriet Washington, Shirlene and Stan's closest friend." She pauses. "And not because the rest of them are dead. Who are you?"

I go with the plan. My real name but a fake relationship.

"I'm Cameron Michaels." I offer my hand. She shakes it with a surprisingly firm grip. "I'm married to Stan's sister's great-great-granddaughter."

"Why don't you have an Australian accent?"

"I'm American. My wife and I moved to Australia from Oregon."

"Humph." She prances past me and positions herself at the foot of the stairs, almost like she's guarding the second floor.

"I don't usually ring the bell," she says. "But I saw the strange car in the driveway."

"Would you care to sit down, Mrs. Washington?"

"Isn't there work to do?" She goes into the dining room. "Stan asked me to put away the Easter decorations before the cleaners arrive." She picks up a basket from the center of the antique dining room table. "They belong in the attic." She passes me on her way to the stairs.

My cell phone rings. It's Shirlene. "Hello."

Shirlene's voice is breathless. "Hattie is coming."

"Yes, I know."

"Is she there?"

"Yes."

Hattie pauses on the stairs and watches me. I wave. She scampers up out of sight at the pace of someone a quarter her age.

"Sorry," Shirlene says. "Stan told me a moment ago. Hattie insisted on helping, and as usual, she wouldn't take no for an answer. Where is she?"

"Upstairs."

"Did she ask you a million questions?"

In case Hattie is listening, I try to sound as natural as possible. "A few."

"Please don't tell Hattie I'm alive. I need to be the one to take care of that in person."

"Don't worry."

"Oh, and Stan told her we have a newborn, so if she asks about the baby, you'll have to come up with something fast. You can't very well tell her the baby is with Mrs. Haddad."

Hattie comes down the stairs. She eyeballs me before going in to grab the baskets from the fireplace mantel. I duck through the dining room and into the kitchen. It's a mess of dirty dishes.

"Shirlene, I can manage Hattie."

"She's going to think we're gold diggers coming to help Stan out of the blue."

Hattie bolts through the door.

"Got to go." I shove my phone back into my pocket.

Hattie opens the dishwasher door. It smells of spoiled food. She pops a tablet into the holder and starts the machine. She begins washing the dishes, which fill the sink and cover the counter. She ought to leave it for the cleaning service, but I sense it's a matter of pride. I open several drawers before finding a dish towel.

"I'll wash." I hold up the clean dish towel. "You dry."

Hattie frowns, and her lips draw into a thin line.

"You know where the dishes belong," I explain.

She snatches the towel away from me. I plunge my hands into the hot water.

Chapter Eight

Shirlene

Stan never relaxes in the hospital. Who does? But now that he's home and in his own bed, he's asleep, propped up on pillows to avoid coughing. I made up the bed in our guest room for myself. It's right across the hall, but I don't want to leave him. I watch him from the old cricket chair. The only light comes from the streetlamp in front of our house.

I'm not sure when Arlene will need me, but I'll stay with Stan as long as possible. I hoped to be more comfortable once I got Arlene and Cameron settled in downstairs and Stan in his own bed up here, but I'm on a balance beam, trying not to fall off. I wonder if I made the right decision bringing everyone together under one roof, but there didn't seem to be any other choice. At least I'm home.

It's a miracle to be in the house I never thought I'd see again. When there's time, I'll touch every object and relish the wonderful memories attached to them. Between the cleaning service and Hattie's fresh flowers, the house looks a bit more as it did when Stan and I were well and able to keep up with it.

This moment to myself is a treat, but with it comes time to brood about my choice to resist the light. Was leaving Danny the right choice? I can't predict how long Stan and I will have together, but he's always been stubborn. I hope it will be weeks instead of days, but when Stan does die, I won't be waiting to greet him with our son at my side. I'll be left here, for who knows how long, without either of them.

Hopefully, it was the right decision for Stan. He begged me not to go, didn't he? It's difficult to recall how it all happened, but now, at least, Stan can find comfort in being surrounded by familiar things. I will hang onto the fact I'm in a body that's able to take care of him in his last days. Otherwise, he'd be alone in some facility. I shudder at the thought. I'll make sure everything is perfect for him—as perfect as it can be when you're dying.

I need to distract myself, so I go to my vanity and open my jewelry box. The streetlamp provides enough light to go through things without waking Stan. My engagement and wedding rings are on top of my clip-on earrings. Stan must have taken them off my body before I was buried.

Buried. My body is really gone. I wonder if I'll ever feel completely myself in this new one. I'm blond and so much taller. Not to mention seventy years younger. I try to put my rings on, but my new fingers are larger. I remove a pendant from a chain and slip the rings on. When I hang it around my neck, I catch my unfamiliar reflection in the vanity mirror. It's eerie to be looking at someone else, but it's me inside. Hopefully, the numerous holes in my ears, over my eyebrow, and in my nose will heal over without scarring.

I remember Rain's sandwich bag of jewelry that I decided to bring with me. I tiptoe into the guest room, where I'll be sleeping, and find the bag in my partially unpacked suitcase. Everything is for filling some hole in my body. Fortunately, she restrained herself when it came to her nipples. As I sort through trinkets—a variety of studs and balls, a dragon, and some pointy things—I find a pretty gold heart on one end of a slightly curved bar with a simple ball at the other. Because of the curve, I assume it's for the holes in the top of my belly button. My cheeks heat up, but I need to find out how this looks. I sneak into the bathroom and close the door before switching on the light. The gold ball doesn't slip off like an earring backing. I toy with it until I discover it screws off. I open my bathrobe, lift my pajama top, and hold the bar with the heart hanging down in front of my navel.

It's sexy, and my libido bids me hello. What the heck am I going to do with it at my age? I laugh loudly and tone it down to a giggle before waking everyone up. Then I wash my hands and put rubbing alcohol on the holes and the jewelry. After I slide the bar up through the bottom hole and wiggle it around, it pops out the top. I screw on the ball, and voilà—my mother would refer to me as a hussy.

On the baby monitor in the guest room, I hear Arlene waking up downstairs. I hurry to turn it off so the sounds don't bother Stan. I've situated the two people with the most potential to upset my husband at the other end of the house. I hope it's far enough away that never the twain shall meet. Experiencing a little schizophrenia, I scurry down the stairs. One minute, I'm watching my ninety-three-year-old husband at death's door, and the next, I'm a young mother with an infant and a belly button piercing.

I go through the den door closest to the crib and farthest from the sofa bed. I found an old folding screen in the attic and situated it so I can't see Cam's bed. He needs some privacy.

I lift Arlene, attempting to ignore the fact that Cam is asleep—or awake—on the other side of the screen, and carry her into the living room to nurse. I settle on the couch, cuddling her, and she latches on like a pro. I curve my body around her. I can pretend she's still inside me where I can protect her. If only I could have protected Danny. No, don't think about that. I concentrate on this miracle who is Arlene. It's quiet except for her satisfied gurgles. A refreshing summer breeze travels through the open windows.

I worry Stan will wake and need me, but he hasn't. So I give myself permission to indulge fully in my baby. I run my fingers across her brow as she concentrates on sucking. This precious little thing is mine.

Chapter Nine

Cameron

The door opens again at the crib end of the den. Shirlene is bringing Arlene back after nursing her. I settle myself and pretend to be asleep behind this folding screen Shirlene insisted I have up at night. It's ridiculous. I've done nothing but toss and turn this first night on the sofa bed. I could have gone to Arlene when she first woke up, but as requested, I waited for Shirlene to come get her.

Shirlene has everyone where she wants them, except me. Arlene is at the other end of the house from Stan, who is home in his bed. But I have a feeling Shirlene would prefer that I were back in Philly. She hasn't said so, but it's obvious because she hasn't let me do much to help.

Stan needs to be moved so we can change the sheets, help him to the bathroom, and make sure he doesn't develop bedsores. After the hospice nurse left this afternoon, Shirlene hauled Stan around by herself. I could do that for her, but she won't allow me upstairs at all. It's like I'm here, but I'm not. Arlene and I are invisible as far as Stan is concerned.

Shirlene stays for several minutes before the door closes. I roll over and punch the pillow into a more comfortable shape. I flip back to my other side. I could text Aimee, who is awake in Europe, or listen to some music with my earbuds, but nothing interests me at the moment.

I get up and throw on shorts, a T-shirt, and my running shoes. Then I grab my reflective vest and head for the front door, encountering Shirlene in the dark foyer.

"You startled me." She tightens her bathrobe.

"Sorry. I thought you'd gone back up." I notice a loose strand of her hair across her shoulder. I have to get out of here. I open the front door. "Thought I'd go for a short run."

"Now? In the middle of the night?" Shirlene frowns.

"Do you need me?" I ask.

"No."

"Shirlene, it's rude of me to be in Stan's home and not speak to him."

She tugs on the belt of her robe again. "Stan needs his rest."

"It won't take but a moment. And I want to do things around here to help you."

"It's late." She's giving me the brush-off, but tomorrow is another day.

"You need some sleep yourself," I say.

"I'm fine. The baby monitor is by my bed, so if she wakes, I'll come back down."

"I won't be long." I step through the open door.

"Be careful."

"I doubt I'll be mugged out here in the wilds of New Jersey."

"But you're a stranger." Shirlene hesitates.

"And…?"

"The police. They don't have people with your complexion around here at night." She stares at the floor. "Running."

"I'll take my chances with the cops."

After I close the door, I take a deep breath. I skip stretching. I have to move, or I'll explode. I take off down the street.

Maybe I'm being foolish, running in the burbs in the middle of the night, but this first day at Shirlene and Stan's has been untenable.

I have to make her see reason and let me help out. I'm also going to find a way to introduce myself to Stan.

Chapter Ten

Shirlene

Both Stan and Arlene have been fed and are napping. I'm cleaning up the breakfast dishes. After insisting I let him mow the lawn, Cam is in the garage, trying to fix the lawnmower, when the front door opens.

"Hello?" It's Hattie.

I knew it wouldn't be long before she appeared. I work to compose myself.

She strides into the kitchen, carrying a plate of homemade muffins covered with plastic wrap. She looks me right in the eyes. There's an ache inside me. I need her to recognize me.

Hattie sets the muffins down without breaking her assessing gaze. She stands silently and looks like she's considering her words carefully. Whether it's due to her superior intellect or her years of navigating a prejudiced world stacked against her, she has had a precise, careful speech pattern. Words are important to her. Even after a few drinks have loosened her up and she throws her head back, releasing a deep, throaty laugh, she never loses her exactitude.

A tear runs down her cheek. "There is something about you that reminds me of Shirlene."

In close to eighty years of friendship, I've only seen Hattie cry three times—when we were kids, when her husband died, and when her adult daughter died. I resist the urge to wail and throw my arms around her. I must be the calm one, for once.

Hattie's hand floats up gracefully to wipe her face, but her voice is rough and unapologetic. "I miss her so much."

I take a step closer. "But I'm right here."

She straightens her shoulders. "Don't you try to take advantage of me, young woman. I may be over ninety, but my mind is perfectly clear." She leans on the kitchen table the same way I've seen her do in court to intimidate a witness. "Tell me what this is all about. What are you doing in my friend's house with her husband?"

I vacillate between lying as the distant relative or continuing truthfully as myself. Hattie might not believe the truth because it is too fantastic, but I've never lied to her in my life.

"You have a heart-shaped birthmark on your left shoulder," I whisper.

Hattie points with a nearly imperceptible tremor in her hand. "How do you know that?"

"Your mom used to call you Hattie Heart because of it."

She moves so quickly around the table that I prepare for her to slap me, but she takes both my hands in hers. They feel cool and familiar. Callused from gardening. She closes her eyes.

It's me. I'm Shirlene, I say silently in my head.

"Why did Shirlene have a tiny scar on the bottom of her chin?" Hattie asks.

"I had a scar from when kids pushed me down for being friends with you. It was one of the only times I saw you cry."

Hattie's eyes fly open. "No one knows that but Shirlene and me."

"Because we never told anyone the truth for fear my parents might try to stop me from seeing you." There's no response. "If you still don't believe me, ask me other things."

"What did I teach you to do if a man grabbed you?"

"To use my fingers to jab the eyes and throat quickly and forcefully over and over. Knee him in his nuts."

"And if he has you pinned?" she asks.

"Bite something, and when 'the bastard' pulls back, jab and knee."

"And then...?"

"Run as fast as my skinny white legs can carry me."

Hattie gasps. "It's really you."

I nod. "Yes, I'm Shirlene."

She threads her arms about my waist and draws me in. When I put my arms around her shoulders, I comprehend how fragile she really is. I thought of her as healthy and strong when she helped me during my cancer treatments, but the reality is quite different. She is skin and bones. Her shoulders poke out of her thin sweater.

"You've lost weight," I say.

"That's what you want to talk about? You're in a completely different body, and you want to assess my lack of body fat?"

I laugh until I cry. She guides me into one of the kitchen chairs, brings the tissue box from the counter, and sits down.

I blow my nose. "You're really old."

"That's not news."

"You're going to die. Stan is near death. I should be dead. How am I going to go on without the two of you?"

"We'll get to that. First, tell me what the hell happened."

After I reveal the details of this bizarre body-switching journey, Hattie gets the strangest expression.

"But what happened to Rain?" she asks.

"I can only assume she's dead."

"She was perfectly healthy and gave up?"

"Oh!" I stand up as if someone shocked my seat.

"What is it?"

"I just remembered a detail I lost in the midst of all this chaos."

Hattie raises her voice. "Tell me."

"It's a little blurry, but I'm pretty sure I heard a voice say, 'Take care of her' right before I went into Rain's body."

"Remarkable. Did Rain know what was happening and speak to you?"

I take out a glass for some water. "Do you want anything to drink?"

"No. Answer the question."

"If it was Rain, it would mean she knew what was going on when I didn't. From what I've picked up, Rain is a lost soul, and I'm sorry for her." I turn on the faucet. "The experience was completely unreal to me. I thought I was dreaming." I gulp down the water and set the glass in the sink. "I don't know why my mouth is so dry." Hattie is staring. "It's unnerving to have you gawk at me."

"I can't help it. You're Shirlene, but you're also this Rain person."

I hurry to my seat across from Hattie at the kitchen table. "Rain is gone. It's only me. I've completely taken over this body."

"Peculiar."

"Tell me about it. Every time I go by the mirror, I think a stranger's in the room."

Hattie leans on the kitchen table with her chin resting in her left hand and her long fingers framing her cheek. It's a familiar and comforting gesture. "Yes. It might be easier if you looked like you when we were twenty, but this entirely new physicality is disconcerting."

Cameron passes the window, pushing the silent mower.

Hattie rises to take a better look. "Who exactly is this guy?"

"He's the baby's uncle, but he's going to raise her. His brother, Chase, is the father."

"His brother got you pregnant?"

"Not me! Rain. They were together, but both of them seem unfit to be parents. Drug addicts. Apparently, when Rain told Chase she was pregnant, he disappeared. She came to Cam."

"Why?" Hattie leans against the windowsill.

"She had no other option. She was basically homeless. Cam convinced her to go ahead with the pregnancy because he wanted the baby."

"Is Cam sleeping with Rain?"

"No. Cam only tolerated her to save the child. He thought she'd take off. Well, in a way, she did. She gave up, and here I am."

"And now he's prepared to help you with Stan?" Hattie asks.

"Yes. I'm letting him mow the lawn at this point."

"I got a good feeling about him yesterday. I'm not happy he lied to me, but you told him to do so."

"Hattie, I couldn't have him telling you I was alive. What would you have thought?"

She grunts. "He was insane."

"See. And I wanted to tell you myself."

"You wanted to see the expression on my face." Hattie's smile is all teeth, and I love it.

"I have another surprise." I stand up.

"Bring it on."

I yank my shirt up to reveal my navel piercing.

"What an adorable belly. Remarkable after just giving birth."

"Hattie!"

"What?" She feigns boredom. "Oh, you mean the holes in your belly button."

"Kind of titillating, isn't it?" I wiggle my belly and hips.

Hattie bursts into laughter. We're both howling when Cameron comes through the back door. I whip my shirt back down and try to act nonchalant.

Hattie switches gears on a dime. "Well, young man, what do you have to say for yourself?"

Cam's eyes dart to me.

"She knows. I told her."

"Lying to your elders," Hattie scolds, but there's a glint in her eyes, like a cat that has cornered a mouse.

"I'm sorry," he says.

"You should be."

"Yes, ma'am." Cameron sounds like a little boy. This amuses me because he's anything but little. I can't help but giggle.

"And what's so funny, Shirlene?" Hattie wags a finger. "Having both your husband and this boy lying for you. Telling me you're some long-lost relative from Australia."

I begin to cackle uncontrollably, and Hattie loses her composure too. Cam gazes at us like we've lost our minds. I wonder if I haven't.

Chapter Eleven

Cameron

Things are quiet after dinner, and the lightning bugs begin to flash in the dusk outside the open windows. I'm hanging out at the dining room table, reading a *congratulations* text from Aimee, sent with a baby-bottle emoji. I don't reply because it's one in the morning where she is. Although we didn't end up married, she's still my best friend.

My phone pings. A text appears, telling me Stan's lawn mower is repaired and ready to be picked up. I'm wondering where Shirlene has gone when I hear her chattering from the den.

I wander through the living room. The door to the den is open, so I step in quietly. Shirlene is lying across my bed with Arlene. Our infant girl is naked on a towel, fresh from a bath. Shirlene kisses the baby's tummy and makes faces. Arlene's little arms and legs joyfully flail. I want to wrap them both up in my arms.

Shirlene notices me and begins to get up. "I'm sorry."

"Relax. It's lovely."

She pauses. "But it's your bed."

"Please don't move."

Shirlene settles back down on the bed and kisses the baby's stomach again. "She's my little piggly wiggly."

I wipe a surprising tear of joy from my face.

"Well, I'd better get her into a diaper before she wets your bedding." Shirlene gets up with the baby.

I join her at the desk-slash-changing table. "I'll diaper Arlene."

Shirlene gets a fresh onesie. "I can't stop gazing at her and touching her soft skin."

I slip the baby into her pajamas. "She's so new. So perfect."

Arlene's eyes begin to close.

"Can I rock her for a bit?" I don't want this moment to end.

"Sure. She loves her daddy."

My chest expands with pride. Cradling my little peanut close, I go to the rocking chair in the living room. Shirlene sits nearby on the sofa.

"How's Stan tonight?" I ask.

"He's sleeping more, which is to be expected. He fights it, though. Afraid he'll miss something."

"You said he was concerned about the grass. Tomorrow, I can pick up the mower from the repair place, and I'll cut the lawn."

"He'll appreciate that."

"I want to tell him myself."

"I'll mull it over." Shirlene shifts on the couch.

This is Shirlene's way of saying no. The baby has fallen asleep. Her head is leaning against my chest, and I'm not up for breaking this intimate spell by pushing my opinion about meeting Stan. It will wait, but not for long.

Shirlene seems to be thinking the same thing. "This is cozy, but I don't really know much about you, Cam. For several days, we've been sharing this house and all the responsibilities of this child, but we're practically strangers."

"Ask me whatever you like." I'm feeling daring. If I share, perhaps she'll answer my questions too.

"Tell me about your brother," she says.

"Wow. Going right for the jugular."

"Sorry."

"I'm joking."

"No, you're not." She leans forward.

"I thought we might start with where we went to high school and work our way to the harder stuff."

Shirlene remains quiet.

"Okay. Chase is six years younger. He wasn't planned. My parents had just bought the real estate business in Los Angeles and moved out there. It wasn't a convenient time for another child. My mother wanted to focus on their new venture, and Dad needed her to work. She nearly had Chase in the office. He was raised by a nanny. My parents rarely saw him."

Shirlene glances down at the Oriental rug. "You said he and Rain were using drugs."

"Chase started very young. While I was still living at home—God, he was only about ten or eleven—I caught him sneaking liquor out of the bar in my father's den. My parents were in denial. Nothing much was done about it. I tried talking to him many times, but he got worse after I came East for college."

"Were things different before Chase was born?" she asks.

"We lived outside Philly then. My grandmother was here, and she was the glue in the family."

"Arlene?"

"Yeah. My dad's mom." The baby wakes, so I stand to rock her a bit. "I spent a lot of time with her at her beach house in Rehoboth Beach, Delaware. Chase did too. Mom plopped us on a plane every summer. This has always felt like home to me."

"So you didn't have a nanny."

"No way. There wasn't money for it then, and because my parents had planned for me, Mom made the time. Dad spent time with me when he could. One child and their real estate business was the strategy. They both took me with them to show properties from the time I was small. Apparently, I was cute."

"I don't doubt that."

I'm both flattered and uncomfortable with her compliment. "My point is they claimed I sold the houses. It was a huge disappointment to them when I became a teacher."

Shirlene frowns. "You a disappointment? I can't see it."

The baby is quiet, so I settle on the sofa next to but not too close to Shirlene. "They built the business for me. At least, that's what they said over and over."

"It's a lot of pressure on you."

"I came out here for college with no intention of ever living near them again. Long distance was the only way to maintain our relationship." I shift Arlene's position and kiss the top of her head. "But enough about me. What about your family?"

Shirlene moves closer so she can take Arlene's hand, which she rubs gently. The three of us are so natural together, a real family. I have to control getting carried away like this. Her husband is upstairs.

"I grew up here in Haddon Heights. Hattie and I went to school together. She's from Lawnside, a Black community that's a sending district for Heights. My father had a dry-cleaning business in town, and Mom was a homemaker. She did the bookkeeping for Dad and took care of my older brother and me." Shirlene hesitates. "Joey was killed during the Normandy invasion."

"I'm sorry."

"Thanks. He was my hero."

"Is he the soldier standing with Stan in the photograph on the piano?"

"Yes." She rises, ambles to the piano, and picks up the picture. "I've known Stan most of my life. He and Joey were buddies since grade school."

"Were you dating Stan when that picture was taken?"

"Sort of, but we kept it low-key. Stan was worried about how Joey would take it." Shirlene replaces the picture and gets a faraway

I resent having to say it's okay, so I simply nod.

He reaches out and takes my hand. "I don't want to miss the time I have left with you."

"What can I do to help you relax?"

He slips his fingers between mine. "It's so nice to be able to touch you without causing you pain." He stares at my hand, continuing to explore my fingers with his.

It's comforting for me, and I hope it is for him. It seems to be. The fight is over, and my tension melts.

His eyes meet mine. "Remember what you used to do when I came home from work upset?"

My throat feels dry. "I can't."

"Please, Shirlene. It will help to soothe me. It may do you some good too."

"But I haven't been able to play in years."

"You have new hands. Play the piano for me." His eyes plead with me.

Arlene cries on the monitor across the hall. She shouldn't be hungry or wet so soon. Our arguing disturbed her. She cries louder.

"Get that baby to shut up!" Stan shouts.

I have no energy to waste on worrying about Stan's anger.

"Coming, sweetheart." I dash down the stairs.

When I round into the living room, the piano calls to me. I pass it on the way into the den and Arlene's crib. I check her diaper—she's dry. She is whimpering in my arms as I carry her into the living room. She's not hungry, but she's in a mood. Both of them are in a snit, and Cam is out for a run.

I gently bounce her while pacing the room. Each time I see the piano, the longing builds in my chest. But reopening old wounds by attempting to play again is terrifying. When my arthritic hands wouldn't do their job any longer, I closed the cover on the keyboard for the last time. Only losing Danny hurt worse. What if Rain's body doesn't have what it takes? I can't risk such a disappointment.

Arlene starts to cry louder. I shift her to my left and sit on the piano bench. Do I dare? With my right hand, I raise the key lid and hit middle C. The sound startles her and pleases me. I slowly play a scale. My fingers are clumsy, but my heart sings along with the notes. My left hand itches to touch the keys too. I notice Arlene's car seat carrier by the sofa. She wails when I settle her into it.

"Just a minute, pumpkin."

I nestle her under the piano and go back to playing scales with both hands, and she quiets down. My reach is excellent as I coax my fingers to behave. My left pinky is especially lazy, which is no surprise. I'm asking these hands to do something I assume they've never done. Despite the extraordinary concentration it takes to persuade my hands into the proper technique, my mind flows with images of moving water as I glide up and down the keyboard.

I become aware of thumping in a different rhythm. I laugh. Stan is telling me to quit the scales and play. I have no idea what he's using to bang on the floor above, but his communication is clear.

"Okay. Keep your pants on," I mumble, opening the music cabinet.

I flip through the top of the pile. Chopin is too challenging. I land on Debussy's "Clair de Lune" as a good starting point. I lift the music desk, and it clicks into position. After settling the sheet music on the shelf, my hands quiver above the keys. I take the plunge, playing a phrase, and the pounding overhead stops. Sensations of nature come to life in my consciousness. The gentle sway of a breeze through pine needles. A Northern Gannet gliding over the waves of the sea. A brook trickling over rocks. After the first page of the sheet music, it all comes back to me. I recall every note.

Chapter Thirteen

Cameron

After mowing the lawn this morning, I still have a penned-up feeling, so I go for a run. I hit my stride, but my mind wanders to Stan. I've respected Shirlene's wishes the first several days here, but it's not normal to be in a house with a man I haven't introduced myself to.

About a mile out, my ankle gives way on an uneven patch of pavement. I manage to stay on my feet, but I'm pretty sure I've sprained my ankle. I head back to Shirlene's, and as I hobble near the house, piano music floats through the open windows. I limp into the hall, and the scene erases any sense of pain.

Shirlene's hands dance over the keys. Her eyes are shut as "Clair de Lune" seems to carry her to another world. She rocks with the tempo. Slowly, Rain has been disappearing. Now, the blond hair is sparkling clean and swept up into a clip. She wears little or no make-up. Her clothes are attractive without being revealing. She carries herself upright with confidence and health. Her skin has taken on a glow. And now that she is an accomplished pianist at her instrument, the transformation is complete. I see only Shirlene with her sleeping infant in the carrier on the floor under the edge of the piano. My niece-daughter is with her true mother.

When Shirlene finishes the piece, she looks up to where I'm standing across the room. She beams as tears well in her eyes. "I can play again."

Although I'm compelled to close the distance between us, I stay still. She'll notice me limping and immediately try to help. This moment is about her joy, certainly not my clumsiness.

"You sure can. You're wonderful."

She wipes her eyes and gazes at her hands. "It was impossible to play due to my arthritis. God, it feels so good. I must work these hands to move properly, but with these longer fingers, I'll be able to play more demanding pieces. I'll have more power."

The energy spinning off her lights up the room.

"I'm happy for you."

"Thank you. I need to contact the piano tuner." Shirlene kneels to Arlene. "She fell asleep as soon as I started, and Stan relaxes when I play."

Stan. I'd momentarily forgotten about him. Again, I imagine Arlene, Shirlene, and me as a family. I hobble over to the couch.

"You hurt yourself," she says.

"I twisted my ankle. No big deal."

"Elevate it. I'll grab an ice pack." Shirlene makes her way to the kitchen.

Her husband is upstairs, listening to her play. He is likely listening to us talking. I decide this charade has to end and make my way to the stairs. Leaning on the railing to keep my weight off my ankle, I make it to the top of the steps and to the open door of Stan and Shirlene's bedroom.

Stan lies restfully in bed. He looks better than I anticipated. He's no longer the robust soldier in the photo downstairs, but there's a strong presence in his weakened body and pale face. I tap on the doorframe.

He opens his eyes. "What are you doing up here?"

I try to walk normally to the bed with my hand extended. "I'm Cameron Michaels."

He shakes my hand. "I can presume that."

I plop down in the cushioned chair and lift my foot onto the footstool.

"What's wrong with your ankle?" he asks.

"I twisted it."

Shirlene bursts in the room. "What are you doing up here?"

"You told me to elevate my ankle."

Stan smirks and then coughs. The baby cries from the living room. Shirlene tosses the ice pack at me and jets back down the stairs.

Stan's eyes bore into me. "You'd better go back downstairs as Shirlene wants."

"Do you want me to leave?"

"Yes. I'd prefer it."

"But I chose to meet you. It's the polite thing to do."

"So, we've met. The Phillies game is coming on in a few minutes, and I'm going to watch it in peace." He coughs again.

I grab the water glass on the nightstand. He takes a sip.

"I want to help. Shirlene has so much on her plate with the baby."

"You and your niece are the problem." He hands the glass back.

"Your dying is the biggest problem."

Stan's mouth drops open.

"I don't mean to be disrespectful, and I'm sorry about Arlene crying now and then. But you're facing death, and I want to be as helpful as possible."

"The most helpful thing you could do is put the pillow over my face." Stan's twinkling eyes belie his words.

"That's not what I meant. I hope you have time left, and during that time, Shirlene needs support. I can do the heavy lifting."

Stan smacks his lips. "I could use more water."

I hand him the glass again. "You're a Phillies fan."

"Afraid so." He takes a sip.

"Great. We can suffer together."

Stan grunts. "You're a bad penny that's going to keep turning up, aren't you."

"Yes, sir."

"Well, I suppose I can't stop you from watching the game up here."

Progress. I sit back in the chair as the game begins and drape the ice pack over my ankle.

Chapter Fourteen

Shirlene

I'm in the basement, taking clean baby clothes out of the dryer. Cam is on the second floor, getting a lesson from Lauren, our hospice nurse, on how to correctly move Stan to use the bedpan, change the sheets, and avoid bedsores. Stan grumbled about it, but he realizes I can't do everything.

I hear Lauren and Cam walking down the stairs. They say goodbye as the front door opens and closes over my head, and footsteps scramble down the cellar steps. Cam appears in the laundry-room doorway. He's smiling.

"I take it things went well with Lauren." I shake out a crib sheet with a snap. "Stan insists on military corners on his sheets."

"Lauren told me."

"Do you know how to make them?" I ask.

"Yes." Cam leans on the doorjamb. "I wish you'd stayed."

"I was in the way."

"Don't be that way."

"What way?" I ask.

"You're angry with me for going up to meet Stan."

"I'm over it."

"Judging from the way you are beating that baby blanket into submission, I guess you're still pissed."

"It's a sheet." I run my shaking hands softly over the fabric.

85

Cam moves closer and rests against the washer. He seems so comfortable in his body, yet there's concern in his eyes. "I should have checked in with you first. I'm sorry."

I begin folding tiny undershirts.

"Do you accept my apology or not?" he asks.

I lay baby clothes in the basket.

"I wanted to do more is all," Cam says.

"Why? Why are you doing all this?"

"I'm not doing much."

"Mowing. Food shopping. Cooking. Changing and bathing Arlene. Now you're going to help with my husband."

"Would you rather I didn't?"

I toss the last pair of little socks into the basket. "I sound ungrateful."

"What is this about, Shirlene?" He steps closer.

I move back a pace. "I'm not used to accepting help from anyone other than Hattie. It makes me uncomfortable."

"I owe you. Think of it that way."

"For what?"

"You have taken on Arlene like she's your own child."

My voice is sharp. "She is mine. I gave birth to her."

Cam reaches out and touches my wrist. My stomach does a flip as I observe his large, warm hand.

He lets go. "Of course you did. But you were under no obligation to take this on. If it weren't for you, I'd be all alone in this baby venture. I can't imagine coping without you."

For a moment, I wish he was still touching me, but I vehemently dismiss that longing and pick up the basket of clean laundry.

Cam takes the basket from me. "Your house, your rules. I won't do anything like that again."

I take a deep breath. "Don't take Arlene up there."

"Can I ask why?"

I notice a lone baby sock on top of the dryer and hold it up to my nose. The sweet smell reminds me of Danny. "We had a son who died when he was very small."

"I'm sorry."

"Stan never..." I look into Cam's eyes. "I need you to agree to this. I can't take a chance on the baby upsetting Stan."

"I won't take the baby upstairs."

"How can I trust you after you went up there to meet Stan? It upset him and me."

"He's getting over it. Although he won't admit it, he likes the male company."

"You're too nonchalant, young man."

"I'm sorry you feel that way. I've apologized, and I promise to check with you first."

"I can't trust you, Cameron."

Chapter Fifteen

Cameron

Ironically, now that Shirlene dressed me down, I'm more comfortable upstairs with gruff Stan.

"Since you insist on being useful, would you shave my face?" Stan adjusts his position in the bed. "I don't want Shirleen doing it. I prefer to shave myself, but it's getting difficult."

I go into the bathroom to collect what I need, feeling as if I'm making headway with Stan. I've never shaved someone else's face, but I am fairly confident I can do it without drawing blood.

When I return, Stan asks, "Have you ever grown a beard?"

"No." I apply shaving cream over the stubble on Stan's face. "My brother has enough facial hair for the both of us."

"I've always thought about trying one, but Shirlene likes my face smooth."

I wait for him to pause before I run the razor down his cheek. "The minute my hair hits my shirt collar, off it comes."

Stan keeps talking, making it difficult to shave without nicking him. "After the war, I kept my hair short. By the late 1960s, all the kids had long hair and beards, but my accounting clients wouldn't have trusted me if I weren't clean-shaven."

"Could you not talk for a moment, Stan?"

"Oh. Of course."

I lift his nose slightly to shave above his upper lip. "Thank you for your service." I tackle his chin. It's the most difficult area on my own face, so I take special care. After I shave his neck, I say, "Shirlene told me you were a pilot."

"I didn't get into it until near the end of the war, but I did fly twenty-six missions over Germany in a P-47."

"Thunderbolt?" I hand him a warm washcloth and a towel.

Stan scowls. "Why do you care about my service? Are you interested in aircraft?" He wipes and dries his face.

"Especially fighter planes. I teach US history." I take the washcloth, towel, razor, and shaving cream back into the bathroom.

As I rinse off the razor, I notice one of Shirlene's hair clips on the sink. Although I'm unhappy with her holding a grudge, the clip reminds me of her beautiful hair. These thoughts about her make me uncomfortable. I have to stop. She's married, and I'm slowly becoming friends with her husband.

When I come back into the bedroom, Stan is rubbing his face. "Feels better."

I sit in the chair. "How old were you when you enlisted?"

"Twenty. I flew my second mission on my twenty-first birthday. I didn't think I'd ever see twenty-two."

"Why did you want to be a pilot?"

Stan's eyes widen. "That's an excellent question. When I was five years old, my family took a vacation to Stone Harbor. We were on the beach, and a guy landed a single-engine biplane right on the sand." He laughs. "Can you imagine such a thing today?"

"It would never happen."

"Not on your life. My older sisters were more interested in the pilot than the plane. They were fifteen and twelve. But I wanted to fly. To my surprise, my mother told Dad to let me go. I was grateful to her. It was a two-seater open cockpit. So I sat on my dad's lap in the front seat with the pilot behind."

"Only five years old." I whistle.

"I was too young to be afraid. The feeling of climbing up into the air was exhilarating. The wind blowing across my face. The sense of speed. And everything looked so beautiful from up there. So when the war came, I knew I had to be a pilot." Stan beams. "I graduated in April of 1944. Second lieutenant Silver Wings."

"Were you dating Shirlene by then?"

"I didn't feel completely brotherly toward Shirlene." Stan raises his eyebrows. "But I kept my admiration a secret for a long while because of Joe being my best buddy. And she was more than two years younger. But by the time I was training in the P-47 at the Millville Army Air Field base, Shirlene and I were getting serious. When I decided to propose, Joe was stationed in England. I wrote to him first, and he gave me his blessing. I'm grateful he did because he died during the Normandy Invasion that June."

"Shirlene told me. I'm sorry."

"It hit me bad, but I was really worried about Shirlene. She was so close to Joe."

"So then you and Shirlene got married?" I ask.

"No. We planned to wait until the end of the war. I couldn't leave her a widow at nineteen. After Joe died, I thought it would be easier for Shirlene to lose a fiancé than a husband. But knowing she was waiting for me, I was determined to stay alive for her."

I can understand Stan feeling this way. Having Shirlene would make a man do anything to return to her. Stan stifles a yawn.

"I'm sorry. You're getting tired."

"It's the most conversation I've had in weeks," he says.

"I'll let you rest. I hope you'll tell me more."

I need to respect that Stan is dying, and talking to me isn't necessarily a priority, but he sure did open up. Maybe he's realized that with so little time left, he doesn't want to waste it being angry with me. But while I've made progress with Stan, I need to focus on finding a way back into Shirlene's good graces.

Chapter Sixteen

Shirlene

"Shirlene?"

I am jumbled about where I am and what time it is.

"Shirlene!" The voice is louder.

I sit up. "Yes."

The hall light is on. Cam is in the open doorway with the baby in his arms. "Arlene has a fever. She's coughing and is completely congested."

I am out of bed and don't care that I'm taking off my pajamas and throwing on clothes right in front of Cam.

He steps into the hall. "I can take her to the emergency room, but I couldn't go without telling you."

"No. I have to go. Will you stay with Stan?" I dash out of the room, buttoning my blouse.

"You're both going," Stan calls from his bed. "I won't have Shirlene driving to the hospital alone in the middle of the night."

"What time is it?" I touch Arlene's head. It's burning up.

"Two o'clock," Cam says. "Her coughing woke me up."

"Cam should stay with you, Stan. What if you need something? I can manage on my own with the baby."

Stan switches on the table lamp by his bed. "I'll phone Hattie. She'd be here in minutes. Now, go! Nothing can happen to this baby."

I can't help but wonder if he's thinking about Danny. I sure am, but there's no time to waste. Cam and I race down the stairs. He settles the baby in her car seat carrier. I notice he's already dressed. I grab my purse on the way out the door.

Cam secures the carrier into the car seat base. "Why don't you sit back here with her? I'll drive."

While I try to soothe Arlene, it becomes clear that Cam had to come with us. I couldn't have stood driving with the baby where I couldn't see or touch her. The fear of losing another child crawls up my throat. My tears land on Arlene's face. She scrunches up her nose.

"It's going to be okay." Cam's eyes meet mine in the rearview mirror as he steers onto Kings Highway.

Arlene coughs and cries relentlessly. Her little face grows redder.

I stroke the top of her head. "Her passageways are so small. I'm afraid she won't be able to breathe."

"Try not to panic. She needs you to stay calm."

"You're right."

Within twenty minutes, Cam pulls up to the hospital emergency entrance. I rush Arlene into the ER while he parks the car. I begin answering the intake woman's questions and signing forms. After Cam joins me, the woman asks for my insurance. Cam hands over his card. Of course, he has the baby covered. I'm so unprepared. I should have planned for this type of emergency.

"Shirlene?" Cam touches my arm.

"What?" I snap out of my racing thoughts.

"I thought you said your name was Rain DeLuca," the woman says.

Cam remains composed. "When Rain gets distracted, I call her Shirlene after her sweet but ditsy aunt. Can we please take the baby in to the doctor?"

"Yes. Of course. In a few minutes."

"It has to be now," Cam insists. His sudden intensity surprises me.

"Sir, you have to wait."

"Thank you." I tug Cam over to two empty seats. "Nice work, Papa Bear."

"She's starting to piss me off."

I notice his right heel tapping on the floor. I try to soothe Arlene while we wait.

"Why is this taking so long?" he mutters.

"Baby Michaels," a nurse calls out from the door.

We follow her to another desk. "When will someone attend to our daughter?" The vein in the side of Cam's neck is pulsing.

"This will only take a moment."

After we answer all the same questions again, we are finally taken into a room, where an ER resident, who looks about sixteen, examines Arlene.

"Is she going to be okay?" Cam asks.

"I need to make sure she doesn't have an infection. She could end up with bronchiolitis or pneumonia."

With the help of a nurse, the resident suctions out the baby's nose, and I can't believe the amount of phlegm coming out. Cam takes my hand, and I let him hold it. It's safe and reassuring. I tell myself this is about Arlene and nothing more.

Once Arlene's temperature comes down, we wait for the doctor in charge of the ER. The sun has already risen when he checks the baby over, reads everything the resident noted, and announces that the baby has a bad cold. We are given detailed instructions on what to do to keep her comfortable. I hug Cam. He holds me close, and I try not to cry. I also try not to feel so comfortable in his arms, but the anger I was holding against him for going up to Stan begins to evaporate. Maybe holding on to it would ease the guilt I have that this horrible night has brought us closer.

Chapter Seventeen

Cameron

It's a little after seven in the morning when we arrive home. Hospice is due in a couple of hours. The house is quiet.

"I'll check on Stan." Shirlene starts for the stairs.

"I'll do it, and I'll let you know if there's a problem. Take the baby into the den. You can rest in my bed. I moved her crib over next to it last night."

Too tired to disagree, she wanders through the living room. I go straight upstairs and notice Stan's eyes are sharp but his face is more swollen. I worry his kidney function is worsening.

"Is the baby okay?" he asks with concern in his voice.

"Yes. She just has a bad cold. She'll be fine."

"Thank God."

"How are you? Did you get any sleep?" I ask.

"Some, but I need to use the bedpan."

After I help Stan deal with the necessities, I settle into the chair and rest my feet on the footstool.

"You look beat," he says.

"I'm a little tired."

"How is Shirlene?"

"She's resting, I hope. It was nerve-racking." I don't mention that the stressful experience brought us closer. "Stan, thank you for asking about Arlene. Shirlene told me you lost a child, and I can't help but wonder why you and Shirlene insist we keep Arlene away from you."

"I haven't been welcoming to your niece. You see, when we lost Danny, I walled up that part of my life."

"I'm sorry."

"I don't like to talk about it, but there's something about you that makes me open up, Cam."

"My students tell me the same thing."

"I was terrified last night that Shirlene was going to lose another child. I'm so relieved your baby is fine." Stan fidgets in the bed. "I need to up my meds. I'm too irritable. Shirlene was so distracted by my bullshit yesterday she didn't have time to notice the baby getting sick. It was my fault."

"Hey, babies can be sick."

"Danny had whooping cough once. Scared us both to death. I don't want anything to happen to your little girl. It's not easy being a father. A lot of work." Stan's mouth tightens. "I don't have enough time left to be a jerk. You could bring her up here sometime. I'd like to meet her."

"I'm sure Arlene will be happy to meet you."

Stan clears his throat. "Well, let's change the subject."

I take my feet off the hassock and sit up straight. "You promised to tell me more about being a fighter pilot."

"Okay. What can I talk about?"

"Did you stay in one place? How long did it take to fly to targets?"

"We moved every three weeks. As the Allies advanced, we relocated from Belgium to Holland and to Germany. We flew in twelve ship squadrons. Sometimes, it took close to three hours to reach our targets, which were often gun bases or tanks giving trouble to our guys on the ground. Sometimes, we targeted trucks and trains. On a dive-bomb run, we'd drop from eight or ten thousand feet to fifteen hundred or a thousand feet to release the bombs."

I shift to the edge of the chair. "It must have been hell when they fired back."

"We flew through flak, and it was the same as flying directly into fireworks. Some pilots got 'flak happy' and had to quit."

"Were you ever hit?"

"Several times. Once, my engine was hit, and on our way back, my flight leader in the ship below mine noticed oil coming out of my engine. He directed me to fly right to base. Right after I landed, the engine froze. I would have gone down."

"That is remarkable."

"I was lucky," he says.

"What happened when the war ended in Europe?"

"I was shipped home in August with orders to report to Sioux Falls, South Dakota, in a month. We were to pick up new models of the P-47 and prepare for the invasion of Japan. The moment I landed in Newport News, Virginia, I found the first phone booth and called Shirlene to tell her we are having the wedding now."

"You decided not to wait until after going to the Pacific?"

"We'd waited long enough. Anyway, the week Shirlene and I were married, the A bombs were dropped. Japan surrendered. I was discharged." Stan laughs. "When Shirlene asked Hattie to be her maid of honor, Shirlene's parents didn't approve. So we eloped with Hattie in tow. It was quite a night."

"I admire Shirlene's devotion to her best friend."

"Her parents were livid, but Hattie came first."

"Shirlene is a pretty tough cookie."

"She is, but she's only human." Stan sighs. "You know, you both have been through the wringer here with a sick newborn and me in hospice."

"Shirlene could have a spa day. I can cover things here."

"Unless you want a spa day too."

"No, sir. I'm not a spa kind of guy."

"You deserve a break." Stan's face lights up. "I'd like you to take Shirlene out to dinner when the baby is over her cold. Hattie can stay with me and Arlene. We'll be fine for a few hours."

Although I hope Shirlene and I got closer tonight, I don't know if she's able to trust me again. "I'd enjoy that, but I'm not sure Shirlene will agree to it."

"Between you, me, and Hattie, she won't be able to refuse."

I hope Stan is right, but I have my doubts.

Chapter Eighteen

Shirlene

As Cam drives us to Tre Famiglia, I can't come up with anything to say. He looks handsome in his khakis and pale-blue shirt. He's gotten a haircut, and he smells good. Although I'm excited to talk about anything other than "the baby has to be changed" or "Stan needs his medications," it feels too much like a date.

I can't believe how Stan and Hattie ganged up on me and set this all up. What were they thinking? Hattie might be up to her devilish ways, but Stan couldn't be considering this a date. I wring my hands because it sure feels that way to me.

"You okay?" Cam asks.

I settle my hands in my lap. "Fine."

"Have you been to this restaurant before?"

"Years ago."

"Wow. Two words." He glances over to me with a smile.

I laugh and decide to be direct. "I don't understand why I'm so nervous."

"Because it feels like a date."

I appreciate his honesty. "Yes."

"Back to one word."

"Sorry. I mean, I am sorry. There, six words total."

"You can't count the first 'sorry' since you said it twice."

"Five words, then."

He chuckles and circles the block in search of a place to park. After he pulls into a spot on a side street, he asks, "Are you sorry to be going out to dinner with me?"

"God, no. You've adjusted your entire summer around Stan and me. You've been so helpful."

"My summer and the next eighteen to twenty years were already transformed when Arlene arrived. So being in Jersey instead of my Philly apartment isn't a big deal."

"It is. I'm grateful."

"You're welcome. Look, I decided to take care of this baby, but you were literally thrown into it. It's as if I won the lottery."

"Why?" I ask.

"You, Stan, and Hattie are a giant improvement over Rain."

I remain hesitant to go into the restaurant.

"Are you unsure because of me barreling through your boundary with Stan? I really need you to be able to trust me again, Shirlene. That means a lot to me." His eyes are so sincere.

I briefly touch his hand, which is resting on the steering wheel. "I'm over it, Cam. After the other night, taking Arlene to the emergency room, I couldn't ask more of you."

"Listen, we're Arlene's parents, right?" he asks.

I nod.

"Parents can be friends, so let's go enjoy dinner as friends."

"Yes, let's." Being friends takes the pressure off, and I can try to have a good time.

Before I gather my purse, Cam hops out and around the car to open my door. Chivalry isn't dead with this young guy. The humid air hits me outside the air-conditioned car, and I second-guess my choice of a light sweater slipped on over the sundress Hattie bought for me. What was that old woman thinking, making me expose so much skin? I hope the sweater doesn't spoil the appearance of the dress. I wonder why I care if it does. Well, the restaurant will be air-conditioned, so I need the sweater either way.

The front dining room has an intimate candlelit atmosphere as the hostess directs us to the only vacant table, located in a cubby with an antique mirror on the wall. For a moment, I assume I'm looking at another couple before I realize it's us. I glance into the second room to the left. It is nearly full as well, and several tables are grouped together.

"We have a wedding rehearsal dinner in there." The hostess hands us our menus. "Your waiter will be right with you. Enjoy your dinner."

Her eyes linger on Cam. She's checking him out, as the kids say. I can't blame her, but it's rude. She has no idea I'm an elderly lady. We appear to be a couple. I'm a smoking-hot twenty-year-old. I take off the damn sweater. The hostess moves on to seat new arrivals.

A moment later, our waiter is telling us the specials and answering questions about the menu. We order. While we wait for our appetizers, again, I am at a loss for words. I twist the linen napkin in my lap. Italian opera music plays quietly on the restaurant's sound system. Cam begins humming along with "Nessun Dorma" from *Turandot* by Giacomo Puccini.

"You're familiar with Puccini?" I ask. There's still so much to learn about Cam.

"Aimee was a voice major at Curtis."

"I went there too."

"Were you there when Leonard Bernstein was?"

"No. He graduated before I started." I'm too curious about this ex-fiancée to reminisce about my days at Curtis. "Tell me about Aimee."

"We're close friends."

"Nothing more?"

"Unfortunately, no." Cam places his napkin on his lap. "Aimee was perfectly clear from the start that her career came first. While I completely supported her, I thought there would be room for me, marriage, and a family. Aimee loves kids but struggles with depression. Managing her performance schedule can become too much for her, so children seemed out of the question."

"I'm sorry."

"It was a difficult decision. She'd love to have a family. I told her I was willing to take on the bulk of the parenting load, and she could concentrate on her work and be able to tour."

"But..."

"When I proposed, she accepted." Cam takes a sip from his water glass. "But about a month away from the wedding, she was becoming more depressed. It hit her that she was getting married to make me happy."

"She must have loved you very much."

"I guess, but she called it off."

"Oh, Cam." My heart breaks for him and Aimee.

"In the end, it was the right decision for her. It wasn't fair for me to try to push my desire for a family onto her when she couldn't manage."

I fidget with my napkin. "What does she think about you taking on your brother's child?"

"She says Rain is bad news, but she understands about the baby. She's happy for me."

"Do you see much of Aimee?"

"I do when she's home, but she's performing on tour in Europe all summer."

Just as I'm wondering how different my situation would be if Aimee weren't away for months, our appetizers arrive. Cam offers me a taste of his sausage and figs. My face heats up when he lifts his fork for me to eat from it. He turns down one of my shrimp, saying he's not one for shellfish.

A thought dawns on me: *If Cam is this close to Aimee, what is she going to make of me?* "So, back to Aimee. Will you tell her who I really am?"

"I have no idea. We have time to figure it out."

"Is she a soprano?"

"Contralto. Her voice is like a sip of rich coffee." Cam takes another bite of his appetizer.

"Rain is a soprano. I was a second soprano, but now I can sing higher without any strain. It pours out."

"I doubt Rain ever sang, other than in the shower."

I set down my fork and stretch my fingers. "I can play any piece on the piano once I get these fingers better coordinated."

Cam sits quietly for a long moment. I sense he wants to ask something.

"What is it?" I ask.

"You have a second chance at everything."

My breath catches. Is he talking about my second chance at motherhood? I only told him we lost Danny. I haven't given him any details.

"What unfilled dream do you have?" he asks.

"I'm getting to take proper care of Stan at the end of his life."

"No. For you. Your music. Because now, you can do it."

I'm relieved this isn't about Danny, and it's obvious Cam feels sincerely excited for me, but my stomach knots up. Why am I frightened by this?

"You can," he continues. "You can be or do anything."

"I wanted to be a conductor," I blurt out.

"Wanted?"

"In my day, women conductors were basically taboo." The old resentment and bitterness constrict my throat.

"That's ridiculous."

"It was also complicated by Curtis cutting their conducting program before I got there. But I doubt I would have gotten in even if it had still existed."

"It might have been tough, but I'm sure you would have been successful," he says.

"I went into education instead."

"Lucky students."

I'm relieved when our dinners arrive. Once we admire the presentation of his beef tenderloin risotto and my crab cakes, we begin to enjoy the mouthwatering flavors. Between the delicious food, the candles, and the passionate music, the atmosphere is too romantic, and I wonder why Stan and Hattie selected Tre Famiglia.

"What about you?" I ask.

"Simple really. Teach, marry my best friend, and raise a family. With Arlene, now I have two out of three." He eats a fork full of risotto.

"Has there been anyone since Aimee?"

"Nothing serious. No one compared."

"You're a wonderful guy, Cam. The right woman will come along."

"Thank you. So are you. Wonderful, I mean. You're wonderful."

My cheeks heat again. "Will you excuse me?"

He stands when I rise. Where did this young man learn such lovely, old-fashioned manners?

The closer restroom is occupied, so I wade past the rehearsal-dinner partyers to determine if the ladies' room over there is free. I find two young women lingering while scrolling on their phones.

"Is there a line?" I ask.

"No, but the bride is in there. We're waiting for her."

"I love your dress," the other one says after scanning me from head to toe.

"Thanks."

I'm likely younger than they are. They could be in their early thirties. Now, women often concentrate on their careers before settling down. So different from my generation, when marriage or becoming a nurse or a teacher were the accepted plans for women. I taught, and I loved working with my high school musicians, but what if I could have been a conductor of a major orchestra? Could I do it now?

The door opens, and the bride-to-be sways out.

"That's it for you, girl," one of her friends says.

"You're right. I don't want to feel crappy tomorrow." She totters to me. "I'm getting married."

"Congratulations." I slip past and shut the door.

I glance in the mirror and am still surprised by who I see. Then I notice an abandoned drink on the sink counter. The smell of alcohol permeates my olfactory senses. Immediately, nothing else exists. Not Arlene. Not Stan. Not my music. Nothing. Just the drink. The liquid shimmers in the glass. The entire world narrows down to the siren call of the alcohol.

Someone knocks on the door. I drag my eyes away from the glass. Tears brim. I grab a tissue and blot.

The knock again.

"Yes, I'll be right out." I toss the alcohol down the toilet and flush. I set the glass back on the counter and unlock the door.

"Are you all right, dear?" the older woman who was waiting asks.

"You saved my life."

The woman's eyes widen. I tremble as I maneuver through the restaurant toward Cam. He jumps up and dashes around the table to my side.

"What's wrong?" he asks.

"I apologize, but I have to leave."

"What happened?"

"Can I explain outside?"

"Of course."

The desire to run outside compels me quickly toward the exit.

"Have a nice night," the hostess says as we pass.

I ignore her.

Cam stops. "Let me ask if Stan covered the tip."

"I'll wait out front."

"Will you be okay for a moment?"

"Yes. I just need to leave."

The sticky summer night embraces me. It's a relief to be out of the air-conditioning. As I warm up, the shaking slows. I take a deep breath and relax my jaw.

Cameron comes out quickly, carrying my sweater. "You forgot this."

"What do you know about addiction?" I ask.

"Plenty. My brother has screwed up his life with drugs."

"It's a disease, Cam."

"I agree."

"What about Rain?"

He shrugs. "She was using, but I assume she had some control because she quit cold turkey when she got pregnant."

"Was she irritable?"

"Yes. Whether she was drinking or not."

As I explain to Cam what happened in the ladies' room, we hike toward the car. "I haven't had a drink in sixty-five years. Haven't thought about it in a very long time, but because I have Rain's body, I have her addictions."

"I'm sorry, Shirlene. Are you okay now?" Cam opens the car door for me and jets around to the driver's seat.

"It could be it's all this stress, but I need to get to an AA meeting."

Cam immediately digs out his phone. His thumbs fly over the keyboard. I lean my head against the window. I need this like I need a tumor. Great. What if Rain's body is also predisposed to cancer? I can't go through that again.

"There's a meeting about to start at a church only a few minutes from here." Cam starts the car. "I'll wait for you outside."

After the meeting, I open and close my purse as Cam drives us home. Inside is a list of meetings, including ones online. It felt weird to be sitting in the circle of chairs again, smelling coffee brewing and staring at people from all walks of life. As when I attended AA in my old life, it was comforting to realize I wasn't alone. Everyone in the room was in the same ocean but in different boats.

"Do you need to talk?" Cam asks.

"Just feeling sorry for myself. Between the baby and Stan, it's going to be difficult to attend meetings."

"I'll cover for you. Hattie will help too."

Cam's generosity and support nearly bring me to tears. "Thanks. I'll try an online meeting tomorrow and find out what it's like. It's much more convenient."

"I'm sorry you have to deal with this."

"Me too." I find myself tapping the armrest and stop. "I wish I understood the main cause. Rain's physical chemistry? My past? All the stress? But wondering why is a waste of time. It is what it is. I'll manage." *I did before. I can do it again*, I think.

"Shirlene, what am I missing here? Outside the restaurant, you said you hadn't had a drink in sixty-five years."

"My dad's father was an alcoholic, so it's in my chemistry. The war added to my need to escape, especially after Joey was killed. There was a lot of pressure at Curtis."

"Did Stan know?"

"He was drinking, too, but he doesn't have the disease. He can take it or leave it." I am getting perilously close to the events surrounding my son's death, so I switch topics. "I admire Rain for staying sober during her pregnancy. It's astonishing how she did it, given the overwhelming power that drink in the restroom had over me. She must have loved this baby a lot."

"Loved?" Cam scoffs.

"When I took over Rain's body in the delivery room, I heard a voice say, 'Take care of her.' It was Rain asking me to take care of her baby."

He steers into the driveway. "Really? That's amazing."

"Love has more power than alcohol or drugs."

"I guess so."

"I know so."

He comes around and opens my door. "I had a nice time."

"If this was a fun date, I'm sorry for you."

He shuts the car door. "I thought this wasn't a date."

Why isn't he at least dating anyone? I wonder if his continued friendship with Aimee isn't what's keeping other women away. He's handsome, intelligent, kind, hardworking, and funny. He's damn near perfect.

"What are you thinking about?" he asks.

I notice I haven't moved from the car. "I wonder how Hattie managed while we were out." I move toward the front door.

Cam opens and shuts the rear car door, catches up, and holds the front door open for me. Once in the foyer, he hands me a takeout box.

"What's this?" I ask.

"Four desserts. During your meeting, I popped back to the restaurant. I got enough for everyone."

"I'll grab plates from the kitchen. Maybe Hattie is in there."

"I'll check on Arlene."

The kitchen is empty. I take out small plates, forks, and napkins. I run into Cam in the dining room.

"The baby isn't in her crib." He takes the plates from me.

My stomach tightens. "Where is everyone?"

We race up the stairs. Hattie sits in the cricket chair, reading. Stan has the ball game on the TV with the sound off, and Arlene is asleep in his arms. For a moment, I can see him holding Danny as a young father and fight back tears.

"What's going on?" I ask.

"Sh," Stan scolds. "She's sleeping."

I can't believe my husband is holding the baby and clearly enjoying it. This change in Stan is miraculous.

"We have dessert." Cam opens the box to reveal four beautiful treats.

"I'll skip it." Stan kisses the top of Arlene's head.

"I'll eat his." Hattie lifts two onto her plate.

After we finish dessert, Cam takes Arlene down to bed. Hattie goes to clean up the dishes, and I settle Stan in for the night.

"Did you enjoy yourself, Shirlene?" He yawns.

"Yes. Thank you for the night out. Now, go to sleep. I'll fill you in tomorrow."

I wonder if I can keep the AA meetings a secret from Stan. I have no intention of dredging up old pains. In the kitchen, I find Hattie setting the dishes in the dishwasher.

"Whose idea was it to take the baby upstairs? Yours or Stan's?"

"Now, don't get your knickers in a knot." Hattie presses a button, and the dishwasher's low rumble fills the room.

"Answer me," I say.

"It was Stan's."

"You're joking."

"No. He's really a marshmallow inside."

I take Hattie's hand. "He hasn't much time left."

"I agree." Hattie hugs me.

"What am I going to do without him? I should have stayed with Danny. I'd be there now, waiting to greet him."

Hattie furrows her brow. "What else happened?"

"I hate that you can read my mind."

She waits.

"I ended up going to an AA meeting."

"And you were worried the evening was going to be too romantic," she quips.

"Yeah, right." I shake my head. "Apparently, I've inherited a body with addiction issues."

"Oh, Shirlene."

I pace across the kitchen. "I thought I was through with all of this. Plus, I had to lie at the meeting."

"What do you mean?"

"I said 'Hi, I'm Rain, and I'm an alcoholic.' I can't be Shirlene. She's dead." I sink into a kitchen chair. "Oh my God. This is insane."

Hattie reaches across the table and takes hold of my hand.

Chapter Nineteen

Shirlene

During the week following our dinner at Tre Famiglia, Stan has slept more and stopped eating. Now he is becoming nearly unresponsive.

"Don't you dare die now! Fight it!" Tears stream down my face. "Please fight it."

Stan gently pats my arm. It's light as a feather. He musters a smile. I can tell it takes a great deal of effort.

"Why didn't you let go when you had the chance?" he whispers.

I bite back the anger that roars to be released. It's his fault I'm stuck here for another sixty or seventy years without him and Danny. I lay my head on his chest, giving in to the sobs. I feel more pats on my back now, soft and otherworldly, like he's reaching from far away, but I can hear his heart faintly beating.

After a moment, he says, "Shirlene."

I adjust my head to stare up at his face.

He speaks with a surge of presence. "Tell me. Why did you come back?"

"Because you begged me to."

"I did no such thing!" His face gets some color.

"Yes, you did. You said, 'Shirlene, don't leave me.'"

Stan's eyes become clear again for the first time in days. "My love, I didn't say that. I called your name, but I never said not to leave me."

My cheeks burn. "You must have thought it, then."

"I most certainly did not. Do you think I'm capable of that level of selfishness?" He pauses, looking as if he's recalling the moment when I died.

I open my mouth and close it. I'm speechless. Did I imagine it or dream it? Was I so codependent I thought he couldn't survive without me?

Stan runs the backs of his fingers along my cheek. "Don't try to make this my responsibility. You chose to come back. Now make the most of it."

His thin body shudders with weak coughs, and his eyes close.

"No!" I shout.

He opens his eyes and gestures across the room to the bedroom door. "Tell Joey to sit down, and give him a drink."

I examine the room, expecting to find my brother. Stan must be seeing the dead.

Forcefully, I grab his face in my hands. "Stan! Don't go to Joey. Stay a few more minutes."

I am that selfish. I was the one to go after what I wanted. Stan let life happen. His lack of decision was his decision, but in the end, he was more selfless than I.

"Red?"

My fingers relax, and I run my thumbs along his temples. "I'm sorry. Did I hurt you?"

"You returned for the baby, not for me."

"But I had no idea I'd take over a pregnant body. Danny tried to warn me, but I didn't understand that I couldn't reoccupy my old body." I kiss his forehead. "I couldn't leave you, Stan. You're the world to me."

His eyes search my face. "You saw Danny?"

I can only nod. Tears drip down my cheeks.

"Why didn't you tell me he was there?"

"I'm sorry. You stopped talking about him many years ago, so I was trying to avoid upsetting you."

"I'll be with him soon."

"Yes." I blow my nose in a tissue.

Stan starts tugging at the top sheet. "Listen, I have something to tell you. I made a selfish decision after Danny was killed."

"Don't upset yourself."

"No, I have to say this. You longed for more children." Stan grabs hold of my hands. "I kept you from having another child. I'm sorry I denied you that joy again."

"I don't understand. We tried. I couldn't become pregnant again."

"I thought you were drinking when the accident happened."

The ancient torture of our marriage beats its drum again. "I told you a million times I was sober. I would never drive drunk with Danny."

"Nevertheless, on some level, I was punishing you. I blamed you for our son's death. Forgive me." He thrashes around in the bed.

"Stan, try to calm down. It doesn't matter now."

"Shirlene, I have a confession."

"Try to relax, my darling." I stroke his arm in an effort to soothe him.

"I had a vasectomy."

He's not making sense. "What?"

"I wasn't able to trust you."

I yank my hands away. "You had a vasectomy?"

He speaks rapidly. "It was the only way I could touch you again. To love you, to be with you again." He has to stop to catch his breath. "I love you, Shirlene, but I had to be sure there'd never be another child to lose."

"You had a vasectomy without talking to me?" Anger burns in my belly. "Without telling me?"

head back in her characteristic fashion and laughing in that deep, throaty way with all her teeth showing. I laugh too. It feels good.

When we settle down, I say, "Stan believed I came back for Arlene, but I had no idea I was going to have a baby. I assumed I'd be back in my old, sick body. I wasn't gone very long."

"In this sort of event, time is impossible to track. You could have been gone longer. Either way, your body couldn't support you returning."

"I needed to take care of Stan."

"And you got to. You were with him as long as you were supposed to be."

I can't believe what Stan did.

"Shirlene, you said Stan had a confession?"

"He admitted to having a secret vasectomy after Danny died."

"That must have been a nasty procedure. It's fairly minor now, but back then..."

"I hope it was painful." I grind my teeth.

"You're angry with him."

"Damn right, I am."

"How did he manage to hide it from you?" she asks.

"It wasn't difficult. We weren't sleeping together after Danny was killed."

"Because you were injured."

"Even after I came home from the hospital, Stan wouldn't touch me for a long time. He slept on the sofa. I felt abandoned. So alone. Remember, we were living in that tiny apartment in Oaklyn. I should have told you when it was happening, but I was too ashamed."

"We don't often have secrets, but I understand you keeping this one." Hattie ponders for a moment. "It could be that's the reason you came back from the dead and took over Rain's body. Stan needed to be absolved of his guilt."

"He did ask me to forgive him."

"Can you?"

I clench the top of the bed sheet. "I don't know. I'm angry with a dead man. So angry, Hattie."

"That he had a vasectomy or that he didn't tell you?"

"He lied. All these years, he's been lying. He said he forgave me, but he never did." I don't want to cry, but tears slip down my face. "The only way he could make love to me again was to punish me each time by knowing he'd never impregnate me again." I snatch a tissue from the nightstand and blow my nose. "Without my knowing, he kept me from getting pregnant again. Each and every month, I held onto hope for years. I grieved every time I got my period. We had planned on having more than one child. We were already trying when Danny was alive." I pound my fist on the mattress.

"Shirlene." Hattie wraps her arms around me.

The memory I fight to keep at bay forces its way back. "I was distracted by Danny's sweet voice. He was learning to sing 'Row, Row, Row Your Boat' with me in rounds."

"It wasn't your fault," Hattie reminds me, as she has all these years.

"I thought God was punishing me when I couldn't get pregnant again, but it was my husband."

Cam drives Hattie and me to Locustwood Cemetery in Cherry Hill. I had hoped Stan would be willing to be cremated so I could scatter his ashes at one of his favorite fishing holes, but he insisted on being buried next to me in Locustwood. The idea of seeing my own grave is more than a little discomforting.

Hattie puts her hand on my shoulder as Cam pulls up behind the hearse in the left-hand turning lane at Cooper Landing Road. I glance at Hattie. She seems so little, sitting in the back seat. She's the only one left of all our close friends and family. Only a handful of people would have attended the internment, so it is private. I can't pretend to be the distant great-great-grandniece right now. I am Shirlene, who is burying her husband.

After the casket is placed, the funeral director leads us over to chairs set up next to the plot. Luckily, the green outdoor carpeting and flowers cover my grave and hide the marker with Shirlene Foster on it. I'm grateful for small mercies.

Since Stan and I attended events at Hattie's Unitarian Church, her minister willingly says a few words at the cemetery. He talks about Stan's service in World War II, his love of fishing and the Phillies, and his volunteer work. When he mentions Stan's beloved wife, Shirlene, who died recently, my head spins. As when I died and looked down at Stan and my body from the ceiling of my hospice room, I am now watching Rain with Cam on her right and Hattie on her left. Rain slumps over. Cam holds her against his chest and rocks her gently in a desperate attempt to revive her.

"She just had a baby a month ago." Hattie gently pats her face.

I hover above, searching for Stan and Danny in the brightly lit tunnel, but they are nowhere in sight. With a sudden jolt, I'm back in Rain's body.

"She's coming around," Cam says with relief.

I try to focus on Hattie, but Stan's casket is a few feet away, balanced on two thick straps over the open grave. This can't be real. I close my eyes again.

"Shirl. Rain," Cam says.

I want to go to sleep against his chest and never wake up.

Chapter Twenty-One

Cameron

Since the funeral last week, Shirlene moves around the house like a rudderless ship. She's lost to a different dimension. She resurfaces a little when Arlene needs something, but even when she's holding the baby, her eyes are far away.

When my grandmother died, I shoved the grief into a tiny pocket somewhere, and when Aimee ended our engagement, I found myself grieving both losses. I would begin to grade papers at my desk on a Saturday and find myself in the kitchen, unloading the dishwasher, with no recollection of stopping one task to begin another. At school, my students and colleagues tethered me to the day. Still, there were moments when someone would be talking to me and I would check out for an unknown stretch. Sometimes, I could piece the conversation together, but often, I had to swallow my pride and ask the person to repeat what they said. I have some small hint of the grief Shirlene feels. I want to help her.

I ask Hattie to meet me at the Legacy Diner on the White Horse Pike. She wanders in a few minutes after I'm seated in a brown-and-tan vinyl booth with paper placemats advertising local businesses.

"I'm sorry I'm late." She slips in across from me.

"I just got here myself." I hand her one of the menus our waitress left.

"I was talking to Shirlene, and I couldn't invent an excuse to hang up the phone. I thought it could complicate things if I told her I was meeting you."

After our waitress takes our orders, Hattie asks, "So, what's up?"

"I need your opinion on something."

"I'm happy to give my opinion. More often than not, it's unsolicited."

"I want it. I have a house in Rehoboth Beach, left to me by my grandmother. I was planning on taking the baby and Rain, if she was still around, down there for some vacation time. I never mentioned going there to Shirlene because there was no telling how long Stan would be with us."

"Are you going to ask me if I think Shirlene would go now?" Hattie asks.

"Yes. It could be too soon for her to leave home."

"A change of scenery would be good for her. Plus she loves the beach."

"I was hoping you might say that. We have the rest of July and the entire month of August left. Of course, you're invited too."

"I would love to come for a couple of weeks, but if Shirlene can manage, I plan to take my trip to Ireland in August."

The waitress brings our food, and we dig in.

"It would be best if you tell Shirlene about our lunch." Hattie lifts her burger, which is almost bigger than she is, and takes a bite. She sure can pack it away for an elderly, petite thing.

I swallow a french fry. "Absolutely. I don't want to keep secrets from Shirlene." I've managed to win her trust back, and I can't jeopardize it again.

Hattie plops her mega burger down and wipes her mouth with her napkin. "Let me ask you something."

"Shoot."

"How do you feel about Shirlene?"

I nearly choke on my sandwich. I haven't allowed myself to consider this question for too long, let alone talk about it with someone else. After I swallow, I ask, "What do you mean exactly?"

"What do you want from Shirlene?"

I can't answer.

She grins. "I have eyes."

"What do you think you're seeing?" I begin tapping my right heel on the sticky diner floor.

"I asked first. What are your feelings for Shirlene?"

"I admire her. She's an amazing mother to Arlene. You have no idea what an improvement she is over Rain."

"So you had no relationship with Rain?"

"Nothing more than trying to help her out in order to take care of my niece."

"But it's different now that Shirlene is in her body." Hattie takes another bite of her lunch.

"Completely," I blurt out. "I mean, I have faith in Shirlene. She's a devoted mother."

"She depends on you too." Hattie takes a sip of her milkshake and scrutinizes me. "I sense there's more developing."

"On her part or on mine?" I take the last bite of my sandwich and try to appear laid-back.

Hattie sets down her glass. "Even though Stan is gone, he's still in her head."

"So you're talking about me."

She nods.

"Have you talked to Shirlene about this?" I'm feeling like a high school sophomore.

"Not directly. She'd snap a nerve."

"So why are you bringing it up with me?"

"Because I'm a practical woman. While I'm healthy for my age, I'm not going to live forever. You are all Shirlene has. She acts strong and independent, but she's only human. What are your intentions? I mean, you're a young man. Eventually, you're going to desire someone significant in your life. Am I right?"

"I suppose so." I wipe my forehead with my napkin. "I haven't given it much thought lately."

"You must have been hurt in the past."

"Hattie, I think the world of you."

"But...?"

"I'm not ready to talk about any of this."

She shrugs her narrow shoulders and finishes her milkshake. "Are you ready for dessert?"

The woman weighs no more than ninety-eight pounds. Where does she put all this food?

At least for now, I'm off the hook, but Hattie's interrogation makes me wonder what the hell I'm doing. I assumed Rain would eventually abandon Arlene and leave her with me. Sure, I'd be a man with a child, but that wouldn't be unappealing to some women. Eventually, I'd be ready to trust again. I pictured myself married with more children down the road.

Things are very different now. Shirlene isn't going to give up Arlene. I would never ask her to. The question is, what do I really want from Shirlene? It scares me to consider it. I want something Shirlene isn't ready to give. She's grieving the loss of Stan. I'm sure Shirlene isn't going to reciprocate my feelings, and I can't go through that again. So I need to do a better job of burying those desires.

Chapter Twenty-Two

Shirlene

I open Stan's side of the closet and inhale. When we got married, Stan insisted we keep an organized closet. On his side, all the long-sleeved shirts are hung together going in one direction, as are his short-sleeve shirts. Vests and pants are also in separate groups. I gave in, not that I had a choice, and my side is also arranged by category of dresses, skirts, slacks, and blouses. I move hangers across the bar, flipping through Stan's shirts, and smell his oakmoss scent. I finger my favorite sweater vest of his. It's a powder blue that brought out the color of his eyes. Someone could use these clothes, but I can't bring myself to offer them to Goodwill. It feels too much like erasing Stan from my life. I close the closet door, lean against it, and slide down to the floor.

I haven't attended an AA meeting since the day before Stan died. But I don't care to speak to anyone right now. I don't want to do much of anything except drive myself to a liquor store. Although it might be helpful to talk about things at a meeting, I can't exactly say my elderly husband recently died, because they believe I'm Rain, who is twenty.

Our bed looms across the room. Hattie changed the sheets with a different bedspread, but I'm still sleeping in the guest room. I can't be in our bed alone. In fact, I don't want to be up here at all. It's nearly time to feed Arlene anyway. I haul myself up off the bedroom floor. When I reach the bottom of the stairs, I hear Cam in the kitchen.

"Just one more minute, sweetheart, and I'll have your bottle warmed up."

I find him cradling the baby in the crook of his arm and testing one of the bottles of my breast milk on his wrist. It's such an intimate gesture.

He notices me. "I thought you might be napping. I tried not to disturb you."

"No. I was just... It doesn't matter."

"Would you prefer to nurse her?"

"You go ahead and have some time with her. Let's go in the living room."

Cam settles into the rocker with Arlene. I sit on the piano bench and hit a key.

"I don't know what to do with myself." I rise and peer out the window.

"Well, I have a proposal," he says.

I pivot to watch him feeding Arlene. My baby. His niece. His daughter. My confusing situation was manageable until Stan died. Now it seems disjointed and absurd.

"Good girl." Cam kisses Arlene's head. "I told you about my grandmother's shore house in Rehoboth Beach. Well, I was planning on spending some time there this summer, but I didn't bring it up because I knew Stan needed to be in his own home."

I look out the window again. Across the street, children are playing in the sprinkler.

Cam continues. "Hattie and I met for lunch today, and we think a change of scenery might be good."

"Tell me about the house." I sit on the sofa.

"It's the last one on the block, right at the beach. There are four bedrooms, but it's nothing fancy."

"Is there a porch?"

"A screened porch. And upstairs is a deck off two of the bedrooms. You have a wonderful view of the ocean from both."

I wander back to my piano. "Although I haven't been able to touch this, I can't be away from the piano for several weeks."

"My grandmother's upright is there."

"Can Hattie come?"

"Already invited."

This could be the lifeline I need.

My stomach churns. I shouldn't be running away to the beach. I should be grieving the death of my husband and processing the anger I'm experiencing about the vasectomy he kept secret from me. I need a drink.

As Cam, Hattie, Arlene, and I approach Rehoboth Beach proper, we enter a business district filled with tourist shops and a variety of restaurants. The festive atmosphere doesn't distract me from my problems, and I keep an eye out for a liquor store.

What am I doing? I glance back at Arlene and try to calm myself without the promise of a drink to settle my nerves.

Pedestrians and traffic slow our progress in the busy summer resort town until Cam drives south. The residential streets are quieter and lined with lovely homes, some large remodels and others older cottages. After turning right and traveling toward the ocean, Cam drives in behind the last house before the beach. It's two stories high with white clapboard siding. While Cam comes around to open the door for Hattie, I release Arlene's infant car seat.

"I'll unload the car later. First, I want to show you the house." With a spring in his step, Cam leads us past the enclosed outdoor shower and up the path to the back door.

We enter a good-sized mudroom, which contains a washer and dryer. We follow Cam into a charming seashore-themed kitchen with a stencil of seashells painted along the top of each wall, likely done by Cam's grandmother.

"The living room is through here," Cam says.

We follow him into a large room. A handsome brick fireplace graces the wall facing the street, with plenty of cozy seating surrounding it. Much of the furniture is antique. There's an eclectic collection of art on the walls.

Cam points to a stairway opposite the fireplace, next to a dining table, sideboard, and chairs. "There's a tiny powder room under the steps."

The upright piano sits next to a heavy wooden door leading to a screened porch. I wander toward it, hoping that if I can play, I'll be more in control. My hands quiver as I reach for the keys but don't touch them.

Cam opens the door. "We need to get some air in here. It's been shut up since last fall." He begins opening living room windows. Salty air floats in on an ocean breeze.

Hattie is the first one onto the porch. "What a view!"

I bring Arlene out with me. She wakes up wiggling her nose at the sweet smell of the sea. "She loves it here," I say. Everyone is happy but me.

Cam comes to the doorway. "Let me show you the upstairs."

Hattie leisurely follows Cam. "I'm glad I brought so many books to read."

The second floor is light and airy with pastel wall colors and lots of windows.

"You two can have the front rooms with the ocean view. I'll take the back." He disappears into the back bedroom, and I hear him opening windows.

"I claim this one." Hattie goes through the door closest to the bathroom.

I poke my head into what will be the nursery before wandering into the other front room. It's cozy and has a dormer with a door leading to a deck. As I carry Arlene through the door, Hattie comes out onto the deck from her room.

"Now I have a problem," she says, staring out at the ocean.

"What?"

"I can't decide if I want to be on this deck or on the porch."

"Life is rough." The sea breeze whips my hair around.

Hattie leans into me. "This will help, Shirlene."

"Hattie, I want a drink in the worst way."

She slips her arm around my waist. "Let's find you an AA meeting today."

I nod. "I need it, and we also have to tell Cam that if there's any liquor in the house, it has to go."

Chapter Twenty-Three

Shirlene

After the AA meeting, Hattie and I saunter arm in arm along the boardwalk. It's a clear evening with a gentle ocean breeze. It becomes more crowded as we get closer to town. Families, couples, and bunches of teenagers are out enjoying amusement rides, video arcades, miniature golf, and beach-memorabilia-filled shops. The smells of popcorn and pizza fill the air. Folks are coming up from the sand and hosing off at the open showers that dot the boardwalk while some diehards lounge on the beach and bob in the easy waves before sunset.

"Do you mind telling me how the meeting went?" Hattie asks.

"I couldn't say I was Shirlene, and I'm an alcoholic, and my elderly husband died moments after telling me he had a secret vasectomy. I'm in this young body. So I said that I was Rain, and I'm an alcoholic. I told them my father, who died recently, told me a horrible family secret. It was as close to the truth as I could manage."

"I'm sorry, Shirlene. This must be so awful for you."

"I'm angry at Stan. Angry with myself for not waiting with Danny, and I'm angry I ended up in the body of an alcoholic. It's not fair."

Hattie pats my hand.

"The meeting did help a little. I'm going to another one tomorrow. It's going to have to be every day for me to stay sober."

"You did it before. You can do it again," she says.

"Enough with the self-pity. I'm grateful to be here with you at the beach. I'm grateful to have Arlene. Cam is very kind and helpful. I'm going to relax and enjoy this vacation—"

"I'm noticing something, Shirlene," Hattie interrupts in a whisper. "There are a lot of same-sex couples here. It's nice they can be comfortable together."

"Can you imagine it in our day?"

"Never. Hey, maybe people will suppose we're a couple."

"Hattie, you're seventy years older than me."

"Oh, I forgot. Well, there's nothing wrong with a May–December relationship." Hattie squeezes my arm. "Or an interracial relationship. I'm seeing a number of them here too. It's a very inclusive beach town."

"So different from when we went to the beach in Atlantic City as teens," I say.

"Blacks were confined to a two-block stretch of sand between Missouri Avenue and Mississippi Avenue. It was the only place we could go together."

"We stayed near the edge of it, so the Blacks ignored the two of us."

Hattie nods toward two teens near the Playland Arcade. "Hey, those boys over there are checking you out."

"Don't be ridiculous. And since when do you say, 'checking you out'?"

One of the boys eyes me. Embarrassment warms my cheeks, and I look away.

"See? Don't you just love this new, young body you have?" Hattie asks.

"Besides dying for a drink?"

Hattie's hand flies to her mouth. "Sorry!"

"No worries. I wasn't really back to that. No, I'm talking about getting my period again. The bloating and cramps. Yuck."

Hattie lets out a little squeal. "When you stop nursing, you're going to need birth control."

"I am not having sex with anyone."

"You never know."

"Hattie, stop it."

"Don't forget, you ovulate before the first period. You can get pregnant."

"Again, a moot topic."

"Shirlene, don't be dense. It's obvious Cam has feelings for you."

My stomach knots up with irritability. "I don't want to talk about this now."

"Oh boy!" Hattie drops my arm and scurries over to a mechanical Zoltar Fortune Teller inside a glass booth.

I weave between tourists to catch up. Zoltar has a black pointy beard and handlebar mustache. He's costumed in a turban, a bright-yellow shirt, a paisley vest, and shiny jewelry. His hands hover over cards, coins, and a crystal ball.

"Let's have our fortunes told!" She roots in her purse for money.

The creepy eyes of the mechanical man start moving, and he says, "What are you waiting for? Let Zoltar tell you of your happy future."

I jump at the booming voice, and Hattie breaks into convulsions.

This makes me more annoyed. "What would Zoltar have predicted about me a year ago?"

Hattie imitates Zoltar's voice. "You are going to die and come back in someone else's pregnant body!" She laughs more, slipping a dollar into the machine. Eerie harp music plays.

The voice speaks again. "The Great Zoltar here with a word of wisdom for your fortunes. Remember, it is a great deal better to do all the things you think you should rather than to spend the rest of your life wishing you had. Live it up, my friend, and start by giving me more money for more wisdom, no?"

"That's no better than a fortune cookie," I complain. "In fact, it's worse."

"Oh, you're no fun." Hattie waits while the machine spits out a fortune card.

Zoltar Speaks is printed on one side of the card, with a picture of the fortune teller. Hattie quickly flips it over and reads, "Your deepest desires will be realized."

I roll my eyes.

Hattie shrieks with delight. "I'm going to meet the love of my life in Ireland. That's my deepest desire."

"Bernard was the love of your life. Remember, your husband?"

Hattie plunks more money into the silly machine. "Let's discover what more Zoltar has to say about you."

The fortune teller's voice sends a chill down my spine as he says, "You are missing someone who has a message for you."

I gawk at Hattie with my mouth open.

Her eyes are huge. "Maybe Stan is trying to tell you something?"

"This is way too creepy for me."

"You're right." Hattie grabs my hand. "Come on—let's find some bumper cars or a scary amusement ride. I, for one, am going to take Zoltar's advice. I don't want to regret what I could have done."

Hattie is right. I am dampening the mood of our girls' night. She won't be in Rehoboth Beach very long. She needs to enjoy her stay. "What do you say to hennas?"

"Chicken. Why not tattoos?"

"Hattie, if you get a tattoo, so will I."

"You wouldn't."

"Try me. I already have three. What's one more?"

Hattie's face becomes serious. "What's your deepest desire, Shirlene?"

"To send Stan a message: 'Go to hell for punishing me with a vasectomy you kept secret."

Chapter Twenty-Four

Cameron

After a package arrives from Land's End, Shirlene comes down the stairs wearing a one-piece turquoise bathing suit that matches her eyes. Her legs go from the floor to Canada, and her hair is pulled back into a long braid. God, she's beautiful. Burying my feelings isn't going to be as easy as I'd hoped.

"Nice." I toss aside the book I'm reading.

"Thanks. I'm going to the laundry room for a towel. Want to join me for a swim?"

"Sure. I'll change. Grab me a beach towel, will you?" I race up the steps.

Arlene is napping in her crib. I knock on Hattie's door.

She replies, "Have it covered."

As soon as Shirlene and I maneuver around all the beachgoers, with their colorful umbrellas and chairs and coolers, and reach the ocean, she tosses her towel in the sand and runs into the water. I hurry to catch up. She dives under a wave and surfaces with a delighted yelp. We work our way out past the breakers, and she begins swimming down toward town. I keep up with her but wonder how far she's planning on going. After passing three lifeguard stands, she turns back.

I tread water in front of her. "Rain isn't in any kind of shape. You're going to be sore."

She pauses. "I know. Isn't it wonderful? Cam, it's so amazing to be able to swim again." She takes off, heading back toward the section of beach in front of my cottage.

By the time we reach our beach, I can feel the burn in my shoulders. I haven't been swimming since last summer.

Shirlene bops up and down. "How far did we swim?"

I can touch the sandy bottom and float up with each swell of the surf. "About a quarter mile."

"I'm going to work up to two miles."

"Not today." My heart races.

"Soon." She swirls around. "This is pure heaven."

Salty water trickles down her face, and I resist the sudden urge to kiss it dry. "When was the last time you were able to swim?" I ask.

"A few years ago."

"In your late eighties?"

"I belonged to the community pool. Until I got sick, I did laps nearly every summer morning during the senior swim."

"You're amazing." In so many ways.

"But I haven't been in the ocean in ten or fifteen years. The surf got to be too much for me to handle."

A wave swells up beyond us. "Watch out." I dive. While I'm under the water, the surge of the surf plays with me. I kick my legs to regain momentum and rise to the surface.

When I break out of the water, Shirlene throws her arms around my neck. "Thank you for bringing us here!" she shouts over the ocean roar.

Since she made the first move, I hug her tight. "I'm glad you're here."

We stare into one another's eyes. My desire to kiss her is overwhelming, but she's so vulnerable, between Stan dying and her battle with alcohol. It would be selfish of me. I release her as a wave crashes over us. When I surface, Shirlene is swimming to shore. I work to catch up with her.

Chapter Twenty-Five

Shirlene

Following a phone conversation with my new AA sponsor, I wait impatiently on the front porch, holding two pairs of binoculars I brought from home. Tall ornamental grasses block the view of people strolling along the beach-level boardwalk. Tops of colorful umbrellas peek above the sand dune. The blue sky is streaked with wispy white clouds, and the ocean goes on forever. I listen to one of my favorite sounds—the mixture of surf and happy voices of children playing in the sand—and it settles me a bit.

Cam bounds onto the porch and takes hold of Stan's binoculars. "Geez, these are heavy."

"Well, they're old, but they work fine."

We march up onto the boardwalk, where he raises them to his eyes. "Wow. Those boats look so close. I can see the people on them."

Hattie waves from the deck. "Have a nice time. Arlene and I need a little alone time."

Yeah, right. Cam and I nearly kissed when we were in the water a few days ago. I've never been so grateful for a huge wave. I used its momentum to swim away. I've been on eggshells ever since and have avoided being alone with Cam as much as possible—until today, when Cam suggested we go for a bike ride. I couldn't resist the idea of soaring along on a bike. I haven't done it in many, many years. I suggested we bring binoculars because I'm sure there are lots of birds to watch where we're going. I hope, with the bikes and the binoculars between us, no other awkward moments will arise.

Cam and I hike into town to Bob's Rental Bikes. The sign on the white building with black trim says it's been in business since 1934. The store has bikes of every color, and the older fellow working there is quite colorful too. The more he talks, the more I think we're never going to get to Cape Henlopen State Park to go birding. When he slips in a few curse words to make his point about tourists and the crazy things they ask, Cam raises his eyebrows. Finally, we pay, and some other customers catch the man's attention.

"That guy may have been drinking his lunch," Cam says good-naturedly. When I frown, his tone grows serious. "I apologize, Shirlene. That was insensitive."

I put on my rental helmet. "Don't worry about it. Let's go."

We both roll our rental bikes over to the street. I stow my binoculars, my water bottle, and an apple in the little basket of my purple bike. "I haven't ridden a bike in over thirty years."

"It will come back to you." Cam playfully taps the top of my helmet.

At first, my bicycle wobbles. I pedal a little faster, and my balance improves. "I can't go too slowly, or I'll fall over."

Cam stays next to me on his bright-red bike until I gain confidence. My new body amazes me. I'm beginning to feel it's really mine and not Rain's. Sailing along on a bike makes me giddy.

I notice Cam smiling. "What?"

"It's nice to see you happy."

"It feels good." I brush the guilt away. I deserve to enjoy myself. I deserve to be alive.

We leave Rehoboth Beach and cycle along Ocean Drive past the high-end houses in Henlopen Acres. In a short distance, we reach the entrance to Gordon Pond Trail. An egret is standing by the water's edge of the pond. I stop and straddle the bike. Cam circles back to a halt next to me. I lift my binoculars.

"See the white bird?" I point.

"Yes." He observes through Stan's binoculars. "It has yellow feet."

"Good spot. It's a snowy egret. The great white egret is taller and has black feet. There's one on the other side of the pond."

Cam scans the water. "It does seem taller in relationship to the seagull next to it, but since it's across the water, I can't really tell the size difference between the egrets."

"Welcome to the fun of birding. And for the record, there are no seagulls. There are gulls with specific names. This one is a laughing gull with the distinctive black head and red beak during mating season." On cue, the great white egret takes off and flies right over us. "No yellow feet."

"I see." Cam seems pleased with his observation. "I find it hard to believe I grew up here and never noticed all these birds." Cam shifts his binoculars onto one of the two World War II Observation Towers that break up the flat terrain of green vegetation and sand closer to the beaches. "We built eleven towers on the Delaware side during World War II to protect the Delaware Bay, Wilmington, and Philadelphia from Nazi naval threats. There were another four on the Jersey side. The guns were in batteries along the beach." He points.

I nod. "After the Japanese attacked Pearl Harbor, the threat of the Nazis reaching the East Coast was very real."

Cam studies me. "Because you look so young, I forget you lived through World War II."

We cycle farther along the trail between scrubby pines of various sizes. We zoom by the Biden Environmental Training Center and reach the World War II Observation Tower that's open to visitors. Long, thin, rectangular openings circle the cement structure at the bottom and again more than halfway up. Toward the top, I notice two observation slits facing the ocean.

"How tall is this?" I take a sip from my water bottle.

"This one is seventy-five feet. They range in height along the coast. The diameter of this one is sixteen feet. The walls are one foot thick. Ready?"

"Yes."

The temperature is immediately cooler behind the heavy walls. As we climb the steel spiral staircase, I'm not losing my breath or feeling pressure in my chest. At the top, we step into the open air, where a chain-link fence surrounds us. A sea of green shrubs with occasional open patches of sand encircles us below. There isn't a cloud in the sky, but a light wind keeps us cool in the strong sunlight.

A section of my hair is blown free from my braid. Cam tucks it behind my ear, and energy runs down my spine. I can tell by the gleam in Cam's eyes that he feels it too. Before I let myself kiss him, I pull away. Cam drops his hand, but the pleasant and unnerving charge remains on the back of my neck. He's so much younger than I am. I'm grieving Stan, and I'm angry with Stan. This is not something I can let happen, but the tug toward Cam is only growing stronger. What will I do when Hattie leaves for Ireland? Cam and I will be living on our own in the beach cottage with Arlene.

Chapter Twenty-Six

Cameron

We pedal in silence toward Fort Miles. I guess I freaked her out a little on top of the tower when I pushed her loose hair back. I'm becoming so comfortable with Shirlene that it was a natural reflex, but we both felt the energy. Her pupils dilated when I touched her. Her skin was beginning to glow from the sun.

This situation is impossible. She's just lost her husband. I have to remember she's ninety and not twenty. It feels like she is somewhere in between. Ninety minus twenty is seventy, divided in half is thirty-five. That's only seven years older than I am. It's no chasm at all. Am I really considering what I think I'm considering?

We stow our bikes at Fort Miles and begin exploring the World War II military post. We stroll into a long concrete-block barracks.

"Pretty meager," Shirlene says. "But probably better than the boys in Europe ever saw." We wander along the paths leading to several large guns, which vary in size and capability. "This is huge." She gestures to the sixteen-inch gun.

"A turret on a battleship would have carried three of these sixteen-inch guns, and I can't imagine the noise when they were going off. They're capable of hurling a two-thousand-pound projectile about seven miles."

Shirlene becomes quiet again.

"Is there anything you want to talk about?" I prepare myself to be told to keep my hands to myself.

"This is making me wonder about Joey and what he was up against, trying to make it onto Omaha Beach."

I don't know for sure if it's only Joey or if she's upset with me touching her. "Are you sure there isn't anything else bothering you, Shirlene?"

She knits her brows. "What's going on here?"

"What do you mean?"

"We've nearly kissed twice. What's happening?"

I don't mean to smirk, but I do. After all, it's perfectly clear to me what's going on. We're attracted to each other.

"Is this a joke to you, Cameron?" Her eyes bore into me. I can picture her in the classroom with an unruly kid.

"I'm not one of your students."

"Then don't act like one. There's nothing funny about this situation."

"No, it's not funny at all." I choose my words carefully. "I'm getting serious about you."

"Well, don't. This is a recipe for disaster." We can see where we left our bikes from here, and she starts toward them.

"That's it? We're not going to talk this through?"

"Not if you're going to act childishly." She gets on her bike.

"You're the one shutting down and pouting. Maybe we ought to wrap this up." I wheel my bike into position and swing my leg over the seat.

"Yes. Let's go home."

She keeps ahead of me the entire ride back to Rehoboth Beach. I rerun the argument in my mind. Shirlene has feelings for me. Otherwise, she wouldn't be so defensive. While I can understand why she's holding herself back, I'm not going to hold back any longer. I can't keep denying the truth. I'm falling in love with her.

Chapter Twenty-Seven

Shirlene

Ever since our ride out to Cape Henlopen today, I sense Cam's lowered a barrier when it comes to me. I thought I'd put him straight about my feelings—a relationship would be a disaster—but he set the dinner table tonight with his grandmother's good china from the buffet drawer, as if he was celebrating something. When Hattie says she's taking Arlene for a stroll on the boardwalk after dinner, I'm concerned about being alone with Cam. I don't want to argue again, and I sure want to avoid any discussion about us being involved, so I try to make small talk while he and I clean up.

"These plates with the tiny roses are lovely." I stack the last one in the dishwasher.

"My grandmother said they were her mother's. Chase and I were under strict orders not to mess around with them." He dries his hands.

"They must be as old as my china," I say. Cameron has to understand I'm old enough to be his grandmother. In fact, I'm likely older than she would be.

Cam leans against the counter next to me. He smells fresh from the shower he took before dinner. "Grandma insisted my brother and I take turns doing the dishes. Chase hated it. Thought it wasn't a man's job."

Chase sounds like a piece of work, to use the kids' language. I hope Hattie doesn't stay out too long. I store the salt and pepper shakers away in the cabinet and begin straightening the spices so the labels face front, as Stan liked them.

"We weren't brought up that way, but Chase developed his own opinion on things. One time, he broke a dish, and he buried it in the sand. Grandma never knew until she found it washed up on the beach." Cam laughs. "My happiest memories of my brother are from here in Rehoboth Beach. Otherwise, it's pretty dismal."

"Why was it happier here?" I close the cabinet door.

"Grandma ran a tight ship. She established more structure than Chase had at home. I'm sure if he'd lived with her full-time, things would have been better for him." Cam lowers his head. "I wish I'd done more for him."

"You were a kid. What could you have done?"

"I'm a lot older. I should have forced him to listen to me." He begins tapping the heel of his right foot.

"You aren't responsible for your brother."

"What if he ends up permanently homeless or sick or both?"

"Then he'll be homeless. He's made choices. He'll continue to make them."

"My parents never treated him fairly." Cam paces in front of the sink.

"How is that your fault?"

"I was the golden boy. I did well in school and sports. My parents had no time for him."

"This is survivor's guilt. You survived your parents' mess, and he didn't. If Chase were a kid, that would be something else, but he's an adult."

Cam takes a bottle of ginger ale out of the refrigerator. "Barely. He's only twenty-two."

His statement irks me. After all, my husband was fighting the Germans when he was Chase's age. I was married and had a one-year-old boy by twenty-two, and I was only a few years older when Danny was killed. Oh, Danny. My guilt is constantly simmering beneath the surface. I don't want to think about that now. I need to stay focused on Cam's brother.

I pace over to hand him a glass. "Chase is accountable for himself. The only person you're responsible for is you." I'm standing too close to Cam, so I move to the stove. "And Arlene. When she's grown, she's her own responsibility."

Cam's eye's narrow. "Isn't that something."

"What do you mean?"

Cam sets his soda and glass on the counter and strides to my side of the room. "You felt responsible for Stan. Still do even though he's gone."

"I don't understand."

"I sense there's more going on than grief, Shirlene."

My jaw tightens as he comes perilously close to the truth. "Stan and my situation is different from yours and Chase's."

"Why?" He leans in toward me.

"It just is."

"Not good enough."

Cameron can't begin to understand the damage done to a marriage when a child dies. The guilt that lives coiled in my stomach hisses and slithers up into my throat. I begin coughing.

"What's wrong?" Cam's voice is filled with alarm. "What can I do?"

Nausea rises in my chest. I'm embarrassed to throw up in front of him, so I rush out of the kitchen and into the little powder room under the stairs. I avoid looking in the mirror and splash cold water on my face for a several minutes. Finally, the queasiness subsides. I dry myself with a hand towel and find Cam waiting outside.

He's holding a glass of water for me. "If you're not ready to talk about it, I respect that."

"I'm going for a walk." I leave Cam with the glass in his hand.

I find a nearly deserted beach. Most people have headed home for dinner. The few stragglers are blocks away. I tramp through the sand to the water, picking up several small stones on the way. The breeze whips my hair. Herring gulls reluctantly move from their repose on the sand and out of my way. One or two complain as they shift. I palm one good-sized stone. It's white and smooth. I hurl it into the waves. I throw one after another as tears stream down my face. I can't keep the story of my boy from Cam any longer. Telling it will be a relief. It could make me more vulnerable to Cam and my growing feelings for him, but I'm so alone.

I sense Cam coming down the beach. Instead of rushing away, I run to him. He envelops me in his arms. He feels solid and sure. I melt into the warm comfort of him and cry.

"It's probably too soon for you to process everything with Stan's passing," Cam whispers in my ear.

"No. It's fine. I want to talk. I need to tell you what happened to Danny."

He releases me. "Oh. Should we go back inside?"

"It's better out here." I need space to breathe. I pick up more stones, carry them a good distance above the high-water line, and dump them. Without asking why, Cam begins collecting stones too. As we continue to wander the beach, gathering pebbles and bringing them to the pile, he waits until I'm ready to talk.

"Danny died because of me." I examine one particularly pretty stone. "I used to drink. Well, you know that. But I was completely sober the day I was taking him with me to the store. He was only four, with rusty-brown hair and the cutest rosy cheeks. We were singing. We didn't have car seats back then. He was right next to me in the front passenger seat. His voice was angelic. I turned to look at him and missed the light changing to red. I drove into the intersection, and a delivery truck came from the right and hit us broadside."

I release the stone into the heap. It makes a sharp sound as it hits the others. "Danny was killed instantly. At least he didn't suffer, but he was crushed into my lap. My pelvis was broken. I knew my arms were also broken, because it hurt so much to hold him, but I kept kissing his bloody face and talking to him."

I search for more stones. "Stan assumed I had been drinking. I mean, who drives through a red light?" Cam keeps pace with me as he wipes his eyes. "I told him I was sober, but he didn't believe me. I said I was sorry a million times. He wouldn't forgive me. But he couldn't imagine his life without me. So we kept going. I wanted to be pregnant again, but Stan slept on the sofa." I add more stones to the mound. "Eventually, he did come back to my bed, but I never conceived. I didn't deserve another child." A hard, biting laugh escapes my mouth. "Talk about survivor's guilt. Why couldn't the truck have been coming from the opposite direction? It would have killed me. My child might have lived."

I notice several more pebbles and reach for one. I cut my finger on a piece of hidden shell and put pressure on it with my thumb.

"Just before Stan died, he confessed that he'd secretly had a vasectomy."

Cameron gasps.

"It was the only way he could return to our marriage as we'd known it, but he couldn't trust me ever again with another child." I have avoided eye contact with Cam, but now I stare directly into his concerned eyes. "Stan asked me to forgive him, but before I was ready to do that, he died. I wish I'd lied and said the words he needed to hear."

Cam speaks for the first time. "I can't begin to tell you how sorry I am."

"Thank you."

"Can you forgive Stan?"

"Not yet." I pick up a small rock and heave it into the sand. It makes a dull thud. "Damn him. Selfish bastard. It was an accident, Stan. An accident!" I scream.

Cameron takes my shaking hands in his. "It's going to take time to work through these feelings, but for your own sake, I hope you can."

I nod and look away. I'm getting too close to this young man. I wish I hadn't unloaded on him. I'm a complete mess, and aside from our age difference, I'm in no condition to start a relationship.

"Are you okay?" he asks.

"I need a break from all this."

As we move away from the beach, Cam says, "May I ask a question?"

"Yes."

"Is there a plan for all those stones?"

"Yes. I'm making a labyrinth."

Chapter Twenty-Eight

Shirlene

The next morning, Arlene sleeps in her stroller under the beach umbrella while Hattie and I gather more pebbles and Cam clears debris from a thirty-foot area. After it's done, I'll walk it until I can forgive Stan, and I'll try to forgive myself. I've never been able to do that. I realize the labyrinth won't be permanent. An extremely high tide or storm will wash it away, but I hope it will last as long as I need it to.

Once we have what I hope are enough stones, I decide where the center will be for our classical seven-circuit labyrinth, leaving more space toward the top for most of the paths. With a thick stick, I draw the cross.

I begin the four *L*s, and Hattie says, "Make it big. It would be nice if there's room in the center to leave shells, feathers, or wildflowers."

I nod. "Exactly."

I add the four dots and begin drawing the lines. I want enough room to cover these lines with the stones and have at least a foot-and-a-half-wide path.

I step back to examine my work. "Some of the curves aren't evenly spaced."

"We can make adjustments with the pebbles," Hattie says.

Cam brushes sand off his hands. "Where did you learn to do this?"

Hattie picks several stones up from the pile. "The first time was when my throwback-hippie granddaughter begged us for one in her parents' yard."

"You had a granddaughter? Were you married?" Cam asks.

"Of course I was married. Who do you think you're talking to?"

"Sorry, ma'am."

Hattie has always known how to manage people. She hands me a small pile of stones to place. "My husband and I had a daughter. He died thirty-two years ago, and she passed ten years ago."

"I'm sorry, Hattie." Cameron watches my progress for a moment and begins placing stones along the lines I drew in the sand.

"My granddaughter, Cassy, now lives in Washington State, and she's due to deliver twins while I'm in Ireland." Hattie hands me more stones from the pile. "Hey, Shirlene. Be careful. You're distorting the curve over there." Hattie points at the section I completed.

I try to fix the stones, but Stan's confession consumes my thoughts. I kept hoping and grieving every month when I didn't get pregnant. How do you do that to someone you supposedly love?

"What about your family, Cameron?" Hattie asks.

"My parents are in California. I have no idea where Chase is, and I don't really want to know."

Hattie's eyes widen. "You really don't have anything to do with him?"

"I tried. For years, I tried to help him. He's a drug addict."

"I'm sorry." Hattie straightens some of the stones I just placed. "If I had a brother, I couldn't give up on him."

Cameron sets his shoulders back. "He can't come anywhere near Shirlene or the baby."

"I understand, but you're in better shape than he is for some kind of reconciliation." Hattie stops working and massages her lower back. "Shirlene, honey, you're off the line again with the stones."

I step out of the labyrinth. "I can't concentrate with you two chattering all the time."

Hattie's mouth opens, and Cameron lowers his head.

"I need to wait until I'm in a different state of mind to do this," I say.

"What's wrong?" Cam straightens up and holds his hand over his eyes to block the sun.

Arlene snoozes in her stroller. The salt air smells heavenly. I gaze out at the horizon, where the sky meets the ocean. Are Stan and Danny out there, waiting for me?

"I need to go to a meeting. Once I get my head on straight, it's best I build the labyrinth by myself."

I scurry off the beach, feeling torn between this world with Arlene and Cam and my afterlife with Stan and Danny. I'm not sure where I belong. I am sure I need to escape this pain.

Chapter Twenty-Nine

Shirlene

I find Hattie in her bedroom, packing her suitcase to go home. She's leaving for her trip to Ireland in two days. A cool ocean breeze pushes through the open deck door.

"The two weeks have passed so quickly. I hate to see you go." I sit on her bed and outline the summer-quilt squares with my finger.

"Me either. If it weren't for my trip abroad, I'd be happy to stay." She folds the last blouse. "However, it's for the best."

"What are you saying?"

"You and Cameron need time alone."

"For what?" My throat tightens.

"I'm in the way of you two figuring out how this is all going to work."

"You're not in the way. I need you here."

She sits next to me. "Shirlene, what are you afraid of?"

I fold my hands and sit up straighter. "Nothing."

"Bull."

"Don't start bullying me."

She takes my hand. "Holding onto this grudge is a way of keeping Stan alive. But he's gone. You must start living again. It's time to make some decisions. You've been given this new life. You need to live it."

"I don't know where to begin."

Hattie dips her chin down and peers over her glasses. "I think you do know."

"Don't look at me like I'm stupid."

"I think you do know because you're not stupid. In denial possibly, but not stupid."

"Surely, not with Cam. He so young, and I'm confused about so many things."

"Then where?" she asks.

"I need to finish the labyrinth. I promised myself I'd walk it until I can forgive Stan for the vasectomy."

"Okay. Start there."

I rise and pace to the deck door. "Will you at least come back here after Ireland? Being alone with Cam is too much for me."

"You're actually admitting to being attracted to him?"

"No!" The ocean breakers are rough today. "Yes. I can never keep anything from you, Hattie."

"When was the last time you really let go of those tight reins you hold onto for dear life?"

"I can't remember."

"Probably not since before Danny died."

I walk back to Hattie. "But Stan hasn't been gone very long."

"You were sick for a couple of years, and then you were Stan's nurse. That part of your relationship ended long ago. Plus, your new body is young. It has needs." She stands. "Do you feel you'd be cheating on Stan?"

"That's definitely part of it." I sit back down on the bed. "If Cam is attracted to me—"

"There's no doubt about it."

"If he's attracted to me and we... act, what happens next?"

"You live happily ever after."

"You're too damn intelligent to think this is simple!"

"Things are only as complicated as you make them." Hattie closes her suitcase.

"I'm not ready for another relationship, and I certainly don't want to be a wife again. I did it for seventy years. Seventy! It's a friggin' long time."

"Wow."

"Yeah. Wow. Cameron sees himself married and with a family. I don't want to lead him on."

"Marriage with Cam would be quite different from what you experienced before. Times are different. You're different."

"I loved Stan. I still do. I don't regret marrying him. But that kind of commitment feels stifling now." I stand up. "I need you to come back, Hattie. The minute you land in the Philadelphia airport."

She lifts her luggage. "The twins are due to arrive while I'm in Ireland. Cassy's mother-in-law has the first shift, but I need to be there a few weeks later."

"Let me carry those down for you." I take her baggage. "But you'll stay here again first."

"I'll try."

I haul Hattie's larger suitcase to the stairs. "Cam said he'd be ready to drive up to New Jersey in about an hour."

When we reach the living room, Cam comes in from the outside shower with only a towel wrapped around his waist. His dark hair is in tiny wet curls. His chest and arm muscles are beautifully defined. My eyes follow the line of chest hair that becomes soft as it travels down his solid abdomen and disappears into the towel.

"Is this your going-away present for me?" Hattie cackles. "Trying to make sure I come back?"

"Hattie!" I shout.

"I'm sorry." Cam heads for the stairs. "I thought you were both in Hattie's bedroom and I could go back to my room without bothering you."

Hattie fans at her face. "Bother all you want."

I slap her arm. "You're being sexist, Hattie."

"Oh, I don't mind." Cam winks at Hattie.

I turn away to avoid watching his tight bum and strong thighs travel up the steps.

Hattie leers. "You poor thing. Left alone with that hunk."

Chapter Thirty

Cameron

When I was carrying Hattie's bags into her Lawnside house yesterday, she broached the topic of Chase again. She recommended I reach out to him, so this morning, I begin to consider the implications of doing that. I can't tell him about Shirlene. I definitely can't have him anywhere near Arlene.

So how do I do this without him becoming involved with what I now consider my family? First, I may not be able to find him. Second, he's likely using, and I need to get a handle on that.

I consider talking to Shirlene about this, but since Hattie left, you can cut the tension between us with a knife. Adding my family baggage to the equation will likely cause additional strain. First, I'll try to find Chase and determine what shape he's in and if he's willing to meet me up in Philly. Otherwise, I don't see the point of stressing her.

I dig up his old cell phone number and briefly text him that I'll be up from the shore three days from now on Thursday morning for a school meeting with my department. I ask if he could meet me for lunch. It's unlikely he's in the Philly area, but this gives him a few days to pull it together if he is around and does want to meet up.

Then I head down to my first breakfast with only Shirlene and the baby. The quiet at the table is deafening. Shirlene says nothing, so I can hear every crunch of my cereal. I decide to take a run to blow off some steam. I jog past the incomplete labyrinth and hit my stride on the hard, wet sand by the surf.

After covering about a mile, I run home. When I jog into the backyard, orchestral music is playing through the open windows. Shirlene must have turned on my grandmother's home stereo system. While taking a quick shower outside, I recognized the piece as *Appalachian Spring*. I begin humming along. Maybe my relationship with Aimee and her tutelage in classical music were preparing me for a life with Shirlene.

I dry off and wrap the towel around my waist then enter the laundry room through the back door. When I tried to slip past in just a towel yesterday, I got a kick of Shirlene's clear embarrassment, which I hope was attraction to me being half naked. Today, it's a good idea to throw on clean briefs, shorts, and a T-shirt from the dryer. Humming along with the Copland piece, I hurry through the kitchen.

From the doorway, I see her. Shirlene faces away from me and conducts an imaginary orchestra. Chills run up my spine as the timpani pounds in response to her gesture. We're nearing the end, and I wish I'd finished my run sooner. Her right hand indicates to the flute to play that heartbreakingly tender phrase. The first violins reply. Each string section layers and builds. The last few notes are added like raindrops on the xylophone. She holds the orchestra until the sounds fade. I've seen Shirlene transported at the piano, but conducting is complete ascension.

She lowers her hands. Applause comes from the speakers. A commentator begins talking about this particular live performance, but I pay no attention to the details. This woman must go back to school. She has returned for more than Arlene and—hopefully—me.

Shirlene turns off the stereo and seems to sense me in the room. Our eyes meet. My grandma's clock ticks from the wall. My inner voice urges me on: *Don't be a fool. Why are you waiting?* I open my arms, and a miracle occurs. She comes to me. Her fingers thread through my hair on the back of my head as she guides my face to her lips. I am overwhelmed by a desire to completely inhale her, but I purposely slow down.

Even so, she suddenly draws back. "What am I doing?" She strides to the porch door.

"Don't go." I wait for her reaction.

"I'm sorry, Cam. I shouldn't have kissed you."

"No harm done. We weren't struck by lightning." From her expression, I immediately regret my words. "I didn't mean that."

She starts for the stairs.

I'm dealing with a caged animal. "I hope we can talk this through."

She pauses on the second step. "About what exactly? The kiss? This insane situation?" Her hand rests on the railing.

I take a chance by going to her and putting my hand on hers. She blinks. Her eyes soften.

"You feel it too," I whisper.

"I don't want to hurt you."

"I'm a big boy."

"It's better if we keep this simple."

"We are way past simple, Shirlene."

She takes a deep breath. "Less complicated. If we get involved, it becomes more muddled than it already is."

"You're right, but I'm willing to take the chance."

She sits on the steps and wraps her arms around her knees, almost in a fetal position.

I crouch down in front of her. "Tell me what you're thinking."

She releases her graceful hands and gently shoves at my shoulders. At first, I sense she's pushing me away. But as I roll back onto the floor, she crawls on top of me, kissing me. Her fingers are in my hair again. My hands travel down her back. Her full weight is on me, and she must feel my reaction against her pelvis. I am consumed by her mouth. Our tongues communicate the longing we have for one another, but she needs to guide this voyage. She has to be the one making the decisions, or I'll lose her.

"Upstairs," she mutters against my mouth and keeps kissing me.

"Are you sure?" I whisper.

"Hmm."

I gently roll her to the side of me, scoop her up, and stand.

"I want to go on my own two feet," she says.

I set her down. She takes my hand and leads me up to my bedroom.

Chapter Thirty-One

Shirlene

T he baby's cry wakes me. I'm in Cam's bed.

"I'll get her," he says.

I watch his naked butt go out the door. "What have I done?" I mumble.

But it was glorious. My feelings for Cameron are stronger than I imagined. Once I unleashed control of my physical craving for him, so much more burst into my awareness.

It's amazing to take what I understand about sex after living ninety years and practice it in a twenty-year-old body. Everyone over eighty should have this experience at least once as a reward for living so long. Rain's body, my new body, responded to everything Cameron offered. My wise, old brain knew how to relax and enjoy the ride. I've never had so many orgasms in a row.

But what about Stan? Although he was fond of Cam, I can't imagine what he'd think of us making love. My eyes well up, and I curl on my side. Guilt gnaws at my gut. Hattie told me to move on with my life, but now I'm more torn between Stan's world and Cam's world than I was before. I long to be in Shirlene's world, but I'm not sure where that is.

And now, what will Cam expect? I should have waited. For what—some guarantee? A sign that Stan approves? My own forgiveness of Stan for stopping me from having another child? Cam used condoms, but I suppose I'd better go on birth control. Lord! I could have more children. We could be a family.

But I shouldn't get any closer to Cam until I understand what the hell I'm doing. I'm not sure about another commitment. After seventy years of compromises and concessions, freedom is very appealing. I don't want to take advantage of Cam.

His arrival with our little peanut cradled in his big arms halts my racing mind. "She's all cleaned up and ready for her grub."

He hands her to me. I have no compulsion to cover my breasts now when Arlene latches on. Cam adjusts my pillows before settling into the bed next to me. "You are my beauties."

I look at him. "What?"

"You're beautiful, Shirlene."

He said it when we made love too. I'm beginning to believe him, and it scares me.

Chapter Thirty-Two

Shirlene

I t's Thursday, and Cam's meeting at school was postponed, so he went food shopping about ten minutes ago. I sing to Arlene, who is nestled in her crib. As I rub her back until she dozes off, I admire the line of her cheek. I remember Danny's chubby, round face at this age. Ever since I told Cam about the accident, it hasn't caused me as much pain as it did.

A door opens downstairs. Cam must have left the shopping list behind. I shut the nursery door and pad to the top of the stairs. I tiptoe down for fear of waking Arlene.

"Cam?" I say quietly from the living room. "Did you forget something?"

"Sort of."

It isn't Cam's voice.

A tall man with long, thick black hair and a bushy beard emerges from the kitchen while guzzling from a can of soda. At first, he looks surprised. He quickly reconfigures his face into a smirk.

I freeze. I spy the front door, but I can't abandon my child.

He sits in a chair. "Aren't you going to say hello, Rain?"

Chase. The dark coloring and broad shoulders are similar to Cam's, but his eyes are agitated, and his nose was broken at some point. His face is hollowed out, and he lacks Cam's healthy glow.

After finishing the soda, he belches and really focuses on me for the first time. His eyes travel up and down my body in a way that makes my skin crawl. He sneers, exposing brown teeth.

"You're looking good. Different. What'd you do with your hair?"

I don't answer.

He stands. "What's the matter? Aren't you glad to see me?"

He saunters up to me. He smells of stale cigarettes and sweat. His hand rises. I flinch. He toys with a strand of my hair. I don't make eye contact, figuring it might provoke him as if he were a mad dog.

"So, did you have the kid or get rid of it?"

This question forces me to stare into his eyes. They are much paler than Cam's. Milky. Dead.

I begin to sense it's better to stand up to him. That's how Rain survived him.

"You can't see her."

"You had it? I'm surprised."

"You will never see her!"

"Why so protective?" He grabs my arm hard. "I have a right."

I can't let him near Arlene. "You'll have to kill me first."

He shoves me up against the wall. My head whips back and hits the plasterboard. The wind is knocked out of me, and the room spins. When he starts yanking at my clothes, my mind races. He's not going to kill me, at least not before forcing himself on me.

Chase presses his mouth on mine. He tears my shirt open. Even in Rain's young body, I'm powerless. I'm at least eight inches taller than I was, but it means nothing. I remember Hattie's words, but he has me pinned in such a way that I can't knee him in the balls. I push against his chest uselessly. He takes his mouth off mine and gnaws at my neck. I gasp for air. I have to interrupt his violent progress. I notice his vulnerable ear and bite it hard.

"Shit!" He jerks away, holding his ear.

Ignoring the taste of blood in my mouth, I begin jabbing at his throat. Before I can knee him, he stumbles toward the fireplace, coughing.

I take a chance with what I say next. "We've had some rough sex, but you've never raped me."

He hesitates. I hope I've hit the mark.

I shout, "Get out! Now!"

I dash into the kitchen for my phone. I grab the big knife out of the block and rush back out to stop him if he's heading for the stairs. I find him sitting on the raised hearth with his head in his hands.

"You pissed me off so much I lost control," he mumbles.

"Get out." I point to the front door with the knife.

He looks up.

I drop the knife. "Leave now. I'm calling 911." I punch the phone buttons.

"You aren't going to call the cops, Rain."

"You don't know me," I hiss.

The 911 operator answers.

"There's a male intruder in the house. I'm Shir—I'm Rain DeLuca."

Chase stands and swipes the mantel clean of knickknacks. "You've become a real bitch." He strides through the porch, leaving with a slam of the door.

I realize I am holding my breath and take in a deep lungful of air as I shoot across the room to shut and lock the door. "He's left. I'm locking the doors," I say into the phone as I run to check the back door.

After I answer all the 911 operator's questions, she explains, "The police are on their way. I'll stay on the line with you until they arrive." I concentrate on keeping my hands steady to avoid dropping the phone, grateful she's talking to me.

Chapter Thirty-Three

Cameron

I'm impressed with Shirlene's composure as the two officers question her. She had the forethought to stay in her torn clothes. She covered herself with one of my work shirts, but when the police ask to take pictures and she reveals the damage Chase did to her blouse, trying to force himself on her, I picture strangling him as I clench and unclench my fists.

Our father drilled into us that you never lay your hands on a woman or a child. Women are equal and, in some ways, superior, he reminded us. They are to be respected. I knew my brother once but no longer.

One of the cops, who seems about my age, starts asking Shirlene the same questions his older partner asked. He's checking to see if she's consistent. She keeps her cool and answers. As she describes everything again, I want to hunt down my crazy brother, but I can't have Shirlene dealing with these cops by herself. Chase thought she was Rain. I'd be enraged if it had been Rain or any woman, but it's worse because it's Shirlene. My Shirlene. And it's my fault. I opened the door for him with my text to meet in Philly. Then the bastard snuck down here to rob me, or whatever, while I was supposedly at school. He intended for me to be out of the way.

I am forced out of my thoughts when the older cop asks, "So you're living with his brother?"

For the first time during this interrogation, Shirlene appears unsure. The implication is clear in his voice: *You're sleeping with your former boyfriend's brother, so what do you expect?* The panic in Shirlene's eyes guides me to speak up.

"My irresponsible brother abandoned Rain when she told him she was pregnant with his child. She came to me, and I decided to raise my niece. We are parenting this newborn together because Chase has no interest and no integrity. Now he comes in here and tries to rape Rain because he's pissed off. I don't care how angry a man is about something. He has no right to lay a hand on a woman. Wouldn't you agree?"

"Oh, well..." He clears his throat. "Yes, of course."

Jesus, what women go through.

I stand closer to Shirlene, whose eyes are welling up. "So let's stay focused on who has been attacked and not wander into conjectures implying she somehow deserved it."

"Of course not. That's not what I meant." He scratches his balding head.

The younger cop takes the lead. "When was the last time either of you had contact with him?"

Shirlene quickly comes up with something. "When I told him I was pregnant."

"That was the last time you saw him?"

"Yes."

"And you?" The bald cop glares. I can tell he's not happy I called him on his crap.

"Rain and Chase stayed at my apartment in Philadelphia for a brief time. They left about ten or eleven months ago."

The officer keeps writing things down. "And that's the last time you saw your brother?"

"Yes." I decline to offer the information about texting him a few days ago. He never answered me, so what's the point?

"Will he come back?" the younger cop asks.

"Knowing Chase, I think not. Well, unless he needs money or a place to sleep because he's on the street again. But I didn't imagine him capable of this, so it's anyone's guess."

"You said he let himself in. You didn't open the door for him?"

"No," Shirlene says. "As I said before, I was upstairs when I heard someone come in. I thought it was Cameron—that he'd forgotten the shopping list and had come back."

"Chase does have a key, but I never expected he'd show up unannounced. I'll change the locks today," I say.

"Are you sure you don't want to press charges?"

Shirlene sits down. "I don't."

"Are you sure, Shirlene?" I ask. "I would, but it's up to you."

"I just want to move past it."

The younger cop puts his notebook away. "Contact us if you need us."

"Thank you." Shirlene stays on the couch as I direct the two men out and lock the door behind them.

Arlene sounds her little waking-up cackle.

"I'll go change her," I offer.

Shirlene doesn't move.

"Shirlene, I think I should take you to the ER."

"No. I'm not hurt, but I'd like to take a shower now."

"Let's go upstairs. I'll take care of Arlene while you shower."

"Will you stay up there until I finish?" she asks.

"Of course."

Shirlene turns to me on the top step. "Did you lock the doors?"

"Yes."

She heads to the bathroom.

Arlene's cackle has ramped up to a full-out howl. I hurry into the nursery. "It's okay, sweetheart."

After changing her diaper, I sit in the rocker with the baby while her mother showers off my brother's stench. No, I can't let myself go there. The baby will sense my tension and become distressed.

Shirlene comes in wearing her robe. "She must be hungry."

"I can offer her a bottle if you need to rest." I stand.

"No, thank you. I want her in my arms."

"Go ahead and sit." I hand the baby to her after she's in the rocker. "God, I never put the groceries away. Are you okay with me doing it now?"

"Yes."

"Shirlene, I'm sorry to tell you this now, but you should know. When Hattie was here, we talked about me contacting Chase."

Shirlene's mouth opens. My gut tightens up.

"I didn't tell you I texted him at an old cell number because I thought it was silly to worry you before I knew if I could find him."

"Why did you text him?"

I run my hand through my hair. "I feel so stupid now." I'm not blaming Hattie. Although she encouraged me, it was my decision. "I was in a generous mood or something, but I didn't mention Rain or the baby. I wrote that I was coming up to Philly for a meeting, and we could meet for lunch. I never heard from him. I assumed the cell number wasn't in service. So I didn't bother telling him the meeting was postponed. I figured he could be anywhere."

Her face darkens. "So he thought you were in Philly."

"And while I was supposed to be there, he came here to steal something to sell for drug money." I kneel in front of her. "I am so sorry."

"Don't keep things from me. You should have told me about texting Chase."

"I blame myself. If I hadn't texted him, he might have gone on with whatever he was doing. Instead, he took advantage."

"You'd better put the food away before it spoils."

I get up. "Shirlene, can you forgive me?"

"I need some time, Cam."

I want to hug her and comfort her. "Is it okay if I kiss the top of your head?"

Her eyes pool up. "It's thoughtful of you to ask, but I need space to process this."

"You are calling the shots on any physical contact."

"You should have warned me, Cam. Don't keep things from me. It's too similar to Stan."

"I promise. No more secrets."

"Go deal with the food."

Like a schoolboy, I slink out of the room. When will she forgive me?

Chapter Thirty-Four

Cameron

During the first few days following Chase's attack, I've been sticking close to home. I don't go for a run, which is not helping the hostility I have toward my brother. I think about texting Chase to warn him to never contact Rain again, but Shirlene isn't comfortable with that. She worries it will only provoke him. Since she's the one who was hurt, I respect her decision, but I want to bash his head against the wall and see how he likes it.

Shirlene is sleeping in her own room now. I understand on one level, but I wish she'd at least talk about why. If it's the assault, that's one thing, but I have the feeling it goes deeper. Does she regret our making love?

As I check my school emails on my laptop at the dining table, I can watch Shirlene and the baby through the open front door. They are just feet away on the screened porch. There's a *ding* on my laptop. My principal is moving up the meeting at school. Damn, I have to go to Philly. This really sucks right now.

Shirlene flinches when I come out onto the porch.

"I'm sorry." I sit down in the rocker next to her. "I should have said something."

"It's okay. I was so focused on Arlene that I didn't hear you coming. I'm a little anxious."

"That's understandable. It'll take time. Would going to an AA meeting and talking about it help?"

"I'll consider it."

"I have to ask if you're upset about my texting Chase and not telling you."

"You apologized, and I'm over it." Shirlene bites her lip.

"So it's the attack."

"Cam, you need to back off. I'm not ready to talk about it with you or at an AA meeting. I need some space."

"I'll try, but I have an issue to discuss. I'm afraid my department meeting has been rescheduled, and tomorrow, I have to go up to Philly for the day. Why don't we make an overnight trip and stay in your house?"

Shirlene's eyes widen. "Why can't I stay here for the day?"

"Frankly, I'm uncomfortable with you here by yourself. If you're in Haddon Heights, Chase has no idea where you are. You'll be safer."

Tears immediately pool in her eyes. She glances away. "I can't go there right now. It's too full of memories and anger with Stan, which I can't process now on top of everything else."

"Shirlene, when I have to go back to school at the end of this month, where do you expect to live?"

Her eyes become steel. "I want to stay here."

"If you can't face your home, at least stay in my apartment, where the Haddads are downstairs."

"Let's not worry about it now. We have a little time." She rocks the baby in her arms.

"But I have to go up for this meeting tomorrow."

"I'm staying here. I'll be okay for the day. You'll be back for dinner. The police are alerted. The locks have been changed."

"I'm not comfortable with this." I touch her arm. It feels wonderful to have some contact. Any contact.

Shirlene shifts the baby so she can pat my hand. "Cam, I'll be fine. We'll both be safe. You're worried, but I must be able to take care of myself. A few hours alone might help me to sort some things out."

I don't ask her what those things are, but I hope our relationship is on the list.

Chapter Thirty-Five

Shirlene

I wake with a start and check the clock—7:23 a.m. Cam has already left for Philly. As I make my bed, I remember hearing a female voice in a dream. It wasn't Hattie's or my mother's voice, but I'm sure I've heard it sometime before. It said to finish the labyrinth.

When I started the labyrinth with Hattie and Cam, I was so consumed with anger about Stan's secret that I never went back to it. I've been running away ever since. And since Chase's attack, I've been hiding in this beach house. My heart races at the thought of being outdoors, but it's time to stop procrastinating.

Once Arlene is settled in her infant stroller under an umbrella, it only takes me a couple of hours to finish constructing the paths lined with stones and pebbles. During the late afternoon, I am drawn back to the beach. After setting Arlene up again near the entrance to the labyrinth, I find a pretty shell and take several deep breaths to clear my mind. I set an intention, as Hattie and I learned to do when we researched labyrinths. The proportions of the designs are based on sacred geometry, which can be used as paths of healing and spirituality, especially if you set a clear intention. I step into the labyrinth asking for ways to forgive Stan and myself, to recover from Chase's assault, and to figure out my feelings for Cam.

I walk the path at my natural rhythm, keeping my mind clear and open. I focus on each step and not on what's up ahead or getting to the center. It's a journey of being in the present. I breathe deeply and release stress and tension along the way. When I reach the center, I place the shell down as a gift of thanks and wait for what I am open to receiving. A chill travels up my spine, and I suddenly feel someone is watching me. I watch the baby asleep in her stroller only ten feet away. I'm annoyed to lose my focus on being in my labyrinth, but the sense of being watched grows more intense.

I scan the beach. The lifeguards are observing the people in the water. A family of four is collecting shells a good distance away. An older couple and friends are gathering up their beach chairs and wandering toward the path a block away. Above the dune grass, I see the tops of people's heads strolling along the boardwalk. No one is paying attention to me.

I would prefer to convince myself that it's Danny and Stan communicating that things will eventually work out, but my knotted stomach is warning me it is something or someone else. I'm grateful Cam will be back from Philadelphia at any moment. All my bravado at being able to take care of myself seems to be draining away.

I hurry the last few steps out of the labyrinth and sigh when Cam comes down the path to the beach. Our eyes meet, and his smile brightens. "How was the meeting?" I ask when he reaches Arlene's stroller and touches her hand.

"Unfortunately, one of our veteran teachers has suddenly decided to retire. His wife isn't well, and he will be her main caregiver."

"I'm sorry. You and I understand the challenge of caregiving."

"After they advertise the position and find some candidates, they'll have me back up for two days of interviews. Not what I planned to be doing the last days off in the summer. Hey, you finished the labyrinth. It's great."

"Did you see me from the house?" I ask.

"No. When the house was empty, I felt a little worried, but I thought you might be on the beach. I saw you for the first time when I came along the path."

"It's odd."

"What's going on?"

"I walked the labyrinth and had an intense feeling that someone was watching me, but no one was." I can tell by the way Cam starts scanning the area that he's concerned his brother is nearby. "I didn't notice anyone. Everyone is a good distance away on the beach or up on the boardwalk."

"There are such things as binoculars." He squints up at the deck of his house.

"You don't suppose he got in somehow and is hiding somewhere in the house?" My stomach does a flip.

"You locked all the doors?"

I dig the keys out of the pocket of my shorts and jingle them.

"Good. Let's go back up, but you stay on the front porch while I check the entire house."

As we hike up the path, cross the street-level boardwalk, and roll the stroller to the front porch, Cam and I are both on high alert. It doesn't take him long to check every room, inspect each closet, and try every lock.

"No one's here." The relief on his face as he joins me on the porch calms me.

"You know, I'm going through so much right now—it was probably just my imagination. I'm sorry I worried you."

Chapter Thirty-Six

Cameron

On the way to the Rehoboth Beach Post Office, it occurs to me that things are starting to get somewhat back to normal. Shirlene and I haven't made love since Chase's attack, but I am never going to push on that issue. She'll make that call if and when she's ready.

I wave to the employees behind the counter and unlock my mailbox, expecting the usual forwarded bills and junk mail, and on top is a handwritten envelope addressed to Rain. It's my brother's handwriting. The return address is a recovery place in Malvern, Pennsylvania.

I wondered where the snake was hiding, but I certainly didn't expect rehab. I close the box and go out front. Why is he writing to Rain? My fingers itch to open the letter, but it's not addressed to me. It's addressed to his dead girlfriend. But Shirlene is the closest thing to Rain, so I hop in the car and zip home as quickly as I dare without getting a ticket in our tourist-packed town. Just when I thought we were getting past this, he's back, as my grandmother used to say, like a bad penny.

I bound up to the back door. Shirlene is in sight, placing laundry in the washer. I have keys, but I tap lightly on the glass. For a split second, her face is worried.

She unlocks the door. "Hi." She frowns. "Why are you out of breath?"

I step inside. "It couldn't have been Chase watching you in the labyrinth a few days ago."

She turns on the washer. "How can you be sure?"

"He's written to you from rehab."

"To me?"

"Well, to Rain." I hold out the letter.

She stares at it.

"Aren't you going to open it?" I ask.

"It's Rain's, not mine." She darts out of the laundry room.

"Aren't you curious about what he's up to?" I follow her into the living room.

"Not in the least." She jerks a chair away from the dining table and flops into it.

I tear open the envelope, nervously tapping my heel on the floor. When I finish reading, I look at Shirlene.

"Go ahead," she says.

"He went into rehab the day after he was here. He apologizes for hurting you."

She bolts out of her chair. "Too little, too late!"

Her intense reaction surprises me. "I understand."

She shakes her fists. "No! No, you don't. Stan would have chopped off his hand before laying a finger on me in that manner!" Tears spill as if someone flipped a switch. "Even when I broke my husband's heart, he never hurt me physically."

She begins to collapse, and I catch her in my arms before she falls. Instinctively, she shoves at my chest, but then she relaxes. I hold her while she sobs.

I whisper, "I'll never hurt you."

"I need to sit down."

I guide her to the sofa, and she sinks into the cushions. I hand her a box of tissues. She blots her eyes and blows her nose, but the crying scarcely abates.

"You've been holding this in for too long. Let it all out." I consider my words carefully. "Is it okay if I ask you a question, Shirlene?"

"Why not?" she says through her tears.

I sit at the other end of the sofa. "Why did you say you broke your husband's heart? Do you mean when Danny died?"

"Yes." Her hands tremble as she wipes her eyes again. "Stan thought I was drinking."

"You weren't."

"No, I wasn't."

"And yet you continue to punish yourself as if you'd been drunk. Stan believing you weren't sober and caused the accident doesn't make it true."

Shirlene's crying begins to subside. "Why would Stan choose to believe I wasn't sober? Why would he need a reason to blame me?"

"I can't imagine." I wish Stan were alive so Shirlene could ask him.

Shirlene squares her shoulders. "I wonder if it was easier to have a reason for the accident than face the fact that we have no control. Life is completely unpredictable. That's difficult to accept, especially for someone as controlling as Stan."

"Maybe."

"So he found a way to control things by getting the vasectomy. There'd be no more children that could be taken away." Shirlene stifles another sob. "I wish he'd been able to tell me how frightened he was. We wasted years with this pain between us."

"Stan wasn't perfect. None of us are."

"No. We aren't perfect." She takes a deep breath. "I suppose there should be forgiveness, including for Chase."

I pick up Chase's letter from the table. "He wants you back. That's why he's in rehab."

She jumps up. "What about Arlene?"

I regret bringing this back up. She was just calming down. "Don't worry. I'm not handing Arlene over to him."

"But he can fight you in court."

"Shirlene, he's not a fit or safe father. He poses no threat to us. I hope he does recover and pulls his life together for once, but that's as far as it goes."

"I should have pressed charges. It would be a legitimate mark against him."

"The police report will help."

"How soon will he be out?"

"He doesn't say, but he asks you—Rain—to write to him."

"That's not happening." Shirlene sits again. "Where is the rehab located?"

"Outside of Philadelphia. According to his letter, my parents are paying for it. That's something at least."

Shirlene gasps. "Do you think he's told them about the baby?"

"They won't bother us."

"How can you be sure?" There is panic in her voice.

"What's upsetting you?"

"Rain has a terrible track record too. What if your wealthy, successful parents want to take the baby away?"

"Trust me. They have no interest in the baby."

I hope I'm right. I could ask them directly, but Chase might not have told them about the baby yet. I'd be opening a door I'd rather keep shut. I need to stop avoiding them like the plague. But for now, I'm going to let sleeping dogs lie.

Chapter Thirty-Seven

Shirlene

I lean against the doorjamb of Cam's room, watching him reluctantly toss clothes into a duffle bag. I haven't been across the threshold since his brother assaulted me.

"I wish you'd come up with me. I wouldn't worry so much about your and Arlene's safety."

"Chase is in a rehab facility over two hours away from here. Nothing is going to happen."

He paces back to his closet and selects another dress shirt. "Well, it's only for two days and one night." He closes his luggage. "I'll have my things packed in the car and drive back immediately after the second round of candidate interviews tomorrow." He passes me and pauses before going down the stairs. "I'll text when I get there."

I follow him. "Drive carefully."

He grabs his keys from the kitchen counter. "Traffic shouldn't be an issue this early." He kisses my forehead. "First interview isn't until late this morning."

"Don't worry about us."

"I'll try."

He goes through the laundry room and out the back door, which I lock behind him. I wave and watch him drive out. I walk through the kitchen and living room to check the front door. It's locked too.

The baby cries from upstairs. When I reach the nursery, she's wide awake. After changing her, I sit with her in the rocker and try to relax, but being in the house alone feels uncomfortable. I practically pushed Cam out the door, and Chase is nowhere near, so I don't understand why I'm feeling unmoored.

I try to focus on Arlene. "Are you hungry, sweetie?"

I'm nursing her when the feeling of being watched returns. Although Arlene and I are the only ones in the nursery, I glance around. Arlene whimpers. I hope I can chalk it up to nerves.

How's she doing? I hear the question in my head, but I'm not the one asking it. In contrast to the warmth of Arlene cuddled up against my chest, a chill runs up my spine.

"She's fine," I say.

Good, I hear.

I have finally lost my mind.

Arlene becomes restless and stops nursing. I lift her to my shoulder and pat her back gently.

You're good at this.

"I've done it before," I reply.

I know, with your little boy.

"Who are you? How do you know my son?"

The chill drains away. All conversation stops. Arlene burps. I shift her back down into my arms.

"Did you hear anyone talking?" I ask her.

She blinks.

"I guess that's a yes."

She's never stopped nursing before. Arlene roots around my breast again. I help her latch back on and try to grapple with what happened to me. Then it hits me. It was the same voice that told me to take care of the baby when I was going into Rain's body. It's Rain. The implications of hearing voices are too terrifying to accept, so I decide I must have imagined it. Otherwise, I'm losing it.

I keep myself busy, but as the afternoon wanes, the anxiety returns. I should have gone up with Cam. I decide to try to eat some dinner. When the water bubbles for pasta, I sense, again, that I'm not alone. Well, I'm not. Arlene is in her carrier. It's only the baby who is watching me, right?

I shift her around so she can't see me. Of course, she starts to fuss. The feeling that someone is watching me intensifies. I close the blind on the kitchen window. What if someone is in the yard? What if Chase has left the rehab? I check the back-door lock once again, and of course, it is still locked. Arlene loses patience and begins to cry. I hustle back to the kitchen and lift her. She immediately settles.

"You got what you wanted, didn't you?" I say to her.

She coos.

I've lost my appetite and turn off the stove. I carry Arlene into the living room, which suddenly feels chilly.

You got what you wanted, didn't you? I hear in my head.

"What?" I ask.

A baby.

I inspect the room. No one is there. My arms begin to shake, and I'm worried I'll drop Arlene. My knees buckle as I stumble to the sofa. I'm losing touch with reality.

You're not nuts.

I hold my daughter tightly. "What do you want?"

To talk to you about my body.

It is Rain. Or maybe this is simply guilt. All along, I've wondered why I ended up in Rain's body. But she gave no fight. I had no sense of her struggling when I was sucked into the vortex that landed me in her body. She said "Take care of her" and gave up.

"You're dead," I say.

There's no reply, but the chill remains.

I wonder what would have happened if I, Shirlene, had gone to the light. Rain would have died in the delivery room. Arlene could have died too. The thought horrifies me. It could be that's why I was sent into Rain's body—to save Arlene. Rain chose to die, but she wanted the baby to live.

I won't hurt Arlene.

I sit up straight. "I won't let you."

It's good how protective you are of her.

"Are you Rain?"

Yes.

"Why are you here?"

Being on the other side has changed me.

"A little late for that."

Not really.

"What do you mean?"

I want my body back.

Chapter Thirty-Eight

Shirlene

I feel neither sane nor safe anymore. I can't possibly tell Cameron that Rain is talking to me in my head. If I have any more episodes with the former resident of my body, I'll begin to believe Cam and Arlene would be better off without me.

To avoid any visits today, I fill every moment with activities. I take Arlene for a long walk in the stroller and speak to more people than I have since giving birth to her. Chatting with strangers, going food shopping with the baby, and sitting on a crowded beach seem to have worked. But now, the day is coming to an end, and Cam has ended up having to stay away another day for second interviews. I can't very well camp out in a twenty-four-hour pharmacy all night.

After staring into the refrigerator filled with food, I end up with a bowl of cereal for dinner. What I want is a drink. The craving starts in my stomach, travels up my throat, and settles in my mouth. I need to taste liquor, and without Cam here to watch the baby, I haven't been to a meeting. Although I could use the support, I'm not sure what AA folks would do with me if I told them I was hearing voices in my head.

The baby cries, and I dash upstairs. When I reach the nursery, the chill returns.

"No way!" I say to no one.

I stand with my back against the crib. I'm not sure if I can protect Arlene against her, but I'll die trying.

Why are you frightened, Shirlene? I'm not going to hurt you or the baby.

"You want me dead." She doesn't reply. "That's true isn't it?"

Technically, yes.

"So if you want me dead, how aren't you a threat?"

We can work this out.

"It *was* your body. Now it's mine."

Another technicality.

I stamp my foot. "There's nothing technical about it. My body and my baby." I pick up Arlene, who is now screaming.

How is she your baby? Rain asks.

"I gave birth to her. You abandoned her." I gently rock my child. "You're upsetting her. Go away!"

Chase and I conceived her.

"Oh, he's a real prince. He came here and tried to rape me."

I don't believe you.

"Isn't that typical."

Well, I admit he can be an ass.

"There's something we do agree on."

She laughs. *I like you, Shirlene. You're savage.*

I'm not sure what she means, but I scan the room for some sign of where she might be. "Can you do anything to show me where to look when addressing you? I'm tired of talking to the air."

I can't. I'm in your head.

Arlene finally settles, and I decide it might be to my advantage to understand Rain better. "Why would you waste your time on Chase?"

I didn't think I deserved better. Now I know differently.

"He wants you back."

He does? That's sweet, but I'm not interested anymore.

"And I suppose Cam is of interest? Do you think you deserve him now?" I am surprisingly territorial.

Mike? She scoffs. *Don't get me wrong. He's a nice guy, but he's never been my type. Besides, I need to stand on my own two feet.*

"How do you plan to do that? You don't even have a high school diploma."

Who told you that?

"Cam."

Of course he'd say that. I finished high school, Shirlene. Barely, but I did.

"How can you support Arlene?"

One way or the other, I'll figure this out. If you give me a chance.

"I need time to mull this over."

Try to hurry.

"Hey! I'm not saying I'll agree."

It will be easier if you do.

The chill leaves. I'm not convinced Rain won't or can't hurt the baby, so I move Arlene's crib into my bedroom. I don't sleep, but it helps to have her close by.

In the morning, I hike into town with Arlene in her stroller. At the Lilypad Children's Boutique, I purchase a baby wrap, which I immediately settle the baby into. It's reassuring to have her against my chest as close as possible.

I come back by way of the boardwalk, and as I near the beach in front of Cam's, I'm drawn to the labyrinth. Crowds of people are massed up a good distance away down by the water. A drop of sweat trickles down my face, and the roar of the pounding waves evolves into white noise. I select a small piece of driftwood from the sand and take several cleansing breaths. I enter the labyrinth. When I reach the center and place my gift down, a chill resumes in my spine.

Rain says, *You're afraid in the labyrinth.*

I glance around to check if any beachgoers have wandered nearby and can hear me talking before I mutter, "I'm not afraid of you, Rain. There's nothing you can do, so go away."

She doesn't answer. I hope she's gone. Then I hear, *I've been meaning to tell you Stan and Danny need you.*

My head pounds. "What do you mean?"

Stan is desperate to talk to you.

"Why can't he speak to me the same way you are?"

He's in a different state. You must come to him.

"Die. I must die. That's what you mean."

She doesn't answer.

I kiss the top of my baby's head as she squirms against my chest. "I can't leave her."

And Mike. You're in love with him.

"Leave him out of this."

I wonder if she's manipulating me or if Stan and Danny are really in trouble. I resent the ancient guilt tightening my throat. "No!" I continue mumbling. "I didn't kill Danny. It was an accident. But you lied, Stan. You deceived me. How could you do that?"

I hope the labyrinth is where I can contact my husband to finish the conversation we were having before he died. "Figure out a way for me to talk to Stan, and I'll consider your request."

Rain has gone.

Chapter Thirty-Nine

Cameron

Every day since I came back from Philly, Shirlene has paced the labyrinth. I've watched from the second-floor deck. She talks to herself, or she's whispering to the baby, whom she continually carries on her chest in the baby wrap. She walks to the center of the labyrinth, waits, goes back out, and starts over. When I ask her what she's doing, she only says it's her meditation. I'm losing her to something or someone else. Today, it's raining, so I hope Shirlene won't go to the labyrinth.

Shirlene comes down the stairs. "I've changed and nursed Arlene. She's gone back to sleep."

"How about some breakfast?"

"No, I'm not hungry." She wanders over to the piano. "Did your cell ring in the middle of the night?"

I close my laptop. "I'm sorry it woke you. Aimee called from Italy."

Shirlene sits on the piano stool. "I fell right back to sleep. Is she okay?"

"Her depression is so bad she's trying to be released from her contract."

"I'm sorry."

"I'm worried someone is triggering it, but she didn't go into details. She plans to come home."

"There could be an upside. Since you're the one she's calling, perhaps she's changed her mind."

"What do you mean?"

"Possibly, she wants to start a life up with you again."

My chest aches like I've been sucker punched. "Shirlene, my life is with you and Arlene now."

Shirlene stands. "Oh, I thought... Never mind."

"Aimee and I are close friends. Even if she did have a change of heart, it wouldn't matter to me. I◇"

"I'm going for a walk." She rushes onto the porch, grabs an umbrella from the stand, and goes out into the rain.

She's heading to the labyrinth again, and today, for the first time, she's without the baby. Is that because it's raining or for some other reason? Panic boils up into my chest when it occurs to me maybe she was saying goodbye to her daughter all those other times she went through the web of paths.

I grab the binoculars and go upstairs into Shirlene's room. Through the window, I can see Shirlene from the waist up when she's on the ocean side of the labyrinth. Otherwise, the dune blocks her, and only the top of the red umbrella she's carrying is visible. She comes back around. When she turns toward the cottage, I watch her mouth moving. Although Arlene is fast asleep in her crib next to me, she's still talking.

An osprey calls, and I watch it fly over the house. I look back toward the labyrinth. Shirlene is gone. She must be hidden by the dune, but the top of the umbrella was visible before. There is no sign of it or her. I wait for her to move away from the dune to where I can see her. Maybe she's given up because of the rain, but she isn't coming up the path from the beach either. I scan back over to the labyrinth, and she has disappeared. I toss down the binoculars and race downstairs.

Chapter Forty

Shirlene

After days of working to convince Rain to let me contact Stan, it surprisingly happens. I'm no longer on the rainy, deserted beach, walking the labyrinth. There's a bright light. It's difficult for my eyes to adjust, and I try to block the glow with my red umbrella.

After my eyes become more accustomed, I find Rain. It is disconcerting how she looks like me, not how I am now but how I was when I first took over her body. She's dressed in impossibly short shorts, and her midriff shows below her cut-off tank.

"Where are my husband and son?" I ask.

"Don't worry. They're coming soon."

Stan and Danny appear a distance away in a sunny meadow filled with wildflowers. They hold hands and appear to be searching for someone. Is it me? Do they need me? I call to them, but they don't respond.

"Stan!" I shout. "Are you all right?" I'm unable to move any closer, and they seem to be floating away. "Wait, I need to talk to you."

I struggle to run to them, but a powerful, invisible force holds me back. I'm desperate to ask Stan why he allowed me the hope of getting pregnant month after month for years, why he told me about the vasectomy right before he died—why he didn't take the secret to his grave. But I can't shout these things in front of Danny. My son and husband begin to evaporate.

"Make them stay!" I yell at Rain, who is also gliding away. "You said I could talk to Stan."

"He couldn't find you. Only if you let me have my body back."

She is gone. I cry with frustration, and I'm suddenly on the sand path again between the circles of stones. The rain taps on the top of my umbrella.

"Damn you, Rain!" I don't sense her presence in the labyrinth, but she's definitely forcing me to choose. I won't gain answers to those questions unless I give up her body and die. The wind whips the mist into my face. By the time I make it back to the cottage, I'm drenched and freezing cold.

Cam yanks open the back door. His beautiful body fills the open doorway, so solid and strong with his dark eyes and chiseled features. I drop the umbrella and run into his arms. He guides me into the laundry room and shuts the door with his hip. I selfishly need his warmth. I kiss him. He immediately responds. Our mouths consume each other. We tug at one another's clothes until we're naked. I allow him to lift me onto the washer. I wrap my legs around his waist as he glides inside me. I dig my fingers into his muscular shoulders. His hands grasp my lower back and pull me closer. My head falls back with pleasure. I'm alive. I'm alive. I'm alive.

It continues to rain. Cam is asleep. As I tiptoe out of his room, where we ended up making love again, I feel that I took Cam in order to fulfill my own needs. It was stupid and selfish. Something Rain would do. I'm not sure who I am anymore. After navigating the creaky steps downstairs, I punch in Hattie's number.

"Hello?"

Hearing her voice floods me with hope. "Welcome home from Ireland," I whisper.

"Thanks. It was a fabulous trip, but why are you whispering?"

"The baby is sleeping."

"So move to another room. My hearing isn't as good as it used to be."

"It's perfect. And I'm in a complicated situation. I'll explain later when you come back down here."

Hattie hesitates. "I won't be able to come for a few weeks at least."

"You're not coming back, Hattie?" I slide into a chair.

"My granddaughter had her twins, and with the other children, she's overwhelmed. She asked me to come out to help as soon as I got back from my trip."

"You said her mother-in-law had the first shift."

"That was the plan, but her mother-in-law fell and broke her ankle. Now I have to go."

"But I need you, Hattie. So much is happening to me." My throat constricts as I fight back tears.

"I'm sorry, honey. Do you need to talk?"

I take a deep breath. I can't afford to lose control. Where do I begin to explain things to Hattie? With the practical.

"I need you to update my will so everything is left in trust to Arlene and Cameron is the trustee with power to take out funds for Arlene's needs."

"Can't it wait a few weeks until I return?"

"No."

"You're a healthy young woman."

"I could be hit by a car."

"What's really going on, Shirlene?"

I would prefer to tell her this in person, but given the circumstances, I can't wait. "This is going to sound nuts, but Rain is back."

"Back where? How?"

"I've had full conversations with her."

Hattie's voice rises. "I am beginning to question your state of mind, Shirlene."

"I don't blame you. I might be insane, but please believe me, Hattie."

She sighs. "Tell me the details."

"It began the first time I was alone here. I felt like someone was watching me. It was very unnerving." I bite my lip. "Then she began talking to me."

"Is she a ghost? Can you see her?"

"No. She's not a ghost. Well, she's dead, but she's in an altered state."

"Shirlene, I don't trust her. She wants something."

"So you believe she's actually talking to me? I'm not losing my sanity?"

"I'm not certain, but after everything that's happened, I'll go with it." Hattie pauses. "Why is Rain back?"

"Try not to overreact. She wants me to die and let her have her body back."

"What?"

"I know. It's upsetting."

"Holy mother, you could say that. Hold on—I need to sit down." There's shuffling on the phone. "Okay. Go ahead."

"The more I talk with Rain, the more she makes sense. I finished the labyrinth, and we've had a lot of conversations there. She had an especially disturbing childhood and had to run away right after high school. I'm beginning to understand how she ended up with Chase."

"Shirlene, she's playing to your codependent and caregiving nature."

"But being in the spirit world has changed her. She wants another chance."

"Are you willing to lose Arlene in order for Rain to come back?" Hattie shouts.

"She promises to take care of her this time." I can't believe I'm defending Rain.

"Bull! No, no, no! You can't do this." Hattie takes a breath. "I'd like to tell Rain a thing or two."

"You're right—Rain's likely full of it. But she also said Danny and Stan are in trouble. What if she's telling the truth?"

"What happened to letting go of the past and moving on with this new life you've been given?" Hattie asks.

"Well, that's just it. What if this was temporary and I was supposed to take care of Arlene until Rain got herself together? Rain didn't really mean to die. She felt overwhelmed and took the escape offered to her. Now, she regrets her choice."

There is silence on the line except sniffling.

"Hattie? Don't cry, because I'll start crying too."

"You are seriously considering dying?"

I shudder at her word choice. "I haven't decided, but yes, I am considering leaving. I want answers from Stan."

"You can't leave me, Shirlene. Not again. I need you. Arlene and Cam need you."

"Please, Hattie. This is hard enough."

Hattie's voice becomes stern. "You have to tell Cam. That young man is in love with you. You owe him that much."

My heart pounds. "I don't know for sure yet. But if I decide to go, I can't tell him."

"You're going to let go and leave him with Rain in your body without any warning?" She's shouting again.

"I have to."

"Why?"

"Because I've let him get too close." I can't fight the tears back. "He'll ask me to stay, and it will kill me to leave him and Arlene."

"After all these years and all the brave things I've watched you face. Losing Danny, for God's sake. I couldn't believe how you got your life back together. But I'm going to tell you that in this situation, you are being a coward."

"I'm sorry you feel this way, Hattie."

"I do. And if you don't tell Cam—warn him—I'll make sure he knows. I'm giving you twenty-four hours, Shirlene. You have to tell him, or I will."

Chapter Forty-One

Cameron

When I finally reach my street, the constant drizzle becomes a downpour. There are only a few cars parked on our block. These couple of days of bad weather have chased everyone away. I ease the baby carrier out without waking Arlene and shield her from the wet with a baby blanket. When I open the back door, the house is still. I slip the blanket off the baby. She barely moves. I carry her into the empty living room.

"Shirlene?" I call quietly. There's no answer.

Shirlene immediately withdrew again after we made love yesterday. I hoped when she initiated sex that she'd come to terms with something. Maybe I was just projecting my wishes onto her. For fear of Shirlene's reaction to me spying on her, I never mention her disappearance while she was in the labyrinth. Then this morning, she backed out of running errands together. Said she wasn't feeling well. I took the baby with me to the post office and bank, but the entire time, I felt uneasy.

Shirlene might be napping, so I creep upstairs to the nursery and settle Arlene into her crib. I go to the back of the house, foolishly hoping to find Shirlene asleep in my bed. There would be nothing more inviting than getting under the covers with her while the rain taps on the roof. But my bed is empty.

"Shirlene?"

My belly churns. I dash back down the hall. The front bathroom door is open. I sprint into Shirlene's room. Her bed is also empty.

Where has she gone in this storm? I scan the boardwalk and beach from the window. No one is out there, but something is floating in the rough surf. I grab the binoculars off her nightstand, furiously adjusting the focus. Long blond hair thrashes in the foamy water.

I skip every other step to the first floor, run to the beach, race across the sand, and force my legs through waist-high surf.

"Shirlene!"

I'm engulfed by a wave but continue to push forward, finally reaching her. I wrap my left arm around her waist and lift her across me. I kick furiously with my legs and plow my right arm into the water doing a sidestroke. When I can touch the bottom, I drag her onto the beach. Her face is nearly as blue as her bathing suit.

I begin CPR, with two breaths into her mouth and thirty compressions on her heart. Water comes out of her mouth. I roll her onto her side.

"Come on, Shirlene." More water gushes out. I flip her onto her back and put my mouth on hers. Then I pump my hands on her heart. "Please live. Please."

Adrenaline courses through my system. I'm having difficulty breathing. I must concentrate.

Suddenly, she coughs. I flip her on her side again. She spits up more water and opens her eyes.

"Thank God." I allow my tears to flow now.

She gasps for air. "Mike?"

Chapter Forty-Two

Cameron

Arlene fusses in my arms while I pace a three-foot stretch of hall-way in the Lewes Beebe Medical Center. Between the freezing air-conditioning, my wet clothes, and my anxiety, I can't bring myself to sit down in the waiting area, so I remain as close as is permitted to where they are working on Shirlene. During this hellish hour and twenty minutes, no one has been able to tell me what's going on, and I'm trying but failing to keep my worry from traveling to Arlene. She needs her mother. I need her mother.

Double doors clang open and shut as a doctor pushes through. "Are you here for Rain DeLuca?"

"Yes. How is she? Can I see her?"

"You may visit her in a few minutes." The doctor, whose long black hair is tied back in a ponytail, eyes the whimpering baby.

I move Arlene up onto my shoulder and rub her back. "I have no one to stay with her."

"Ms. DeLuca is disoriented, but she's doing okay. Were you the person who administered CPR?"

"Yes."

"Your quick actions made the difference. She isn't showing signs of permanent brain damage, but we're giving her oxygen until her blood tests return to normal. She needs to stay for observation. Lung problems, such as pneumonia, can develop within the first twenty-four hours after submersion."

"Please let me see her now."

"In a moment. You need to be prepared. It may not make sense, but Ms. DeLuca could be depressed. Near-drowning survivors can have several emotional issues. Try not to become alarmed. Stay calm. Avoid asking her questions at this point." She frowns at Arlene. "If you can keep the baby quiet, you may follow me."

The doctor's stern demeanor does nothing to calm me down. I'm led past several sets of drapes before the doctor glides one open. Shirlene's eyes are closed, and she looks frighteningly pale.

"Doctor, can she hold the baby?" I whisper.

"Only if she requests to do so. Otherwise, do not overstimulate her." The doctor leaves, closing the curtain.

I sit as quietly as I can in a chair, but Shirlene opens her eyes.

"Hi," I say.

She coughs. "My throat is sore."

I notice a plastic cup with a straw in it. Balancing Arlene in the crook of my left arm, I hold the straw to Shirlene's lips with my other hand.

She takes a swallow. "Did you haul me out of the ocean?"

I nod. A million questions rush to my mind. Why was she swimming in the pouring rain? What happened to cause her to nearly drown? Why did she call me Mike before passing out? I fight the fear that she's Rain and not Shirlene but restrain myself and follow the doctor's orders by not asking questions.

"We're both grateful you're alive." I shift Arlene around to face her mother.

Shirlene reaches out and touches the baby's arm. "This is Arlene."

This declaration is odd, but the doctor said she might seem confused.

"Hello, baby girl." Shirlene closes her eyes again, and her deliberate breathing indicates she's falling asleep.

A nurse opens the curtain. "We have a bed open. We'll be moving her shortly."

The baby breaks into a full-out cry, but Shirlene doesn't stir. I desperately dig through the bag of things I brought in search of a bottle.

"Can you take the baby away?" the nurse asks.

I glare at her.

"We need to keep Ms. DeLuca quiet. It may be best if you go home and sleep. Updates will be available during the night. If she is released tomorrow, it will be a challenging day for her. You'll need to prepare. Light foods, rest. There will be instructions in the discharge papers."

I curb my desire to bundle Shirlene up in my arms. Instead, I lightly kiss the top of her head and move lethargically out and through the double doors.

Before leaving the ER, Arlene reminds me she's hungry. I sink into the nearest empty chair. She drinks as I try not to cry. The doctor warned me the survivor could be depressed, but I wonder about the rescuer. I'm beyond thankful Shirlene didn't drown. I should be happy. I can't put my finger on it, but something's not right.

When the baby is done, I burp her and slip the bottle into the bag. The rain has stopped, but Delaware humidity waves over me as I stagger out of the hospital. I shuffle through the thick air and become aware of my damp clothes clinging to me. My skin and hair are covered with sticky salt. I need a shower and some sleep.

After I set Arlene in her car seat, my phone pings. A text from Aimee.

I'm definitely coming home. My agent is threatening to drop me because I'm not completing my contract. He's a dickhead anyway. I need to see my therapist. I'm crashing, Cam. I have a lot to tell you, but it has to be in person. You have your hands full with the baby and Rain, but I wanted to tell you.

Sorry, I text back. I remember her apartment is sublet to someone. *Do you have a place to stay?*

Yes. Nancy, who is subletting my place, is okay with me staying in the spare room. Better if I'm not alone.

This doesn't sound good. I text back, *Let me know when you arrive. Safe travels.*

I can't begin to tell her everything that's happening with me. She obviously has more than she can handle already. Otherwise, there's no reason she would be cutting her tour short and pissing off her agent. She didn't say exactly when she'd be back. I hope things will be calmer on my end by then.

Chapter Forty-Three

Rain

The nurse comes in again to make me inhale and exhale as hard as I can into some weird thing, which makes a little white ball rise and fall. She tells me to concentrate, but all I can think about is how that bitch Shirlene nearly killed me. Without a body, we would have both died. Why would anyone go into the ocean in the pouring rain? But she dove under the breakers and swam out. I never learned to swim. My mother wasn't exactly signing me up for lessons at the pool or baking cookies for my lunch bag. What a laugh. But I sensed Shirlene was vulnerable, so before she got any deeper, I moved into my former body. But the stupid ass started fighting me. By that time, we were drowning. Then, unexpectedly, Shirlene gave up. I thought I was going to die again when I realized I was back in my body and going under. It was nothing short of a frickin' miracle I was still alive when Mike pulled me out of the surf.

I try as hard as I can to make the ball go up so the nurse will leave me the hell alone. My lungs hurt, and I can hardly lift my arms or move my legs. If I felt stronger, I'd make a run for it, but part of me wants to find out if I can handle this mothering thing. A pretty cushy deal. Living in a beach house. Not having to scrounge around for a meal or have sex with a stranger to have a roof over my head. The baby is cute. I mean, how hard can it be? If I can handle the mother role, it makes more sense to stick with Mike. I'd better keep my mouth shut. The longer he believes I'm Shirlene, the longer I'm on easy street.

Chapter Forty-Four

Cameron

When I reach the beach house, I find a voicemail from Hattie, who is helping her granddaughter in Seattle. Newborn twins and two older kids. Honestly, I can't fathom how she has the energy. She needs to talk to me. As much as I want a hot shower and some food, I dial the number Hattie left in the message.

"My dear boy, how are you?"

"Well, Hattie, are you sitting down?" It's best if she's not standing when I tell her we nearly lost Shirlene. At least, I hope to God it's Shirlene I rescued.

"I am. What's wrong?"

"Shirlene is fine, but she nearly drowned."

"Oh, good heavens!"

"They're keeping her in the hospital overnight. Likely, she'll be released tomorrow."

"What happened?" Hattie asks.

"I was running errands, and Shirlene must have decided to take a swim. When I got back, something caused me to look out the window, where I saw her body in the surf."

"Where were the lifeguards?"

"It's been raining here. No one was out there. When I dragged her to shore, she was unconscious."

Her voice quivers. "Thank God you saw her."

"Luckily, a woman jogging on the boardwalk called 911 when she realized I was going into the ocean to rescue someone. After the

Rehoboth Beach EMTs loaded Shirlene into the ambulance, I sprinted into the house for the baby and drove to the hospital."

"Is Shirlene going to be okay?"

"The doctor told me there's no sign of brain damage." To avoid alarming her more, I don't bring up the odd things Shirlene has said.

Hattie exhales. "Have you talked to Shirlene?"

"Only briefly. The doctor was adamant about not upsetting her with questions or stressing her. Apparently, near-drowning survivors can experience emotional issues."

"Yes, I've read about that." Hattie hesitates. "Cameron, has Shirlene been different in any way?"

"If you mean peculiar, not herself, yes, she has."

"Oh dear."

"Hattie, what do you know?"

"Is it from the near drowning?"

"The doctor would have me believe so."

"Was she herself before she went in the ocean?"

"Withdrawn but that's all." I can't tell Hattie that Shirlene disappeared while in the labyrinth. It might panic her. At times, I think I imagined it. I never discussed it with Shirlene, either, for fear of her reaction to me spying on her with binoculars.

"Shirlene called me and told me something she was considering doing, but I shouldn't be the one to tell you. You must ask Shirlene as soon as she's well enough to talk about serious issues."

My stomach flips. "Hattie, you're freaking me out. Are you sure you can't tell me?"

"I'm sorry. It needs to come from Shirlene."

Once we wrap up the call, I'm left with the problem of when to ask Shirlene to tell me whatever she's ready to tell me that she already told Hattie. Damn.

Chapter Forty-Five

Rain

As Mike drives me home from the hospital, I try to figure out how to pretend to be the uptight ninety-year-old lady. I guess I can start by saying please and thank you all the time. I laugh to myself because I've played lots of roles to survive in my life but never the good girl. Never the smart girl. And never the old girl. How am I going to pull this off?

"You're quiet," Mike says, interrupting my thoughts.

"I'm very tired." I hope he won't bug me if his precious Shirlene isn't feeling great.

Arlene giggles from her car seat in the back.

"She's happy you're coming home," Mike says.

I crane my neck around to glance at the baby. "I'm happy to be coming home, sweetheart."

Mike gazes in my direction with nothing but love and admiration in his eyes. A man has never looked at me the way he is now... now that I'm Shirlene. Oh, screw Shirlene. I want a man to love me for me. I deserve it as much as any other female walking the planet.

When we drive in behind a white beach house, Mike bounds around to open my door. I'm perfectly capable of getting out of the car unassisted, but he does this sort of thing. Or maybe he's doing it because I'm just out of the hospital. My head is dizzy with how to respond like Shirlene. I feel like I have heavy weights on my legs and arms.

The salty air smells refreshing. Birds fly and cry out over my head. "God, those seagulls are loud," I say.

Mike scowls. "You said they aren't seagulls. They're gulls, and each type has a specific name." He shields his eyes from the sun to stare up at the frickin' birds. "Those are laughing gulls."

Oh God. Shirlene had a pole up my ass. Unsure of what to do, I wait by the car while Mike gets the baby out of her car seat.

"After you." Mike gestures at what must be the back door.

Although my spirit was here, talking to Shirlene, I have no idea about the layout of the house. I try the doorknob. It's locked. "Do you have the key?"

"Oh, I forgot. Yes." He hands me his keys.

I sort through them and make a guess. Lucky me, the door opens. We come into a laundry room, and I can see the kitchen. I wander in. Shirlene would know where to find the glasses and which drawer has the silverware. I could blame the near drowning for some memory lapses. Shirlene would also know where the baby food is stored—but wait. She's nursing. Gross. I have no clue how long I can pretend to be Shirlene.

"Are you hungry? How about a cup of tea?"

Oh yes, let's have a tea party. "No, thank you."

"Do you want time with the baby or go up and rest?" Mike gently rocks Arlene in his arms and makes faces at her. He is one dumb lug of a guy.

As much as I need time alone to try to get my shit together, Shirlene would want to be with Arlene. "I'll hold her."

"Why don't you sit on the screened porch."

I wander into the living room. Luckily, from there, I can see the porch through the windows. I try the door. It's locked. This place is a real Fort Knox. I flip the bolt, and it opens. Mike follows me out, and after I sit in a rocker, he puts the baby in my arms. She immediately begins to cry.

My throat tightens. "What's wrong with her?"

Mike looks surprised. "She probably needs to be changed."

I can't face a poopy diaper. "You know, I should go rest." I stand up, hand Arlene back.

"I'll manage the baby. You take a nap."

There are stairs in the living room, so I go up them. I walk into the first room and peek out at the sea through a door with little windows.

"Why are you in here?" Mike followed me up to change the baby.

"Oh, it's a nice view from here."

He tilts his head a little to the left. "You have the same view from your room."

I hold back from asking him if he's the room police, because Shirlene wouldn't say that.

"You called me Mike on the beach." His eyes seem to bore right through me.

I keep my mouth shut.

"After I lugged you out of the water and gave you CPR."

"I don't remember," I lie. I slip out and into the room next door.

Since Mike disappears without further comment, I figure I'm in the right room. It's reassuring to close the door. He's suspicious. I have to remember not to call him Mike. And the way the baby reacted to me, she knows. She wants Shirlene, not me.

I wish Arlene liked me. I knew she wouldn't. I'm no mother. Look at the role model I had. That's why I gave up my body and the baby in the first place. I couldn't face all this. But it's a woman's prerogative to change her mind. I regretted throwing my life away. I needed another chance to do whatever it took to stay alive.

Another door with glass windows, similar to the one in the first bedroom, leads to a deck. When I open it, I hear the waves crashing on the beach. My skin crawls with fear. I push the door firmly shut.

I sit on the bed and run my fingers along the neat stitches connecting a bunch of squares in a quilt. It amazes me someone sewed all this together. Well, Shirlene and Mike must not be sleeping together—not in this little bed. At least I won't have to pretend to be her during sex. God, what would she do? Probably nothing kinky. I tug up the dull T-shirt Mike brought me to wear home from the hospital and touch my belly piercing. Shirlene did wear this. Shocking.

I open the closet to check out the rest of her stuff. Shirlene has her boring clothes organized by category. Shirts are all hung together going in one direction. Pants are also in a group. There are a couple of okay sundresses. Nothing of mine is in here. All my thongs are missing from the underwear drawer too. Several one-piece bathing suits are in the next drawer. New shorts and T-shirts folded in the bottom drawers. No halter tops. Nothing revealing. I wonder if any of my things are back at Mike's Philly apartment.

"My stuff better be someplace," I mutter, tightening my fists.

I open a box on top of the dresser and find two wedding rings and a diamond ring on a chain. There's a sudden knock on the door. I jump, dropping the chain and rings onto the floor.

"Give me an idea of when you want lunch," Mike says outside the closed door.

My stomach growls. I didn't eat much of the breakfast at the hospital. "Now would be good."

"Sandwiches okay?"

"Yes." I remember not to say "yeah." I need to say thank you. "Thanks."

I hear no reply. He must have already gone down.

I roam back to the door and glance out at the ocean. The view is nice from this room, but I have no desire to go near the water. Judging from the number of bathing suits I found, Shirlene was a swimmer. I'm going to have to use the fact that I almost drowned as an excuse.

When I come down, Mike appears at the kitchen door. "If you're up to it, could you set the table?"

"Yeah. I mean, yes. Sure."

"Thanks." He gives me an odd look before going back into the kitchen.

On one side of the living room is a table and a long cabinet with drawers. I begin opening the drawers to find the plates and silverware. The dishes are old and grandmotherly. I handle two plates with roses on them as gently as possible.

"Sure, use the good stuff. We're celebrating your survival." Mike is carrying a bowl filled with chips.

"Shit. You almost made me drop these plates." I suppose Shirlene probably doesn't say "shit," based on the frown Mike gives me.

"I'll use them for the sandwiches." He whizzes back into the kitchen with the two plates.

Even though I don't know if we'll need them, I set forks and knives on the edges of placemats with linen napkins.

Mike comes back with the sandwiches and a pitcher. "Don't you want to eat on the porch?"

I scramble for a reply. "Not with the good dishes."

"Right." He sets the plates down. "Arlene is napping."

"Good."

He locates two crystal glasses. "Lemonade? I also have iced tea out there."

What I want is bourbon. "Lemonade would be lovely." Lord, I've never said anything was lovely in my life.

"How about a stroll on the beach this afternoon?" Mike pours lemonade from the pitcher.

I'm not going near the water, and I need to avoid the labyrinth. I could possibly hear from Shirlene in it. "I'm too tired from everything that happened to me."

"Okay. It's best you don't push yourself." Mike takes a bite of his sandwich.

My sandwich is ham and cheese. I hate ham, but I'd better eat whatever Shirlene does.

Chapter Forty-Six

Cameron

After lunch, Arlene wakes up hungry.

"I'll go up," Shirlene says.

It worries me how long it takes her to walk up the steps.

I go back to my book on British women spies during World War II, but I can't concentrate because Arlene hasn't settled down like she usually does the moment she nurses. I wait a few more moments before going up to check out what's happening.

Shirlene is sitting in the nursery rocker with Arlene, who is flailing her arms and screaming bloody murder.

"She won't grab on."

I nearly dissolve, seeing so much pain in Shirlene's eyes. "Just let the baby have a moment. With you in the hospital, she's been on the bottle for a couple of days straight."

Tears trickle down Shirlene's cheeks. "I'm doing it wrong."

"Don't beat yourself up." I kneel close to try to soothe both mother and baby, but the smell hits me. "Didn't you change her first?"

Color rises in Shirlene's face.

"It's okay. The doctor warned us that—"

"To hell with the doctor. The baby hates me."

I've never seen Shirlene lose it. She's been angry with Stan and me but never with the baby.

Shirlene pushes Arlene into my arms.

Before she leaves the room, I reach for her hand. "It's going to be okay. It takes time."

She jerks away. "I'm not trying to nurse anymore." She gives the baby a nasty glare. "She's going on formula."

She is so different from Shirlene that I decide to test her with the task of diapering. "Why don't you change her now."

Shirlene puts the baby on the changing table. As I watch her struggle to diaper Arlene while the baby fights her with kicking feet, I realize denial is a powerful thing. Near drowning or not, this woman isn't Shirlene.

"Hold still, you little monster."

"Try humming to her," I suggest, to see if she'll sing.

The woman darts me an exasperated look. "My throat is sore."

"Do you want me to help?"

"No! I mean, no, thank you." She avoids my eyes. "I have no idea why I forgot to change the baby before nursing her. And I can't seem to work this diaper right now." She gives up and steps back. "Would you? Please?"

I long for this person I rescued to be the woman I love, but she doesn't move like Shirlene. She tries to speak like her but fails. I've hesitated to say I'm suspicious, because the last thing I intend to do is upset her if she is Shirlene. But I have to face the truth.

I take over the diapering, and Arlene immediately settles down. "The doctor said you might be confused, but this is ridiculous. You don't remember how to change a diaper?"

"The baby wouldn't hold still."

"Don't blame Arlene. Shirlene would never criticize her daughter." I lift the baby off the changing table and stare intently into this woman's eyes. "Tell me who you really are."

Her cheeks grow rosy. "You know perfectly well who I am."

"I know who you're pretending to be."

"I'm going to lie down."

I block the door. "Who did we name Arlene after?"

"Your grandmother."

"And who else?"

She hesitates. "My grandmother."

"Maternal or paternal?"

"My mother's?"

"Wrong."

Her voice becomes sharp. "Stop! I'm screwed up from practically dying. Now, move out of my way."

I remain in the doorway. "Why are you named Shirlene?"

She jabs at my chest with her finger. "Move."

I allow her to pass, and I set Arlene in her crib.

The woman scurries down to the living room. I'm not going to let her get away with this.

I pursue her. "Who wrote *Rhapsody in Blue*?"

She spins around to face me. "Screw you!"

I grab her arm. "Where's Shirlene?"

She glares with cold eyes. "She's dead."

My grip tightens on her skin. "What did you do?"

"Come on now, Mike. You're not the violent brother."

It's Rain. I make a fist to punch the wall, but she's right. I don't do that. I release her arm. "What the fuck did you do?"

"It wasn't me." She backs away toward the fireplace. "Honestly. Shirlene wanted to go."

I spit out the next words through gritted teeth. "She would have told me."

"Well, she didn't."

"So, just like that? Poof, you're here, and she's gone?" I pace away, praying this is a nightmare I'll wake up from.

"Not exactly." Rain gets a coy expression. She's enjoying this. "Shirlene and I have been talking for a while."

"In the labyrinth?"

"Yep. But in here too. When you were away. After you came back, we had to talk in the labyrinth."

Although doubts are pouring into my mind, I repeat, "She would have told me."

She glides onto the sofa. "Sorry, big boy. Wrong again. Sweet, innocent Shirlene had secrets from you. She needed Stan and Danny more than you."

I try to shake out my clenched fists. I stride around the room. Pressure is rising in my chest. I've never hurt a woman, and although Rain is more of a devil, I can't let myself unleash this fury on her.

"Get out!" I shout.

Her eyes widen. "You said if I had the baby, I could stay as long as I was clean and sober."

"But you didn't deliver the baby. Shirlene did. She's Arlene's mother."

She jumps up. "I carried that kid for nine months. I labored with her for hours. Shirlene pushed me out and did the easy part."

"You gave up. You died. You're dead!" I think my head might explode.

"No, I'm alive and well. I'm also clean and sober and ready to be a mother."

"Like hell."

"I realized my mistakes, Mike. Shirlene understood me," Rain pleads as she moves toward me. "We became friends. She chose to give me a second chance with Arlene."

"Lies!" I yell. "These are all lies!" I have to have some space between us. I cross to the fireplace.

Rain's voice becomes soft. "Be reasonable. Doesn't school start around next week? You need someone to take care of the baby. Who better than her mother?"

"You are *not* her mother." Spit shoots out of my mouth. I run my hand across my lips.

Rain's voice remains calm. "Okay. Arlene has two mothers. Shirlene was one, and I'm the other."

The room begins to spin as my phone rings. The caller ID says Penn Medicine. What the hell? I answer the phone.

An official sounding voice says, "I'm trying to locate Cameron Michaels."

"That's me."

"You're listed as the contact person for Aimee Bellerose. We found your name in her wallet."

"Yeah." I wish this guy would make his point.

"Ms. Bellerose has had a stroke."

The cell slips from my fingers. I snatch it from the floor. "A stroke? Is she alive?"

"Yes. She's in stable condition. I'm calling from Penn Stroke Center at the Hospital of the University of Pennsylvania. Can you come in? Her doctor wants to discuss her treatment plan with you."

I grab hold of the fireplace mantel so I don't fall.

"Can you come in to talk with her doctor?" he asks again. "Tomorrow at ten a.m. if possible."

"That works. Will I be able to see Aimee?"

"Of course, but the doctor requests talking to you first. Are you familiar with where we're located?"

"Yes. I live in Philly."

After I disconnect, I collapse into the easy chair by the fireplace and rub my hands up and down both armrests. My right heel taps involuntarily. So often, I watched Shirlene nurse Arlene in this chair. But she's gone, and the baby will be drinking formula because the woman standing here is dried up in so many ways. And now Aimee has had a stroke.

"What's happened, Mike?" Rain asks with concern in her voice.

I can't bring myself to look at her. "Pack up. We're going back to Philly."

"Can't I stay here at the beach?"

I leap out of the chair. "Absolutely not."

"Are we coming back here?"

"No." I bolt out of the room. I shove my shock and pain over Shirlene's death deep down inside. There's no time for it. My best friend needs me. I have to close up the beach house and get home quickly.

Chapter Forty-Seven

Rain

Now that Mike has some kind of crisis on his hands, I'm safe for a while. He'll need me to take care of Arlene. I figure I've won some time before he throws me out, so I don't ask questions.

While Mike unloads everything from the refrigerator into a cooler and packs his belongings, I grab all Shirlene's—now my—clothes and the baby's things. I'm not used to having so much stuff. Shirlene wasn't showy, but it takes two suitcases to carry out all her clothes. Everything I had fit in one backpack. I make about a hundred trips to the car, carrying all the baby crap.

Mike's face is stony, and he's silent the entire drive back to Philly. He could ask his landlady to take care of Arlene and toss me out. I can't let her be involved. Besides, I'm clued in on a few things now—for example, changing before feeding. I decide to try to be a decent mother. Since I've been given a second chance, it's the least I can do.

When we reach Spruce Street, Mike pulls over to the curb, and we unload everything but the baby.

"Here are my keys. Start carrying stuff up. I'll help as soon as I find parking."

Before I can argue, he takes off with Arlene. He's going to have to trust me with her at some point. I gaze up at the four steps leading to the front door. I figure I'd better load things into the downstairs hallway so no one steals anything while I'm upstairs. This way, Mike will be back, and I won't have to make too many trips up to the second floor. So far, being responsible isn't feeling great, but I start lugging things up and in through the heavy double doors.

"Hi, Rain. I'm surprised to see you. How's the baby?" It's Mrs. Haddad, wearing her weirdo head-scarf thing.

"Fine."

"School starting soon for Cameron?"

"Yes."

She looks past me at the pile on the sidewalk. "You have a lot to bring in. I'll find my husband so we can help you."

"No. I don't want your help."

Her mouth opens in shock. Then it crumples. Who is she to be hurt?

"Rain, I thought we'd become friends."

"You're wrong. Now, I have to move this stuff off the street before someone steals it."

Mike rushes in with Arlene in her carrier.

"There's that sweet child." Mrs. Haddad reaches for my baby.

I snatch the carrier handle and the keys from Mike's hand. "I'm taking Arlene up." Mike can bring everything the rest of the way. I'm not his servant.

Before I unlock the apartment door, Mike says, "She's back to her old self, I'm afraid. I'm very sorry."

"My husband and I can at least bring your things in here."

"I'd appreciate that."

"He's in the back, working. It's taken him all summer, but he's nearly finished the studio apartment."

I let myself into Mike's place. It's good to get away from his landlady's chatter. The apartment smells stuffy. But before I open the windows, I lug Arlene into the spare bedroom. She's beginning to fuss. She probably needs to be changed and fed again.

I set the baby carrier on the floor to open the nursery window and go into the other bedroom to open the two windows in there.

Quickly, I peek into Mike's closet, where I expect to find my old clothes and whatever else Shirlene bought to wear, but it's filled with his clothes. Of course—Saint Shirlene was breastfeeding, so she slept with Arlene and got up at all hours of the night. Well, I'm clearly sleeping in the baby's room, too, if I plan to convince Mike to let me stay. Arlene lets out a howl. I shuffle back to deal with her. My stomach lurches when I remove her diaper, and I worry I'll never be used to this smell.

Mike comes into the room, carrying his luggage. "Oh, are you staying in here with Arlene?"

"Yes." I snap up Arlene's little outfit. "If you don't mind, put my stuff in here."

He disappears back down the hall.

Arlene continues to cry loudly. I go to Mike's bedroom door. "I have to feed her."

He quickly wipes tears from his face. "There's a bottle of breast milk in the cooler. Everything in it needs to go into the fridge."

Once in the kitchen, I warm up her bottle the way Mike did before we left the beach house. With Arlene's high-pitched wails from the nursery pounding in my head, I only shut the cooler lid rather than empty the food into the refrigerator.

Mike swings into the kitchen with Arlene in his arms. He begins to soothe her but gives me the stink eye.

"I'm getting her bottle. I can't do two things at once," I say.

Arlene's piercing cries settle to a moderate fussing. I hand him the bottle. She quiets the moment the nipple touches her lips.

I lean on the counter. "She's going to have to toughen up."

Mike scowls. "Don't be ridiculous. She's barely three months old."

"If you spoil her, she's going to cry all the time."

"And you're the expert on this?" he barks.

"Life isn't fair. The sooner she learns that, the better." I move past him. "I'm going to unpack."

In the nursery, I sit down on the rocker. Gripping the armrests, I rock forcefully back and forth. My mother had a terrible childhood, and she made sure I did too. I want to be different with my baby, but I don't know how.

I wipe tears from my cheeks. "Crybaby."

I begin emptying the two suitcases of Shirlene's clothes. As I'm wondering what she did with my stuff, I notice my torn jeans pushed to the back of the closet. I tug off the shorts I'm wearing and pull on my jeans. I open the bottom dresser drawer and find my halter tops and bras and thongs. I whip off this boring T-shirt and throw on my favorite top. Plenty of boob shows, and my jeans are nice and tight. I grab my jewelry and refill every pierced hole that hasn't closed, forcing through a couple that resist the wires. I look in the mirror. I add eye shadow, liner, mascara, and bright-orange lipstick. I step back to recognize myself. Now I'm more than a mother. I'm hot again.

Chapter Forty-Eight

Cameron

After filling Mrs. Haddad in on Aimee's stroke and asking her to keep an ear out for Arlene in case Rain decides to let her cry instead of soothing her, I arrive at Penn Stroke Center. I'm ushered into a small conference room by a friendly young woman in scrubs, but everyone wears them, so I'm not sure of her position. There's a table with three chairs. She offers me a seat and asks if I could use coffee or some water. After I decline her offer, she leaves. I tap my fingers on the table. I become more aware of my heart racing, so I try to distract myself by rising to examine the pictures of two Philadelphia riverfront landscapes hanging on the pale-green wall. The room is windowless, which doesn't help my pent-up emotions.

Moments later, Aimee's doctor comes in, a tall Black man who appears to be in his fifties. He wears a concerned yet warm expression as he shakes my hand. "Hello, Mr. Michaels, I'm Dr. Manning. Please sit down."

I take a chair, and he sits across from me. "I understand you're Aimee's friend."

"She's my best friend. She hasn't any living family members, so I'm also her power of attorney." I shift in the chair.

"Thank you for talking with me. Aimee suffered a stroke that has affected her ability to communicate. She can't speak. Nor can she write, draw, or gesture to convey what she can't say. She knows when people are talking to her, but her ability to express herself is—hopefully only temporarily—disconnected."

"Hopefully?" This is much worse than I anticipated. "What are her chances of recovering?"

"Every patient is unique. A lot of it will have to do with her desire."

"Are you aware she has a history of depression?"

"Yes. We accessed her records and her medications. The woman who is subletting her apartment and who called 911 was helpful. Aimee's treatment plan will include ways to deal with her depression."

I force my right heel to settle on the floor. "She contacted me from Europe... I can't remember clearly how many days ago. I've lost track of things."

"Take your time," Dr. Manning says. "You've had a shock."

"It took several days for her to get things together before leaving the tour, but she said she was crashing emotionally and was coming home." I am confined to the chair, and there's very little room to move. I lean forward. "Frankly, I'm worried about whether she'll have enough willpower to fight through. She's always been sort of fragile."

"From what I can tell, her initial willpower, as you said, is surprisingly good. Sometimes, we find an inner strength we didn't know we had."

"I hope you're right."

"Now, when you see her, be yourself and remain calm. Reassure her. Obviously, don't ask questions. That will only frustrate her. We can't imagine what it's like to be trapped in a body that won't express what we're thinking or feeling. But do communicate what you are thinking and feeling."

"How can I expect her to react to seeing me?" I ask.

"I'm sure she'll be happy you're here, but being unable to communicate those feelings may make her angry or cause her to cry. Simply reassure her that displays of emotion are to be expected after a stroke."

After we talk some more, Dr. Manning directs me to Aimee's private room. The heavy door creaks when I open it. When Aimee sees me, her teary eyes look panicked. I rush over and wrap my arms around her.

"Aimee, sweetheart. I'm sorry this has happened." I run my hand through her adorable pixie-cut dark-brown hair. I wipe her wet cheeks. She keeps crying. "No matter what happens, I won't leave you. We're going to make it through this together."

It's baffling to be talking to someone who can't offer me any indication of whether they understand what I'm saying, but her beautiful green eyes continue to search my face as if I know an answer.

"I can tell that you want to communicate something."

She can't even nod, but I sense her answer is yes.

"I can imagine how frightening this is for you, but try to relax." I take both her hands in mine. They are cold and clammy. "I met with Dr. Manning. He explained this is temporary. You'll work with therapists in the hospital's rehab facility to heal this part of your brain. When you're released, I'll work with you. I promise to take care of you, Aimee. Please don't quit."

A nurse comes in. "She needs to rest."

"I understand." I release Aimee's hands, and she immediately shifts around on her bed like an agitated, frightened animal. "I'm coming back tonight."

I hope having a sense of when she can expect to see me will help her to calm down. She lets her eyes close, and I quietly slip out into the hall.

As I drive back down toward my neighborhood, I remember that the eggs, butter, condiments, and breast milk I hastily packed up from Rehoboth Beach yesterday are the only food in my apartment. I find parking down the street from my place and hike toward the Acme on Fifth, but I find myself wandering over to Washington Square, where Shirlene first told me she was a ninety-year-old woman who died but came back to life in my brother's girlfriend's body. She had resisted the light in order to take care of her elderly husband. I was impressed with her level of devotion, but now that devotion has taken her away from me.

My head feels woozy, and the trees begin to move. Not sure I can hold myself up, I sit on a park bench. Shirlene is dead. She gave up Arlene, me, and life itself for Stan and Danny. I laugh at my foolishness. I believed if I had any advantage over Stan, it was that I was alive. I could hold her, kiss her, and make love to her. Apparently, there's no competing with a grieving widow's devotion for her recently deceased husband. Hattie might argue that Shirlene didn't go back to be with Stan but to confront him about the vasectomy. Either way, she needed Stan more than she needed me.

I blink and try to clear my head. My vision goes back to normal. Stress. This is all too much stress. My brother, who wore his heart on his sleeve until he dulled the pain with drugs, resented how I could compartmentalize my feelings. Although that coping mechanism isn't healthy, I have no time to grieve over Shirlene. Too many people are depending on me. I have to keep my shit together.

I'm numb by the time I enter the downstairs hall and start hauling my grocery bags up to my apartment.

"Everything was quiet upstairs. How's Aimee?" Mrs. Haddad asks from her doorway.

I set the bags on the steps and come down to her. "After she's released from the hospital, she'll be in rehab. I need a place for her to live where I can take care of her."

"She's not going to be able to manage on her own?"

"The stroke affected her ability to communicate."

"I'm so sorry." My landlady points to the door down the hall. "How about the studio apartment?"

"That would be great, but I'm going to have to take the semester off from work to take care of Aimee. So I can't afford the rent."

"We'll work something out. Besides, my husband needs a deadline to make him finish the rehab."

My eyes burn with emotion. "Thank you. Aimee will have some privacy, and her visiting therapists can come and go without disturbing the baby."

"And I'm right here." Mrs. Haddad briefly touches my shoulder. "If Rain won't allow me to help with Arlene, I'll do what I can for Aimee. In fact, count on me to be her personal chef."

Mrs. Haddad is tough and compassionate. She reminds me of my grandmother. "Thank you for always being so kind," I say.

"Go upstairs and check on your baby." Mrs. Haddad ducks into her apartment.

Chapter Forty-Nine

Rain

My blood boils when Mike tells me about his ex-fiancée. So much for trying to be a better person.

"What do you mean she's going to live here?"

"Not here. Downstairs."

"Same thing."

"No, it's not." He finishes burping Arlene and sets her down on a blanket on the floor. It's obvious he doesn't want to argue with her in his arms. When is this kid going to start dealing with real life?

"How are you going to help with the baby when Aimee will need you all the time? And I'm not going to start taking care of her when you're at school. Arlene is more than enough."

Mike marches across the room to his desk and opens his laptop. "I won't be at school."

"What? Why?"

"You're right. I can't do all of it, so I'm taking the semester off."

"What about money?"

"We'll be fine." He begins typing.

"What are you doing?"

"Emailing my principal and my superintendent."

I remember the money Mike promised me if I delivered the baby. "Give me my ten thousand dollars now."

Mike spins about in his chair. "You must be out of your mind!"

"It's my money. You said I could do what I want with it."

He stands. He's taller than Chase and intimidating. "You lost that when you died. And you doubly lost it when you caused Shirlene to die so you could come back." His hands are shaking.

Still, I don't back down. I've handled his drug-fueled little brother. I can manage this jerk. "That's not fair."

"I'll tell you what's not fair. The woman I love is gone, and you're back. You're lucky I don't throw you out. You've got a roof over your head and food to eat because of my generosity."

"The law is on my side. I'm the mother of the baby. You can't throw me out without throwing out Arlene, and you won't do that."

"A mother with a terrible reputation."

"But your precious Shirlene changed everything. Now I have a good track record."

He laughs. "And who would attest to your 'good' record? What a joke."

He has a point, so I shift gears. "You need someone to take care of Arlene. You may be Mr. Perfect, but even you can't manage an infant and an invalid."

"Don't call Aimee that."

"But you follow my drift." I watch him put two and two together.

"Fine." He sits and goes back to his email.

"'Fine,' I can have my ten thousand?"

"Absolutely not. Shirlene closed the account and put the money back into my account. She canceled your credit card too. Now I need the money since I won't be working for a few months."

Well, it's clear I'm not getting the money right now, but I'll find a way to weasel it out of Mike.

Chapter Fifty

Cameron

A couple of weeks later, I wait for the train to arrive at the PAT-CO Speedline stop. A crowd of people starts coming up from the lower train level, and I spot Hattie's spry gait behind a young family. When she reaches me on the other side of the turnstile, we hug.

"Hattie, I've missed you more than you can imagine."

"I've missed you, too, my dear boy." She stretches up and pats my cheek. "I can't wait to see Shirlene and the baby. How are they? Has Shirlene fully recovered from almost drowning?"

"I'll fill you in, but first, how are your granddaughter and her children?"

"Everyone survived my visit."

I guide Hattie toward the elevator, but she gives me the stink eye. We take the stairs to the street level and go around the corner toward my place.

"Was your flight back okay?" I ask.

Hattie slaps my arm. "Why are we making this small talk, Cameron? You're worrying me."

I take her hand and squeeze it. "Hattie, we're going to talk in a minute. There's my apartment coming up."

Once we're inside the building, I walk toward the studio apartment in the back. Aimee hasn't moved in yet, and it will provide us the privacy we need to talk. I hope I don't have to hold Hattie back from going up to my apartment and strangling Rain.

Hattie pauses in the hall. She observes the stairs. "Shirlene said you live on the second floor."

I open the studio door. "Hattie, we're talking down here."

Her hands flutter to her throat. "Shirlene's not here, is she?"

Hattie begins to collapse. I dash to catch her before she hits the floor. When I lift her tiny body up into my arms, she seems to weigh as little as Arlene.

"Hattie, are you all right?"

She hasn't passed out, but she buries her face in my shoulder as I carry her into the one-room apartment. There's no furniture yet, but Mrs. Haddad and her husband have set up a card table with two chairs. They've left a pitcher of lemonade and a plate of cookies.

"Can you sit?" I ask.

"Yes."

I set Hattie down in one of the chairs and pour her lemonade. She takes a hankie out of the handbag dangling on her thin wrist and dabs at her eyes.

"What happened?" she asks.

I take a seat in the other folding chair. "When I thought that Shirlene had nearly drowned..." It's difficult for me to say this out loud. "Rain took her body back. I'm very sorry, Hattie. Shirlene is gone."

Tears stream down Hattie's cheeks. "When we talked on the phone, you said Shirlene was going to be all right."

"It was Rain pretending to be Shirlene."

"Bitch."

I agree but remain quiet. Hattie clutches her purse to her chest for a shield and cries silently. Seeing her mourn brings tears to my eyes. My efforts to compartmentalize my grief disintegrate. I wonder how Arlene, Hattie, and I will ever move past this loss.

"Please forgive me, Cameron." Hattie's intense stare unsettles me. "I knew. I knew, and I didn't warn you."

I don't appreciate the sound of this. "What are you talking about?"

Hattie sets down her purse and takes my hands in her tiny ones. "Before the near drowning, Shirlene called me. She told me Rain was talking to her."

My stomach tightens. "So it's true—Shirlene hid this from me."

"I insisted she had to inform you about what was going on. I threatened to tell you myself. That's why I left the message for you."

I gently pull my hands from Hattie's. I don't intend to upset her, but my head is spinning again. "Why didn't you tell me the truth when I called you?"

Hattie dabs at her eyes with her hankie. "You'd just rescued who we both thought was Shirlene from the ocean. I didn't want to put more on you. But most of all, I thought Shirlene should be the one to tell you she was considering giving her body back to Rain. I had no idea it had already happened."

I shift in the chair. "I wish you had told me, Hattie, because Shirlene was acting withdrawn for a couple of weeks before I found her—or the person I thought was her—floating in the surf."

"I'm so sorry. I really should have told you everything. Maybe Shirlene would still be alive."

"There's more?"

Hattie's eyes well up again. "Yes. The reason Shirlene was considering letting Rain have her body back was because Rain had convinced her Stan and Danny needed her."

I fly out of the chair. "But they're dead. Arlene and I are alive. We're the ones who need her."

"I do as well. But I suspect what took Shirlene away was her need to confront Stan. There was too much unresolved between them after his deathbed confession."

I stride to the window. "Shirlene left me for Stan. Clearly, she still loved him and not me. But Arlene. How could she leave her daughter?" I wipe my wet face.

Hattie blows her nose.

"You don't happen to have another handkerchief, do you?" I ask.

"No, and I've soaked this one."

I notice a roll of paper towels on the kitchen counter. I flip on the faucet, splash cool water on my cheeks, and blot my face dry. "We are a fine pair, aren't we?"

A tiny smile plays at the corners of Hattie's mouth. She takes a sip of lemonade. "Shirlene also asked me to draw up papers putting her assets in a trust for Arlene with you as the trustee. I did it, but she never had the chance to sign."

I need to be closer to Hattie, so I sit again. "Then why would she give up her body before signing them? If she chose to protect Arlene and make sure that Rain didn't obtain control of the house and financial accounts Stan placed in Rain's name, why didn't she wait to go back?"

"We'll never know."

"Hattie, I'm grasping at straws here, but don't you think Shirlene would have left me a note if she meant to leave?"

Hattie sighs. "I'm not sure."

"But there's hope."

Hattie, who usually sits up straight, straightens herself even more. "Hope for what? Rain forced her out? Shirlene didn't really want to go? Where does that leave us? She's gone." She wipes her eyes. "There's nothing to hope for, young man. We need to let go of hope, which is nothing but a slippery slope, and we must grieve."

I wipe another tear from my face. Hattie is right. Shirlene is gone. The baby cries in my apartment above us. Hattie's face lights up.

"Arlene is ready to see you."

"But is Rain up there?"

I nod.

"I can't meet that woman." She makes a tiny fist. "I'll punch her lights out."

"I'll bring the baby down. Wait here."

I take the steps two at a time. When I reach the nursery, Rain is wearing earbuds and sleeping. Arlene coos from her crib. I quickly change her, warm a bottle, and go back down to the studio apartment.

Hattie opens her arms the moment she sees our little peanut. "Oh, my girl. I missed you so much."

I pass the baby to Hattie, along with the bottle.

"Let's see my big girl drink this all up."

As I watch my daughter cuddled in Hattie's embrace, I try to pretend everything is normal. My weird normal. Raising my brother's child and loving a ninety-year-old woman in the body of my brother's girlfriend. Crazy, but it worked. Now I can't figure out how anything will work.

"Cameron, time got away from me out in Washington State. School is back in session, isn't it?"

"Yes, school has started, but I'm on a leave of absence." I sit at the card table. "Do you remember Aimee, my former fiancée?"

"The vocalist."

"Yes. Well, she had a stroke."

"So young. I'm sorry."

"She's in rehab right now, and she'll be living here in this studio where I can take care of her."

"So you had to leave your job?" Hattie shifts Arlene in her arms.

"I can finish feeding her."

"Hands off, Daddy. She's all mine. Go on."

"I took a family leave, which meant I had to write on the form that Aimee and I are engaged again. It was the only way to move the paperwork ahead." I lean back in the chair. "I'm not sure how Aimee will feel about it."

Hattie knits her brow. "Why haven't you told her?"

"Because she has aphasia. She can't communicate. I don't want to upset her and have her unable to communicate her feelings. It'll frustrate her at this point."

Hattie plunks the baby's bottle down on the table. "The poor woman."

I rise and pace around the tiny apartment. "The physical therapists have gotten her to raise her chin as a response. It's a little unclear because it sometimes seems to mean yes and other times no. Aimee has also started grunting in reply to us, but obviously, she can't function on her own."

"So you'll have Aimee down here and Rain and Arlene upstairs." Arlene burps. "Good girl." Hattie cradles the baby in her lap. "You're managing a lot. Tell me how I can help."

"Thank you, Hattie." I stand next to her. "The Haddads are being amazing, as usual. They're renting this studio to me for about half what they should be getting, because I'm not working."

"Let me help with that." She kisses Arlene's nose.

"Only if I need you to. Right now, I'm all right."

"It's a shame you can't use Shirlene's house." Then Hattie asks, "Does Rain have any idea that Stan's new will gives her access to Shirlene's property and assets?"

"Hell no. I haven't told her."

"Let's keep it that way. We have to come up with a way to force Rain to sign everything over to Arlene's trust." Hattie begins to cry again. She hugs the baby close. "I don't know what I'll do without Shirlene."

Chapter Fifty-One

Rain

As I push the baby carriage along Spruce Street, I spot a man watching me from across the street. He's wearing a sports jacket over a white T-shirt and jeans. His hair is short and his face clean-shaven. After turning onto Fourth Street, I glance back. The man follows me. I'm uncomfortable and search for someplace where there are other people. I roll Arlene into Three Bears Park on Delancey. Toddlers are playing as their nannies and parents are lost on their cell phones. When he comes close, I spin on him, and then I recognize him.

I whisper through clenched teeth, "What the hell do you want?"

Chase blushes. I've never seen this before.

"Just to talk." He glances around as if someone might be paying attention to him. "Don't be afraid—I won't hurt you again."

I'm not sure what he means exactly, but I relax a little.

"Can we sit?" He points to a bench.

I shrug. He broke my heart, and I hate that I'm glad to see him.

I wheel Arlene over with us and sit. "You look so different all cleaned up."

"You do too." He assesses my clothing. "Well, you did at the beach house." He lowers his head. "I'm sorry about that day. I was completely high. Not that that's an excuse. There is no excuse."

I don't understand. "Okay."

"It will never happen again." He grimaces. "I bet my brother wants to kill me."

To avoid looking brainless, I shrug again. Why can't I be more like Shirlene, *in* control of myself and my life?

"That was the bottom. When I could hurt you, it was a wakeup call for me."

"I've seen you at the bottom before, Chase."

"Not really."

Then I remember. Shirlene said Chase tried to rape her, but I didn't believe her. He was that out of control.

"I feel shitty about it. I'll never lay a hand on you again. I'm getting my life back together. I'm sober one month today."

"That's good." I try not to sound shocked, but I am.

"You're surprised, aren't you?"

"I never thought you cared about being sober." I adjust Arlene's carriage so the sun isn't in her eyes.

"I have a reason to now. How about you? How long have you been clean?"

"Since I found out I was pregnant, so I don't know. A long time." I'm embarrassed that I can't remember how old Arlene is to figure this out. Being dead really screwed with my sense of time.

"Rain, that's great."

I'm unused to this nice a conversation with Chase. With any man, really. He must need money or something. "What do you want?" I ask.

"My parents asked me to come out to stay with them. They're offering me a job. If I can stay sober and prove myself, they'll consider leaving the business to me."

"Damn!" I say. Chase has talked about his parents' obsession with their successful LA real estate business. "You're going to be rich."

"Eventually. It's going to take time, but I can turn my life around now that I have a chance."

He sniffs, and it's not a cocaine sniff. Chase hasn't ever been vulnerable with me. I'd better pinch myself to be sure this isn't a dream.

"My counselor at rehab wouldn't let me blame anyone for my problems. I'm an addict, but I used the drugs to avoid what he called 'unresolved pain' over my mom and dad." Chase uses air quotes. "After I worked through my own shit, he encouraged me to contact my parents and talk about it. They paid for the rehab, so I opened up to them. That's when they offered to have me come out there to start over."

"Did you tell them about me and the baby?"

"I did. They look forward to meeting both of you. But I need you to wait. Let me go out there and find out how I do. Okay?"

My stomach flips with disappointment. I'd leave with him this minute. So much for playing hard to get.

"Rain, you really are the only woman for me. But it's not smart for any woman to trust a man who's hurt her. But if I can keep my shit together, I hope you'll give me a second chance. And if you want to keep the kid, that's okay. My parents will hire a nanny."

"Would you like to hold her?"

Chase's hands shoot up. "No. Not really." His voice softens. "Hey, let's take this slow. I have no idea how to raise a kid. And I'm working on staying clean. God, every minute, I'm dying to get high. Let's see how this job works out first."

"I understand. It's not easy."

"But you're doing it."

"I'm trying. It's not easy with the kid and everything."

"You've got a lot of months under your belt, and you're doing a great job with the baby."

He doesn't know that I've been a mother for only a few weeks.

"Yeah, sort of. Do you plan to talk to Mike?"

"Not yet." He rubs his hands together. "I will, but later."

"Should I tell him I saw you?"

"That's up to you, but I need to prove something to myself before I can face Mr. Perfect."

"You need to forgive Mike for being who he is. He's really not so bad."

Chase leans back. "You sound the same as my counselor."

I laugh. "No way."

"Rain, what do you want to do with your life?" he asks for the first time in our relationship.

I'm not used to this touchy-feely Chase. I squirm on the bench. "I wish I knew."

"You could go to school to be a counselor. You could relate to people really good. You've been through a lot, and they'd listen to you."

"You're nuts."

"No, I'm not. I believe in you, Rain." He touches my arm, and my skin tingles.

I stand. "Well, I've got to go back, or your brother will worry I've run off and kidnapped his kid."

Chase gets up. "She's yours."

"She's yours too."

He glances at Arlene, who is asleep. "I don't feel that way. I'm sorry."

"You can't help how you feel."

Chase pulls me close and kisses me, and it reaches all the way to my toes. I lean into the kiss. Everything feels different with him now. New.

He releases me and hands me his phone. "Give me your cell number."

I tap in the number for the phone Mike gave me.

"I'll be in touch. I promise," he says.

As Chase leaves the park, he takes off the sport jacket. His butt is still hot.

Chase believes in me. No one ever has, ever. I can't believe how turned on I am by his clean-cut look. I sit down again, dizzy with possibilities.

Chapter Fifty-Two

Cameron

For the first time, Rain says she's clearing the table after dinner. I don't want to look a gift horse in the mouth, but my defenses go up. While I answer an email from the teacher covering my classes, Rain puts everything in the dishwasher. I'm attaching a file for my sub when Rain hovers nearby.

"Can I talk to you?" she asks.

What's she going to lay on me? "Okay."

"You're wondering what I mean to say."

"Rain, just spit it out."

"Okay. Jeez. I need to figure out what I'm doing with the rest of my life."

"That's good." I wait for the other shoe to drop.

"I hate the idea of those AA and NA meetings, but I might need them to get started. You'd have to take care of the baby for me while I went to a meeting."

I'm astounded. "Of course."

She is surprised. "Thanks."

That's the first time the real Rain has said thanks. It makes me long for Shirlene, but I shove that feeling away quickly. "They have online meetings now too."

"How do you know about this shit?" she asks.

"I don't live in a bubble. I'm a schoolteacher. My brother is an addict." I don't mention Shirlene's problems. It's none of Rain's business. "Just tell me when. I'll work out taking care of Arlene."

"Speaking of the little princess, I'm going to go chill out before she wakes up again."

As I watch Rain disappear down the hall, I wonder what has brought this on. She's never shown any interest in self-improvement before. I doubt that it has to do with Arlene, although it should. Something is up. My gut churns.

On the morning Aimee is released from the Penn Medical Inpatient Rehab, I follow the young woman pushing her wheelchair into the elevator. Once inside, Aimee reaches for the button to the third floor.

"What's she doing?" The woman, whose name tag reads Krissy, selects the ground-floor button.

"I don't know." I shift to look at Aimee. "We're going home. You'll be back for outpatient rehab, but we're going down to the street level now."

The elevator begins to go down, and Aimee reaches around Krissy and aims again for the buttons.

"What's on that floor?" I ask.

"It's the hospice unit."

"Sweetheart, I'm taking you home."

Her eyes pool with tears. She points to herself.

"Aimee, you're not going to die. You don't need hospice."

The elevator settles to a halt on the bottom floor.

Aimee slumps as she's wheeled to my car in the pickup zone. Krissy stops pushing, locks the wheels, and helps Aimee stand. I open the car door, and Aimee slides onto the passenger seat. I shut the door, thank the woman, and dash around to the driver's side. As I steer out into traffic, I sense Aimee tense up. I reach over and place my hand on hers.

"It's okay. I'll drive carefully." I hate repeating things to her, but I'm not sure she remembers. "Now, we're not going back to your apartment. I've worked it out with Nancy. She's going to keep subletting and have her sister come in to use the other bedroom."

Aimee grunts and raises her chin.

"I want to make sure you understand what's going on."

She raises her chin again.

"I brought everything I could think of from your place and put it in the studio apartment in my building." I'm about to say she should tell me if there's anything she doesn't like, but she can't do that. "I'll be right upstairs, and the Haddads are right next to you."

We don't have far to go, and by some miracle, I find a spot right in front of my place. Mrs. Haddad, who usually welcomes everyone who comes in, told me she'd stay out of the way until Aimee was settled. She thought it might overwhelm her. I agreed.

Aimee's eyes glisten when we come into the hall. She stares upstairs.

"You're down here." I unlock the door to the studio. "Here is a set of your own keys for the front door, this door, and there's one to my apartment just in case."

Once we're in her new place, she immediately sits down on the small sofa and leans her head back.

"So, I'd show you around, but it's all right here. The bath in there." I gesture to the door next to the refrigerator. I move over to the bedroom side of the studio and open the double doors to the closet. "I hung some of your clothes in here. You can rearrange things. As you can see, I hung up some of your framed posters of favorite operas and performers. My feelings won't be hurt if you want to change something."

I'm talking too much. But if I don't talk, it's more obvious that Aimee can't. I sit next to her and force myself to stay quiet, and she sets her hand on my knee. I experience a rush of love for her and the need to bundle her up in my arms, but it's not good to overwhelm her.

Arlene begins to cry upstairs. Aimee stands and gazes at the ceiling.

"That's the baby," I say in an effort to calm her. "Rain will deal with her."

Aimee opens her mouth. Her eyes are squeezed shut. I assume she is trying to make a sound. It's heartbreaking to watch. At first, she growls. With a ton of effort, she says, "R."

Although I don't know what she means, this is a huge step. "That's wonderful, Aimee."

Aimee lifts her chin and says again, "R."

When it's clear I can't possibly understand her, she dashes out the door and up the first few steps to my apartment.

I follow. "R? Arlene?"

Aimee halts. "R."

"Do you want to meet the baby?"

She lifts her chin again.

I'm not up for putting Rain and Aimee together. "I'll bring her down."

The baby cries again.

"R!" Aimee stamps her foot.

"Okay. You go back to your apartment."

Aimee grunts and passes me on the stairs.

When I reach my apartment, Rain is bouncing Arlene in her arms. "She won't stop crying. I've changed her. I tried to feed her. Nothing makes her happy."

"Let me take her downstairs for a while."

Rain immediately hands Arlene to me. "Thanks." She makes a beeline for the nursery, probably to sleep.

Usually, Arlene settles for me, but she continues to cry as I go down the stairs. Aimee immediately opens her arms. In seconds, the baby is quietly cuddled in. Peace settles over the room. Although Aimee can't express it, I sense joy in the way she cradles Arlene and kisses her forehead while sitting on the sofa.

Watching them, Shirlene with Arlene comes to mind, but Hattie is sure Shirlene is gone. She said hope is a slippery slope. There is no hope for Shirlene. I need to move on.

Aimee wanted children, but she was afraid her bouts of depression would ruin their lives. Has the stroke changed her? Maybe after I grieve my loss of Shirlene, there's a future for Arlene and me with Aimee. The problem is I'm too busy taking care of Aimee to grieve.

Chapter Fifty-Three

Shirlene

My baby. My baby. My baby. She smells so good. I kiss her and kiss her and kiss her.

Chapter Fifty-Four

Rain

Mike texts me that he has to run over to Jersey to visit a friend. I have to "hold down the fort." Who says that? Whenever Mike takes the baby, she's quiet. Every time she's alone with me, she screams. The pediatrician says there's nothing wrong with her. I know it's because she doesn't like me. On cue, the baby is crying again. I can't stand another minute of this.

Banging begins below me, which makes the kid cry louder. What the hell is that? Is Mr. Haddad working on something? I carry the baby down the stairs, where I hear the thumping again. It's not coming from the Haddads'. It's back in the studio, where the former fiancée is living. The door to her place is open, and she's standing with a broom in her hand, hitting the ceiling with the tip of the handle. I go in. She notices me, tosses down the broom, and opens her arms.

She looks about Mike's type. Collegiate and wholesome with short brown hair, pale skin, and fierce green eyes. She growls and shakes her open arms. She nods at the baby with her chin.

"Here, take her." I hand the kid over.

In moments, the baby has completely changed. She's smiling. Why can't I make her smile?

"I guess you're Aimee, Mike's big first love." I figure this woman is never going to talk again, so I can say whatever I want. "That is until Shirlene took over my body." Aimee's eyes dart up to me and narrow. I hit a chord. "Yep, I died, and Shirlene, this old lady, was living in this body of mine. Mike fell for her. Can you imagine? It's

242

pretty sick. Anyway, I wanted my body back. After my childhood, I deserved a second chance. I thought I could handle the mothering thing. I mean, I'm trying. She doesn't like me. She sure likes you. Why is that?"

Aimee rocks Arlene. I wander around the tiny apartment. I wouldn't mind it in here. Get Aimee to move upstairs with Mike and the kid. I'd have some peace and quiet down here.

This chick must think I'm crazy, but I don't care. She's mute. "So, Shirlene was married when Mike got the hots for her, but her old husband died. She had a boy who died a long time ago. Very tragic. But Shirlene needed to see Stan and her son more than she wanted to be with Mike and Arlene. She made her choice. She broke Mike's heart."

Aimee's stare drills into me.

"And you broke Mike's heart. What happened? Why didn't you marry him? He's taking care of you now. Obviously, he's devoted to you. What's it take to make a guy feel that way?"

Aimee's glare is giving me the creeps. She knows something I don't.

"Stop looking at me that way."

She doesn't stop.

"I've got a guy. Chase. Mike's brother. He's straightening himself out. He's working out in California with his parents. They're going to give him their real estate business if he can keep it together, which he can. Because he's doing it for me. For me and Arlene."

Aimee stands up and stamps her foot. I'm pissing her off, but I don't really intend to. She's the perfect babysitter. I don't have to pay her, and she can't complain. I decide it's best to retreat upstairs without the baby.

Chapter Fifty-Five

Cameron

For the first time since Shirlene died, I pull into the driveway of her Haddon Heights house. This is Hattie's idea, not mine. She's been sorting through Stan and Shirlene's belongings and making donations. She also has the legal papers to fulfill Shirlene's wish that everything go into a trust for Arlene. If we can't find a way to push Rain to sign these papers, Hattie feels it's important to clear the house of personal items. I agree, but now she's left boxes for me to go through in case there are things I want to keep for Arlene.

I hoped Hattie would be here, but the wily woman has purposely left me to my own devices. She knows I haven't had time to process Shirlene's death. I suppose she feels this will help. Well, I'm here. I might as well deal with it.

As I step into the foyer, there remains a faint sweet aroma that's Shirlene's. I notice various small boxes and bins on the dining room table. I can't bring myself to begin my job of sorting through what's left of her and Stan's lives. So I go over the property first.

Although Hattie is taking remarkable care of the house, I check for water in the basement. Then I make sure the washer and dryer are unplugged, the pilot lights on the stove are on, and the lamp timers are working. The hole in my chest gapes open as I run my hands over things Shirlene touched and used her entire married life with Stan—the kitchen chairs, the stair railing, and especially, her piano.

When I walk into the den, my chest tightens. I can picture how cute Shirlene and the baby looked playing on my bed the time I discovered them. It's too hard to breathe in here, and I need to get to work, so I go back to the dining room table.

The first box I open is filled with envelopes whose postmarks indicate they are the letters Shirlene and Stan wrote to one another while he was a fighter pilot during the war. Do I keep them for Arlene? I consider Shirlene to be Arlene's mother, but I can't fathom how I will explain that to my daughter when she is old enough to understand.

The letters are organized in chronological order. Convinced Shirlene was the one who did that, I tap the first envelope Shirlene wrote to Stan. Do I have the right to read this? Do I really want to? It will either help my grieving process or make things a million times worse.

I slide the writing paper out of the envelope. First, I examine Shirlene's neat penmanship. It's strange how someone is dead but something as personal as their handwriting lives on. I run my fingers over the words she penned as a very young woman. I press the letter to my chest because I desire my own letter from Shirlene. With trembling hands, I hold it to read.

Dear Stan,

I miss you, especially your goofy sense of humor. I miss laughing, but as long as you are in harm's way, I'm so unhappy. Please don't take any crazy risks. Flying a fighter plane has its own risks, but be careful.

Nothing much to report here. Hattie and I went to the library and took out books on cooking. It might sound silly to you, but I'm not a very good cook. I want to do a better job of it when we're married.

Love, Shirlene

I open the next letter.

Dear Shirlene,

You need to have fun. Be happy. If I'm learning anything because of fighting in this war, it's that life can be cut short. Don't waste time wor-

rying about me. I'm fine. I know what I'm doing. I should, after all the training I went through before being shipped over here.

We'll be moving up again soon. The Allies are gaining ground. This war is going to be over soon, and I'll be home, and we can have our wedding.

Thanks for writing to me, Shirlene. Your letters offer me hope. Keep writing, darling, even if you don't hear from me for a while. Don't be frightened. When we move, it takes longer for your letters to reach me and for mine to reach you.

All my love, Stan

Their innocence and sincerity blow me away. Although they're coping with war, separation, and fear, they remain idealistic. I decide to skip ahead to some later letters.

Dear Shirlene,

I'm sorry to tell you my buddy Tom was shot down yesterday. I feel the loss deeply. I'm not worried about myself. Somehow, I'm coming home to you when this is over. But seeing Tom's plane hit, I felt so helpless and angry. I wanted to fly my plane right into the German who hit Tommy, but I thought of you waiting for me. I knew I didn't want to die, but I don't know what to do with all these feelings. I miss Tom. He was a hell of a good guy. As I told you in other letters, he enjoyed playing practical jokes. He came up with the craziest ideas. Boy, he could make me laugh.

Yours faithfully,

Stan

Stan didn't tell me about Tom. We talked about his experience as a fighter pilot. But I didn't ask about his buddies, and he never mentioned any of them. I wonder how many survived.

I open the next letter from Shirlene.

Dearest Stan,

I'm sorry Tom was shot down. I can't imagine watching your friend die. I wish I could hold you in my arms and let you talk about it.

I feel guilty, but I'm grateful it wasn't you. Forgive me for saying that. I don't mean to minimize your loss, and I honor Tom's memory. But if you die, I can't go on. I've allowed myself to fall so deeply in love with you. At times, my depth of commitment gives me strength, and other times, it makes me so vulnerable.

I know you would tell me to go on. To love again. Get married. But in my heart of hearts, I'll never love anyone as much as I love you.

I can't read any more. My answer to the big question I've been asking since Shirlene chose to die is right here. Whatever it was Shirlene felt for me, she decided to give it up, along with her life, to be with Stan again. Shirlene walked away from Arlene, from me, and from all her second chances. You'd only do that for your soulmate. Stan is it for her. It's time I accept that and let go.

As I store the letters away in the box, a hardness comes into my chest. I'm sealing over the pain and sorrow. I've read enough to find out what I needed to know. I will save the letters for Arlene, but I'll tell her Shirlene was the woman who took care of her when she was first born, and that's all. The chapter is closed.

Chapter Fifty-Six

Rain

Ever since the ex-fiancée moved in downstairs, she's either pounding with her broom when she hears the baby cry, or she's singing. Mike told me I have to deal with the opera music. Apparently, she was some big-shit singer who toured the world or something. Half the time, it's not in English. The only good thing is when she sings, Arlene calms down. She's a more pleasant baby when that voice is traveling up through the floorboards.

My cell phone beeps. It's Chase. My heart flutters, and I try to stay cool.

Hey, how you doing?

I type back, *OK. You?*

It's amazing out here, babe. I can't wait until you come out. I'm actually into the real estate business.

Cool, I type.

I'm going to meetings and keeping myself clean, Chase writes.

I'm going to meetings too.

Rain, that's great!

The little dots are pulsing. I wonder what he's writing.

I'm bonding with my old man and old lady like I never did growing up.

Lucky you, I tell him.

What will make me truly lucky is if you allow me another chance. I miss you.

I crack my knuckles, wondering what to say.

Me too, I admit.

I'll be in touch soon about you coming out here. It won't be long.

The idea of starting over out in California is exciting. I have a clean slate. Chase is actually holding down a job. He's proving himself to his parents. It makes me mad and happy at the same time. My parents are dead to me even if they draw breath. But if I go out to California, Chase's parents might like me. I could call them Mom and Dad.

Chase didn't mention bringing the baby. He didn't ask about her at all. So do I bring her? If I have to ask this question, that probably says a lot about my answer. A real mom wouldn't ask. The answer would be definite. I don't feel that way. Plus, I have an option. Most women don't have anyone else who wants the kid. I do. Mike is fully committed to this baby. Aimee holds her all the time. The poor kid deserves someone who's into this. She deserves more than I have to give. My NA sponsor tells me not to beat myself up. Whatever I feel is okay.

Chapter Fifty-Seven

Cameron

When I let myself into our building, Aimee is singing "Ava Maria."

Mrs. Haddad pops out of her apartment as usual. "She has the most amazing tone. It's like dark chocolate.

"I hope it's not bothering you. She's singing a lot."

"Are you kidding? My husband and I have stopped watching television or listening to the radio. Who needs WRTI when we have this going on?" She gestures toward Aimee's door.

We both listen for several minutes.

When Aimee finishes, Mrs. Haddad sighs. "This is real progress. I'm so glad her therapists thought to have her sing."

"They do it with other stroke survivors with aphasia, not just singers. Aimee isn't singing to communicate. That's not clicking yet. But I hope it's helping."

"It sounds as if she could perform. What a loss that people can't listen to her now."

"It's difficult to predict how she could handle performing, even here in Philly, without being able to talk to anyone."

"You could do it for her. You and Arlene could travel the world, doing it."

"You mean quit teaching?"

"You'd miss it."

"Yes, I miss it now, but Aimee does make a lot more money than I do." I laugh. I'm joking, but it's true. We could live on Aimee's former salary.

Aimee begins "Cara Sposa" from Handel's *Rinaldo*.

"It's been quiet upstairs. The baby likes the music." Mrs. Haddad goes back into her apartment.

Since it seems Rain has things under control upstairs, I head to Aimee's apartment. On the drive back to Philly, I decided it's time to tell her about my relationship with Shirlene. That will be a step in letting go, getting closure. Aimee's door isn't locked, and she pauses when she sees me.

"Please continue. You sound beautiful."

She is beautiful. Aimee runs her finger along the music and catches back up with the rehearsal track. The cheeks of her porcelain skin become rosy. The tiny furrow between her eyebrows tightens when she concentrates. A thrill zips up and down my spine as she sings.

When she finishes, she comes over to me at the door and hugs me. I sense she longs for me to kiss her. I do. She returns my hunger. We haven't kissed like this in well over a year. In fact, we've never kissed quite like this. I don't know what's more exciting—that she's communicating through the kiss or that the kiss tells me she has feelings for me.

I take her hand, and we sit together on the sofa. "I won't understand the full meaning of that kiss until you've recovered. But I have to admit it gives me hope for us as a couple." Aimee lifts her chin, and I continue. "I need to share something with you. I never really stopped loving you, Aimee, but I did fall in love with someone else this past summer."

She shifts her position and looks directly in my eyes. I can't tell her Shirlene was in Rain's body. That's too much to explain when Aimee can't communicate her reaction.

"Her name was Shirlene. She died."

The dark centers of Aimee's green eyes dilate. If we can possibly fall back into love—if what kept us apart has changed for Aimee, with or without her aphasia—Shirlene can't be between us. So I continue.

"We didn't have much time together, but I hoped it would be a lifetime. I told her all about you and our relationship... that we were engaged and why it ended but how we stayed best friends. She was excited about meeting you when you got back from tour. She was very good to Arlene. They were very close."

Aimee begins to cry.

"Oh, honey. Please don't cry. I'm not telling you this to upset you. It's over, and not just because she unfortunately passed away. This morning, I recognized it's time to put it all behind me. You and Arlene are the loves of my life."

Aimee wipes at her tears. I take her into my arms, and she wraps her arms around my waist.

"Darling, please understand. I love you. I always will."

Aimee tightens her arms around me. We kiss again and hold on to one another. It's a lifeline for both of us. I realize that I'm trying to draw out her ability to communicate what she's feeling, while she is trying to pull me into her head so I can understand her.

Chapter Fifty-Eight

Shirlene

I'm right here, Cam. Please don't say it's over. Don't put me behind you. Damn. How I wish I could tell you that I'm not Aimee while there's still time. I must find a way to communicate who I am and that I love you. Perhaps it is too late.

Chapter Fifty-Nine

Cameron

Aimee and I stroll into her speech therapy appointment, holding hands.

Linda, Aimee's therapist, grins. "How long has this been going on?"

"First time around or this time?" I laugh.

Aimee smiles. She actually smiles.

"This is excellent physical progress." Linda writes a note on Aimee's chart. "I'm positive the verbal and written are coming soon. Right, Aimee?"

It takes a moment, but Aimee nods.

"Good job." Linda asks me, "Seriously, how long have you two been holding hands?"

I have to think back to the day we kissed in her apartment. "A couple of weeks. I should have told you."

"It's fine. Any kissing?" Linda asks.

"Lots."

Aimee's cheeks redden.

"Nothing more. I'm waiting until Aimee can tell me it's okay."

Linda winks at Aimee. "That's quite a motivating prize."

Aimee buries her face in her hands.

"Oh my God, you two are too cute." Linda takes Aimee's arm. "Let's get to work so you can get back to kissing."

Aimee musters as much of an embarrassed expression as she can.

I mouth, "I'm sorry."

I watch Linda take Aimee through her routine. After her appointment, I maneuver around the Philly traffic and double park to let Aimee off directly in front of our apartment building. "You go ahead in. I'll hunt for a spot, and then I need to go up to my apartment to check on Arlene."

"R," she says before climbing out of my car.

After parking in a space in the next block, a lightness fills my step that's been missing a long time. I hurry up the stairs with the intention of taking Arlene down to Aimee's. Rain will happily relinquish the baby for the rest of the day.

But when I bound into my apartment, I discover my brother sitting on my couch next to Rain, who is holding Arlene. Despite the fact that he's shaved and cut his hair and is wearing clean clothes, adrenaline bolts through me.

"Get away from them." I grab his shirt, haul him up, and pin him to the wall.

"Hey, man. It's cool. I'm not here to hurt anyone." He relaxes against my hands pushing his shoulders back.

"Why the hell are you here?" I spit out the words without releasing him.

"Mike, chill. I came to talk to you."

"About what?"

Rain stands. "Mike. Let him go. He's sober."

I step back but stay between Chase and Rain, who still cradles the baby.

Chase straightens his shirt. "Good to see you, Mike."

"The last time you showed up, you attacked Sh... Rain."

He lowers his head. "My bad. Since then, I've been in recovery. I take full responsibility." He stares me in the eye. "I'm here to make amends."

"We have a police report because of what you did at the beach house."

"I wasn't myself."

I speak to Rain. "Why did you let him in?"

She gives my brother a look that is nothing short of pure admiration. "It's what he said. He's changed."

What the hell? I widen my stance and set my fists on my hips.

"May I move?" Chase asks.

"Yeah, but stay away from the baby. In fact, hand her to me." I hold out my arms to Rain. If she wants to toss her life away with my loser brother, I don't care, but I'm not giving up Arlene.

"Take her." She hands Arlene over to me.

"You're not getting the baby," I say to Chase.

"I'm not here for her. I'm here for Rain. If she chooses to bring the kid, it's up to her." Chase sits down and crosses his legs.

His arrogance unnerves me, but I focus on Rain. "He shows up today, and just like that, you're going with him?"

"This isn't the first time he's shown up."

Nausea roils in my gut. "You've been here with my daughter?" I tuck Arlene closer to my body.

"No, he met me on the street." Rain sits next to him on the couch.

"When were you going to let me in on your little plan?"

Chase rubs his hands together. "When I was ready. I had to prove to myself I could handle this."

"Handle what exactly?"

"I'm clean. I go to meetings four times a week. I got a sponsor. Mom and Dad have hired me. If I continue to prove myself, they plan to leave me the business since you've turned it down."

His transformation is remarkable and exactly what I wanted for him. "Really?"

"Yeah. The parents aren't so bad."

"I'm shocked our parents have changed so much, but that's good, Chase."

"Thanks, Mike. We're finally connecting."

"Wow." My pounding heart settles, but I'm having trouble taking this all in.

Chase uncrosses his legs and leans forward. "You were a great brother. I'm sorry I couldn't live up to your expectations or Mom's or Dad's. But I'm trying to now."

"I'm happy for you, Chase. You and Rain have my blessing, but I'm making this perfectly clear: Arlene stays with me."

Rain stands. "There's nothing you can do. She should be with her parents."

My jaw tightens. "I have a lawyer and too much documented information on why you are both unfit parents."

Rain laughs. "The old Black woman?"

I clench my jaw and point my finger at her. "That attitude is only one of the many reasons I won't have you raising Arlene."

"Well, what about my money?" Rain moves closer. "You owe me ten thousand dollars."

"You expect me to buy Arlene? She's not a commodity."

She shrugs. "People do it all the time, Mike."

I don't answer. I worry this could blow up in my face if I say too much about my financial concerns with not working, paying for two apartments, and taking care of Aimee's medical copays. I have to talk to Hattie.

"You're out of here for the time being."

"Both of us?" Rain's face blushes.

"No. You can stay. Chase, I'll talk to you later."

Chase grudgingly rises and goes to the door. "I have to go back to work on the West Coast soon. I'll be in touch, babe." He leaves.

"Rain, if you try to disappear with the baby, I'll slap kidnapping charges on you."

She runs to the nursery and slams the door.

I grab some baby formula and the diaper bag before going down to the studio. As soon as I open the door, Aimee takes Arlene to cuddle her. The baby coos.

"I need to leave Arlene with you when I'm not able to be home. Okay?"

Aimee's eyes widen.

"You need to keep your door locked. I'll knock and use my key. I'll ask Mrs. Haddad to do the same. Otherwise, no one gets in here, including Rain."

Aimee tilts her head. She must be wondering why I'm spitting out all these instructions in an obvious panic.

"My brother showed up today. He's asked Rain to move out to the West Coast with him."

Aimee leans her shoulder and arm over the baby protectively.

"Rain wants ten thousand dollars for the baby. I don't have it now. My finances are tapped. What the hell am I going to do?" Anxiety rises in my chest as I stride around the small apartment. "I can't handle all this much longer." I run my hand through my hair. "Maybe the baby would be better off with Rain. She is her mother, and Chase is her father."

"N... no!" Aimee stamps her foot.

Before I can congratulate her on saying her first word, she carries the baby into the bathroom, slams the door, and locks it.

I go to the door and tap lightly. "Aimee, open up. Please."

I can hear her crying. Damn.

"Aimee, don't cry. I was only thinking out loud. I wasn't seriously considering letting Rain take the baby to California. I'm just frustrated. I'm talking crazy."

Aimee comes out of the bathroom and crosses to her apartment door. She opens it.

"Do you want me to go?" I ask.

She nods.

"I'm sorry I said that. I'll never let Rain take Arlene. I promise." Aimee holds the baby tightly. "G... go!"

"Okay. I'll go. Lock the door. But let me in. Okay?" She can't respond. "I'll go to Hattie. She'll help me figure this out." I point at the diaper bag I brought down. "There's everything you need for a while in there."

She stares out the door. I go. She locks it behind me. While I'm jogging to my car, I call Hattie.

When I reach Shirlene's house, I vault out of my car into the house, passing large trash bags on the portico. "Hattie?"

She comes down from upstairs, dragging a full black plastic bag. She looks exhausted. "This is the last of the clothing donations."

I take hold of the bag before she collapses. "You're wearing yourself out."

"Be a good boy and stick this bag out front with the other donations. The veterans are picking the stuff up any minute."

"Go sit down in the dining room. Do you want some water?" I ask.

"I'm fine. Just do as I say." She eases herself into one of the chairs at the table.

When I return from dumping the bag with the others, Hattie says, "You haven't given me a hug."

I squeeze her tiny shoulders before sliding out the chair adjacent to her. "Hattie, Chase is back. It seems he's gotten himself pulled together. But he's here to take Rain out to LA with him."

"They're not taking Arlene!"

"No, she's safe with Aimee for the time being. But when Rain showed up at my apartment pregnant and asked me to pay for an abortion, I told her if she delivered the baby and stayed sober, I'd give her ten grand. Now, she demands it, and with all that's happened, I'm nearly tapped out. What legal rights do I have if Rain tries to take Arlene away?"

"Will she fight for the baby if you don't pay her?"

"She threatened."

"The fact that she is offering to leave the baby for money will help your case in court."

I exhale. "Good."

"But..."

I tap my fingers on the table.

"Arlene could end up in foster care until this gets settled."

I fly out of the chair. "No way!"

"I said 'could.' It's not definite, but a judge might want the child someplace neutral."

"Could you take her?"

Hattie scrunches up her nose. "I would, but if you are asking me to represent you—"

"I am."

"Then it's a conflict of interest."

I lean against the table. "Arlene already lost Shirlene. She can't be placed with strangers."

"To make sure it doesn't happen, let me provide the money to pay off Rain."

I can't believe what I'm hearing. "Hattie, I came over here for legal advice. I'd never dream of asking you for money. No. Absolutely not."

She rises and takes my hand. Hers is tiny but holds a warm energy. This legal discussion has revived her. "You didn't ask me. I offered."

"I won't take it."

"Not for Arlene?"

I take my hand away. "Now you're not being fair."

"How about a loan. You'll pay me back when Aimee is well and you're working again."

I run my hand over my mouth while I consider this. "Do you believe we can really force Rain and Chase to go away for money?"

"From everything I've heard about them? Absolutely. And to gain their money, they'll have to sign the consent forms relinquishing Arlene."

"Is it legal?" I ask.

She waves her hand like she is swatting a fly. "Don't ask questions, Cameron."

"Oh boy." I sit back down.

Hattie gives both my shoulders a motherly pat. "Stop worrying."

"Hey, what about having Rain sign those trust papers so she can't try to get ahold of this house and Shirlene and Stan's assets?"

"I'm one step ahead of you, but we need to convince both the mother and father to sign consent forms relinquishing Arlene."

"How long will it take to have those drawn up?"

"Not long for me." She winks. "I'll manage the paperwork for you today."

"Hattie, you are a legal life saver, but I won't let you loan me the money. I'll come up with it some other way."

"I respect your decision, but my offer stands."

"I hate to rush, but I left the baby with Aimee. The way she was acting, she'd kill Rain and Chase if they try to take Arlene."

"She's able to express more physically?"

"Yes, and she said 'no' when I made the mistake of thinking out loud." I can't admit to Hattie that I actually said Arlene might be better off with Rain and Chase.

"She spoke!"

The joy in the midst of all this chaos finally hits me. I grin. "She did. Like a toddler, the first word is *no*."

"I like Aimee. She sets boundaries."

I scratch my head as I lumber up. "Funny, she's never been very good about doing that. She always tried to do too much for everyone else."

Hattie walks with me toward the front door. "She's caring."

"To a fault. That's why when she was finally able to say no to me and marriage, I had to respect how difficult it must have been for her. It nearly killed me, but at the same time, I was proud of her."

"She trusted you enough to be herself and say her truth."

"Yes. And now we'll have a second go of it. I'm giving myself the chance to open up and fall in love with her again."

Hattie wipes her eyes. "I'm so happy for you, Cameron. I want nothing more than your happiness."

"But you wish it were with Shirlene."

"Shirlene is gone. We must honor her by living our lives. I'll be dancing at your wedding with Arlene in my arms."

"Hattie. There's no one who can make me believe in miracles but you."

"You and I may be shopping for an engagement ring in the near future."

"Unless Aimee's willing to use the first one I gave her, I will need a loan from you."

"Do you still have the ring?" Hattie asks.

"Aimee does, I guess. When she called off the wedding, I told her to keep it."

Once I get into my car to drive back to Philly, I begin wracking my brain for a way to raise the money without Hattie's help. I have nothing to sell that would begin to cover it. I could take out a bank loan, but it requires too much time. My parents have it, but I won't go to them, especially when they're doing everything for Chase. It's way too complicated. But there is my 401(k). I promised myself I'd never touch it, but I might have to.

Chapter Sixty

Shirlene

I hear Rain coming down the stairs. I've locked my apartment door, but I cringe as her footsteps fall closer. There's no way in hell that woman is taking Arlene to the other side of the country. The front door of the building opens and closes. With Rain out, it's my opportunity to take Arlene someplace she and Chase don't know about.

I tiptoe with the baby up to Cam's apartment and let myself in with the key he gave me, "just in case." He never said exactly why, but this situation qualifies. I remember seeing a backpack in Cam's hall closet. I pack as much of the baby's necessities as I'll be able to carry. I go quietly back downstairs to cram what I can of Aimee's clothes and medications into the backpack. So far, I haven't disturbed Mrs. Haddad, who constantly pops out into the hall when she hears anything. Now, getting past her door and out of the building will require more than a miracle. I swing the full pack onto my back, adjust the straps, and pick up Arlene. I peek into the hall before starting out. I take the stroller, and once down the exterior steps, I put Arlene into it.

My stomach flutters with mixed emotions as I roll the stroller toward the closest PATCO entrance. I feel free, but my mind buzzes with worries. What if I run into Rain and Chase? What if someone asks me a question? I can't talk to ask for help. I'm kidnapping a child. Cam will be worried and likely angry, but I need to transport Arlene to a safe place.

I haven't been on the PATCO Speed Line to New Jersey in years, and after navigating the carriage down the stairs into the station, I discover they've changed the ticket machines. I'm taking too long reading each step in the directions when the man behind me says, "Can I help you?"

I nod.

"Going to New Jersey?"

I nod again. Since the shock of possibly losing Arlene prompted me to say "no" and "go" to Cameron, perhaps I can try to say "thanks" to this kind stranger.

"Tanks." Well, it was close, and he is so focused on getting my ticket from the machine that he doesn't seem to notice. When he hands me my ticket, I nod.

Once we're on the train to New Jersey, Arlene fusses. I lift her out of the stroller. No one speaks to me. When my stop is announced, I slip the backpack on and push Arlene, in the stroller, to the door. I take the escalator, and a young fellow offers to balance the stroller for me. I sigh. I want to be able to thank him. It takes great concentration, but I do manage to say "Tanks" again. I'm making progress, and I try to keep faith that I will be able to recover completely.

It's a long way to my home. I neglected to take a water bottle with me. Luckily, it's a cool autumn day and not one of those ninety-degree humid days we seem to have well into October nowadays.

It's reassuring to stroll Arlene down familiar streets. Some of the trees are beginning to show beautiful golds and oranges. The closer I come to my house, the more assured I feel. I trust there's still a key hidden in the garage. I can't very well ask a neighbor for help. Aside from not being able to talk properly, I don't look like Rain or Shirlene. I hope no one calls the police when I am snooping around the place.

My lovely Colonial-style home comes into view. I speed up my pace. The front door opens, and Hattie comes out.

My heart soars. "Ha... ie!" I can nearly speak her name.

She turns in my direction. I wave. She seems baffled and tilts her head. Hattie hasn't ever met Aimee, but as I push the stroller closer, she recognizes Arlene.

She rubs the baby's cheek. "My little one. How are you?" Hattie adjusts her assessing eyes to me. "Are you Aimee?"

It's difficult to hold back this burning desire to throw my arms around her. I ache to hold her close. I'm terrified I won't be able to speak again, but I must try to tell her who I am. "Shir... Shir..." I begin to cry. "A... mee body." I pat my chest.

"Anybody?" Hattie says.

I give my head a violent shake. I've tried and tried to tell Cameron and was unable to, but now that I've gotten out a few words, I must be able to tell Hattie who I am. Frustration builds, and I clench my jaw. My speech therapist has repeatedly told me that won't help. I take a breath and relax my mouth. "Shir... een." I point to my heart. I slap my arms. "A... mee body."

"Aimee's body?" Hattie whispers. Recognition widens my dearest friend's eyes. "Where did you have a scar?"

"Ch... chin."

"What birthmark do I have?"

"Hear... sh... aped." I swallow and try again. "Heart."

"Shirlene!" She throws her arms around my waist, leans her head against me, and begins to weep. "Shirlene. You're alive."

I slip the backpack off, letting it drop onto the lawn, and hug Hattie tightly. We shudder with sobs as we hold each other. Arlene whines in the stroller.

"We'd better go inside and pull ourselves together before a neighbor notices us out here blithering," Hattie says.

While Hattie warms up the formula I took out of the backpack, I bounce Arlene in my arms to try to keep her occupied. I scan my kitchen. There's the tired old wallpaper Stan and I put up ourselves. I peek out at my backyard where we planted so many flowers together.

Hattie sits at the table and holds her arms out. "Let me feed her."

I hand Arlene over and sit down.

Hattie coaxes her to take the bottle. "Several months ago, we stood in this room, and you explained how you ended up in Rain's body. I hope you can tell me what happened this time."

"Stu." I can't get the word out.

"Stupid?"

I nod. I was so stupid to go for that swim.

"Are you trying to explain how you ended up in the ocean?"

I nod again.

Hattie's lips are tight. "I agree. Stupid."

It takes every ounce of concentration to try to put my words together, so I move around the room. I'm dying to tell Hattie what happened in the ocean, how I lost control of Rain's body, what Stan told me when I did go to him, and how I ended up in Aimee's body, but I can't say the words.

"R... ain." It's so damn frustrating.

"Breathe, Shirlene. Let me try to ask questions."

"O... kay."

"When you died, did you talk to Stan?"

I nod.

Hattie sighs. "You will be able to tell me what he said later, but I'm guessing he sent you back again."

I nod and wipe tears from my cheeks and eyes with a napkin. "T... to a body in cha...

"In chaos? Aimee's stroke."

"Ru... rush hos... pital."

"It must have been terrifying."

Exhaustion washes over me as I drop my head into my arms on my kitchen table.

Chapter Sixty-One

Cameron

I knock on the studio door. "Aimee? It's Cam." There's no answer. The door isn't locked, and the apartment is empty. I bound up the stairs and open my apartment door. "Rain?"

Silence. I race to the nursery. Arlene is not in her crib. I nearly trip rushing back down to my landlady's door. I knock. There's no answer.

Where the hell is everyone? I look for the baby's stroller, which we keep tucked under the steps. It's gone.

I've never had a panic attack, but from the way my heart is hammering and my hands are shaking, it sure seems one is coming on. I sit on the steps and try to focus. I take deep breaths, but my mind continues to swirl in a tempest. Where is Aimee? Have Rain and Chase taken the baby?

Mrs. Haddad arrives at the beveled glass front doors. I leap to open them for her.

"Hello, Cameron."

Before she can say more, I rattle off questions. "Do you know where Aimee is? Where's the baby? Did you see her leave with Arlene? Have you seen Rain and my brother with the baby?"

"Oh my goodness. Try to calm down." She shuts the doors. "Tell me what's happened."

"I can't find the baby. I'm afraid Rain and my brother have taken her."

"I'm so sorry I wasn't here. I've been at my son's new apartment. My husband and I have been helping him move."

I run my hand through my hair. "What should I do?"

My cell rings. It's Hattie. "Excuse me, Mrs. Haddad. Hello, Hattie?"

"Yes. It's me. I'm sorry to ask you to come back over here, but you have to."

"What's going on?"

There's a pause. "Aimee is here with the baby."

I sigh. "Thank God."

"Cam, please come."

"I'll be there right away." I disconnect.

"Aimee and the baby are with Hattie in Haddon Heights."

Mrs. Haddad wrinkles her brow. "Why would she go there?"

"I'm not sure, but I've got to go."

"Drive carefully. You're very upset."

"If you run into Rain, tell her Aimee and I are out with the baby. Do not, under any circumstances, tell her we're in New Jersey."

"I'll handle things on this end."

While I hightail it to my car parked three blocks away, the pieces of the puzzle begin to fall into place. I am the world's expert on compartmentalizing and denial. What a fool I've been. Aimee knows nothing about the Haddon Heights house. She can't be Aimee. Which means she's Shirlene, and my Aimee must be dead.

Chapter Sixty-Two

Shirlene

When I carry Arlene upstairs for a nap in Stan's and my old room, I breathe deeply to take in the familiar smells, and I experience acceptance rather than sorrow or anger over Stan. There's no crib here, so I open a deep dresser drawer, expecting to find my old clothes. I'm surprised to discover it's empty. I'll have to learn if Hattie knows where they are. I set the drawer on the bed and take a soft throw from the chair to cushion the bottom. With a clean sheet from the hall linen closet, I get the baby settled before going downstairs.

Hattie sits in the dining room, where hot tea steams out of two mugs. As she lifts her teacup, I notice her hand shaking.

"Are you o... kay?" I ask.

"You're not going to be happy."

"Spit... it out."

"I called Cameron and told him Aimee and Arlene are safe."

Panic immediately aggravates my stomach. "W... why? Ax... ask me?"

She tips her chin down and stares over her glasses. "I knew you'd say not to, but the kid must be worried sick. He has no idea where Aimee and his daughter are. He was here earlier, in a frenzy, asking me if his brother and Rain can take the baby away. I couldn't leave him hanging."

"Did you t... tell him?"

"That you're Shirlene? No." Hattie pushes the other mug toward me.

I ignore the tea.

Hattie leans her elbow on the table, with her chin on her hand. "I told him to come back here."

I stand up. "What?"

Hattie's mouth opens. "You didn't stutter."

"Not im... important." I stop. The words are flowing better.

Tears begin again. I can communicate. My speech therapist told me the connection in my brain would heal. It would take time to talk normally, but after all the hard work I did in therapy, she said it was bound to happen.

"I just had to piss you off. If I'd known, we could have had you talking sooner." Hattie tosses her head back and laughs.

"I am m... mad at you." I worm past her to look out the dining room window. No sign of him yet.

"It won't take long at this time of day. The traffic shouldn't be too bad." Hattie sits at the dining table again and sips more of her tea.

I turn away from the window. "I'm not ready t... to tell him who I am."

Her eyes narrow. "How can you not? He loves you. He believes you're dead and is grieving terribly."

"No. He l... loves Aimee again. He's let go of me. He t... told me, I mean Aimee."

She shifts her chin back, which she does when she thinks I'm being stupid. "How are you going to pretend you're Aimee? How does Aimee know about this house? Although I didn't say you're Shirlene, he has to be putting it together by now."

I dismiss this with a wave of my hand. "He's too stressed to s... see the nose on his face. I've obv... obviously been Shirlene. Simply noticing how the baby reacts to me, he sh... should know. But he doesn't. He's b... blinded by everything that's going on."

Hattie stands up and plants both her hands on the table. "Listen to me, Shirlene. You tell him, or I will. End of discussion."

"Why do you g... get to decide?"

"Because I didn't tell him about Rain talking to you, and that bitch messed with him, pretending to be you. I let him down. I'm not making the same mistake again. He's a wonderful man. He deserves the truth."

Her anger rattles me. "You're right. I'm s... sorry. But I'm a... afraid of how he's going to react."

"He's going to be thrilled. He's going to take you in his arms and kiss the hell out of you, and I'm going to enjoy watching."

"Yes, you m... must stay. I can't do this alone."

Moments later, Cam's car screeches into the driveway. He parks behind Hattie's car and rockets across the lawn. My palms begin to sweat.

Hattie opens the door. He glances into the living room and then sees me in the dining room.

"Shirlene?" he snarls.

I want to fly to him, but his expression is clouded. "Y... yes." My throat tightens. "Yes, C... Cam. I'm Shirlene."

He moves toward me with the dining table between us. "Is Aimee dead?" His voice breaks with emotion.

How could I not have thought about this? If I'm alive, it means Aimee is dead. I speak slowly. "I'm s... sorry. Yes, she is. I feel t... terrible about it."

"Can she come back so you can fuck me over again?"

I'm too shocked to speak. I glance at Hattie, whose mouth is agape.

Cam tugs at his hair as if he's going to tear it out. "Well, you've got what you wanted. The baby." He bolts toward the den.

"She's upstairs," Hattie says.

I rush into the foyer and watch him bound up two steps at a time.

"Go after him." Hattie shoves me.

"This isn't g... going the way you said. He was supposed to be happy and k... kiss me."

"Give him time. Now, go up and talk to him."

My feet are concrete blocks as I climb the stairs. I wipe my hands on my pants when I go into the bedroom.

"You're angry with m... me," I whisper.

"Damn right, I am."

Stan held his anger inside, where it festered. He expressed it by punishing me. I won't repeat this with Cam.

"That's okay. Be angry. It's b... better to let it out."

Cam seethes and waves his arms. "And you can suddenly talk. How long have you been hiding that from me?"

I step toward him. "You saying you're giving my daughter to Rain and Chase shocked me into t... talking. How c... could you even consider that?"

"I was in a panic. I didn't mean it. But you hid other things from me."

"I haven't hid... den anything from you."

"How about the fact that Rain was talking to you at the beach house? You walked the labyrinth to communicate with her. Another detail you kept from me." Cam paces back and forth next to the bed I shared with Stan for seventy years.

"I'm s... sorry."

"How could you leave Arlene?" Cam's eyes brim with tears.

"I t... tried not to."

"I don't believe you."

Anger rises in my throat as I stride away. This is too much of a re-peat performance with Stan after Danny was killed—me explaining and apologizing to someone incapable of understanding.

I slam my hand down on the top of my dresser. "Then d... don't believe me, you s... selfish prick."

Cam's mouth drops open, and his eyes widen.

"I'm not p...putting up with this shit a second time. I didn't fight my way back in poor Aimee's damaged body to be treated like sh... shit. Go ahead, don't believe me, b... but it's the truth."

"Why did you leave me?"

"That's what this is really a... about, isn't it? Not Arlene but how I c... could abandon you?"

"Yes." He takes a deep breath. "And Arlene."

"All right, I'll tell you what ha... happened, but only if you're willing to t... trust me. I'm only going to tell you the truth."

"Okay."

I move back to him. "I ad... admit I did consider going back to Stan and Danny but only because I n... needed answers from my husband. I did see Stan."

Cam stiffens. "Why didn't you tell me you were trying to contact Stan? You hid all of that from me," he says. I touch his arm, but he jerks away. "I can't deal with all of this."

"S... so that's it. You won't listen to my ex... explanation."

"Not right now." He picks up the baby, who whimpers.

"Cam, p... please don't take her back to Philly."

He stops at the door. Arlene begins to cry.

"Rain and Chase d... don't have any idea where she is if she's here with me. She'll be safe until you can pr... process all this."

I watch his broad shoulders lift and fall as he sighs. He rounds to me. I go over, reaching for the baby. Cam's eyes hold nothing but pain and turmoil. I long to say I'm sorry. I want to tell him I love him, but it's not the right time. He hands Arlene to me and pounds down the stairs. The front door slams shut.

I set the baby back into her makeshift crib. I gently rub her back.

Hattie comes into the room. "Are you all right?"

"He wouldn't t... touch me."

"Not after you explained things?"

"He wouldn't l... listen." Arlene goes back to sleep. "Please, let's not t... talk about this in here. I won't upset the baby anymore." I go across the hall into the guest bedroom.

Hattie closes the door. "What do you mean he wouldn't listen? That's not like Cameron."

"I t... tried to tell him, but he said he couldn't handle it. He's blaming me for Aimee's death. He completely rejected me. He h... hates me." I collapse on the bed.

"No, he doesn't. He couldn't."

"I j... just want to go to sleep and never wake up."

"Don't say that. You fought back so hard after the stroke. You can't quit now."

"Fought b... back for what? Cam doesn't love me anymore."

Hattie crosses and sits next to me. She positions her arm around my shoulder.

I lean into her. "I understand he's just lost Aimee. I know that kind of p... pain, but he was unreasonable. I don't need this c... crap."

"Well, I'll find him and explain things." Hattie moves.

"No, you won't. Maybe I'll tell him when he's con... contrite." I rub my temples. "Hattie, I've had it with explaining myself. First Stan, now Cam won't l... listen to me."

"He'll listen to me." Hattie gets that determined glint in her eyes.

"I n... need you to promise you won't try to f... fix this."

"But I want it fixed. You two should be together, especially after everything you went through to come back to him."

"I appreciate that, Hattie. But I n... need a pinky swear on this."

"You're kidding, right?"

"I need your w... word you'll leave things be. It isn't yours to fix. C... Cam and I have to fix it. If we can."

Chapter Sixty-Three

Cameron

Incapable of driving, I pull over a few blocks from Shirlene's. I never give in, but I have no choice. The hole in my chest shatters open, and my body rocks with grief. I cry longer than I've ever cried in my life and feel like I'm going to throw up. My dearest friend is dead. Aimee is gone. The stroke killed her. She's been dead for weeks, and I didn't know. I was the fool again. I repeatedly slam my hands on the steering wheel until they might break.

Shirlene pretending to be Rain. Rain pretending to be Shirlene. Shirlene pretending to be Aimee. Rain threatening to take Arlene to LA with Chase. Aimee gone. For the first time in my life, I think I'd be better off dead. It would relieve this never-ending spinning.

Chase. I shake my head to clear the mess in my brain. This is how Chase felt. He drank and used drugs until the pain stopped. He threw his entire life away. A sardonic laugh escapes my throat. We've switched places. Now Chase is the golden son, who will inherit the real estate business, and I'm incapable of functioning. I lean my head back on the headrest as exhaustion overwhelms me.

I wake up to knocking on my car window. I'm startled, concerned it's the cops, but it's Hattie. She must have been driving home and saw my car on the side of the road.

I put down the window.

"What are you doing here, Cameron?" Her sweet face is full of concern.

"Get in."

She hustles around the front of the car and settles into the passenger seat. "Are you okay? I thought you were dead."

"Hattie, I wish I were."

"Oh dear."

"Exactly." I muster the miniscule amount of energy I have left in my body to keep from crying again. I absolutely will not fall apart in front of someone.

"How can I help?"

"Hattie, you are the kindest person, and I don't mean to sound melodramatic, but I'm beyond help. I really am. Nothing makes sense anymore, and I've lost everything." I jam my thumbnail into the pad of my other hand to fight back tears that are determined to fall. "Aimee's dead, and I didn't know." I try to bring myself to look at Hattie, but I only manage a glance. "I wanted to marry her, and when she couldn't, I loved her so much that I stayed friends, which had its costs. Now, she's gone."

"I am sorry for your loss. It makes no sense to see someone young, and with their whole life ahead of them, die."

"Like your daughter," I say.

"Yes. Like my girl."

"How did you ever get through that?"

Hattie doesn't answer for a moment. "I don't know. Losing a child..." She sighs. "Shirlene and I somehow stumbled through it together. At least my daughter got to grow up, start a career, marry, and have a baby. I have my granddaughter and her family. It helps. Poor Shirlene missed all of it."

Anger, rather than empathy, heats up my body. "Please don't talk about Shirlene right now."

"Why are you blaming her?" Hattie asks.

"Because she left me and Arlene. She abandoned us." I clench my teeth. "And now she's taken over Aimee's body. Why? Why the hell couldn't she have stayed dead?"

Hattie zips open her large purse and dabs at her eyes with a hankie.

"I'm sorry. I didn't mean to make you cry." I pat her arm.

"I know. You can't help it right now."

"You mean well, Hattie. But it's best if you leave."

She straightens up in her seat. This means she has more to say, and I'm not looking forward to it.

"I'll go in a minute, but, Cameron, I need to ask you some questions."

"Great." I rapidly tap my right heel against the car floor. God, I'm twelve years old again.

"What about Arlene? Are you going to let Rain take her?"

"Of course not. I'll take the money from my 401(k) and pay off Rain. I already got in touch with my finance guy."

"Let's go." She fastens her seat belt. "After we go to your financial planner to acquire the money, I have to stop at the law firm to pick up the consent forms relinquishing Arlene. We need to make Rain and Chase sign them now."

"How could those papers be ready so fast?"

"I talked to the right people after you left this morning and called in a few favors. As your lawyer and friend, I'm with you in this, Cameron. These papers are the first step for you to adopt Arlene."

It's the lifeline I need. "Thank you, Hattie."

"You'll have temporary custody until we take the next steps."

"I sense there's a hitch."

Hattie clears her throat. "Arlene needs to stay with you, but Shirlene isn't going to let you take her away." She touches my arm. "Arlene needs both you and Shirlene."

"No way."

"It's the only way, Cameron. You're going to have to make this work to protect Arlene."

I drop my head back on the headrest. "I suppose I'm moving back into the den at Shirlene's house."

She slaps her hands together. "I was hoping you'd come to that conclusion. Now, drive."

As I hoped, Chase and Rain are packing up her belongings when Hattie and I enter my apartment.

"I have your money, Rain." I hold up the envelope.

Rain reaches for it.

"Not until you sign these." Hattie waves the papers in front of Rain. "You too, Chase."

"Who the hell is this?" my brother asks.

"I'm Harriet Washington, lawyer for the adoptive father." She places papers on the coffee table and holds out a pen. "Who's first?"

Rain cracks her knuckles. "I want more money."

"You're not getting it."

"If you don't fork over more money, then you're not getting the baby."

Hattie waves her finger. "Listen to me, Rain DeLuca. You haven't even asked where Arlene is right now! Any decent parent would be worried sick about their child, but all you ask about is money. I have documented records of your addiction, your homelessness, and your thieving, and that of your boyfriend as well. This case is airtight. You are both unfit parents."

I point at my brother. "I've been raising the baby since she was born. *I* was in the delivery room. Where were you, Chase?"

My brother's eyes bug out. "Forget about the money, Rain. I'll have plenty. Our lives will be completely different in LA. Let's just sign the papers so we can get out of here."

Rain pouts. "I demand my ten K." She sits down and writes her signature wherever Hattie indicates.

Chase does the same. I relax when Hattie folds the papers up and stows them in her big bag. Next, she draws out more papers and additional hundred-dollar bills that are a surprise to me.

"Ms. DeLuca, this money can also be yours if you sign another document." Hattie lays the pen back down next to the papers.

"What's this?" Rain asks.

"Some minor assets were signed over to you in trust for Arlene. But since you've given up Arlene, you must sign this trust over to Cameron."

"What kind of assets?" Rain asks.

"Nothing substantial." I hope to convince her. "This is cash in your hand."

Rain reluctantly picks up the pen and signs.

Hattie adds the papers to her purse and hugs it close to her chest.

"Can I send birthday presents or a card or something?" Rain tugs at her T-shirt.

I don't know how I feel about that. "We'll work out the details later."

Rain's demeanor softens slightly. "Thanks for taking me in the night I showed up here pregnant, Mike."

For a moment, I see Shirlene in her, but that's a lie of my mind. "You're welcome."

Chase clears his throat. "I was an ass my whole life, Mike. You always tried to help me. I hope someday, you can forgive me."

"Little brother, I really understood you for the first time today. No hard feelings."

Chase reaches his hand out for mine. I take it, and we shake.

"You may think I'm a jerk since I'm giving up Arlene, but she's better off with you. I'll try to be a good uncle to her."

"Okay, man."

Once they are out the door, I grab hold of Hattie and lift her off the floor.

She giggles. "We did it."

"Hattie, *you* did it. Thank the Lord for you, but how much do I owe you for the second signing?"

"That's on me. I love that little girl. Now, let's pack up what you need to move back in with Shirlene."

I clench my jaw. "This isn't a good idea, Hattie."

"You're doing it for Arlene."

Chapter Sixty-Four

Shirlene

With Arlene safely snuggled between cushions and pillows on the sofa, I sit and play "Summertime" from *Porgy and Bess*, and the joy of feeling the keys beneath my fingers brings me to tears. Aimee's fingers immediately work better than Rain's. I assume she played piano.

I have the urge to vocalize, and I begin to sing along. I remember Cam describing Aimee's voice as drinking rich coffee. The therapy singing paid off. I'm less and less hesitant in my mind-and-mouth connection. Arlene giggles before nodding off, and I allow myself to escape into my music.

The doorbell interrupts my bliss. What if it's a neighbor? My stomach knots up when I cross into the foyer and reach for the doorknob. How am I going to explain who I am and what I'm doing in Shirlene and Stan's house?

I open the door and see the last person I expected. I'm thrilled and terrified at the same time. Cam's holding the baby's car seat carrier. I'm afraid he's going to insist on taking Arlene back to Philly. That would mean I'd have to go with them.

"Can I stay in the den?" His voice is even. His eyes are clouded with tension.

"Yes." I step aside to let him pass. That's when I notice he has his duffle bag.

He lingers at the arch into the living room. "The sections of her crib are tied to the roof of my car. Should I set it up in the den or upstairs?"

"Upstairs."

"Okay."

These one-word answers are going to make me scream. "It's ob... obvious you have no desire to be here, so w... why are you?"

"Hattie convinced me it was better for Arlene."

"You t... talked to Hattie?" I wonder how much she's intervened when I told her to stay out of it.

"Yep."

He marches into the living room and kisses the baby. She coos. He sets down her carrier and deposits his duffle bag in the den. When he passes me at the front door to move more things out of his car, I can smell his citrus scent. I jam my hands in my jeans pockets to keep from reaching for him. His stiff body language makes it clear that even if Hattie tried to make him listen to reason, he doesn't want to be touched.

"I'll find sh... sheets and a blanket for the pull-out sofa."

He doesn't respond.

I gather what I need from the linen closet upstairs. We pass in the downstairs foyer. He's carrying in boxes.

"Here's Aimee's music. Should I leave it by the piano?"

"Yes. Thank you." There are other boxes in my foyer. "What's in h... here?"

Cam sets the boxes of music down at my piano with a thud. "Aimee's clothes and all the other stuff you were using in the studio apartment."

"I'm sorry you ended up lugging all this over in your c... car." Here I am apologizing again. "I carried wh... what I could on the train. Arlene's things were most important."

He stands still in my living room with his back to me. "So you let yourself into my apartment and took her things?"

"Cam, please l... look at me." Tears burn in my eyes.

He pivots around.

"I needed Arlene to be safe from Rain and your b... brother."

He moves toward me. Hope springs in my heart, but he passes me. "I have to take the crib off my car."

"Let m... me help."

"No. I've got it." He exits out the front door.

I want to shout after him, but I hear Hattie's voice reminding me to give him time. I carry one of the boxes of Aimee's clothes up to the main bedroom. When I consider opening the closet to find Stan's and my clothes from a previous life, I'm afraid the sight of them will make me dizzy. Soon, very soon, I will empty it out and take the clothes to Goodwill. Other people could use them.

I run my hand over the bed Stan and I shared. I'm at peace with him now, but I will not sleep in here. It would feel as if I were going backward. I need to find a way to move ahead. So I decide to stay in the guest room. I start to carry the box of Aimee's clothes across the hall and run into Cam as he is holding sections of the baby's crib.

He stops in his tracks. "Which room?"

We're only inches apart. I remember us kissing in Aimee's studio apartment. My chest feels as if the only way it won't crumble into a million pieces is to be pressed up against him. My inner thighs tingle. I notice his breath quicken. But he was kissing Aimee. He loves Aimee, not me. He's come back here for Arlene's sake, not for me.

"Which room?" he repeats.

"Cam, would you be more c... comfortable if we went back to the beach house? I mean rather than s... staying in my house?"

"I'm not comfortable anywhere right now. My own skin doesn't feel right."

I refuse to say I'm sorry again. "Then since you've brought everything in, let's make Stan's and my room the nursery. We can ch... change her on the bed."

His brow wrinkles. "Are you sleeping in there?"

"No. I'm in the g... guest room." I drag myself away from him to start depositing Aimee's things in the guest room closet, which, to my surprise, has been emptied. There wasn't much in there, but I wonder why it's not there. I'll have to ask Hattie about it and the dresser drawer.

Cam returns with the rest of the crib sections. It will go more quickly if I help, so I cross the hall. He's brought up Stan's tools from the basement workbench. Cam is kneeling on the floor, and he stares up from beneath his curly black hair. He sighs, and I go over to steady one side and the foot of the crib while he attaches parts. We work in silence until the crib is assembled. Our fingers brush when we put on the clean bedding. Goose bumps run up my arm.

He steps away. "I'm going for a run."

Arlene fusses from the living room. "I'll t... take care of her."

We both go down the stairs and into the living room. He continues to the den, where I hear him rooting through his duffle bag for running gear. I pick Arlene up, and she yawns.

I smell her bottom. "You need to be ch... changed."

Once we are upstairs, the front door thumps shut. I go to the window and watch Cam jog away down the street.

"What are we going to do about your d... daddy?" I ask Arlene. Gas escapes from her butt. She wrinkles up her face. "Let's clean you up and find a bottle."

The phone rings, and I pick it up.

"How are things going?" Hattie asks.

"You p... promised not to talk to him."

"All I did was explain why it was best for Arlene if he stayed at your house."

"Well, he's here, but he's m... miserable."

"Listen, I submitted the papers Rain and Chase signed relinquishing their rights to Arlene."

"Really? They s... signed them?"

Hattie sounds surprised. "Didn't Cameron tell you?"

"No."

"And I paid Rain to also sign the new trust I wrote up, so all of Stan's assets that were left to Rain while you were in her body are now in a trust for Arlene. You—as Aimee Bellerose—and Cameron are the trustees."

"I can't believe that so m... much has been resolved." I plop onto the bed. "What is it with these passive-aggressive men in my life? Cam is holding b... back information that would obviously offer me relief."

"The kid's head is spinning. He probably forgot. I don't believe he consciously decided to withhold this good news."

"Subconscious or conscious, it doesn't m... matter."

Arlene starts crying to be changed. While cradling the phone between my ear and neck, I set a pad on the bed and take off her dirty diaper.

"Give him—"

"Time. I know. But I won't be held hostage for t... too long. I allowed Stan to control my life with guilt and blame. I won't d... do it again."

Hattie clears her throat.

"You don't agree with me?" I ask.

"I do agree with you. You've found your voice now. You never fully used it in your first marriage."

"Hattie, in order for my m... marriage to Stan to be my first, it means I've remarried. Last time I checked, Cam and I are barely speaking, let alone walking d... down the aisle."

"Now, listen. I've talked to a judge friend of mine who hears a lot of adoption cases. He said one way to sway things in your favor is for you and Cam to be married."

"Hattie, have you been l... listening to me? He's a giant block of ice."

"He'll eventually melt."

"So far, I'm not s... seeing it."

"Cam is a very different type of man than Stan was. I believe he'll come through for you."

"You're not hearing me. I'm not marrying s... someone who can't move fully and completely past this. I loved Stan."

"I know you did, honey."

"But I was married a d... damn long time. It is work. I may never marry again."

"Well, at least you could get engaged."

I don't reply.

"For Arlene's sake. It could keep her safe from Rain and Chase changing their minds. Or Cam and Chase's parents trying to take her."

I drop the baby-powder container to the floor. When I snatch it back up, Hattie says, "Shirlene, are you there? Are you okay?"

"I'm here." I adjust the phone against my ear and finish changing Arlene. "You almost g... gave me a heart attack."

"I'm sorry, but you need to face the facts. Those grandparents have rights."

I can hardly swallow at the thought that Cam's parents have rights to Arlene.

Chapter Sixty-Five

Cameron

Aimee is dead. Aimee is dead. I repeat it every time one of my feet hits the pavement. That woman back there with my niece-daughter is Shirlene, not Aimee. Shirlene is alive. Shirlene is alive. Aimee is dead. How do I reconcile Aimee's death when she looks alive? I lost Shirlene. I lost Aimee. Now I have Shirlene in Aimee's body.

Although a stiff autumn wind is blowing and leaves make scuffing sounds as they scurry along the streets, sweat trickles down my back. I'm running for the first time in weeks, and I don't intend to stop until the desire to sweep her up and make love to her is drained out of me. I'm not ready to open up again. Letting her close would kill me.

How did I let Hattie talk me into returning to Shirlene's house? But she's right. It's best for Arlene, both emotionally and legally. I wish the temporary relief I had when Hattie convinced my brother and Rain to sign those papers hadn't faded. I feel as if I've been beaten with a club.

I stop dead in my tracks. I never told Shirlene they relinquished their rights to Arlene. I should have told her the moment I arrived at her house. I reach for my phone. It's not in the pocket of my running shorts. I forgot to bring it. I begin running back. Shirlene has a right to know one step has been taken to protect the baby.

I see Shirlene's house and push harder to make it as quickly as possible. When I'm closer to the door, I hear her singing. She sounds like Aimee. I stop and fight off a dry heave. Aimee is dead. Shirlene is alive. I have to rest, but I must tell her. I bound into the house, slamming the front door much louder than I intend.

She bolts up from the piano. We both listen for the baby to cry. Things remain silent.

I lean over with my hands on my knees, breathing like a freight train. "I forgot to tell you." I swallow hard. "Rain and Chase relinquished their parental rights to Arlene. Hattie has their signatures. And she had Rain sign the trust fund you wanted for Arlene." I can't catch my breath.

Shirlene is so still that I worry she can't communicate again.

I step into the living room. "Are you okay? Can you talk?"

"I'm fine. Did Hattie call your cell? Did she make you come back to t... tell me?"

My breath is beginning to calm down, but my heart is thumping in my chest. "No. I forgot to take my phone." I shoot past her and grab my phone from the den. She follows me and watches me pick it up from the table by the pull-out sofa.

"Oh." She seems conflicted.

"Did you want me to have the phone with me and only tell you the truth because Hattie forced me?"

"Of course n... not. I'm glad you came back to tell me. It's very good news." She rushes into the living room.

I pursue her. "You'd be happier if I'd withheld the news purposefully. I can read it in your eyes." She is going to play games now.

She sits on the sofa, folding her hands in her lap. This body is really housing Shirlene. Neither Rain nor Aimee would do that.

"You're pushing me away, Cam. When Hattie t... told me about your brother and Rain signing the papers, I did think you'd neglected to tell me on purpose."

I lean on the fireplace mantel. "I'm not Stan."

"And I'm not Rain. She's the one who tried to fool you into believing I was s... still in her body."

I'm hearing her, but I am weary.

She continues. "In the very beginning, I had no choice but to pretend to be Rain b... because I had no idea what happened to me. I didn't mean to lie to you, but I was afraid you'd have me committed and I'd never find Stan and I'd l... lose Arlene. When I ended up in Aimee's body, she was having a stroke. I tried to let you know I was Shirlene, but the aphasia prevented me. Do you remember me trying to push the hospice floor button on the elevator at Penn Medical? I hoped you'd realize I was Shirlene b... because that's where I died before taking over Rain's body. It was heartbreaking for me that you thought I was Aimee."

"Why did you end up in Aimee's body?"

"Timing, I guess. There was the horrible swirling vortex again. Just before I arrived, Aimee's stroke occurred." Shirlene takes a breath. "Once I was in her body, it was chaos. I was t... terrified. I felt as if I was underw... water, the same as when I was drowning. All I wanted was to be with you again, and I couldn't tell you." Her hands tremble in her lap. "I... I love you, Cam."

I can't catch my breath again. "Shirlene, I'm not ready for this. I believe what you've told me, but I can't right now."

Chapter Sixty-Six

Shirlene

After several long, intense days working with my speech thera-pist, I'm able to speak normally most of the time. Sometimes I have to search for a word, but I'm used to that from when I was an elderly woman. I'm also working on my writing, which is coming back more slowly.

At the end of the day, I normally collapse into bed and fall into a deep, satisfied rest, but tonight, a noise wakes me. I sit up in bed and listen to the baby monitor. There's a rustling coming from it. I can't swallow for fear Chase and Rain have found us and are taking Arlene. Without grabbing a bathrobe, I race across the hall to face whoever is in with my baby.

Cam stands, rocking Arlene in his arms.

I don't care that I'm barely covered in the tank top I wore to bed. "What's wrong?"

His eyes drink me in. He takes a breath. "She has a little fever."

I rush closer and touch Arlene's head. It's warm. "Why didn't you w... wake me?"

"You were sound asleep." He sits down in the cricket chair.

"Why did you come up here?"

"I heard her crying."

"I can't believe I didn't wake up."

Cam's eyes soften. "It's okay. You've been working for hours to re-gain your full speech. Don't worry about it."

That's the most civil thing he's said to me since I told him I was Shirlene.

"Did you take her t... temperature?"

"Yes. It's only ninety-nine."

I sit on the bed and notice my cleavage is popping out over the rim of the tank and my new shapely legs are exposed in my sleeping shorts. "Excuse me a moment." I dash over to toss on a bathrobe and hurry back. "Thank God her temperature isn't high like the time we rushed her to the hospital."

"It's going to be fine. Try not to worry."

I stand there awkwardly. I can't get comfortable.

"Why don't you go back to bed. I'm awake. She's settling down. I'll wake you if anything changes."

"I can't fall back to sleep." I notice the television Cam moved up here for Stan. They used to watch baseball games together. "I wonder if there's anything on." I hope the distraction will relax me.

"I'm enjoying the quiet."

The lines of his well-defined muscles push through his T-shirt. Arlene is safe in his strong arms. He has one leg bent and resting across his other knee, like men do. Our eyes meet. He's been watching me admire his masculine beauty. My stomach does a flip.

"Are you sure she's all right?" I ask.

"Definitely. Go back to bed."

I cross the distance between us to kiss Arlene's head. I feel Cam's breath on my shoulder. I turn to his face. The corners of his mouth turn up slightly.

Okay, that's enough. I attempt a graceful exit, hoping he's watching my—well, Aimee's—round bottom through the bathrobe.

Of course, I can't sleep. I toss and turn, worrying about the baby and wondering if Cameron's cold heart has melted a bit. Hattie says hope is a slippery slope, but I can't help but hope.

Chapter Sixty-Seven

Cameron

Shirlene left about an hour ago. I've been listening to her tossing around in the guest room bed. I try not to think about her alone in there in Aimee's body. I was hopeful for a second chance with Aimee, but it was really Shirlene kissing me in Aimee's body these past weeks, not Aimee at all. Did I want Aimee again, or did I sense on some level it was Shirlene? My brain is going to explode with confusion, guilt, and anger.

To distract myself, I decide to check Arlene's temperature again. She squirms a little but doesn't wake up. It's back down to ninety-eight degrees. I hold her a while longer. She's the most precious thing in the world. I try to focus on what's right in my life, but the loss of Aimee carves a hole in my chest. I snuggle Arlene a little closer before putting her back in her crib. She sleeps on, and I decide it's okay to go down and get some shut-eye.

I tiptoe out into the hall and take the stairs carefully. They creak in this old house. The street light slices through the living room windows, casting a glow on Shirlene's piano. I'm first drawn to her wedding photo with Stan. Her original body is tiny but shapely. Her wavy red hair just hits the shoulders of her white gown. Stan remarked on how beautiful his wife was.

I step back to examine Shirlene's piano. I remember how a few months ago, when I sprained my ankle on a run, I hobbled back here and found her playing for the first time in Rain's body. The transformation was mind-blowing—the shiny blond hair, the healthy, glowing skin, the passion with which her fingers wrung every emotion from her instrument. And Arlene was sleeping in her carrier under the piano. My heart broke open, and I never again thought about Shirlene being in Rain's body—she was completely Shirlene.

By the time I crawl into the sofa bed in the den, I'm wide awake in more than one way. "Not now," I grumble and roll over onto my side.

If I could love Shirlene in Rain's body, why can't I accept her in my Aimee's body? Shirlene made a gorgeous tall, lean blonde. Now she's wandering around in the middle of the night, revealing luscious curves and killer green eyes.

"Damn it. This is not helping my current condition." Time to take a cold shower.

Chapter Sixty-Eight

Shirlene

When Hattie hears Arlene had a temperature last night, she's over here in a flash.

"I promise you..." I pause. "We need to define your position in Arlene's life. You're aware I'm more spiritual than religious, but would you be her godmother? I'm sure Cam would approve."

Hattie beams. "I'd be honored, but let's ask Cameron." She sits at the kitchen table with the baby in her arms.

"I promise you your goddaughter is fine."

"I know, but I don't need an excuse to visit my sweet girl." She kisses Arlene's head. "Where's Cam?"

"He had to go into school to take care of some things with his substitute teacher." My mind wanders to last night, and I find myself smiling.

"What's going on?" Hattie asks.

I lean against the counter. "I saw a little chink in the armor."

"Tell me the details." Hattie's dark eyes dance with delight.

"Well, the old spark was there. We were in close proximity, checking the baby's temperature in the middle of the night, and I could feel it. He smiled a tiny bit."

"Progress."

"He was definitely turned on by Aimee's body."

Hattie shifts her chin back. "Well, that's a little weird. It's practically a ménage à trois."

"Hattie! That really bothers me."

"That I said it or that it's true?"

"Both." I fold a dish towel. "I need Cam to love *me*."

"Explain to me how it's different from him falling in love with you in Rain's body. You're still you. You're just in Aimee's body."

"Because he never loved Rain. In fact, he disliked her until I took over. I transformed her into me. But now, there's so much more confusion because he loves Aimee. She's dead, but because I look exactly like her, who is he falling for—me or Aimee?"

Hattie laughs. "It's absurd, but you make perfect sense."

My house phone rings.

"Aren't you going to answer it?" Hattie asks.

"Since it's not you or Cam calling, no."

"How do you know it's not Cameron?"

"Because he's in a meeting at school at this moment."

It keeps ringing.

Hattie hands Arlene off to me. "I'll answer it. Hello?" She listens. "Yes, Aimee is here." Hattie cover the phone. "It's Mrs. Haddad. Apparently, Cameron gave her this number."

"You talk to her. I don't feel like pretending to be Aimee right now."

Hattie rolls her eyes. "Mrs. Haddad, although Aimee's speech has improved, she's not comfortable speaking on the phone, but I'm her friend Hattie. Can I take a message?" Hattie's jaw drops. "He said he was who?"

Mrs. Haddad's voice goes a mile a minute, but I can't make out what she's saying.

"Okay. Yes, you did the right thing. I'll tell Aimee. Thanks for calling. Goodbye."

She hangs up the phone.

"What is it?" I'm going to jump out of my skin.

"Hold onto your hat, Shirlene. Supposedly, Aimee is engaged."

"What?"

"Her fiancé came searching for her. He went to her apartment, and the woman subletting Aimee's gave him Mrs. Haddad's address."

"Where has he been all this time?"

"On tour. He claims it's where they met." Hattie takes Arlene and sits down.

"Is he aware of her stroke?"

"I have no idea. But Mrs. Haddad said he left very angry that Aimee wasn't there."

"Well, he can't find me here."

"Unfortunately, Mrs. Haddad let it slip that Aimee was in Haddon Heights, New Jersey. That's why she called. To warn you. She refused to give him the exact address, but he's going to be looking for her—you."

I crumple into a kitchen chair. "You can't be serious. How can Aimee be engaged? Cam and she were best friends. Surely, she would have told him she was engaged, but he's never mentioned it. Also Cam said that with her depression Aimee couldn't handle marriage. That's why she called it off with him."

Hattie tickles Arlene's belly. She giggles. "Cam wants children. Possibly, this guy doesn't, and she thought she could manage only a husband."

"It was her career and nothing more. And that became too much because she left the tour early due to depression. How does a fiancé fit in with all this?"

"It could be he's the reason she got so depressed." Hattie winks. "Some men can be a pain in the ass."

"Tell me about it."

Arlene starts yawning.

"We should put her down."

I follow Hattie up to the nursery. I glance out the window to check the street for strange cars.

"That's my girl." Hattie settles the baby into her crib.

We tiptoe out and close the door.

I go across to the guest room and lie down on the bed. "I wish I could hide under these covers."

"That's not like you, Shirlene."

"Lately, I just long to stay in bed."

Hattie lies down next to me as she did when we were young and when Stan died. "What are you going to tell Cameron?"

I stare at the ceiling. "After the improvement last night, I'm not looking forward to telling him Aimee agreed to marry someone else after ending her engagement with him. He's so fragile right now."

She sits up. "But if you don't tell him..."

"Oh, I must tell him. I'm just earning his trust again. There can't be any secrets. Cam needs some warning before this fiancé shows up."

"If he finds you." Hattie lowers her head onto the pillow next to mine.

"I have a bad feeling he will."

"Mrs. Haddad said he was a very determined guy."

Chapter Sixty-Nine

Cameron

I push Shirlene's front door open so hard it slams into the foyer wall. Steam must be coming out of my nostrils. I close the door shut with a thud, flip the deadbolt lock, and throw my keys on the hall table.

Shirlene jets out of the kitchen. "What's going on out here?"

"There's a man outside who says he's looking for his fiancée, Aimee Bellerose." I try to relax my jaw as I watch Shirlene's hand fly up to her throat.

"Shit." She dashes to the front dining room window and glances out.

"How long have you known about this guy?" I ask from the foyer.

Shirlene steps away from the window but stays near the dining table. "Mrs. Haddad called about an hour ago to say a man claiming to be engaged to Aimee showed up searching for her."

"When did you plan on telling me?"

She snatches up a napkin from the table and blots her palms. "Don't start with me, Cam. I didn't want to text you something this significant. I planned to tell you as soon as you got home."

"Well, he beat you to it. Apparently, he's a singer. He claims to have been on tour with Aimee and that he proposed before she broke her contract and came home. He says the tour ended, and he's come to see her."

The doorbell rings.

"How the hell did he find me out here?"

"He says after my landlady slipped that Aimee was in New Jersey, he saw mail for me with this forwarding address on the hall table of my apartment building. He put two and two together." I start for the door.

"Wait!"

"For what, Shirlene?"

"Who am I supposed to be?" She tosses the napkin on the table.

I lick my lips. "Aimee, I suppose. You're going to have to break up with him."

"No kidding," she snaps.

The doorbell rings again. There's a loud knock.

"If you don't, I'll do it for you. Aimee can't be engaged to two men at once."

Shirlene crosses into the foyer and comes within two feet of me. Her eyes are wild. "Are you and Aimee engaged?"

Pain shoots up my neck. "As far as my school administration knows, yes, we're engaged."

"Well, that's news to me. Do you usually treat a fiancée like shit?"

There is pounding on the door. My head vibrates from the sound.

"Just open the damn thing before he knocks it down," Shirlene growls.

I'm frozen. Shirlene bounds past me. She unlocks and opens the door. Her hands fall limp at her sides when the tall, trim, bearded redhead I met outside takes her into his arms. "My Aimee. My Aimee." He nuzzles her neck.

My fingers itch to rip him off Shirlene. "Take it easy, man."

He regards me like I am the third wheel on a Harley. "Could Aimee and I be alone?"

"Absolutely not." Shirlene steps away from him.

"Who is this guy?" the redhead asks.

"I'm Cameron Michaels, Aimee's fiancé."

The man squares his broad shoulders. "You aren't her fiancé. I am."

"I'm sorry, but I didn't catch your name." I force my fingers out of a fist.

"I'm Tristen MacKinney."

If I weren't so pissed, I'd laugh. Tristen. What the hell kind of name is that?

Arlene begins wailing from upstairs.

"Where's Hattie?" I ask, hoping she can soothe Arlene.

"She went home." Shirlene moves toward the steps.

"Whose baby is making all the racket?" Tristen tries to step past me, but I don't budge.

"Um." Shirlene grips the railing. "Cam's niece. We're going to raise her."

Tristen shoves past me to reach Shirlene. "But, Aimee, we agreed not to have kids. I told you I have no desire to have children."

Well, that explains a little about why Aimee apparently agreed to marry this jerk. She wasn't feeling pressured to have a family. I should have given in on that, and we'd have been married. Maybe she'd be alive. My stomach rolls with guilt, and my chest fumes with rage. Aimee didn't tell me about her engagement. The women in my life love to keep their secrets.

"Our careers come first. It's what we discussed." He reaches for Shirlene's hand on the railing. Arlene wails.

"I've got to go to her." Shirlene goes up.

"Can't you deal with your niece right now?" he asks me.

"Listen, pal. You're pushing your luck."

"Aimee," he calls up after her. "I need to talk to you. The woman who is in your apartment told me you had a stroke. Why wasn't I notified?"

I push between him and the steps. "Notified? Who do you think you are?"

He grabs the top of my shirt. I shove him with all my power, and he slams against the newel post.

I look up at Shirlene, who is coming down the steps, holding our screaming baby. Shirlene's face is bright red. "Get out of my house!"

"Yeah, get out," I repeat to Tristen.

"Both of you!" Shirlene shouts. I've never heard her yell. "You've upset the baby. Both of you, out of my house now."

She balances the baby on her hip, shoves me with her other hip, and grabs Tristen's shirt. The two of us tumble out onto the ground, and the door slams shut. I swing at the body entangled with mine.

"No, wait. I have a new headshot scheduled for tomorrow. I can't have my face messed up." Tristen stumbles up onto his feet. "The day after tomorrow, I'll be only too happy to kick your ass."

"Are you joking, pretty boy?"

He dashes to the car parked across the street. "This isn't over!" he yells as he drives away.

"Damn right, it's not."

I brush the grass from my pants and go to the front door. It's locked. She's really throwing me out too. I dig for my car keys, but my pocket is empty. I dumped them on the hall table. No phone either. I didn't take it out of my back pocket. I scour the yard. It fell out when I landed on the ground. At least I have it. I hit Hattie's number.

"Hattie, it's Cameron. Shirlene has thrown me out."

"I'm not surprised."

"You're not?"

"Frankly, young man. I'm not."

This was not the reception I was expecting. But I need a good talking-to. "Hattie, can I come over?"

"Of course."

I'm dressed for the meeting with my sub at school, and my running shoes are locked in Shirlene's house. It will take me longer to cover the roughly three miles walking than running, but I start toward Lawnside. I could call a cab, but I think better when I'm moving on foot.

I've lost my perspective on everything. Why am I so angry with Shirlene? Maybe I'm angry and taking it out on Shirlene, which is stupid as shit. When I reach Warwick Road, I run the last stretch to Hattie's. These shoes are going to kill my feet, but I can't stand going this slowly.

"Where's your car?" Hattie asks when she lets me into her well-kept house.

"At Shirlene's." I grimace. "My keys were inside after she tossed me out."

"Too proud to knock?"

"Afraid she wouldn't answer."

"Probably wouldn't." Hattie goes to her kitchen, and I follow.

Although I've never been in her home, it looks much like I imagined it would after dropping her off here a few times. It's filled with photos, African art, and books, and everything is neat and clean.

I peek out her back door to her lovely garden. "Your mums are beautiful."

"I have some iced tea, and we can sit out there. Or would you prefer a beer?"

"A beer, please. You're going to set me straight, and I need a little fortification."

Hattie throws her head back and laughs.

The phone rings. "Hello." Hattie hands me a bottle and bottle opener.

She listens, and I have the feeling it's Shirlene.

"He's here." Hattie snags herself a beer. "No, I won't. He's staying here." She turns to me. "You're staying in the guest room, aren't you?" She doesn't wait for an answer, and I'm honored to be invited. "Cameron's taking me out to dinner. I'll bring him back over in the morning. I'll talk to you then. It's like Peyton Place around here with you two." She ends the call, opens her beer, and pours it into a tall glass. "Come on out back."

I follow her into a lush garden in its final bloom. We sit at a patio table.

"Hattie, this is beautiful."

"Thank you. It's my slice of heaven."

"That's evident." I take a sip of my beer. "So, what did Shirlene have to say?"

She rolls her eyes. "Flowers arrived from the other fiancé."

"Man, he doesn't waste any time." I grind my teeth. "And why didn't Aimee tell me about him? I thought we were best friends, but she never mentioned being engaged. Now, this guy is trying to win her back, only it's Shirlene he's wooing."

"He must have driven directly to—or phoned—a florist after she threw you both out."

"He had his car keys." I drink more beer.

"True. He also has another advantage." Hattie smirks slyly.

"What the hell, Hattie? You're not making me feel any better."

"I'm not trying to."

"What's his advantage?"

She chuckles. "You're acting like—"

"An ass?"

"I was going to say, 'a man.'"

"And this Tristen isn't?" I take another swig of my beer.

"No. He's acting like a lover. That's his biggest advantage at the moment."

Two monarch butterflies flit and flutter around the nearby flowers.

"But Shirlene isn't in love with him. I hope she's still in love with me."

"There's only so much malarkey Shirlene is going to tolerate from you. You're taking your anger out on her. Stan, although he was a wonderful husband in many ways, passive-aggressively took out all his unresolved feelings on Shirlene after Danny was killed. I can tell you with confidence that she won't go through it a second time."

I quickly polish off my beer as the butterflies float away.

"But Shirlene can't be taking this guy seriously. What's she going to do—pretend to be Aimee, or tell him the truth? It's ridiculous."

Hattie tilts her head and peers over the rim of her glasses. "The distraction of a doting, handsome man is never ridiculous."

I wipe sweat from my eyes. "So you're saying that although Tristen—God, I hate his name—doesn't really have a chance, he's making me look bad."

"Only because you've lost your way, Cameron. You used to be practically perfect. Shirlene and I couldn't imagine why you were single."

"Aimee." I realize there are tears, not sweat, on my face. "I couldn't get over Aimee."

"And the fact that she hurt you deeply."

I can only nod.

"Until Shirlene. You finally risked again, and you assume she abandoned you and Arlene for her dead husband and son."

I struggle to speak. "She did."

"No!" Hattie's sharp voice takes my breath away.

I nod. Guilt gnaws at my gut. "I know. Shirlene tried to explain it to me, but..."

Hattie's hand comes down on the glass-top table. "Shirlene explained to Stan that she wasn't drinking when Danny was killed, but he never believed her. Don't you see? She can't stay with a man who refuses to believe her."

"I don't know how to move past everything," I admit.

"I recommend you go to the beach house. Alone. The sea air will help."

Chapter Seventy

Shirlene

I wake up and hear someone in the house. Cam and Hattie are back. I intend to apologize to Cam for throwing him out with Tristen. It was a mistake, but I was angry with the both of them for fighting and upsetting Arlene. I toss on a bathrobe and hurry down. I find Hattie alone, making tea in the kitchen.

"Where's Cam?"

"On his way to Rehoboth Beach. He packed up what he needed and left."

My heart sinks. "Why didn't you wake me up when you brought him here?"

"He asked me not to."

"He didn't say goodbye." Even though I just woke up, I'm exhausted and plop into a kitchen chair.

Hattie pours two glasses of orange juice. "It's not permanent. The boy is confounded. Being at the ocean will comfort him." She sets a glass in front of me. "I saw the roses in a vase on the dining room table."

My hand flies up to my mouth. "Did Cam notice them?"

"If he did, he didn't say anything."

"It seemed a waste to throw them out. I'm sure they were expensive." I drag myself out of the chair and open the refrigerator door. "How about some scrambled eggs?"

"Sure." She glides into the dining room and smells the roses. "Mind if I read the note?"

305

I laugh. "Tell me you didn't already read it while I was asleep."

"Guilty as charged."

"Ha. So much for privacy." I whip the eggs and transfer them into the pan.

"Are you going to use the number he wrote on the card?" She comes to the kitchen table and pours our tea. "Are you going to have dinner with him?"

"Why the hell would I go to dinner with a man I've never met and pretend to be someone I'm not?" I lower the fire and stir the eggs.

"Sounds fun."

"Sounds exhausting to me."

After I dish out the eggs and grab the salt and pepper shakers, I join Hattie.

"So, when did the roses arrive?" Hattie digs in.

"A little after I settled Arlene back down. She was so upset by those two foolish men fighting in the foyer. I noticed Cam's car remained in the driveway, and his keys were on the hall table. When I went outside to find him, a florist truck arrived with the roses from Tristen."

"The poor man. Aimee's dead."

"I can't very well tell him that, so I have to break his heart by calling off our engagement." I swallow a bite of my eggs.

"It's not going to be easy." Hattie adds sugar to her tea. "So, what's this guy look like?"

"He's tall."

"That's it?"

"He has red hair and a close-cut beard."

Hattie nods. "Ahh, a ginger."

"Whatever his hair color, I have to write Tristen a letter to break it off, but I have no idea where to send it."

"You need to tell him in person." Hattie insists.

"Why?"

"A Dear John letter? It's cruel."

"I suppose."

Hattie finishes her eggs and carries her empty plate to the dishwasher. "You can gain some information from this guy."

"Like what?" I push my remaining eggs around the plate with my fork.

"Well, for one thing, why didn't Tristen come back with Aimee when she became so depressed she left their tour?" Hattie takes my plate and rinses it. "When she needed him most, he kept with the tour. What kind of fiancé does that?"

I join Hattie at the sink and wash the frying pan. "Knowing the little I do about Aimee, she likely insisted he not break his contract."

"But why wasn't he in touch?" Hattie sits.

"I have no idea what happened to her phone after the stroke. Because I couldn't communicate, it was ignored. I assume it's among her belongings at her apartment. He could have been texting like crazy, worried sick."

Hattie leans on the kitchen table, with her chin resting in her left hand and her long fingers framing her cheek. Her eyes sparkle. "We should go over to Aimee's apartment and search for the phone."

"For what purpose?"

"We'd learn if Tristen tried to be in touch. We'd see what kind of romantic things he wrote."

"Hattie, you're incorrigible. And nosy."

"Enquiring minds want to know."

"You're enjoying this Peyton Place more than I am."

Hattie's throaty laugh makes me smile. "Touché."

"I want things back to normal—well, my peculiar normal. I have another new body to adjust to, but I'm back with Arlene." I slide into my chair. "And I hope I haven't lost Cam."

"Speaking of Cameron, when he stayed with me, he was worked up that Aimee never told him about being engaged to Tristen. We could find out why Aimee kept this from Cameron."

"How are we going to solve that mystery at Aimee's apartment?" I ask.

"The phone texts, or we might find a journal."

"I suppose it would be helpful to Cam if he understood why Aimee didn't tell him."

"You ought to go out to dinner with him."

"How? He's gone to the shore." I put away the salt and pepper shakers.

"Not Cameron. Tristen."

"Are you out of your mind?" I slam the cabinet door.

"It's the kinder thing to do. Break it off with him as gently as you can, but get some answers to our questions."

"*Your* questions."

"Come on, Shirlene. What's happened to your sense of adventure?"

"I'm so tired."

"Are you taking Aimee's antidepressants?"

I bite my lip. "Yes, but I discussed cutting back the dosage with her doctor. I thought I could handle things differently than Aimee."

"Because you're a superwoman or something?" Hattie's voice rises.

"Okay. I'll be in touch with the doctor."

Chapter Seventy-One

Shirlene

I finally agree to meet with Tristen. I insist it be for lunch. Dinner has too many romantic implications attached to it. I text Cam, because he won't answer his phone, and tell him I'm having lunch with Tristen as Aimee to break off the engagement. Cam doesn't reply, but at least I'm not doing anything behind his back. No secrets.

I go through Aimee's clothes that Cam brought from her apartment. It's all very casual because up until now, she—I mean, I—was only going out to doctor and rehab appointments. Most young people would wear jeans to lunch, but I don't care to. Although I doubt I have appropriate clothing in my former Shirlene wardrobe, I go across the hall to my old bedroom closet to check. Stan's clothes will be in here as well. I take a deep breath and gasp when I find it empty. Completely empty, the same as the dresser drawers. I forgot to ask Hattie about them. She must have gone through everything when she thought I was dead and donated them. It makes sense, but it's a little shocking.

My hand flies to my throat. "The letters?" I dash to the steps. "Hattie?"

Her face appears at the bottom of the stairs. "Sh! You're going to wake up Arlene."

"Where are the letters Stan and I wrote to each other during the war? They were in a box in my clothes closet."

"Cam took them for Arlene."

"Did he read them?" My voice goes up into a soprano range.

"I don't know."

"You don't know?"

"I really don't. What's the big deal if he did?"

"The letters are personal. Private. Did you read them?"

"No. I absolutely didn't." She begins to cry. "But I did donate your and Stan's clothes because I thought you had died."

I go down and put my arm around her thin shoulders. "It's fine, Hattie. Nothing to cry over. You saved me a lot of work."

"You sure? Do you forgive me?"

"Hey, I was dead. I couldn't expect you to keep all my stuff." I laugh, trying to help Hattie relax.

She blows her nose on a tissue she pulled from her pocket. "What are you going to tell Tristen at lunch today?"

I shrug. "I'm going to blame everything on the stroke. Why I no longer have feelings for him. Why I suddenly want a child. Why I love Cam again."

"I hope he's convinced."

I hesitantly enter the Treehouse Coffee Shop in the nearby town of Audubon. Tristen stands and gives me a wave from the back corner. It's the most private spot in the local hangout. I wander around the eclectic collection of unmatching tables and chairs and unsuccessfully dodge a kiss on the cheek. "Hi."

He slides out my seat. "It's good to see you, Aimee."

I sit as he pushes in my chair. His hair is perfectly styled, and he's wearing a green Izod shirt and khakis. I could understand how some women might find him attractive, but there's something skeevy about him.

"Thanks for coming to lunch. Things got a little out of hand at that house." He scrutinizes me. "How did you end up there?"

Here it goes. Lie number one. "Cam was friends with the older couple who owned it until their deaths. They left it to him."

"A nice neighborhood." He lightly drums the table with his perfectly manicured fingers.

"It suits me."

"So, you're subletting your Philly apartment?"

"Yes. When the lease is up, Nancy, who is the woman subletting it, plans to stay there."

"She was nice when I showed up there expecting to find you." His eye twitches.

I spot the passive-aggression in the comment. "I'm glad Nancy was able to help you."

Tristen glances around. "I wonder why no one has bothered to bring us menus."

"We have to order up at the counter."

"There's no waitress?"

I ignore his snobbery and stand up. "Come on."

We inch past the laid-back display of local, organic jarred salsas and applesauces for sale and toward the counter crowded with yummy-looking homemade muffins and cookies.

He scans the list of lunch items on the chalkboard. "What's good here?"

"The wraps and paninis."

"I can't eat that stuff." He slaps his flat stomach. "Salads. Which salads are good?"

Aimee would know he must keep trim to perform in public. "They're all good."

A young woman wearing a bandana over her hair comes to the other side of the counter. "Are you ready to order?"

Tristen flashes her a grin. "We'll have two avocado chicken salads with no added dressing."

I don't say a word about him ordering for me. Perhaps Aimee liked it or let him.

"Anything to drink?" she asks.

I speak before Tristen can speak for me. "Unsweetened iced tea for me."

He squints. "Since when do you drink caffeine?"

"I'll bring the salads over." The young lady points to a table. "Silverware and napkins are there."

"Thank you." Tristen sneers before taking my elbow and steering me to our corner.

"They make fresh-brewed iced tea here." I'm quickly regretting meeting him in person. "Sometimes, when I'm not on tour, I drink it."

"I thought it made you jumpy."

"You're making me jumpy." I laugh to make it a joke.

He looks surprised.

"I'll grab utensils." I take deep breaths to settle myself as I move away, snatch up what we need, and sit back down.

Tristen sighs. "I couldn't wait to be with you without that guy around. We need to talk privately. That's why I sat us here." He scans the coffeehouse. "Away from the odd assortment of customers."

I giggle at his pretentiousness. Stan and I were regulars here. I decide to try to keep him talking rather than asking questions. "How did the remainder of the tour go for you?"

"Paris was wonderful, but it wasn't the same without you." He reaches for my hands.

I slip both of them onto my lap. "How were the audiences?"

"Fine. Your replacement was adequate." He sniffs. "You lost out on so much."

"Tristen, you seem angry I came home from the tour. I couldn't help it, and what if I'd had the stroke over there? It would have been a nightmare."

"I'm sorry," he says. "I missed you."

"Well, it wasn't about you. It was about my mental health and my physical health."

Tristen's mouth opens. "You've changed, Aimee."

I'm guessing Aimee never put him in his place. What an ego he has. "I have changed, in more ways than you can imagine. That's why I'm breaking off our engagement. You wouldn't want to marry me the way I am now."

There's a sadness around his eyes, but his mouth is tight. "But I love you. You love me."

"Not any—"

Our food arrives. I'm not hungry, but I gulp down half my iced tea.

For several moments, Tristen doesn't take his eyes off me. Finally, he takes a bite of his chicken salad.

"How's your lunch?" I ask.

"Thank God I asked her to hold the dressing. It already has too many calories."

I taste my salad. "Hmm. Delicious."

"You must be kidding. Too much mayonnaise."

I wonder how Aimee could have given up on generous, kind Cameron for this self-centered piece of work.

Tristen pokes at his salad. "Why didn't you find a way to tell me you'd had a stroke?"

"I couldn't communicate. For weeks, I was unable to talk or write."

He sits back in his chair with an incredulous expression.

"If you don't believe me, read the doctor's report."

"Doctors." He scoffs. "They don't know what they're talking about. They have you convinced you're depressed—"

I've had it with him, so I stand up. "It's over, Tristen. I have no idea what I saw in you before, but I've woken up."

He stands. "I'm not letting you go, Aimee."

I am either going to slap his face or run for my life. I dash toward the door.

"This isn't over," he calls after me.

By the time I reach my house, my heart is beginning to beat normally. I run to the house, practically fall through the door, and lock it behind me. Hattie leaps up from the sofa, dropping the novel she's reading.

"What's wrong?" She crosses to me in the foyer.

"Tristen is going to cause me another s... stroke." I stumble into the dining room and sit.

"You could use some ice water." Hattie disappears into the kitchen.

I run my hand across my brow to wipe the sweat off. "C... could you bring me a cold, wet dishrag?"

I hear her opening the drawer to find a clean cloth and run the tap. I concentrate on slowing my breathing down. Hattie returns and sets down the glass. She hands me the dishcloth. It feels cool against my face and neck.

"You're red."

"With anger."

"Should I call the doctor?"

I wave my hand. "No. I'm calming down."

"What the hell happened?"

"Tristen is a control freak. He's obnoxious and, frankly, scary."

"Take a drink."

I wipe my face again and swallow some water. "I'm sure Aimee left the tour to escape him."

"Wow!"

"Or he made her so depressed she thought about killing herself. Honestly, how she got mixed up with him, I'll never know."

"I'm sorry I pushed you to meet him."

"I'm okay, Hattie. Listen, I agree we should go over to Aimee's apartment. Cameron deserves to know the details of Tristen and Aimee's engagement."

"Broken engagement, right?"

"Yes, I broke it off."

"How did he react?" Hattie leans in.

"He refused to accept it."

"We need to learn more about this guy—not only for Cameron's sake, but you need to know who you're dealing with."

"What is it about Aimee that makes these men so obsessed? Although Cam isn't crazy like this guy, he never got over her, and this man is fanatical about her." I glance down at myself. "I mean, she's cute, but she's no bombshell. Maybe it's her talent that attracts them."

"You're missing the boat, Shirlene."

"What do you think it is?"

"They think she needs to be rescued, taken care of."

I lower my head onto the table. "Ugh."

"Are you okay?"

"I want to go to bed." I start for the stairs. "Was everything okay with Arlene?"

"She's an angel. Should I stay?"

My arms and legs feel heavy, and I sit on the steps. "I can't make it upstairs."

"I'm calling 911." Hattie moves toward the phone.

"No. It's not physical. It's depression. With everything with Tristen, I haven't contacted the doctor about raising Aimee's dosage back up." I slowly stand up. "What are the chances I'd inherit one body with addiction issues and a second one wired for depression?"

"Well, I'm not leaving you and Arlene."

"Thank you." My entire body aches as I hoist myself up one step at a time.

"Can I phone Aimee's doctor and ask about upping your dose?"

"Let's see how I am at dinnertime," I say from the top of the stairs.

The doorbell rings. I freeze.

"I'll set this ginger straight," Hattie says as she flings open the front door.

I come down a few steps to find Hattie shutting the door with her hip because her arms are holding a large arrangement of sunflowers.

She drops the flowers on the floor, opens the card, and reads, "Dear Aimee, forgive my behavior at lunch today. I promise to behave. Please meet me again. Yours, Tristen."

I cringe. "When is this jerk going to give up?"

"Were you completely clear that the relationship is over?" Hattie asks.

"Oh, I was abundantly clear, as anyone at the Treehouse can attest to."

"What should I do with these?" Hattie points to the sunflowers.

"Throw them out."

"But I'm saving the card for evidence in case you need a restraining order. He's sounding more and more like a stalker."

"You're making me more nervous than I already am, Hattie."

"When are we going to Aimee's apartment?"

"The sooner the better. I'll contact Nancy to schedule a visit as soon as possible."

Chapter Seventy-Two

Cameron

Once I step out of my car behind my grandmother's beach house and smell the salt air, I feel less jumpy. Before unloading, I jog up to gaze at the ocean. It's a crisp day in autumn—my favorite season at the shore and a time I rarely spend here because of teaching. The sun warms my skin despite the cool breeze. Some people are sitting in beach chairs and lounging on blankets. The lifeguards are gone for the season, and no one is swimming anymore. A group of laughing gulls circles above. Their black, feathered heads are turning white, and they've lost the red breeding color on their beaks. I've learned these specifics because of Shirlene.

I glance in the direction of her labyrinth. The dune blocks it from view, but the thought of it makes me tighten my jaw. I hope a high tide has washed it away. I plop down in the sand. In so many ways, it was the best summer of my life. With Shirlene, Arlene, and Hattie here, I had a family. Once Hattie had to leave for her trip to Ireland, things began to unravel. No. That's not accurate. Shirlene and I made love. We were getting closer until my brother showed up. That's when it all began to go to hell.

My throat burns with bottled-up tears. I have to let this pain out, so I let them fall. It's the real reason why I'm here. I haul myself back across the boardwalk, wiping my eyes. Ignoring my stuff in the car, I go directly into the beach house. It's always been my respite. I can sense my grandmother's supportive spirit here. I go upstairs to what was Shirlene's room for the summer. I collapse onto the bed and cry myself to sleep.

I wake up to darkness. Wondering how long I've been asleep, I check my phone. There's a text from Shirlene. She sent it late this morning telling me she's having lunch with Tristen to break off the engagement. Great. I'm two hours away, and she met this asshole for lunch. I wonder how things went and why she hasn't texted to tell me.

My stomach growls. There's nothing in the house to eat. I need to go food shopping but not tonight. After a shower, I wander toward town for a burger or whatever I'll find appealing. I decide to take the boardwalk.

A fair number of people are wandering the boards. Things are open, not like years ago when the shore shut down after Labor Day. Rehoboth Beach is pretty much a year-round resort now. Kids are carrying ice cream cones, and the bells and lights of the arcades are ringing and flashing. Zoltar, the animatronic fortune-telling machine, catches my eye. I've gone past him a thousand times, but I haven't bothered to stop since I was a kid. I saunter over, hoping no one I know sees me. Zoltar's yellow shirt, paisley vest, and gaudy jewelry seem to glow behind the glass.

I stare at his face. What do I want? There are so many layers that I have no idea where the hell to begin.

I'm startled when the fortune teller's hands move over his crystal ball, coins, and cards, and his voice says, "What are you waiting for? Let Zoltar tell you of your happy future." It costs a dollar now to receive some silly card. What do I have to lose except one buck?

"The Great Zoltar here with a word of wisdom for your fortunes. Remember, it is a great deal better to do all the things you think you should rather than to spend the rest of your life wishing you had. No, do not be leaving this place with regrets. Live it up, my friend, and start by giving me more money for more wisdom, no?"

A card slides out of the machine. It reads Zoltar Speaks on the front. I flip it over: *You are a strong believer in fate. You feel you have no control over your destiny. You've had trouble this year.*

No shit, Sherlock. I wasted a dollar for confirmation that my life sucks. Although it hasn't pinged, I check my phone again. I'm right—no word from Shirlene about how her lunch with Tristen went earlier today. I can't believe Aimee would be involved with this jerk, let alone engaged. As I search the boardwalk for the greasiest burger I can find, I consider texting Shirlene to ask how she handled Tristen, but I don't want to be in touch with her until I figure myself out. I loved Aimee for a long time. Loving Shirlene in Aimee's body is really bothering me.

I kill my phone. No contact until I get my act together.

Chapter Seventy-Three

Shirlene

After dropping Arlene off at Mrs. Haddad's, I drive Hattie around several blocks in search of a parking spot in the Fishtown neighborhood of Philly, and finally, a place opens up not far from Aimee's apartment.

"Are you trying to be a celebrity?" Hattie points to the sunglasses I'm wearing and the hat I've pulled down as far as it will go. "You're going to draw more attention this way."

I take hold of her arm. "Sh! I can't afford to run into anyone Aimee knows. Now, walk normally."

"How else would I walk?" Hattie yanks away.

We scurry into the building without incident.

"I hope it's worth all this," I mutter as we approach Aimee's door and ring the bell.

An attractive Asian-American woman in her midtwenties answers the door. "Aimee, it's so good to see you're feeling better."

"Thanks for letting us stop by."

"You called at the perfect time because I work from home on Fridays."

"This is my friend Hattie."

She shakes Hattie's hand. "Hi, I'm Nancy. Please come in."

We enter a cozy living room that opens to the kitchen and includes a small dining table by one window. There are three doorways to the right of the kitchen area. One is closed, and beds are visible through the other two.

We both settle in on the sofa, and Nancy sits in a chair across from us. The walls are a soft pale green with several framed photographs of seascapes and rivers hanging around the room.

Nancy points to one of the two open doors. "Well, all your stuff is in the second closet in my room. Whatever opera and music posters Cam didn't bring to your studio apartment are in there. I hope you don't mind me taking them down."

"Of course not. Your photographs are lovely."

"Thanks—a hobby of mine. Now, the things you brought back from Europe but weren't well enough to deal with are in suitcases and two boxes in my sister's room. She's at class right now."

"Where does she go to school?" Hattie asks.

Nancy smiles with obvious pride. "She's working on her master's in bioengineering at Temple. My sister needed a place. I was glad to be able to help her out."

I notice a laptop and several files on the table by the window. "We're interrupting your work."

"Oh, I don't mind," Nancy says.

Hattie wanders around, snooping like a detective. "Were you here when Aimee had her stroke?"

"Yes. Lucky thing too. I recognized what was happening and called 911 immediately." Nancy looks at me with surprise. "Don't you remember?"

"No, I don't recall." I try to sound apologetic.

"You poor thing. It happened shortly after you arrived. While we were waiting for the EMTs, I thought you'd died."

Just like Rain in the delivery room.

"You closed your eyes, and you stopped breathing, and I couldn't find a pulse. Suddenly, you took a deep breath and opened your eyes."

"I remember that."

"You became panicked. You kept trying to say something, but you couldn't talk."

It all floods back to me. After leaving Stan and Danny, I experienced that sickening vortex again, and then I was sitting right where I am now, staring at Nancy but not knowing who she was, who I was, or where I was. I tried to ask her, but my brain had disconnected from my mouth.

"Do you know what happened to Aimee's phone?" Hattie asks.

"I told Cameron when he asked about it. He's a nice guy. It was in Aimee's purse, which I took with us in the ambulance to the hospital, but after the staff took it to keep with Aimee, the phone disappeared."

"Damn." Hattie circles around the sofa.

"I'm so sorry." Nancy's eyes follow Hattie, who is still wandering around.

I glare at Hattie and raise my eyebrows. "It's not your fault, Nancy."

Hattie finally settles next to me. "What about her passport and credit cards?"

"They were in a separate travel pouch. You took them off right after you came in the door. I stored them in one of the boxes."

"Well, we'd better start sorting through my things. I need to get my life back together."

"Are you going to go back to singing?" Nancy leads us into one of the bedrooms.

"I'm not ready to make a decision." I hesitate to open either set of closet doors because I'm not clear which contains Aimee's things. "Could you remind me where I should be looking?"

"Sure." Nancy opens the closet to the left. "This is yours, and everything else is in suitcases and boxes in the next room. I'd better go back to work." Nancy starts to leave.

"What can you tell us about Tristen?" I ask.

"Who?"

"The big ginger." Hattie crosses her arms across her chest.

"Oh, that guy." Nancy stares at me. "Well, you're the one engaged to him. What could I possibly know that you don't?"

There's cotton in my mouth. "Well, Nancy, my memory is off from the stroke. Some things remain a little vague."

Her eyes soften. "I'm very sorry."

"Did I talk about him before my stroke?"

Nancy sits down on her bed. "Yes, you did." She looks at Hattie. "I didn't know Aimee before she sublet her apartment to me. We had a mutual friend who recommended me to her." She turns to me again. "I thought it was unusual for you to open up to me when you arrived after leaving your tour. You were trying to explain why you needed to stay here so badly." She pauses. "You don't remember any of this?"

"No."

"You told me you needed to get away from this guy. He wasn't mentally healthy. You seemed real scared, and he had gotten into your head. *Manipulated you into an engagement* was what you said."

Hattie nods in my direction. I reply with raised eyebrows. Tristen is bad news.

"What else did I say about Tristen?"

"Not much, because one minute you were talking, and the next, you weren't. You sort of zoned out. You couldn't respond to me, so I called 911."

"Thank you. If I hadn't been with you, things could have been much worse."

Hattie clears her throat. She's going to cross-examine. "Nancy, what was your impression of Tristen when he showed up here?"

Nancy pressed her lips together. "He's a real charmer, but he put me on edge. He was too charming, if you know what I mean. Maybe it was because you said that he manipulated you, but I saw red flags when he was here."

I shiver.

"Is he still bothering you?" Nancy pats the bed.

I sit. "I broke off the engagement. He's not accepting it."

"Before your stroke, I suggested you do that, but you were too frightened."

"Well, I'm not Ai... I mean, I'm not the same Aimee. Recovering from the stroke. I'm stronger."

Nancy touches my shoulder. "Good for you." She rises. "I really have to work."

"Thanks for your time." Hattie shuts the door after Nancy goes back to her computer.

"I know how to pick 'em, don't I?" I begin going through the clothes hanging in the closet, mostly sweaters and heavier winter things that Aimee didn't take on her summer tour. "First Chase and now Tristen."

"You didn't pick them, Shirlene. These mixed-up young women did." She heaves a box out from the closet floor. "Let's discover what's in here."

We root through and find school yearbooks, memorabilia from her Curtis performances, books, and photographs with friends and with Cam. An engagement photo of Aimee and Cam shows her holding out her hand to reveal the ring. It makes me sad and a little jealous.

"This wasn't helpful at all." I plop on the bed again.

"I disagree. The photographs with Cameron tell us that she held onto them. She still had feelings for him." Hattie tosses shoes out of the closet. "We need to keep searching."

"You're right. Cameron needs to know Aimee wasn't in love with Tristen. She was vulnerable and manipulated. That's a big difference."

"Hold the phone." Hattie spins from the closet with a grin on her face and a jewelry box in her hands. She sits next to me and opens the lid.

"We're intruding now. This is personal stuff, and jewelry isn't going to tell us what we need to know."

Hattie ignores me and gently moves aside several pairs of earrings and a bracelet to reveal a small velvet-covered ring box. Inside is a contemporary-style diamond engagement ring.

I pick up the ring to examine it more closely. "Cameron told you he didn't take it back when she called off the wedding. My heart aches for him. He hoped she'd change her mind, and just when he thought she might, he found out she was dead and I was here instead. He must hate me."

"No time for pity parties right now, Shirlene."

"Yes, ma'am. Let's find out what's in the other room." Before leading Hattie through the living room, I pocket the ring to show Cam that Aimee kept it. Nancy doesn't look up from her work. I shut the bedroom door.

Hattie stands over Aimee's suitcases and some boxes in the corner. "Okay. This is all the stuff she had with her on tour. We'll find better information here." Hattie opens one suitcase on the bed. "More clothes, toiletries—oh, medications."

I examine the labels. "Antidepressants and antianxiety meds."

"Is it possible Aimee told her doctor about this guy?" Hattie opens one of the boxes.

"The doctor has never brought up Tristen—or much about Cameron, for that matter. He mostly talks about finessing my medications."

Hattie holds up what might be a journal. "Bingo."

I take the notebook with a cover design of musical notes and flip to the last entry.

"Read it aloud." Hattie sits on the floor.

"This isn't story time, little girl."

"Just read."

Aimee's handwriting has jagged edges. The pen was clearly pressed hard onto the page.

I begin. "I caught Tristen reading this. I'll make sure he never sees it again. He claims that in order to help me with my depression and to protect me, he needs to know everything. I don't agree at all, but I couldn't speak. I freeze up with him, and I'm afraid that's going to happen to me on stage. I feel completely trapped by this relationship, and the only way out is to end it all. But I think of Cameron and how hurt he'd be." I look up. "Oh, Hattie."

"Go on."

"I'm doing a sucky job on stage. I have to break my contract before we go to Paris, which is where Tristen says he's buying a ring for me. I can't face that possibility. I need to get away from Tristen now. I hope I can convince him to stay with the tour until it's over. I need to see Cam. He'll know how to handle this."

"Well, it's confirmed," Hattie says. "You need to talk to Cameron."

"I will."

"You're being evasive."

"Don't put me on the witness stand, counselor."

"Give me the diary."

I hand it over and go through the second box while Hattie flips through Aimee's writings.

"Hey, listen to this." Hattie points to a page. "This is back in July. 'How have I gotten myself into this situation? Tristen proposed. I said I don't love him, but he didn't seem to believe me. The entire company believes we're engaged because he told everyone we are, even though I didn't agree. He ignores whatever I say that doesn't go along with his plans. It's making me suspect my sanity, which of course is up for grabs anyway. If I was going to marry anyone, it's Cam.'"

Hattie pauses and looks at me. I can't catch my breath. Aimee still loved Cam.

She continues reading. "I want to tell Cam about Tristen, but I'm worried it will hurt his feelings. Plus, he has so much going on in his life this summer with his brother's girlfriend having a baby whom he's taken in. He doesn't need this extra stress. But what am I going to do?"

Hattie rolls over onto her knees and waves one arm. "Help me up, will you?"

I take her wrist and guide her onto her feet.

"Thanks."

"Anytime."

She pushes the diary into my face. "If you don't tell Cameron, I will this time."

"Okay." I sit on the bed, wondering if this will only make Cam feel worse about losing Aimee and getting stuck with me.

"I'm serious. I worried he wouldn't forgive me for hiding your conversations with Rain."

"Yeah, he's not generous with forgiveness."

Hattie frowns. "You shouldn't blame him."

"Sh. Keep your voice down, Hattie. I have to deal with Tristen first. Tell him it's really over."

"You did that. What would be different this time?"

"I didn't stay calm at our lunch. He surprised me, and I became angry. That only turns a controlling person on. They want to win. If I remain in control of myself, I can get through to him."

"What if he refuses to accept it?" Hattie asks.

"I need a backup plan."

"I have a plan."

I can tell Hattie's plotting something.

"Tell him the doctor says you could have another stroke anytime. I bet money he'll be running for the hills if he thinks he'll be saddled with caregiving. He's no Cameron."

"Don't start sweet-talking on Cameron right now. I don't need Cam or any man."

Chapter Seventy-Four

Cameron

I try to keep my right heel still on the floor as I read a letter from my parents that's been forwarded to the shore address.

Dear Son,

Hold on to your hat. We've been in family therapy with your brother and Rain. It's been eye-opening to say the least.

We buried ourselves in our business and nearly lost both our sons. We desire to reconnect with you, Cameron. More than holiday and birthday cards. We'd also like to be whatever part you decide we can be in the life of your daughter. We won't interfere with you adopting her, and neither will Chase or Rain.

We apologize for not showing respect for your career and life choices. We are immensely proud of you being a teacher and positively affecting young people's lives.

If you can forgive us, we look forward to being a part of your life.

Love, Mom and Dad

Needing some air, I take off for the beach. When I pass over the dune, I discover that Shirlene's labyrinth has been washed away. I'm both relieved and sad that it's vanished with the tides. I jog a hundred feet along the dunes to another clearing. My parents have asked me to forgive them. I lean over and pick up a good-sized whelk shell.

What will it cost me to let go of my anger toward them? I gather more shells and small pieces of driftwood. Why wasn't my becoming a teacher good enough for them? Why wasn't I good enough for

Aimee? My chest tightens. Shirlene never loved me as much as she loved Stan.

I take a deep breath and reach for more shells to add to my pile. A speck of sand blows into my eye. I drop my load and let my eye tear up. I can hear my grandmother's voice saying, "Don't rub at it, Cameron. Let the tears wash it out."

I begin to cry and not from the sand. Glad that the beach is nearly empty this morning, I plop down in the sand and watch the surf, blinking until the sand is washed from my eye.

Here I am, beginning a labyrinth just as Shirlene did. I'm grieving Aimee's death like Shirlene is grieving Stan's. I have a lot of forgiving to do. Like Shirlene, I need to begin by forgiving myself. I go back to gathering beach treasures to line my labyrinth paths.

Chapter Seventy-Five

Shirlene

A few days later, I enter the Legacy Diner, and Tristen waves to me. He appears handsome and pulled together, sitting in front of two cups on a table. He smiles broadly.

I take a deep breath and go to him. "Hi, Tristen."

"Hello, darling." He kisses my cheek before ushering me into one side of our booth. He sits across from me. "I ordered for you. Decaf."

It's coffee, and I prefer tea, but I'll pick my battles. "Thank you."

"I'm so glad you agreed to meet me. I apologize for my behavior." He drinks his coffee.

"I accept your apology, but it doesn't change the fact that I'm not the same after the stroke. I want different things."

"Like what?" He stares without blinking.

My stomach starts to do flips. He knows how to push my buttons, but I won't allow him to goad me.

"When we were together on tour, I relied on you. You were a wonderful support."

He lifts his eyebrows. He wasn't expecting a compliment. "Thank you. I tried my best."

"I'm very grateful."

"You're welcome. I'd do anything for you, Aimee."

I finger the corner of my paper placemat. Then, knowing I must not appear vulnerable or anxious, I force my hands into my lap. "You are the perfect man for a woman who needs guidance and advice. I used to be that woman, but I'm not now."

"You don't need me?" His lower lip pushes out slightly.

"Honestly, I don't. My priorities have changed. I nearly died, and I want to do things differently now that I have another chance."

"Why can't I be a part of that?"

"Because I'm not in love with you anymore."

"You're crazy about me."

Wow. He is truly delusional. Okay, now what do I say? "My stroke changed everything. I need to be completely clear. It's over between us."

His facial expression darkens. "You'll be sorry in the end."

I keep my voice level while holding my hands under the table and picking at a cuticle. "You need to understand that I won't be threatened. I won't hesitate to get a restraining order, but I don't know what that will do for your career."

He sits back and studies me. He laughs. "I wasn't threatening you. I think you'll regret your decision later."

"Possibly I will."

"There won't be any second chances with me."

"No, I understand. Your career comes first. We had agreed to that on tour, but I'm in a different place now."

He gazes down at his coffee. He's sulking.

"You'll make it big, Tristen. You're incredibly talented."

He feigns a modest expression, and I fight the urge to gag.

"I wish you the best." I'm hoping this is it.

He shifts his gaze up and glares. "It's that Cameron guy, isn't it? He is the hero because he nursed you back from your stroke, but I didn't know you were sick. I would have come at a moment's notice."

"No, you wouldn't have."

"What?" He sounds indignant.

"Oh, be honest, Tristen. You couldn't have given up the tour. Work comes first for you, as it should. You're very dedicated."

"True."

"So let's not play games. I insisted you finish the tour when I had to leave. You agreed. It was for the best."

"But I texted you every day. Why didn't you reply?" Tristan appears to be fighting tears. He's an excellent actor.

"My phone disappeared at the hospital. I'm sure you were worried sick."

"Oh. Yes, I was."

A waitress nears our table. I wave her away.

"And I appreciate it. It's unbelievable how you managed performing when you were concerned about me." I'm laying it on thick, but it seems to work with him.

"Well. I'm—"

"Amazing is what you are. And you deserve everything in your career. I'm no longer the woman to help with that."

"Are you sure?"

"Yes, Tristen. You deserve someone who will put your career first." I decide to use Hattie's idea for safe measure. "The doctor tells me I could have another stroke, and I won't let you give up your dreams to take care of me."

He takes a moment to calculate what I said. "Okay. I understand."

He looks relieved. I just gave him a Get Out of Jail Free card.

"Thank you, Tristen. I appreciate that. You've always been so understanding and supportive."

"Good luck, Aimee. I hope you're happy."

"You too." I dash for freedom.

I burst through the door and find Hattie feeding Arlene in the kitchen.

"I was brilliant. I made it seem as if it was for his benefit that we break up—for his career—and he took the bait, hook, line, and sinker."

Hattie pats her heart. "I'm so thankful."

I sit at the kitchen table. "He was easy to manipulate once I understood his agenda. He caught me off guard the first time. I fell right into his trap. Poor Aimee. She couldn't get away from him. He's a real operator." I jump up for a gingersnap.

My phone dings. I dig it out of my pocket.

"Your expression changed. Is it Tristen?" There's a tremor in Hattie's voice.

"No, it's Cam. So he's finally responding to my texts and calls."

"Thank God. Answer it."

I tap the answer icon. "Hi, Cameron."

"It's good to hear your voice, Shirlene."

"Didn't you listen to it on the numerous messages I left?"

Hattie frowns. I dart out of the kitchen, through the dining room, and into the living room.

"I'm sorry I didn't return your messages or texts. I was a mess," he says.

"I guess so."

"You're not going to make this easy, are you?" Cam asks.

"Why should I?" I pace back and forth in front of my piano.

He changes the subject. "How's Arlene?"

"She's fine." I stand still. "I'm not going to do small talk with you, Cam."

"I don't want to either. I understand a lot more about why I got so stupid. I'm calling to ask you, Arlene, and Hattie to come down to the beach house."

"Yes!" Hattie shouts from right behind me.

I jump. "What the hell, Hattie." I slip into the den and close the door. "Sorry about that."

Cam is laughing. "Hattie up to her usual tricks?"

"I need to think about this. I'll let you know by tomorrow."

His reply is slow in coming. "Of course. I want to apologize for everything, and I have some things to explain to you in person."

"Okay. I need a little time."

After disconnecting, I dread facing Hattie in the living room. When I open the door, she's not there. I cross into the foyer and catch her talking to Arlene upstairs. My cookie is calling to me from the kitchen, so I sit down to take a bite.

"You want a gingersnap?" I ask Hattie when she enters. I grab the box and open the refrigerator. "I need milk with these."

I sense Hattie's glare through the back of my head. "Why are you eating so many cookies?"

"Hmm!" I savor a bite of dunked cookie. "These bring back the best memories of autumn. Hattie, sit down."

She stays put. "We're going to Rehoboth Beach."

"I know." I dunk the rest of my gingersnap.

"Then why are you making him suffer?"

"You're ruining these cookies for me, Hattie." I take my last bite and drink my milk.

She peers over her glasses in that way that makes me feel stupid. "This game you're playing is mean."

I stand. "Fine. I'm mean. But he deserves to wait. I'm sick of men. Stan. Tristen. Cam. The entire lot of them can go to hell." I stomp out of the room and go up to check on Arlene.

"Cam doesn't play games. He's confused, but he's honest!" Hattie shouts from the bottom of the stairs.

I stare down at her.

She wags her finger. "You're going to have to forgive Cameron."

"Ha. Like hell."

"Do you know who you remind me of right now, playing this passive-aggressive crap?"

My knees collapse, and I grab the railing and sit on the top step.

"Holding a grudge." She places her hands on her narrow hips.

I bite my lip.

"Say it."

"Stan."

She has cut me to the quick. I resent her for pointing this out to me, but damn, she's right. I'm behaving like Stan. "Okay." I pull my phone out and text. *We'll be down tomorrow after lunch.* I hold the phone up. "There. Happy?"

"I'm going home to pack." She starts for the door like a kid going to camp.

"Hattie, I need you to help me."

She watches me with her perceptive dark eyes. "Shirlene, you don't need me. The same as Cameron, you need some time by yourself. I have confidence you will figure this out."

As she closes the front door, my throat tightens. I can't move and stay glued to the top step of the stairway. Since there's no use trying to stop them, I let the tears flow. I'm not sure why I'm so unhappy and irritable. I should be joyful. I fought to regain my speech and did it. Rain and Chase are gone. I have Arlene. I sniff and wipe my wet cheeks on my sleeves.

After Aimee's—now my—psychiatrist saw how I fought through the aphasia, he agreed with me when I asked to lower the dosage on my medications. In my arrogance, I thought I was stronger than Aimee and could handle the depression. But I'm not. I've known this for days, but I've let dealing with Tristen delay my call to the doctor. Now I'm really feeling it.

I didn't ask the cardiologist to lower those medications. It would be foolish. I'm doing everything the cardiologist recommends in order to avoid having another stroke. So why am I treating the depression differently? They are both diseases. I smooth my hands along my thighs. Rain was addicted. I went to meetings and avoided triggers to address the physical chemistry I inherited in her body. Now I must do the same for Aimee's chemistry.

I haul myself up and go down into the kitchen to reach out to the doctor. He'll ask how many days I've been on the lower dosage of antidepressant, so I'd better check the date. When I explore the kitchen calendar, my stomach tightens. It suddenly dawns on me that I haven't had a period since entering Aimee's body well over a month ago.

Chapter Seventy-Six

Cameron

Right after getting Shirlene's text, I begin to clean. I vacuum and dust the nursery and Hattie's bedroom. An ocean breeze is moving the window curtains in Shirlene's room. The salty smell fills me with hope. I am taking a dustcloth to wipe the top of her dresser when the edge of a shiny object on the floor catches my eye. I pick up Shirlene's chain that holds her and Stan's wedding bands and a diamond ring. She must have taken it off her neck to swim the day she nearly drowned. Somehow, it slipped off the dresser. I angle Stan's simple gold band to see what's inscribed inside. I read the word *Forever*. Inside Shirlene's band I read the word *Love. Love Forever.*

Shirlene will love Stan forever, and that's okay, because I will love Aimee forever. While walking in my labyrinth, I decided I can love both Shirlene and Aimee, and Shirlene is capable of loving both Stan and me—if she loves me after everything that's happened. I set the chain on the dresser.

The image of another ring pops into my head. I'd forgotten about my grandmother's engagement ring. After she died, I stored it and a few other valuables in her bank safety deposit box here in Rehoboth Beach. I wonder...

Chapter Seventy-Seven

Shirlene

The closer I drive to Rehoboth Beach, the more it feels like someone is pounding a racket ball against the walls of my stomach. "Hattie, do you have antacids?"

She rifles through her handbag. "Why are you nervous?"

"I have a lot on my mind."

"You'll feel better once you spend some time by the sea and the higher antidepressant dosage your doctor ordered kicks in." She hands me two Tums.

"Thanks." I chew the chalky pills. "There's something else." I hesitate to tell her.

"Don't keep me waiting."

"When I talked to the doctor, he reminded me that before the summer tour I—Aimee—went off birth control because it could be aggravating my depression."

"So go back on the pill."

"It's not that simple, Hattie." I swallow. "I realized that I haven't had a period since ending up in Aimee's body."

"Are you afraid you're pregnant?"

I nod. "With Tristen's child."

Hattie's hand flies up to her mouth. "No."

"Cameron may be willing to take on his brother's daughter, but I doubt very much he can accept Tristen's offspring."

"Are you certain Aimee was having sex with Tristen?" Hattie asks.

"She never mentions it in her journal."

"Then there's hope that you're just delayed from the stroke. Or perhaps Aimee wasn't regular."

I tighten my grip on the steering wheel. "Honestly, Hattie. I don't get a break with these bodies. Why couldn't I end up with someone who isn't addicted or depressed or prone to strokes?"

"Hey, you could have ended up in my hot bod!" Hattie lifts her boobs with both hands.

I laugh through my tears.

After leaving Rehoboth Avenue, I head south several blocks. I make a left onto Cam's street and turn into the last drive. Seeing Cam's car parked there increases my heart rate. Hattie claps and cheers before hopping out of the passenger's seat to take Arlene from her car seat in the back.

I can't breathe when Cam dashes down the back steps toward us. Hattie is closer to him than I am.

"Welcome back." He hugs her and kisses Arlene's head. "I've missed you, my little peanut."

Our eyes meet over the car. My feet are stuck to the ground. "Hi, Cam."

He moves quickly around to my side of the car but stops a few feet away from me. "Shirlene. Thanks for coming down."

I have no idea what to say. I don't know if I can hug him. He doesn't move. Hattie stares at us before taking the baby into the house.

"It's good to be back," I finally say.

Simultaneously, we step toward each other for a brief hug. He smells of salt air and citrus aftershave.

"Well, we'd better unload the car." Cam opens the door and takes hold of two suitcases. I trail behind him with the diaper bag and Hattie's luggage.

Arlene is cooing when we come into the kitchen. "She's glad to be back," Hattie says.

"Give me my girl." Cam takes Arlene into his arms and kisses her face so many times she's giggling.

Hattie and I carry our things to the second floor.

"I missed this view." Hattie drops her bags and scurries to the front door of her bedroom. She goes out onto the deck, which adjoins our bedrooms.

I drop my luggage and immediately notice the chain with my and Stan's rings sitting on top of my dresser. I caress the wedding rings, remembering how I took them off to swim that day in the rain. If I hadn't gone, I wouldn't be in this mess.

I look in the mirror, surprised by my short brown hair and green eyes. I grin and tug my T-shirt up. I miss my belly piercing. I'm sure there's a place in Rehoboth Beach to have it done.

Hattie appears at the deck door to my room. "What are you snickering about in here?"

"Oh, simply an outing you and I might take together for some girlfriend time." I wonder if I can persuade Hattie to pierce something.

"I'm glad I brought warmer clothes with me. It's much cooler down here than up at home." Hattie flips her shoes off and falls back onto my bed. "Autumn at the shore. I couldn't be any happier."

I crawl in next to her. "Tell me it's all going to work out."

She touches her nose to mine. "I believe it will work out." She notices I'm holding the chain with rings from my earlier life. "Are you going to wear it again?"

I ball the rings and chain up in my hand. "It's time to put them away." I roll onto my side, pull open the nightstand drawer, and place my old treasures in it.

There's a knock on my doorjamb, and Cam says, "Someone's cooing for her mommy."

"Come on in," I say.

Arlene's eyes widen as he sets her on the bed between Hattie and me.

"Was this room yours as a boy?" I impulsively ask Cam.

He blushes. "Yes. Chase was in Hattie's room."

Hattie giggles. "I presume we don't want to begin to imagine what went on in these beds."

I slap her arm. "Hattie!"

"And on that note, I'm going to leave you 'girls' to your own devices. Dinner will be ready around five thirty." Cam exits my room and closes the door for good measure.

Hattie and I roll with laughter, careful not to crush Arlene, who kicks her legs with joy.

Chapter Seventy-Eight

Cameron

The atmosphere is festive while we eat dinner on the front porch. The wind dies down, but Hattie wears two sweaters, which entertains Shirlene and me quite a bit. After cleaning up, Hattie announces that she is going to put the baby down and go into her room to read for the night. Not too obvious, but the dear woman is trying to give Shirlene and me a chance to talk alone.

"How about some Kohr's frozen custard?" Shirlene asks.

"Absolutely."

We both grab sweatshirts because it's after sunset.

"They'll have their pumpkin flavor now." I hold the front-porch screen door open for Shirlene.

"Oh, I love pumpkin anything."

Aimee's body walks next to me up the path to the boardwalk, but Shirlene is definitely inside. I nearly say out loud that for Aimee, pumpkin was for pie only, and every other version was blasphemy. But I don't want to bring up Aimee. Not yet. I'm enjoying the even keel we are experiencing together. It's almost like we've gone back to summer, before Chase and Rain showed up.

Shirlene and I stroll in comfortable silence along the boardwalk. Shops are still open, and people are out enjoying the nice weather. The town will hum along through to Christmas before some places button up for the winter.

"Have you been here at Christmas?" Shirlene asks.

"You were reading my mind."

Aimee smiles at me—no, it's Shirlene. I clear my throat. "I was just thinking about the holidays. There's a big tree set up here." I point to the bandstand as we get close to Kohr Brothers. "It draws quite a large crowd for the tree lighting, and Santa is up on the boardwalk in a small wooden house."

"Sounds lovely."

I take her comment as a good sign. We wait to order our cones. I could easily stay here with Shirlene and Arlene—and Hattie, if she'd like—through the holidays. We could decorate a tree by my grandmother's fireplace. There'd be presents under it for Arlene. Then I'll be back to school in the New Year.

"Sir, what flavor?" The woman in the brightly lit stand hands Shirlene her cone.

"Pumpkin and cinnamon swirl in a cone."

"Yum." Shirlene will have her cone devoured before I start mine.

"Let's sit down." We go to a bench where we can see the beach.

Shirlene shivers. "Could you hold my cone while I slip my sweatshirt on?"

"Is it too cold for ice cream?"

"Never. Look, the moon is coming up over the ocean." Shirlene points.

Moonlight begins dancing across the waves, shifting the mood. I become keenly aware of Shirlene's breathing and warmth close to me. I long to touch her. Her, not Aimee. But I can't ignore that Aimee's body is next to me.

Shirlene devours the bottom of her cone. Aimee would have nibbled at it forever.

"I wonder if the water is too cold for swimming." Shirlene watches the surf.

I'm taken back to summer, when Shirlene dove into the sea with complete abandonment in Rain's body. She was like a joyful dolphin.

Aimee preferred pools. The idea of fish and other living things in the water with her gave her the creeps.

"Ready to head back?" Shirlene gets up.

I finish my custard. "Sure." I look at her face. She isn't wearing any makeup. Aimee wouldn't have been caught dead without makeup. I laugh.

Shirlene's unadorned eyebrows rise.

"Nothing," I say.

I can't tell her I'm amused over the irony that Aimee *is* dead without makeup. Sick. I'm finding humor in the most unfunny things now.

"Do you mind if we go back along the beach? The moonlight is so beautiful." Shirlene takes off her shoes and sinks her feet into the sand. "Ahh."

I remain in my sneakers. It's too chilly for bare feet.

We meander down the deserted beach, watching the waves.

"We have so much we need to talk about." Shirlene zips up her sweatshirt.

My stomach lurches. "I know."

"I've been working with Aimee's psychiatrist."

"Are you depressed?"

She glances over. It's darker now that we've left the lights of the boardwalk, and I can't quite gauge her expression.

"Just like Rain's addiction surfaced, so has Aimee's depression. If one of them was diabetic, I'd be diabetic now."

"I understand. How's it going?"

"You know me—I thought I could cut back because I'm older, wiser, possibly tougher, but chemistry has the upper hand. I take her stroke medications without question, so after a conversation with the doctor yesterday, I'm on the same antidepressant dosages."

"Good. You don't want to mess with that."

"I realize it now."

"How is it talking to Aimee's psychiatrist?"

"When I have to pretend to be Aimee with her doctors, it's extremely uncomfortable. My hands sweat from nerves."

Aimee apologized for her clammy hands on our first date, but I'm not going to mention it to Shirlene.

"It's so weird that my doctor knows more about me than I do."

"If you need to ask me anything about Aimee, I'll tell you what I can."

We reach the stairs to the boardwalk in front of my house. "Okay. Thanks."

But she doesn't ask me anything. At least, not right now. "It's a relief to be able to be me with Hattie and with you," she says.

"And Arlene."

"And Arlene." She waves good night before going into the house. It's Shirlene waving, not Aimee.

I stay to enjoy the moonlight on the water.

Chapter Seventy-Nine

Shirlene

Hattie is out with Arlene this morning, so I snatch up Aimee's journal and start down the stairs, where I meet Cam. We both stop and stare. I wonder if he's remembering the time we first made love. How it began here on these stairs.

"We need to talk," Cam says.

"I know." My grip tightens around Aimee's journal.

Cam goes down to the living room and sits by the fireplace. I remember how his brother collapsed on the raised hearth after attacking me. I shut the memory away. I need to stay positive. I sit across from him on the couch.

"What do you have there?" Cam asks.

"Hattie and I found a journal Aimee kept on tour this summer. I hope you don't mind, but I read it. I needed to try to understand her."

"I get that."

"There are things I feel Aimee would want you to know, especially about Tristen."

"I hate that guy's name. It sounds like the name of a cracker."

"I think it may be more than his name."

Cam smirks. "You're right."

"You're welcome to read the entire journal. It's not mine. As I said, Aimee would want you to understand what she was going through."

Cam leans forward in his chair. "Go ahead and read it to me."

I open to the page I flagged and read aloud. "I can't stop thinking about Cam, and how wonderful he was to me compared to Tristen. If I hadn't had Cam love me, I'd probably accept Tristen and all the awful things he does. I wouldn't know any differently. Cam was always kind and respectful. He saw and accepted me for who I was. Tristen is constantly trying to make me over. He thinks he can 'fix' my depression, or I can, if I do what he says. Tristen lies without knowing he's making things up. He believes what he says, and I begin to believe I'm crazy if I don't go along with him. The falsehood becomes fact. Tristen is delusional. He's made up that we're engaged. I haven't accepted his proposal. I'm not wearing a ring. He just announced to the company that we're getting married. I need to get away from him before he consumes me. I texted Cam I'm coming home. I'm quitting the tour. There doesn't seem to be any other option. I can't wait to see Cam."

I stop reading and check in with Cam. "She might not have been able to give you everything you dreamed of with her, but she regretted breaking off your engagement."

Cam makes fists. "I wish I could have protected Aimee from this Tristen guy."

"She didn't agree to marry him. She didn't even want a relationship with him. Having you in her life helped her to escape."

"I didn't act like it before, but now I'm grateful you were able to go back and talk with Stan. I wish I could see Aimee one more time. It would help to say goodbye."

I lean over and reach for Cam's hand. He lets me take it. "I'm very sorry for your loss."

He runs his free hand over his clean-shaven face. "Thank you. I'm sorry I didn't fully understand what you were going through when Stan died. I can understand now how you became vulnerable to Rain's manipulations."

"And Stan revealing his vasectomy caused it to be more difficult. But, Cam, when you and I made love here, I longed to be with you. I wanted to move forward. It wasn't about dulling the pain."

"Thank you for saying that."

"And then Chase assaulted me, and I lost the foothold I was beginning to get. That's when Rain started to communicate. I began to believe I was losing my mind."

Cam's dark eyelashes are wet. He releases my hand and wipes his eyes. "I wish you'd told me."

"I wish I had too. I'm sorry. I hope you can forgive me."

"I do, but you don't have to protect me."

"Okay," I say.

"I may have gone off the deep end when you told me Aimee was dead, but I'm capable of handling the truth."

"It was too much after everything else."

"It was too much after losing you, Shirlene. When Rain told me that you were gone, the world stopped. For the first time in my life, I thought I could hit a woman. I was that furious with Rain. She killed you, as far as I was concerned, but she looked like you. I'd be hitting you. I wouldn't do it one way or the other, but I wanted to. Then, before I could begin to deal with your death and Rain being back, I got the call that Aimee had had a stroke."

"You dropped everything to take care of her—me."

"I did." He sighs.

"What is it?"

"I remember you telling me that Rain said something to you when she first gave up her body to you."

"She said, 'Take care of her.'" I realize what he's hoping. "I'm sorry, Cam. Aimee didn't speak to me." His shoulders slump. "Her body was in total chaos during the stroke. But I can say she was relieved to go. She wanted no part of what was happening to her body. I sensed she was escaping."

"So she wanted to die." He leans over and holds his head in his hands.

"She was at peace. Cam, at my last appointment with Aimee's doctor, he asked me if I was having suicidal thoughts." I hesitate to ask, but I need to know. "Had Aimee ever been suicidal before?"

Cam sits up. Again, tears well up in his eyes. "Twice since I've known her."

"I can't imagine how difficult that must have been."

"That was her main reason for not having children. Aimee was afraid she'd ruin their lives."

I take the chance. I make room for him on the couch and open my arms. He comes and sits next to me. Then he leans in for me to hold him while he cries. I rub his back, wondering if there was any possibility Aimee suspected she was pregnant. If she was certain she would ruin her child's life, that's another reason why she peacefully let go.

Cam straightens up. "How did Aimee allow herself to get involved with Tristen in the first place?"

"He's the type of narcissistic person who preys on empathetic people. He probably selected her, and she was into it before she realized. She couldn't find a way out except to come back home."

I notice Cam flexing his fists again. I wouldn't blame him for aiming to pound Tristen into the ground.

"What happened when you met with him?" Cam asks. "Do we have to be concerned about him?"

"No. I made him think it was his idea to end the engagement. Let him off the hook because his career needed to come first. I said I wouldn't let him quit to take care of me should I have another stroke."

Cam smirks. "You are one smart woman."

"Well, that was Hattie's idea, and it worked. He wanted no part in caregiving."

"That's a relief."

I prepare myself for the worst. "But there may be another issue about Tristen we have to deal with."

Cam raises his eyebrows.

"I haven't had a period."

Cam catapults upward and moves away. Although I knew this could be his reaction, my heart sinks, and my palms become clammy. The muscles under the back of his T-shirt tighten. I can't speak. Cam takes a deep breath and turns to me. I expect his eyes to be wild, but they are filled with compassion.

"If you're carrying Tristen's child, we'll deal with it together."

Now, I start to cry. He sits next to me and enfolds me in his arms.

"If Aimee came home from tour pregnant with anyone's child, but she was afraid of him and didn't want to marry him, I'd support her. I'll do the same for you, Shirlene."

I press myself closer. "Oh, Cam."

"It's okay. We'll get through this. Have you taken a pregnancy test?"

"No. This may sound stupid, but I'm too scared to get the answer." I wipe my eyes.

"Was Aimee sleeping with him?"

"From what I read in Aimee's journal, I don't think she had a physical relationship with Tristen, but even if she did, is there any chance her periods would have been irregular?"

"I hate to give you false hope, but yes, Aimee was irregular."

I slump back. "I pray that's what's going on." I wipe away the remaining tears and laugh.

"What's funny?"

"Not a damn thing, but I'm sick of crying. Stan often said, 'Laughter is the best medicine.'"

Cam gets up and stretches. I sense he needs some space from me. "I have a confession," he says. "I read a few of the letters you and Stan wrote to one another during the war."

"Hattie told me you saved them for Arlene, but she didn't know if you read them."

"I did go through a few of them. I thought you were dead."

"Why did you need to read them?" I shift around on the sofa, hoping he has a good explanation for invading my and Stan's privacy.

"I..." He stops.

"Go ahead. It's okay. Whatever you're going to say, we'll deal with it."

He lets out a sigh. "I needed to understand why you loved Stan so much you could leave me and Arlene. I thought I might find the answer in your wartime letters."

So that's why he's pacing like an anxious animal. I thought the biggest hurdle would be the idea of having Tristen's child inside me, but it's still Stan.

"I didn't go back on purpose, Cam. The lifeguards were gone because no one was on the beach in that miserable rain. But the water felt wonderful. I dove under the waves and swam out past the breakers. Then I hit a riptide. I suddenly felt powerless against it. That's when Rain saw her advantage and came into my head. I couldn't swim and deal with her stories about how much Stan and Danny needed me. She was fighting to get her body back. At first, I was thrashing around in the water, but suddenly, I became very still. I sensed I was about to drown. I couldn't allow Arlene to become motherless, so I let Rain take over."

His eyes look sad but not angry. "But Arlene knew *you* were gone anyway."

"I didn't know that would happen. Rain had carried her for nine months. There had to be some connection between them. And it was clear that if I didn't stop battling Rain, that body of ours was going to die in the ocean, and Arlene would have no mother."

"What happened then?" He grabs hold of the back of the chair as if to steady himself.

"Stan and Danny were there in the light. I had no choice but to go to them."

"Tell me what Stan had to say." Cam sits next to me.

I smooth the thighs of my jeans with the palms of my hands. "He explained that he told me the truth about the vasectomy to give me permission to live and take this second chance at motherhood, since he took it away the first time. He wasn't placing some burden on me. He was trying to free me. He also asked what I planned to do with my second chance at a musical career."

"What did you tell him?"

"I'm going to be a conductor."

"Congratulations, Shirlene. We'll work that out. Classes. A degree. Whatever it takes."

"Then he sent me back to you with his blessing. It was painful to leave Danny again, but Stan was with him. That helped me to let go."

"He really told you to come back to me?"

"Yes." I nod.

"I always liked Stan."

"And he liked you."

Cam takes my hand. "You took a big risk trying to return."

"Time isn't the same out there. I had no idea if I'd be drowning in Rain's body or if I'd have to fight her or if I'd end up as an elderly Chinese man halfway around the world. But I was coming back to you."

"I'd love you no matter who you were, but I have to admit I'm relieved you're not a man."

"Cam, I brought back more from Aimee's apartment besides her journal." I pull the engagement ring from my pocket.

Cam's eyes twinkle. "Are you going to propose?"

"Aimee kept your ring."

Cam takes it into his large fingers. "Yes. This style didn't appeal to me, but I knew it was what she preferred."

"Do you still love her?"

Cam sets the ring down. "Yes. You still love Stan, right? And Danny?"

"Of course."

"But it doesn't stop you from loving Arlene."

"I love both Danny and Arlene."

"Exactly. We never get over losing the ones we love, but we can move forward. Shirlene, I want to move forward with you." Cam holds me close. He kisses my eyes, my nose, and my mouth.

I grab hold of his wavy hair and sink into the kiss. Like a switch has been flipped, I feel dampness between my legs. Chills run up and down my spine. I let out a soft moan. "God, you turn me on."

He shifts back and smiles in a wicked way. "You are something, Shirlene."

I'm relieved to hear my name and not Aimee's.

Hattie comes in through the screened porch door with Arlene in her arms. "I left the baby carriage out front. Your daughter needs to be changed, fed, and napped."

I can't believe Hattie's timing, but Cam hops up and takes the baby. "Did you have a nice time with Hattie? Woo, someone does need a changing."

I have an incredible urge to pee. "I'm sorry. I'll be out to help in a moment, but I have to use the bathroom." I duck into the powder room under the stairs.

After closing the door, I hear Cam and Hattie whispering, then someone goes up the steps above me, and judging from the sound, it must be Cam taking Arlene to her room to change her.

I pull down my pants. "I've gotten my period!" I holler. I expect Hattie to respond, but there's silence.

The relief of it nearly sends me through the ceiling. Quickly, the elation crashes around me as past experiences of immense sorrow over getting my period stab my heart. I'm overwhelmed with emotion.

"I'm not pregnant," I whisper.

While I'm cleaning up, someone pounds down the steps in a run. "What's going on?" I shout. Again, no answer.

I find the living room empty. "Hattie? Cam?"

"In here." Hattie comes from the kitchen with Arlene and a bottle.

"I got my period."

"Good." Hattie frowns. "How do you feel?"

"Relieved I'm not carrying that sicko's seed. Sad I'm not pregnant."

"I understand, but you're young. You can have another child."

As if on cue, Arlene starts fussing in Hattie's arms. "You need a break," I say. "Why isn't Arlene with Cam?"

"He's busy." She tests the bottle on her wrist. "Now, little missy, it's time for you to be changed and have a nice drink upstairs."

"I'll take her. You've been dealing with her all morning."

Hattie gets a sly expression. She knows something I don't, and she's enjoying it.

"What the heck, Hattie?"

"You need to go to the labyrinth while I continue to love up my goddaughter." Hattie carries Arlene toward the stairs.

I dash after her. "Tell me what's going on."

Reminding me of the Cheshire cat, she says, "Go to the labyrinth, and you'll find out." She carries Arlene up to the nursery with no more explanation.

I stamp my foot. Then I laugh. That's so me. I wonder if Aimee ever did that. I throw on a sweatshirt and go out through the screened porch. A lovely autumn breeze embraces me on the beach. The sun warms my face as I look down toward the labyrinth I built out of stones and pebbles last summer. I wasn't interested in going into it again, but Cam stands in the center. It seems he's waiting for me.

The sea is calm, and several people sit in beach chairs, wearing jeans and jackets. Others wander along searching for treasures tossed up by the tide. It takes a bit longer than I remember to reach the entrance to the labyrinth.

Cam smiles. He shares Hattie's secret. What is going on?

"My last days in this labyrinth weren't good, Cam."

"It's not the same labyrinth. The other one was washed away by a storm. I built this one for us."

I look more carefully and notice this labyrinth is composed of shells and pieces of driftwood. Cam holds out his hand. I take the first few steps into the path.

"Forgiveness." I move ahead, taking the curve of the outer circle, and begin the next section. I forgive Stan. I forgive Cam. I move closer to the center with each turn. I forgive Rain. There's emotion lingering. I stare at my feet stepping along the way. I forgive myself.

When I reach Cam, he kneels, and my heart rate picks up. He reveals a ring box and opens it. Inside is a diamond in a beautiful antique setting. "Shirlene Foster, will you do me the honor of marrying me?"

My hands fly up to my face. Never in my life did I imagine I'd be proposed to again, nor did I think I wanted to be married a second time. Hattie waves to me from the second-floor deck. She blows me a kiss. I recall her saying that Cameron is a very different type of man.

"Shirlene. We'll take it slowly. The engagement can last as long as you need."

"Yes."

Cam takes my shaking left hand and slips the ring on. He rises. His strong arms draw me into his chest. I wrap myself around him and feel the weight of the previous months lifting.

I look into his eyes. "I love you."

"I love you, Shirlene."

We kiss to the sounds of the sea and the call of the gulls.

Acknowledgments

This novel is dedicated in memory of my dear friend Charles V. Osborne, Jr. He passed away at the age of ninety-eight on March 17, 2022. Before his death, we had several conversations about his service as a World War II fighter pilot. With his usual grace and generosity, he shared his stories and experiences flying twenty-six combat missions in Europe and gave his permission to use what I needed for the service of Stan Foster in the story.

Enormous thanks to Lynn McNamee and her team at Red Adept Publishing. My editors, Alyssa Hall and Sarah Carleton, helped to clarify the story and strengthen my writing. Jennifer Klepper, my Red Adept mentor, answered my many questions. Streetlight Graphics designed my wonderful cover.

Writing can be an isolating pursuit. Without the writing communities that support me and my work, I would have had a much more difficult journey. Thanks to the Noveletics Writers Collective, Women's Fiction Writers Association, Eastern Shore Writers Association, South Jersey Writers Group, and Artists Conference Network.

I'm grateful to Kim Taylor Blakemore for the coaching she did on the opening chapters and my query letter. I also received tremendous feedback and critique from my beta readers: Gary Collings, Kay Cyr, Linda Delany, Tawdra Kandle, Cynthia Myers, and Bonnie Neubauer.

My husband, Gary Collings, is always the first to read my work. He listens when I'm struggling, helps me brainstorm ideas, and tries to be quiet when I'm writing on the laptop. I couldn't accomplish any of this without him.

About the Author

Gail Priest has a passion for women's fiction. Her degrees and work in theatre and counseling psychology inspire her stories of healing from trauma and secrets within families. A dash of romance and her love of second chances are always in the mix. The settings of her novels are influenced by her time spent on the coast of New Jersey and the Eastern Shore of Maryland.

Gail lives in New Jersey with her husband and their Havanese dog, Annie. When she's not writing, Gail can be found reading or looking for birds and sea glass along the beaches and bays of the East Coast.

Gail is a member of The Women's Fiction Writers Association, the Eastern Shore Writers Association, the Novelitics Writers Collective, and the South Jersey Writers Group, where she was named Writer of the Year.

Read more at www.gailpriest.com.

About the Publisher

Dear Reader,

We hope you enjoyed this book. Please consider leaving a review on your favorite book site.

Visit https://RedAdeptPublishing.com to see our entire catalogue.

Check out our app for short stories, articles, and interviews. You'll also be notified of future releases and special sales.